The author has worked in a factory, making fire extinguishers for the last 25 years. He wakes early, before four o'clock in the morning, so on the weekends, he writes to keep quiet while his wife sleeps. He loves to go on holidays, which gives him places to write about. He would like to write for a living.

He has grown up in a small town in Wisconsin and is married to a wonderful woman. Don believes there is always a different way to look at things. He is a guy that always has something going on. He has three daughters, in three different states.

Donald Richter

Fairies, Sorcery and the Devil

AUSTIN MACAULEY PUBLISHERS™
LONDON • CAMBRIDGE • NEW YORK • SHARJAH

Copyright © Donald Richter (2018)

The right of Donald Richter to be identified as author of this work has been asserted by him in accordance with section 77 and 78 of the Copyright, Designs and Patents Act 1988.

All rights reserved. No part of this publication may be reproduced, stored in a retrieval system, or transmitted in any form or by any means, electronic, mechanical, photocopying, recording, or otherwise, without the prior permission of the publishers.

Any person who commits any unauthorised act in relation to this publication may be liable to criminal prosecution and civil claims for damages.

A CIP catalogue record for this title is available from the British Library.

ISBN 9781786936929 (Paperback)
ISBN 9781786936936 (E-Book)
www.austinmacauley.com

First Published (2018)
Austin Macauley Publishers Ltd.
25 Canada Square
Canary Wharf
London
E14 5LQ

Chapter One
Jack Robinson Believes

This is the way it started, on a warm July evening, in the large garden of an old man. It was a warm, still night; the lawn was lit with soft moonlight. Jack Robinson, an elderly man, 82 years old, was doing what he had done for 3 weeks in a row, ever since his wife of 53 years passed away of a heart attack. He would sit at the picnic table with a box-trap (You know the one with a box, a stick and fifty yards of string). Jack would sit and drink coffee for hours, not saying a word. He would catch rabbits and relocate them to a forest seven miles from the house, that way he knew that they wouldn't come back. He took them to a nearby park the first few years, but he swore he was catching the same rabbits. Over the years, he relocated at least a hundred.

His wife Emma helped him plant the garden, like she had for the past 24 years, ever since they moved to the small town, where he became the sheriff. They gave nearly 90 percent of the produce to a local food pantry and neighbours. They did a lot of community works. Jack was the meals-on-wheels guy, belonging to the Knights of Columbus, and Emma was a church lady. She was on the finance council, she helped clean the church, did the laundry and worked at the food pantry as well as the animal shelter.

This night was like every other night until he saw a green light whizzing over the trees, down over the lawn. Jack grabbed a Million Candle Spotlight off the table and waited till the light was past the garden and heading right for him. Jack pulled the trigger on the light; the whole back lawn got lit. The light, to Jack's surprise, came right at him. Jack couldn't tell what it was but it was coming fast, really fast. Jack didn't have time to move, he was hit right in the chest. The old man took a step back due to the shock of the impact. He heard a small voice, screaming insanely: "They're going to kill us!"

Jack looked down at the talking bug, it was pointing at a dozen or so blue lights. Jack hit them with the spotlight; they scattered. The green bug was holding onto Jack's collar, screaming at him: "Run for your life! They will kill both of us!"

Jack took a can off the table and hit them with the light again; this time, they didn't scatter. They were coming towards Jack, slowly at first, but when they rushed him, he shot a stream of juice out of the can—down went the blue bugs. They hit the ground and a blue light streamed from them. The green bug grabbed Jack by his dressing gown and pulled. "Step into the light!"

Jack couldn't argue, the bug was strong and pulling him off balance, so he had to step forward. The light swirled around him; Jack glowed for a second, then he went dark again. The green bug sat there, hovering in front of his face, with its hands on its hips, staring at him like she was waiting for something to happen.

Jack asked, "Are you a fairy?"

The bug replied, "Run! There are more blues coming, those were the chasers. They will corner you. Then—"

Jack interrupted with a pull of the trigger on the spotlight that he was holding. A dozen blue bugs started to glow; they were carrying the birdbath, about ten feet above the ground, coming right at him. Jack shot a stream from the can and down they went, crashing with the birdbath. This time Jack walked right over to the crash site to absorb the light. The whole garden lit up with an eerie blue light, there were a couple of a hundred blue bugs hovering out there. Jack said, "Boy, you must have pissed someone off! And what the hell are they doing?" Then he shouted, "Get out of my lawn"

The bugs slowly linked their arms, forming a ball that glowed bright. The green bug that was on Jack's chest started screaming again: "Run!"

A beam of blue power shot out of the ball. The green bug flew in front of Jack, taking the hit. Jack shot a stream of spray onto the glowing ball, which didn't do anything. He then pulled his old service .45 out of his dressing gown pocket, aimed and squeezed, shooting dead centre of the glowing ball. Sparks flew all over. Just for a couple of seconds, the blue bugs broke apart, which was enough for Jack to hit them with a stream of spray. The lawn lit up brightly with blue light. Jack took a step forward and the light came right towards him, swirled around him, then entered his body, lifting him right off the ground. As the power died, Jack settled to the ground. He walked over to the green bug that had saved his life, got down on his hands and knees and picked up the strange little bug.

Jack asked, "Are you OK?" He had it in the palm of his hand and nudged it with his finger. He asked again, "Are you a fairy? You have green, scaly skin, but you have a face like a human, little legs and arms and wings. Hot damn! I think you are a fairy!" The little fairy moved, then wrapped her arms around Jack's finger. Jack said, "Wow! My hand went numb." The little green fairy sat in the palm of Jack's hand and started to speak. Jack put it close to his ear.

The fairy then started over again, "My name is Elizabeth and yes, I am a fairy. You must forget that you ever saw me."

Jack asked, "Why were those blue fairies trying to kill you?"

She answered with, "They wanted to capture me and turn me into a slave. Well, I must be off then."

Just then, a red flash came out of the rose garden and flew right in front of Jack. This was a smaller bug, red in colour, which looked like a huge red grasshopper, but this one had a face like a human too, with arms and legs. It flew up to Jack, six inches from his face and said, "Hi, Jack", then turned to the green fairy, "Hello, Elizabeth. You know the code: Jack must be taken in front of the council, so they can decide what to do with him."

Elizabeth answered, "I don't have time for that. You take him."

Nora snapped back at Lisa, "Oh no, you don't! I'm not going to die for your mistake. This is your doing, you fix it."

The red fairy turned to Jack and said, "Hi, I'm Nora. You're going to have to come with us to the council of fairies to see what they want to do with you."

Jack asked, "Why should I go?"

The red fairy said forcefully: "Now you listen to me, Jack. You might not know me, but I know you. Your name is Jack Robinson, you are 82 years old. You were sheriff for 24 years. Your wife Emma died 3 weeks ago, of what you think was a heart attack, and you have a son and a daughter. I don't know what happened to them, but they come and visit monthly. You have been sitting outside, catching rabbits that have been eating your garden, ever since your Emma died."

Jack muttered, "This can't be happening. What the hell is going on?"

Nora said, "You know the woods where you let the rabbits go? That is where you must go, then we shall take you to see the council."

Elizabeth yelled, "Who do you think you are, telling me what we are going to do? I'm the one in charge here."

Nora asked the green fairy, "What brings you to Oregon?"

Lisa answered, "I was chased here by those blue devils."

Nora then asked, "How did you know that blue power wouldn't kill Jack?", then she turned to Jack and said, "You didn't, did you? You hoped it would kill him, then you wouldn't have to deal with him."

Nora flew within inches of the green fairy and said calmly, "You know the laws of the fairies: once a human has seen a fairy, they must be brought in front of the council."

The green fairy shrugged her shoulders, "If we're going to do this, let's do it."

Jack asked, "Don't I have any say in this?"

The green fairy got right in his face and asked, "Why didn't you die?"

Jack was stunned.

He knew then that Elizabeth was not to be trusted and he didn't have a choice, he had to follow them.

Nora asked, "Jack, do you still have that old hammock?" He nodded. She turned to a fairy that flew up, "I want you to fly home and get a bunch of guys to the car park in the woods behind the riverside bar."

The little fairy stammered, "Some of those blue fairies aren't dead, they're coming around."

Jack said, "There is a rabbit cage on the porch; quarter-inch hardware cloth should hold them."

With that, a red fairy flew up to the porch and picked up the cage, then flew off to the spot where Jack had sprayed the blue fairies. Nora told Jack, "You get dressed, it's getting late."

Elizabeth flew to Jack and said, "I am in charge here. You get out that hammock, put it in your car and get to the woods, now!"

Jack looked at her and said, "I'm getting dressed."

The green fairy flew up to him, grabbed him by the collar of his pyjamas and flew off with him towards the garage. Nora was right behind them, along with the rest of the red fairies. Elizabeth set Jack down right in front of the garage.

Nora protested, "He has to get dressed."

The green fairy put her foot down, "Listen here, if you don't want to have your wings ripped off, you will shut your mouth and do as you are told."

Jack opened the garage door and flicked on the light. Nora flew up to Jack's good ear and talked very quietly, "Where is that hammock?"

Jack answered, "It should be in the corner over there, in the jumble sale stuff"; he pointed to a pile of stuff.

Nora flew to the red fairies outside. In a couple of seconds, they came flying into the garage, up and over the car, then began digging in the pile. All of a sudden, the pile moved, things were falling off the top and a rope hammock came out, with five little fairies flying with it. Jack opened the boot and the fairies dropped in the hammock.

Jack yelled out: "Well, you might just as well put that rabbit cage in here too."

A couple of red fairies picked up the cage very carefully; there were blue arms sticking out of it, trying to touch the reds. They dropped it into the boot. Nora looked then flew to Jack and said, "That cage isn't going to hold them."

Jack walked over and stuck his head into the boot and said, "You're right, they're chewing right through the steel mesh." He grabbed the cage and threw it onto the garage floor, then stepped back and pulled out a can from his dressing gown and squirted it over the cage. All the blues fell right to the bottom of the cage, they died with a wisp of blue light. There were no bodies, they just disappeared. The light came out of the cage and right to Jack. He looked back into the boot and said, "That should do it, let's go." He shut the boot and walked up to the driver's door.

Elizabeth flew up and said, "We will follow you, don't worry about losing us."

Chapter Two
Jack Is Taken to the Forest

With that, Jack got into the big, old Lincoln town car and backed out of the garage. He was on his way down the road when Nora flew up from the back seat. She said, "It will be all right, Jack. Just do as I say and everything will turn out just fine."

Jack said, "Sure, I think I'm losing it. I don't believe in fairies, but here you are. So tell me, where are we going?"

Nora said, "We are going where you release the rabbits—the car park in the forest—and it's no big deal. You're just going in front of a council, every human that sees a fairy does. You know that we don't want anyone to know about us."

Jack asked, "What if they think I'm a threat?"

Nora smiled and said, "Let's not worry about that. We just have to get there while it's still dark."

Jack drove on, then asked, "Why don't you light up when you fly?"

Nora replied, "Well, it's this way, remember when those blues were chasing Elizabeth? She was glowing green and they were bright blue, they were all at full power. Now, the big group of blues that were following were conserving their energy and flying with their wings."

Jack said, "I see, the more power you use the brighter you become. It will be fifteen minutes or so." Nora asked how the car moved and what the gauges were for. Before they knew it, they were entering the forest.

Jack got out and popped the boot. Nora flew up to his good ear and told him to leave the boot open and then Elizabeth flew to his shoulder and started to blink a soft green light. To Jack's surprise, a red light started to blink Morse code—short, then long, fast and then slow. Elizabeth blinked back and forth. Then she fluttered around the car slowly and landed gently on Jack's shoulder and asked: "Can you hear me now?"

Jack laughed softly, "Does everyone know I'm deaf in one ear?"

Elizabeth said, "We have to get going down the path. In about 50 yards or so, there is a small clearing. They will meet us there."

Jack did as he was told and started to walk, but then he realised that he didn't have his cane.

Elizabeth kept pushing on, "Let's go, old man, just around the corner."

Jack took his time making sure of every step he took as he walked the small dirt road; a half-moon lit the way. Once they reached the clearing, Jack asked, "What did that red light say? Is that like Morse code? You guys blinked like crazy! There must have been a lot more to it than we saw here."

Elizabeth replied, "I will tell you in good time. Right now, we must get you in front of the council. Then I can be on my way, I am on a mission."

Just then, red lights blinked on and off, coming right towards them. Jack looked down and there were about 20 fairies, they all glowed a deep red and then they were off. Jack's jaw dropped as they flew off down the path. In seconds, their light was gone. Jack pointed and said, "Did you see that?"

Nora replied, "Yes, Jack. Now it's your turn."

About 50 reds were carrying the hammock and laid it down in the grass. Elizabeth said, "OK, Jack, walk over to the hammock."

Jack asked, "Why?"

Elizabeth started to glow a deep green, "Just do it!"

Jack did as he was told. Elizabeth flew into his face and said, "Do as you are told, old man and everything will be fine. These fairies will carry you because it would take too long to teach you to fly. And it would take you forever to walk."

Nora told Jack to lay down face first on the hammock and everything would be fine. Jack stepped on the hammock, then got down on his hands and knees and lay down. The rest of the fairies grabbed the hammock and glowed lightly, up they went—about five feet—and they were off. Nora was leading the way down the path and then into the wood. They climbed higher into the big pine forest.

Elizabeth flew up to Nora and asked, "Why are you flying so slowly?"

Nora replied, "We have to be safe and he's heavy. Why don't I send you ahead? We will catch up." Nora motioned to a red male, when he flew up to her, she said in a loud voice, "Take this green fairy up the river to the council," and waved to Elizabeth. Off they went, a red and a green light flew through the forest. Nora flew back and said, "Let's go, guys." They turned from a dark red glow to a bright red, almost pink glow. Up through the treetops they went, over a hill and through a valley. Down below the treetops they went, skimming over a small river, then slowing as the river turned into a stream, then into the forest they went.

They laid Jack down in the ferns, the ferns were about five feet high and thick, so he had to spread them to get through.

Nora said to Jack, "Follow as fast as you can, it's just a few feet." So Jack spread the ferns as he walked, not 20 feet from where he was set down, the fairies were busy uncovering an animal. He walked up to see a small horse lodged in the crotch of a small tree. The back end of the horse was stuck in the mud and its head lay on the ground. Nora flew up and said, "Can you get him free?"

The old man grabbed onto a piece of brush and lowered himself to his knees, he reached out to stroke the horse. To his amazement, the horse was white and started to glow. "OUCH!" exclaimed Jack as he shook his hand in the air. The small horse raised it head and turned slowly; it had a single horn sticking out of his head. "It's a unicorn!" Jack gasped.

Nora asked again, "Can you free him? If the green fairy finds out that we're doing this, we'll all die."

Jack patted the unicorn's head, "No kidding! A real live unicorn!" He stroked the little horse as he looked around, as he did this, he could feel energy being sucked out of his body again. Jack said, "Take what you need, little one, we'll get you out of this." The horse's mane shone a bright white, then dulled; it just lay there. Nora flew up and told Jack that the unicorn had been stuck for two weeks now and they had tried everything.

Jack looked around, there was a shovel, a saw and some rope. Jack stood and said, "OK, first we have to get him on solid ground. We need some branches and small logs, something he can stand on." Jack got back down on the ground and took off his slippers and socks. He stood and dropped his pyjama bottoms and then stepped out of them. He walked into the mud behind the unicorn. "We have to break the suction that is holding him here. Hand me those branches." The fairy started to bring branches, Jack was stepping down into the mud that came up past his knees, lifting the horse's tail. He shook his head.

"Bring me the rope." A fairy flew the rope over to him and he tied it to the unicorn's tail. Jack said, "OK. Let me get to the side and then you lift." Jack made his way to the side of the unicorn, then he pushed his arm down around the belly and said, "Lift." The fairies all glowed and slowly, the horse rose. Jack yelled, "Stop! We don't want to break his back." Jack pushed some of the branches under it hooves so he stayed on top. Jack got out of the mud and walked over to the tree. He got down on his hands and knees, wiped off clumps of mud, then he wiped his hands off on the ferns and he stroked the animal. Then he said, "I think it has a couple of broken ribs."

Jack grabbed one tree, pushed with one hand and pulled the other. A voice from behind him said, "Close your eyes concentrate on the tree's power. When you feel it, slowly tell it to bend, then push lightly." Jack did as he was told, the tree bent without effort and stayed that way. Jack opened his eyes to see the unicorn stand and step onto solid ground. The unicorn turned to Jack, "I have been stuck for weeks and I thought I was going to die. Thank you so much."

The unicorn lay down on its side and started to glow. Jack snarled, "Next time, look before you leap." Then he smiled and asked, "Are you OK?"

"I'll be fine. With that power you gave me, I can heal myself," the unicorn replied. Jack looked behind him where the voice came from, standing there was a grey unicorn. The unicorn bowed to Jack and told him, "Get your pyjamas on, time is running short."

Jack was covered with mud from the knees down. Nora called a few fairies over to her; she talked just for a few seconds, then half a dozen fairies picked him up by his shirt and flew him to the stream. Jack washed up, splashing water on himself. He then stepped out onto the shore, where his pyjamas hung on a branch with his socks. He sat down and put on his socks and pyjamas His slippers came flying over, four little fairies carrying each slipper. Jack lifted one of his feet and they slid his slipper on and started to tie it. All of a sudden, there was some shouting and pushing. Nora flew up, hovering in front of Jack's foot; with a wave, the other fairies left. Nora flew to his slipper and tied it quickly. She flew to the other slipper and tied that one too. Then she flew up to Jack's shoulder and said, "We don't have shoes, so they don't know how to tie the laces."

Jack smiled, "Thanks, how do you know how to do it?" The small fairy blushed.

The old unicorn came up to Jack and said, "We have little time and we must go." Jack reached down and stroked it gently, the unicorn started to turn white, but it didn't glow. The unicorn said "OK. Take him to the rock bluff." In a streak of white, the unicorn was gone.

Jack's jaw dropped, then he exclaimed, "Wow! Did you see that?"

Nora flew up and said, "That is the fastest I've seen him go in 50 years. We'll never catch him."

All the red fairies that were there grabbed Jack. Up into the air they went, then flipped him onto his stomach; they were off in a shot. Jack left out a small "I'm going to die" as they shot out of the forest canopy, flying just over the treetops. The fairies started to glow as they picked up speed, flying up to the highest hill, where they slowed, setting him down on a large rock outcropping. Jack took a couple of steps then said, "Whoa, that was some ride! And I have to take a leak."

The old unicorn stood right next to him and said, "Hurry up Jack, they can't stall that green fairy much longer and if she catches us, there will be hell to pay!"

Jack stepped over to a tree. While he was relieving himself, he asked, "So do you have a name?"

The unicorn apologised, "I'm sorry, we haven't been properly introduced, I am Ivan. One of the elders, maybe the last elder. We stay within the forest boundaries these days, it just isn't safe. The blues are everywhere." Ivan dispatched the red fairies and told Jack to climb on his back. Jack said, "You have to be joking! I'll break your back!"

Ivan responded with, "I know what I'm doing, if you want to live, you will do as I say." Jack stepped over the unicorn's back; it only stood three feet high. Ivan said with a shout: "Bend your knees so you don't drag your feet, and hang on."

With this, they were off like a shot, Jack was ducking branches; he wrapped his arms around Ivan's neck and held on for dear life. They went a couple of a hundred yards, Ivan slowed, then went up a hill to a buff that overlooked a beautiful waterfall, this is where he stopped and Jack got off. He exclaimed between breaths: "Don't you people ever go slow?"

Two red fairies came out to greet them. One bowed to Ivan and said, "I put it in the cave."

Ivan asked, "How is the green fairy doing?"

The fairy replied, "She isn't happy, we can't stall much longer."

Ivan asked, "What way are they leaning about Jack?"

The little fairy hovering in front of both of them looked down then shook his head, "I don't think he has a chance."

Jack stepped close to the old unicorn and spoke softly like he was taking to a dog, "Hey boy, how ya doing? What don't I have a chance at?" Jack reached down and stroked the side of the animal.

Ivan looked up, "Your chance of living, of course. Don't worry, I'll get you out of here as soon as possible."

Jack looked at the red fairy and said, "Damn, my hand has fallen asleep again." The old grey unicorn had grown a couple of shades whiter. He asked the fairy what Elizabeth was doing.

The fairy said, "Well, she has stated her case, that she was here looking for her sister Aurora when she was chased here. That is when she ran into you, she didn't let you see her on purpose. I have one of the best guys trying to stall her. But we can't hold her for long. Green fairies have bad attitudes and there will be hell to pay when she finds out."

Ivan told Jack to follow as he turned and walked to the face of the bluff, then up a small path for about twenty feet and around a small boulder. Jack said, "I can't fit in there."

Ivan turned and said, "I said, do as you are told, old man! Get down on your hands and knees; it's only a few feet, then you can stand."

Jack grunted and groaned as he got to his knees, "I'm not going to be any good to you if I can't walk." Jack crawled slowly behind Ivan into the dark; his eyes adjusted and he could see Ivan's horn glowing. The small passageway led to a room that was big enough for Jack to stand in, he looked around to see a small bed made from hay.

"This way," Ivan said as he turned. Jack saw a red fairy shoot across the room and pick up a small package made of tightly woven grass. Ivan stopped at a rock wall and put his horn into a crack. Jack heard a pop, then some other noise like wheels turning as a boulder slowly turned to the side, revealing a hole that was pitch dark. Ivan's horn illuminated the inside; Jack could see a hammock hanging inside as well as some old boxes. Ivan said, "Come here, I want you to sand off the point of my horn, catching the dust on this board." The unicorn walked over to a flat rock.

Jack walked over, picked up a piece of sand paper and exclaimed, "Wow! This stuff is old!"

Ivan said, "I haven't been in this room for at least 20 years. Enough of that! Time is short, get on with it." The fairy flew up with a box of aluminium foil. Jack took the box, ripped off a piece and laid it down on the rock. Ivan put his horn over the top of it and said in a commanding voice: "Let's get on with it." Jack wrapped the paper around the tip of the horn and started to twist it. Ivan said in an irritated voice, "We don't have all day, you know!"

Jack snapped back, "I'm an old man, what do you expect?" Jack tapped the paper onto the foil and some dust fell onto it.

"More," came from the fairy standing on the stone. Jack wrapped the paper around the horn again; this time, he really got into it. Twisting and stroking, dust just drifted down onto the foil. The fairy held up his hand, "That's enough." Jack tapped the paper, then set it down.

Ivan said, "Over here." Jack walked over to where Ivan was standing, there was a number written on the wall. "This is how we can reach Marvin the Magnificent, you must take this number back and contact him." The fairy flew up with a pencil and notebook, both were covered with dust.

Jack reached into his pocket and took out his mobile phone, flipped it open and dialled. He said, "No bars in here but when we get outside, I think we could call."

Ivan said, "Take these two packages, Boris will know what to do."

Jack said, "Boris? Who the hell is Boris?"

The small fairy flew up and said, "I will be your travel companion."

Ivan said as he turned toward the door, "Boris will be my eyes and ears. If you screw this task up, you will be killed. Do you understand? You will follow Boris's instructions to the letter."

Chapter Three
Jack Devotes His Life to the Cause

Jack said, "Yes, I understand. You're saving my life, so I will save yours." Jack dropped to all fours and this time, Ivan wasn't waiting for him, but Jack was right behind him.

Ivan asked quietly, "How're the wrists?"

Jack grabbed onto his wrist, "Hey! They don't hurt at all and I feel really good."

Boris flew up to Ivan and talked, with his hands flying in the air. Ivan shook his head and said, "You have to, about midday."

Jack said, "Yes! We have a signal! Two bars, that should work fine." He called the number that was on the wall, a woman came on, asking who was calling. Jack said, "Put Marvin on please, it is a matter of life or death."

Boris said, "Tell him it is Ivan from the forest."

Nora flew in and told Jack to say, "The horn is getting long and the juice is flowing."

Ivan said, "Just tell him it's Ivan from East Germany."

Jack said, "I hate to tell you, there is no more east and west, it's just Germany now. Oh, here we go."

An old man's voice came on, "This had better be good! It's four o'clock in the morning!"

Jack said, "Hi, this must be Marvin the Magnificent. I am here with Ivan from East Germany; he is a little horse, you do know he's a—"

Marvin cut him off: "You never know who is listening. Is he there with you?"

Jack said, "Yes."

"Well, put him on, we don't have all day."

Jack lowered the phone to Ivan and said, "When you want me to move the phone, just blink." Jack put the phone to the unicorn's s mouth, then to his ear every time Ivan blinked.

They talked in German most of the time, this went on for two or three minutes, then Ivan turned and said, "He wants to talk to you."

Jack said into the phone, "Sir, what is going on here? Is this a dream or am I going mad?"

Marvin laughed. "You're not going mad. I need some paper and a pencil," he yelled. Then he asked if Jack would give him his name, address, social security number and date of birth. Marvin's tone turned sharp, "Now listen here, you promised Ivan you would do whatever asked of you. This is what you're going to do: Ivan will give you two bags, don't open them. You must go home, take a shower and pack quickly. Make arrangements to be gone for a couple of days, go and tell the neighbours, family, anyone that would need to know."

Jack stood there listening and watching fairies buzz around. Nora flew up and started to make hand gestures for him to hurry up. Jack then asked, "Where should I tell everyone that I am going?"

Marvin said in an angry voice, "I don't care, just get there. If the green fairy returns, Juliet will die. How long will it take you to get to the airport?"

The old unicorn walked up to him, cleared his throat and stamped his hoof on the ground. Jack then spoke, "Well, that depends on how long it takes to get out of this forest."

Marvin said, "I'll have a private jet waiting for you when you get there." "Oh yeah," he yelled excitedly, "what is your mobile number and your home phone?"

Ivan gave him a tap on the leg and said, "It's time, Jack." Jack gave Marvin the number to his home phone and apologised that he didn't know his mobile number. Marvin told Jack not to forget his charger and that he once forgot his and... Ivan interrupted, clearing his throat loudly. Jack looked down and told Marvin that he would do what he had to.

Marvin yelled into the phone: "Get going before that green fairy gets back and ruins the whole damn thing. Just do whatever the red fairies tell you and don't trust the green one. It might kill you."

Jack shut his phone and asked Ivan, "Is this was really happening or am I going mad?"

Boris flew up and said, "I brought good news: they drugged Elizabeth, she will be out for a few hours."

Ivan shook his head and asked, "Do you know what you are doing? I once saw a green fairy fly off the handle and kill the whole council, they are nothing to screw with."

Boris came back with: "It's your fault, if he hadn't saved that unicorn stuck in the mud and spent half the night chatting with you, he would be on his way."

Three reds came streaking in, you could see the lines of red light through the forest. They flew up between Ivan and Boris.

Ivan said, "OK, now Jack can leave."

Boris said, "You can't give him that! It's more than half our winter supply, we'll starve!"

Ivan told him: "This is our only chance to survive, we must put our faith in Jack."

Boris flew to Jack and motioned to the other fairies that were holding two bags that were made of grass—tightly woven together—and were about the size of tea bags. "Now take these bags and guard them with your life. Our success in reaching the Magnificent is vital to my people."

The night sky was giving way to the dawning new day. Boris told Jack that it was time to go. Jack said, "It took a hundred red fairies to fly me into the woods and these four don't look that strong." The unicorn that Jack had pulled from the mud came up, kneeled before Jack and thanked him for saving his life. "Oh I see," Jack said, "I'm riding out."

Ivan spoke with a commanding voice: "Take him up and over. Do it quickly."

Nora flew up to Jack's shoulder and told him: "Take off your shoes and tie them to your belt. You're going to get a crash course in flying."

Jack said, "I can't fly!"

Ivan walked over to Jack and advised, "Feel it, search your mind. You took the information from me, use it."

Jack sat down slowly and slowly started to take off his shoes, he couldn't quite reach his shoes. Ivan told Jack to hurry up. Jack said, "I haven't sat on the ground and taken off my shoes in years. I usually sit in a chair, even then it takes me a couple of minutes." Nora flew down and quickly untied his shoes and pulled them off along with his socks. She barked out a couple of commands and the four reds that were sitting in a bush nearby flew down and picked Jack off the ground and set him on his feet. Jack thanked them.

Boris flew over and said, "OK, it's time to fly." Nora flew up and tied Jack's shoes to his belt. She flew off, then right back again, asking Jack to put his socks in his pocket. Boris flew up and hovered in front of the two with his hands on his hips. He shouted: "We have been here twice as long as we should have. Nora stops screwing around! Get him ready and let's go."

Nora pulled a pouch off her belt that Jack hadn't noticed before. She flew down to his feet and sprinkled a few grains of sparkly powder on them, then flew up and sprinkled a few on his hair. Then she asked him to hold out his hands, palms up and sprinkled some on both palms.

Jack exclaimed, "Wow! My feet are tingling like mad!"

Boris turned to the four fairies that were lounging on a bush and shouted: "Grab him. Let's go."

Nora flew to Ivan, thanked him and asked how long they had before Jack went down.

"Three or four hours," Ivan shouted, "This is our last hope, don't fail!"

The fairies grabbed Jack by the shoulders and his waistband. One said, "I hope this shirt holds, if we drop him, we'll be in deep shit."

Nora flew up to Boris, "I don't think his pyjamas are going to handle his weight, we should get that hammock."

Boris snapped: "Shut up and get going!"

Jack was being slowly lifted off the ground and though the canopy of the forest. The trees were old growth and very tall, soon they reached the top and broke free of the trees. The sky was just turning pink. Nora flew up, yelling: "Faster, faster! We don't have much time!" She grabbed him by his collar and started to pull.

Boris flew up, landing on Jack's back. He walked up to his shoulder and told him to "Stretch out your arms and feel the flight. Search your mind, Ivan said you should be able to fly."

Jack reached out and shut his eyes, then let out a little chuckle and yelled: "Show me the way!" He did some big banks, then dove down closer to the treetops; he was climbing and falling, enjoying the freedom of the flight.

Boris landed on his shoulder and yelled like a drill sergeant: "Stop screwing around, move it, move it! If I have to kick your butt all the way to the car, I'll do it."

Jack started to pick up speed, he was going so fast in fact, that the fairies which were a dark brown before, were glowing a bright red, trying to stay in front of him. Nora flew to his side and told him to slow down, the car was just over the hill. She then flew back to the four that had first carried him. They flew up and Jack slowed and started to descend, he slowed to a point where he was falling, that's when the four fairies grabbed him. Nora told Jack, "We are in a hurry. We will have to teach you how to land some other day." The four fairies sat Jack down right next to his town car.

Jack laughed, "Now, that was fun!"

Boris landed right on the roof of the car and said, "We're not out of this yet, let's get going."

Jack was reaching for the door handle when Nora flew up and said: "I wouldn't do that if I were you, can't you feel it? The blue fairy."

Boris turned to her and asked, "Feel what?" Then he said, "You know, maybe we should check the car quickly."

Nora flew over the car slowly, then pointed to the bonnet, "In here."

Jack opened the door and pulled the latch, then he walked around to the front of the car and popped the bonnet.

Nora screamed: "Did you see it?"

Jack pulled his can of wasp spray out of his pocket and asked, "Where?"

Nora flew to Jack's shoulder and pointed towards the carburettor. Jack looked and said, "I don't see anything," but he shot some spray in there anyway. There was an eerie, high-pitch noise, then a blue fairy came out like it was shot out of a gun, it went up about 20 feet and popped like a bottle rocket. The blue sparks pulled together and streamed slowly to Jack. Jack heard hundreds of "Ahhs" coming out of the woods. Boris just stood there, with his jaw hanging.

Nora wasn't that impressed, as she had seen Jack do this before. She said, "Shut the thingy and let's go."

Jack reached up and shut the bonnet, then walked over and grabbed the door handle.

Boris, who was still standing on the roof, asked him, "How did you do that?"

Jack smiled an old man's smile, "Wasp spray works on their nerve system, kills them dead."

Boris said, "No, why didn't you die? I have seen the blues kill many humans in my day, but their power doesn't hurt you. I thought you were dead."

Nora flew up and impatiently said, "Really! That's nice! We are running out of time, let's go!"

She flew under Jack's arm and into the car. Boris was right behind her. Jack slid in, took the keys out of the ashtray and started the car. Boris and Nora were screaming at one another.

Jack asked, "What is the problem?"

Nora flew onto the dash; she had tears streaming down her face. She sobbed, "Boris won't let me come!"

Jack exclaimed: "You're kidding me! Huh! Well, I think I have a say in this. You're coming."

Boris snapped: "Oh no, she is not!"

Jack reached up and turned the car off.

Boris asked excitedly, "What are you doing?"

Jack took a deep breath and replied, "We will just have to discuss this. It might take a while and I don't want to waste gas. She goes."

Nora added, "We don't have much time."

Boris gave in, "Just go. This is a big mistake. Our whole existence is riding on this."

Jack said, "Let's just get home. Maybe I'll wake up and this will have been nothing but a dream."

Jack started the car and headed out of the woods. Boris stood in the passenger seat, Nora sat on Jack's shoulder. Nora was the first one to start talking; she was thrilled to ride in the car. She said that she had watched cars for decades but still didn't know what made them move.

Boris told her, "Be quiet! Let Jack drive."

They rode for five minutes, then they were on the road. Jack turned his indicator on and came to a stop. Nora couldn't help it, she had to ask, "Why did you turn that blinking light on?"

Jack chuckled, "That shows other drivers which way you're going."

Nora said, "That makes it blink on the outside? Oh I see, I always wondered what turned on those lights."

Boris again protested, "You shouldn't have come. Ivan told me to watch Jack. There is a lot riding on this, for God's sake, we're going to starve this winter if we fail!"

Jack put his foot down and said, "She stays and that's the end of it."

Boris started to talk, but Nora just put her finger to her lips and shook her head. Boris shook his head and mumbled to himself; he knew that he couldn't change the old man's mind.

Nora said, "Everyone is going faster than we are."

Jack was doing his normal 45 in a 55. Cars were backing up behind them and were taking their turn passing them. Jack told Nora, "At this age, if I got a ticket, I would lose my licence and never get it back."

That was it for the rest of the ride to his house. He was explaining how the traffic laws worked and she just wouldn't shut up. Jack started telling them about the neighbourhood as they came close to his house.

Nora was full of questions. She asked, "What is that big tower that is in every city? Sometimes, they are different shapes and sizes; there's the one in this town," she pointed to the water tower.

Jack chuckled and shook his head. He asked: "How long have you been coming to town?"

Nora answered, "Not long. Right after the first car came to town."

Boris spoke, "I have been coming here since the first house was built. I was a spirit in the Indians' eyes before that. We used them to kill the bear that ate some of my people. Why do you ask?"

Jack said, "Wow! You're a hell of a lot older then you look!"

Then Nora pointed to a small ranch house down a long drive way, "There's his house."

Boris told Nora to get into Jack's dressing gown's pocket, which she did at the last second.

Chapter Four
Getting Ready for the Flight

Jack pulled up to the house and parked. He stepped out of the car, then had to put his hand on the car to steady himself. "Oh boy, I don't feel so well."

Nora said, "Just get into the house. Quickly, we're not alone."

The old man opened the car door again and pulled out his cane, then started for the front door. He would go ten feet and stop, then ten more. Finally, they reached the door. He opened it and entered the kitchen; there, on the counter, the answering machine blinked a two. "Oh boy, I fired my weapon last night."

Boris said, "No time for that. Now we have to clean you up." Boris had Jack's dressing gown by the collar, almost lifting him off the ground. He yelled at Nora: "You find some water, we have to wash him."

Nora flew up to Jack's ear and said, "You will have to shower."

Jack sat down his cane and pulled up his pyjama pants. He walked over to the table and pulled out a chair, sat down and said, "First, I'm going to make some coffee."

Boris was hovering six inches in front of his face. "No. The first thing you'll do is wash up." The little fairy turned a bright red that glowed.

Nora flew up. "Just do as he said, please."

Jack slowly got to his feet. "Well, I'm not getting undressed in the kitchen." He slowly moved towards the bathroom.

Boris was pissed. "Where are you going?" he yelled at the top of his lungs.

Nora flew up to Boris and said, "He's going to shower, just watch."

Jack turned on the light, opened the shower door and turned on the water. "Boy, did I get dirty! Where are my slippers anyway?"

Nora flew up to him and said, "They're in the car. Just wash up, this is important."

Boris flew into the shower, "Hey, the water is hot!" He flew out of the shower and hovered next to Nora. He asked, "Where does the water come from?"

Nora told Jack, "Just get into the shower."

The old man stood there naked; he had mud up to his knees and dried blood from being whipped by branches. When he stepped into the shower, he adjusted the temperature and stepped into the spray with a long sigh. He sat down in a waterproof chair and scrubbed his legs. Both fairies sat on top of the shower, watching him. Nora flew off, Boris right behind her.

He yelled, "Stop!"

She stopped and turned to him. "Get him ready for travel," he commanded and back to the bathroom he went, up and over the shower door.

Jack was shampooing his hair. Boris shouted: "What are you doing?"

Jack rinsed, then stood and shut off the water. "What do you think I'm doing?" He reached outside the shower, grabbed a towel and dried himself. He reached into a drawer by the sink and pulled out a comb. He started to comb his hair, then stopped. He looked up at the mirror. There stood an old man looking back at him. He muttered to himself, "Yesterday, I was clean-shaven." He stood there, staring at the mirror.

Boris flew up and asked, "What's wrong? We don't have time for this."

Jack looked at the mirror and said, "Yesterday, I was clean-shaven. Today, I have a three-inch beard and my hair is six inches longer. I'm making coffee." Jack walked out into the kitchen in his birthday suit and started to make coffee.

Nora flew up with a pair of underwear and socks. "Jack, I will put these on the table," she yelled as she hovered next to his ear.

Jack finished filling the coffee maker. He stepped over to the table, pulled out one of the chairs and started to get dressed. The phone rang as soon as he pulled on his first sock. He noticed Boris jump and get really nervous, so he said, "Just the phone."

He got up and answered it. Boris sat there and listened to the one-sided conversation. He heard Jack say, "No, I didn't shoot. It must have been a back fire. Good, yeah, that's right. I'm doing fine. OK then, bye." He set the phone back on the rest.

Boris flew over to the coffee maker and watched it drip coffee into the pot. Jack pushed the play button on the answering machine. The first one was a neighbour, asking if he was shooting in the middle of the night last night. Jack pushed delete. The second was Marvin the Magnificent, telling him to call him when he got this message. Jack wrote down the number. The third message was his son again; he must have called while he was in the shower. Nora flew up with a shirt and tie.

Jack looked at her and said, "No, I don't need a tie." He took the shirt from her and put it on, then walked back to the table, sat down and put on his other sock. Then he got up, poured himself a cup of coffee, reached over to the sink and gave it a shot of cold water. He took a sip and a long "Ahh" came from his lips. He then started for the bathroom.

Boris flew up and asked, "Where do you think you're going?"

Jack replied, "To finish getting ready."

Boris asked nicely, "You were supposed to call Marvin."

Jack turned around, walked back to the phone, picked it up and dialled. Then he sat down at the table with a pen and paper. Marvin picked up on the second ring. Jack sat and talked for a couple of minutes, then sat the phone on the table.

Boris was all excited about the phone call, asking, "How did Marvin sound? Is he OK? When are they going to pick us up?"

Jack drank a long drink of coffee and said, "You know, I've been up all night. Let me enjoy this cup of coffee, then we'll get going."

Nora landed on the table, walked up to Jack and asked where his baggage was.

"You mean my luggage. It's in the basement."

Jack picked up the phone and dialled, speaking into it and telling whoever was on the other end that he would be gone for a couple of days. Nora flew down the hall, turned on the lights and went down to the basement. Jack said, "I'm visiting an old friend."

Nora flew up with a suitcase and asked if this was the one he wanted. Jack said that was his wife's but it would do just fine. Nora set it down on the floor. She flew to the coffee pot, then over to the table and topped him off. She had her arms wrapped around the top of the handle and her feet on the bottom to steady it.

Jack turned to Boris. "Nora's pretty strong. She is an asset, you know." Then he thanked her for the coffee.

She asked, "So how is everything going?"

Boris took command and told her, "Jack has made arrangements to leave for a couple of days and he called Marvin."

She asked, "So, when do we leave?"

Boris asked Jack, "When are they going to be here?"

Jack replied, "We have to meet them at the airport in about an hour."

Nora flew to Boris and whispered something in his ear. Boris threw up both hands and yelled, "What? Now you tell me! For the love of God, why didn't I remember that?"

He flew over to the table and asked, "How long to the airport?"

Jack replied, "Fifteen minutes."

Boris turned to Nora and said, "Is that good?"

He asked Jack, "How do you feel?"

Jack said, "Fine. I could use some more coffee."

Nora flew to the coffee maker.

Boris shook his head. "We don't have time. Get dressed, let's go."

Jack said, "They will wait for us."

Nora landed on Jack's shoulder and said, "I hate to tell you this, but you are going to be sick. I mean really sick, for a couple hours."

Boris flew over to the two and yelled in a loud voice (well, the loudest a two-inch fairy could yell): "I am in charge here, you there—" he pointed at Nora, "get his britches."

Before Jack could even take a step, Nora was there with a pair of blue jeans.

Jack shook his head, "I think I should dress up a bit."

Boris hovered in front of him with his arms crossed, staring at him. Jack reached out, took the pair of black slacks that Nora flew up with and put them on. He stood and buttoned up. In the middle of doing this, he stood staring into space. Boris was right there, up on his shoulder, telling him that he didn't have time to lollygag. Jack started for the basement steps.

Boris screamed: "Where in the hell do you think you're going?"

Nora flew up with a glass of water and said: "Drink."

Jack reached out, took the glass and slammed it. Then he handed it back to Nora, thanking her for it. With that, he headed down the stairs, very quickly, may I add.

Nora flew down to the two of them, "What are you looking for?"

Jack told her about a rock collection that his son made years ago. She flew over to shelf and pointed to a box on a shelf labelled rock collection, "Could this be it?"

Jack exclaimed: "Wow, you can read!" He pulled out the box and started to rifle through it, every rock was wrapped in paper. "Ah, there's one," he pulled out a piece of quartz, then another. He grabbed both rocks and said, "Now we are ready." He headed for the stairs, then reached up and grabbed the railing and stopped. "Where is my cane? Oh my God!" He stood frozen with his hand on the rail.

Nora flew up as she said, "I wrapped all the rocks back up but couldn't put the box back on the shelf." Then she asked, "What is going on? Shouldn't we be going?"

Boris held up his hand and raised a finger. "Let Jack realise what's happening to him, it took him long enough," Boris flew up to Jack and slapped him on the back of the head, "Let's go now, we are running behind."

Jack looked up the stairs, Nora streaked in a red flash by him and came down with his cane. She yelled for Boris to take the rocks from Jack, which he did. Then she gave Jack his cane. He slowly raised his leg and took his first step, then used his cane.

Boris flew onto his shoulders, "We don't have time for this, you ran down the stairs!"

Nora flew to Jack and asked how he felt and why he needed the rocks. Jack didn't think about climbing the stairs. He just walked up them as he was talking to her. "I guess we are ready, let me check things over one more time." He walked over to the door, "Let me check and see if Nora packed my drugs."

Boris started to push him toward the door. "We have been here twice as long as we should have. If that green fairy shows up, we're dead; if the blues show up, we're dead."

Jack yelled: "Wait!" Then he walked over to his dressing gown and pulled out a can of wasp spray and set it on the table. He opened the wardrobe door and pulled out a light military coat and slid it on. He walked back to the table, picked up the can and pushed it into a pocket. Then he grabbed the dressing gown again and pulled out his service .45 and put it in his breast pocket. Jack said, remembering his wife, "Emma sewed in a large pocket for this gun, back in the early sixties."

Boris flew into the kitchen and up to Jack. "All our lives are at risk the longer we are here."

Jack stopped staring into space while thinking of his wife. He took three long strides, then jogged to the front door. Nora flew in, then back to Jack; she was carrying his cane. Jack let out a small chuckle. "Did you see that I ran? That's the first time in twenty years. I don't think I need that cane anymore."

Nora said, "Jack, you're an old man, act like one. We can't draw attention to us."

Boris, standing on Jack's shoulder, asked if he could ride in Jack's coat pocket. Jack held open a breast pocket in the coat and Boris climbed in. Nora flew up, handed Jack his cane and flew up to his pocket, the one Boris was holding open and climbed in. Then Boris yelled: "What the hell is he doing?"

Jack said, "I will just be a minute; I need some cash."

He went to the bedroom, into his sock drawer and pulled out an envelope with some cash in it. Nora flew up and opened a cupboard door and took out an old can of dried prunes and sat it on the table; she opened the lid. Jack was back in the kitchen now, holding the charger for his mobile phone. "What do we have here?" he asked.

Nora said, "Emma has been putting money in this can for years."

Jack reached in and pulled out a wad of hundred dollar bills. "Wow!" he muttered, "there must be three grand here. That reminds me—" He pulled out his credit card and picked up the phone, dialling the number on the back. Then he started to push more numbers on the phone. He read a long list of numbers, then flipped the card over and said some more. He chatted with someone on the other end and told them that he was going on holiday. Jack placed the phone back in its holder and chucked to himself.

Nora asked, "What was so funny?"

Jack smiled, "Yesterday, I would have had to use a magnifying glass to read that."

Boris, still in Jack's pocket, waved to Nora. She then flew over. As she was getting in, Jack heard Boris ask, "How long do you think we have?"

She answered with a prayer, "God, I hope he makes it to the airport."

Boris yelled out: "Jack, can you take some water with you?"

Then Jack heard Boris tell Nora, "He needs as much water as we can get in him. His body has many years of poison to get rid of."

Jack pulled a couple of bottles of soda out of the fridge and headed for the door. Jack grabbed the handle and started to open it. Nora yelled to him: "They're here, I can feel them."

Jack pulled open the door and started looking around. "I don't see anything," Jack said as he scanned the porch, with his can of spray firmly held in hand.

Boris spoke then. "Yeah, I feel it too. It's blues, more than one, but they won't attack in the daylight."

Jack slowly stepped down the steps. Nora flew out of his pocket and down to his feet. Three blue lights turned on under the porch. Nora flew straight up, screaming, giving Jack a quick shot at them. He squirted the first one and the other two flew into the stream. All three fell to the ground; the blue light streamed out as their bodies disintegrated. It swirled and came right to Jack's outstretched hand. There was a strange high-pitched sound coming from the tree, kind of like katydids' but eerie. Jack turned back up the steps, grabbed his suitcase, picked it up and said he was going to make a run for it. Down the step he ran, suitcase in one hand, spray can in the other. He made it halfway, when the tree busted with blue light. The leaves started to move, the lights moving closer together.

Jack stood, asking more from himself than from anyone else, "What should I do?"

Boris yelled: "Hit them now!"

Jack calmly said, "They need to be closer, they're out of range." He started to take slow steps toward the car. The tree started to shake.

Boris yelled: "They're making their move."

Jack sat his suitcase down, unzipped the front pocket and pulled out another spray can. He turned from the car and bolted to the tree. He stopped right in front of it, pointed both spray cans up at it and started spraying; it was like hitting a wasp nest. The fairies fell like rain, popping like firecrackers. They attacked, streaming blue lights coming out of the tree. They were all coming right at Jack, but he just kept on spraying and they kept on falling.

Nora screamed: "There, behind you!"

Jack spun around. Sure enough, there were a couple hundred hovering there, waiting; he sprayed them all in seconds. They all fell and the whole front lawn was lit with an eerie blue light, even in the bright sunshine. All the blue light came right to Jack; he slowly sank to his knees.

He said he needed the rocks. Nora flew to his suitcase and came out with one of the quartz stones. She avoided the blue streams that were entering his body as he kneeled on the ground with his head in his hands. He reached up and took the piece of quartz and held it out. It glowed with a blinding light. Jack finally stood. The rock that he held clenched in his hand looked like any other quartz stone.

He stood next to his suitcase and said in a new, stronger voice, "I thought they don't come out during the day."

Nora said nervously, "They don't, I have never seen one in the daylight."

Boris backed up her story that he had never, ever, seen one in the daylight. He said with fear in his voice, "They're frightened of you. Nothing will stop them from finding you and killing you."

Nora said in a meek voice, "You mean us."

Jack smiled, "Well, you have to go sometime." He reached down, picked up the suitcase and headed for the car.

Just as he reached the car, a small boy came riding up on his bike. "Hi, Mister Robinson," the boy called.

"Ah, nuts," Jack murmured. "Jimmy, I'm going on holiday for a couple of days. Would you hold my paper?" he said with a loud voice.

The boy drove right up to Jack and asked if he could help put the suitcase in the car. Jack snapped back: "I can do it myself!" Jack's breast pocket moved as Boris kicked him in the chest. Jack let out a small "Ouch!", then he asked Jimmy, "How much do I owe you for the paper?"

The boy said that he didn't know and he asked, "Did you see a weird blue light over here, like someone was wielding?"

Jack pulled a 20 out of his wallet. When Jimmy was done putting his suitcase in the car, he handed it to him. "Now this should do it. Keep the rest."

Jimmy thanked him and headed back down the driveway. Jack said softly that he was sure he had forgotten something. Nora crawled out of his pocket and up to his shoulder and asked, "Has Jimmy ever seen you without your cane? And you're walking like a man half your age!"

Jack stopped staring out over the lawn. Boris flew out of Jack's pocket to stand right next to Nora. "What is going on here? Nora, you go back to the house and get Jack's cane," he said with a demanding voice. "Now, you!" He said to Jack, "Get into the car. We should have been at the airport a long time ago."

Nora flew across the lawn fast, and I mean real fast; she was holding Jack's cane, "I hope no one saw me."

Jack said, "Yeah, I didn't think you guys came out during the day either."

Boris stood on the roof of the car with his arms folded in front of his chest, tapping his foot. Jack came to the car but instead of reaching for the door handle, he put his hand on the roof, then the other. He leaned against it and let out a groan. Boris got right into Nora's face; he looked like he was about to break down. "See, he isn't going to make it. The whole colony is going to starve."

Nora ran over to Jack, grabbed onto his forehead and lifted. Jack lifted his head and said, "I don't feel so good."

Nora yelled at him, "Well, if you don't get us to the airport, everybody dies! Did you hear me, Jack? Everybody—you, me, the colony!"

Boris threw in, "Everyone except the blues."

Jack pushed off the car. As he did, they heard a jet overhead. It was reversing its engines loudly. Jack pulled the can of wasp spray out of his pocket and got into the car. Nora and Boris flew in and sat on the dash. Jack started the car, turned it around and headed down the driveway. Boris questioned Jack on how he felt and told him to drink water. Jack told him that he had bad stomach cramps and he wanted to turn around and go to the bathroom.

Boris yelled: "That's too damn bad! We're going. From now on, things are going to be done my way. Now you're going to listen to me. Ivan has risked all our lives on this and he put me in charge."

Jack pulled out onto a two-lane county road. He brought the old town car up to his standard speed of 45, when all of a sudden the car kicked into passing gear. Jack's hands tightened on the wheel, you could see his knuckles turn white.

"Oh my God!" he gasped, "The pedal is stuck to the floor." The car's speedometer read 70 and was climbing fast. Nora dropped the water and flew down to the steering column and turned off the car. Both of Jack's feet were on the brakes already, bringing the car to a screeching halt. Boris was standing on the dash; he got slammed against the windscreen. Jack's knuckles where pure white now; his face was close to the same colour. He sat there staring, both feet were still on the brake pedal and hands on the wheel.

Nora flew to his shoulder and asked, "What is going on? Oh my God, do you feel that? There's a blue under the bonnet!"

Jack threw the door open, stepped out, reached in and pulled the bonnet release. Nora flew over to the wasp spray but Jack firmly said, "No, you should never touch that can. If it kills blues, it will kill you." He crawled in, grabbed the can and walked over to the front of the car. Nora was on his shoulder; Boris flew up next to her. Jack reached under the town car's bonnet and started to lift.

"Quickly!" yelled Boris.

Jack threw open the bonnet. Three blues stood on the air cleaner. As soon as the bonnet opened, they flew right at him. Jack reached down and grabbed the can of spray off the bumper and shot it wildly. The can wasn't straight in his hand so it shot to the side instead of forward. He swung his arm, hitting two of them right before they got to him. The third was faster, he hit Jack right in the chest. Jack reached up and grabbed him. There was a small blink of light that came through his fingers. The two that he sprayed flopped around on the engine for a couple of seconds. Then they turned into blue wisps of power and came right to Jack.

Jack came back, held onto the front of the car, hung his head and threw up. Boris yelled at Nora: "I told you!"

Nora put her finger to her lips, then said, "Jack, there's another one in there."

Jack's head came up. "Where?" he said. He started to look around the engine compartment. "Oh, this isn't good. They chewed through the wires," he said, reaching in and lifting a few wires.

"There!" yelled Nora, as she flew and pointed, "Behind that thing."

Jack reached over and pointed. "You mean the battery?" he questioned, as he reached over it and sprayed a good stream around it. A blue light floated right up to Jack, he let out an "Ah! That felt good!"

Jack asked Nora, "Are we good? Is it clear?" Of course she had to ask what he meant by that. "Are there any more blues in the car?" he asked, with that old man crabby voice.

Nora slowly flew around the car. "I don't think so," she said sheepishly.

Jack's mobile phone rang. He reached into his pocket, looked at the number and put it back into his pocket. He then said, "Remind me to call my son." He opened the door and stood there for a few seconds, then let out a loud: "Well."

Boris flew in and Nora was right behind. Jack slipped in behind the wheel. Boris was whispering in Nora's ear. All of a sudden, she was in the backseat, going through Jack's luggage. Jack questioned Boris, "What is going on?" Nora answered by flying up with the last bottle of water.

Boris said, "You must keep drinking; all the impurities must be flushed from your body. And let me tell you this—it is going to be a rough couple of days."

Jack's phone rang again. He wiggled around, trying to get it out of his pocket. Finally, he unsnapped his seat belt and pulled it out. Nora, standing on his shoulder, watched Jack look at it. This time he opened it. Nora questioned Jack, "Who was it?"

He said, "It is the pilot. He said his name was Andre Indroppoff and he was waiting at the airport." Jack told him they were about five minutes away, apologised for being late and told him they had a bit of car trouble. In fact, the check engine light hadn't turned off yet and she was running a bit rough.

Boris flew onto Jack's shoulder and yelled: "There's smoke coming out of the bonnet," pointing to the passenger's side. Jack closed the phone and started to slow down. Boris ordered Jack: "Keep going!"

Jack put the pedal down; the old town car coughed and started to slow down. Jack pleaded to the car, "Come on, baby, you never let me down. Just a few more miles."

Boris asked, "Will we make it?"

Jack said, "I have it to the floor—it must be spraying gas. The fire under the bonnet must be growing."

Nora said, "The airport is right around the corner."

Jack didn't leave off, the big old town car came sliding around it. He could hardly see though the smoke. He said loudly, "Get ready to exit quickly."

The two fairies scrambled into Jack's breast pocket. He whipped it though the gate and out onto the airfield, coming to a screeching halt. Jack threw open his door, then opened the back door and grabbed his suitcase and cane. He turned and sprinted for about ten yards, then turned to watch his car burst into flames. There were men running toward the car with fire extinguishers.

Nora crawled out of Jack's pocket and up to his ear. "Use the cane, Jack! You're an old man."

Jack dropped the suitcase, hunched over, bent his knees and put weight on his cane. A cop came running up to him, out of breath—it was a good hundred yards from the building. "Jack," he puffed, "I didn't think you were going to make it out of there." He put his arm around the old guy. "Hey, I'm sorry about your car."

The cop and Jack watched three men shoot a yellow chemical into the open doors and under the car. A younger man came running out on the field with a long bar; he pried the bonnet open and the flames leaped out. "She's a goner. I know how much it meant to you," the cop said. The men shot streams from their extinguishers and the fire died. A cloud of yellow smoke hung over it.

A man walked up behind them, picked up Jack's suitcase and said, "You must be Jack."

The old man turned to see an older pilot, about six feet, cleanly shaven and in his uniform. The cop took his arm off Jack's shoulder. Jack held out his hand and the pilot took it gently, as introduced himself, "I am Andre Indroppoff, and I will be piloting this flight."

Jack turned to the cop, "Pauly, do me a favour—have Hank come over, pick up the car and make me an estimate for the damages." The cop told him he would do it. Jack said, "You can call the fire service and cancel that fire brigade."

In the distance, you could barely hear the siren. Pauly pulled the microphone from his shoulder and assured them the fire was out. Andre had slid to Jack's side, took him by the arm and started to guide him toward the plane. Pauly jogged up to them and started to question them. He started with Jack, "So where are you headed?"

Jack, being an ex-sheriff, told him just what he needed to. "An old army buddy needs me."

"Where are you going?" asked the cop.

Jack slipped into the old man role again. "I told you, an old army buddy wants my help and he sent a plane. See you when I get back."

"How long are you going to be gone?" the cop questioned.

Jack stopped walking, raised his cane and told him, "Listen here, I'm going to help an old friend and I will be back when I get back."

Pauly turned his attention to Andre. "So this is the first time that I have seen a jet land here. Isn't the strip too short?"

Andre stopped, let go of Jack's arm and stepped close to Pauly. Then he leaned in so his face was about six inches from Pauly's. "Now let me tell you, boy. On the net, your runway was six thousand feet. You're lucky it's three thousand, I damn near killed myself. I have contacted the FAA, three solicitors and your mayor. There's going to be hell to pay." By now, Andre was up on his tiptoes, yelling at the top of his lungs. "Somebody's going to pay for this! What kind of an idiot would do this kind of thing? And if you don't get the hell out of my way, I am going to come down on you like a hammer. I will wipe you out, just like this little town."

Andre grabbed Jack by the arm and stormed toward the plane. He said, "Hurry now! That just stunned him for a couple of minutes. He will realise that he is in power here."

Pauly stood there, wiping the spit off his glasses and watched them walk away. Andre helped Jack up the stairs. When he came back down, Pauly was back being a cop again. This time, he didn't ask. "You're not going anywhere until you answer a few questions," he said, as he put his foot on Jack's suitcase.

Andre stared into his eyes and said, "We're going to L.A. So get your foot off the bag."

Pauly gave him the old, "Not until you answer a few questions first."

A police car came flying up to the plane; Andre rolled his eyes and muttered, "Now what?"

The chief of police jumped out of the car, hurried around it and yelled: "Pauly, what's going on here?"

Pauly told him that he was just asking a few questions, trying to find out what was going on here.

Andre piped in with: "He's holding me here. Do you mind if I tape this conversation?"

The chief grabbed Pauly by the arm and turned him away from the plane. He whispered to Pauly, but not a good whisper. Andre heard most of it. The chief had his ass handed to him by the mayor, who had his handed to him by Andre's flight coordinator and by a fancy city solicitor. Andre reached down, grabbed Jack's suitcase and tossed it into the jet. "We'll be off then." He climbed the stairs, turned and stated that he would be seeing them again.

He started pulling up the stairs when he overheard Pauly yelling: "Don't you make the take-off! The runway is short! Jack, wait!"

Chapter Five
The Plane Ride

Andre climbed into the pilot's seat and looked back at Jack. He said, "Well, that wasn't that bad!"

Jack looked at him and said, "I just don't believe this is happening to me."

"Well, believe it," Andre said, as he started flipping switches. He turned and asked Jack, "Would you like to sit up front with me? We have to get going before they ground us. Did you bring the bags from Ivan?"

Jack nodded his head and asked, "Is there was a bathroom aboard? I don't feel the greatest."

Andre said, "Man, you do look like hell warmed over. Are you going to be all right? It is in the back."

Jack quickly staggered to the bathroom, grabbing the back of the seats on the way. You couldn't stand in the jet, it was only an eight-seater. Andre fired up the engines and started down the runway; he was calling in his flight plan as he drove. There was a strange vibration from the wheels as it rolled. Jack staggered up to the cockpit and asked, "What is that vibration? It feels like you have flat spots on your tyres."

Andre taxied to the far end of the runway, almost on the grass and said, "Jack, sit down and buckle up. The runway is about two thousand feet short, this will be a quick take-off. And yes, we might have flat spots on the tyres. I stood on the brakes on landing."

Andre turned and asked, "What kind of idiot would lie about the length of your runway?"

Jack shrugged his shoulders, "Who knows? They might want this town airport to look big or it may be a misprint."

Andre flipped some switches and ran some RPMs. The plane roared and started to shake. He turned to Jack and yelled, "Hole shot!"

The plane started to slowly move down the runway, shaking violently; the roar was deafening. Jack looked back, everything in the plane was shaking wildly, overhead compartments were opening and spilling their contents.

Andre yelled over to Jack: "Hold on!" as he stepped off the brakes and the jet leaped forward. Both men were pinned back into their seats.

The jet shot down the runway, Andre pulled back on the yoke for a couple of seconds, raising the nose of the plane. He yelled excitedly, "This is going to be close!" Then, he reached up and pulled a couple of things and flipped a few switches. The plane quieted and slowed; he brought the nose down a bit and started to call in his flight plan again. The tower congratulated him for making the take-off and gave him a heading.

Andre turned to Jack and said, "Well, we only have two things to worry about. One, that the tyres weren't on fire when I pulled them up, and two, that we have enough jet fuel."

You could smell the burnt rubber from the tyres, which nearly choked Jack. He said he was going to be sick, so he unbelted himself and headed back to the bathroom. After 10 or 15 minutes, Andre walked back to see how he was doing.

Jack asked him, "What the hell! Who's flying the plane?"

Andre smiled, "It's on auto-pilot, it should be a semi-smooth flight."

Jack lifted his head from the toilet. "That was the all-time worst take-off I have ever had, I thought I was going to die. And let me tell you, boy, when I was in the war getting shot at, mortars landing all around, I felt safer than when flying with you. Now get your ass up front and fly the plane. I tell you, people these days!"

Andre asked, "Is there anything I can do for you?"

Jack said, "Yeah," as he slowly got to his feet. He started to stand but bumped the ceiling. "Just get us there safely," Jack said weakly. Then he said a little prayer, "My God! I feel like shit. Help me though this."

Nora peeked out of Jack's pocket. Seeing Andre walk away, she flew out, landing on the seat in front of Jack and asked, "Are you all right?"

Soon Boris was sitting alongside of her. Jack told them, "This is absolutely the worst I have ever felt."

Boris asked, "Jack, do you have any of that water you packed?"

Nora flew off down the aisle. She spotted Jack's suitcase, which was wedged under a seat. She was pulling it but it wouldn't move. She screamed when Andre grabbed it and gave it a jerk. She ran and hid behind a leg, flattening her body against it. Andre smiled, "I've seen you, so don't be shy."

Nora stepped out and walked into plain view. Andre put his hand down, palm up, so she could walk right into it. He said, "You're a cute little fairy, aren't you?" He carried the suitcase and the fairy back to Jack's seat. Andre asked Nora, "What do you want out of the luggage?"

She told him, "Water."

Andre said quietly, "I have cold water in the fridge."

Boris turned and shouted, "You showed yourself," shaking a fist at Nora. Boris glowed red and the whole inside of the plane glowed.

"Wow, someone's not happy," Andre said.

Boris said, "I need that water now."

Andre turned to walk to the fridge. Boris flew to his shoulder. "Let's get this straight now. Your job is to get us to Marvin's, my job is to take care of Jack. Now, we don't want to put him into shock, warm water will do." Nora had already taken all the water out of the suitcase and handed one to Jack.

Andre stood and looked at Jack, then he asked, "Is he going to make it?" Jack had no colour whatsoever and was drenched in sweat.

Boris asked, "How long before we get there?"

Andre said, "Well, if we don't have to stop for fuel—three hours."

Boris looked at Nora. She said, "Just before dusk." Boris asked Jack for the two bags. Jack straightened one of his legs out, reached into his pocket and pulled them out.

He said weakly, "Take care of them; they are of the utmost importance." Then he fell back into his seat.

Boris snapped at Andre, "Aren't you supposed to be driving this thing?"

Andre turned, started to walk to the cockpit and slid into the captain's chair. Nora, knowing her job was to help Boris, stayed there and helped make a potion, drug, whatever you wanted to call it. Boris had her talk Jack into drinking as much water as he could. Then Boris rubbed this drug on Jack's wrists, neck and a few more pressure points. Jack fell asleep and Boris took some more of the drug and rubbed Jack's temples with it. Jack's breathing quickened; he started to sweat and shake. Nora asked Boris, "Is he going to be all right?"

Boris told her loudly, "Don't worry about it, everything is going according to my plan. And tell me before we get there."

This gave Nora time to talk to Andre, so she flew right up to the windscreen and looked out. "Wow! How high are we?"

Andre smiled, "We're about 20 thousand feet."

Nora told him, "This is the highest that I have ever been."

Andre asked, "Why?"

So Nora told him, "The air is too thin and cold. The blues can fly this high, but they still need air. The green fairies can fly from planet to planet."

Andre said, "Tell me about the green fairy."

Nora flew onto Andre's shoulder and started the story about Elizabeth flying into Jack's lawn and him killing all the blues with wasp spray, dragging Jack into the forest, saving the unicorn, outwitting Elizabeth, drugging her and slipping away.

"Wow! How long before she finds you?" Andre asked.

Nora said, "By nightfall. Ivan would have told her where we were headed."

Andre asked, "Why would he do that?"

Nora said sadly, "Because Ivan doesn't lie." She flew off his shoulder, only to return in a minute, "Boy, I can't stand to watch him like that."

Andre asked, "How is he?"

Nora told him, "He is soaking wet and shaking like he's freezing."

Andre told her, "We are about halfway. We will be landing in about an hour and a half."

She told him, "Tell me when we are a half hour out."

Andre started his checklist of things to look at. Nora asked about what they were and what they did. Andre tapped on the fuel gauge, then called the tower. He told them he was low on fuel and asked if he should stop and refuel, or if he could come right in and land. The tower gave him a heading and told him the traffic was light that day, so he should be able to shoot it straight in. Andre thanked him and told him he owed him one.

Nora asked, "What do you owe him?"

Andre smiled and said, "It's cheaper to give them a fifty-dollar gift certificate in the bar than to circle the airport for hours. How is Jack doing back there? Looks rough."

Nora flew back and talked with Boris for a moment, then flew back to the captain. She said, "He looks rough—like, dead. He is grey and not moving. I mean, you can't even see him breathing." She wiped a tear that was sliding down her face.

Andre stared at her for almost a half-minute, then burst out: "Well, is he going to be all right?"

Nora shrugged her shoulders. Her antennae shot straight up as Boris flew up and slapped her on the back, almost knocking her off the switch that she was standing on. He boasted: "Jack will be fine. I haven't worked like this in decades, it feels good to work on humans again. And let me tell you, this one is going to be a challenge." Then he asked, "How long before we land?"

Andre said, "In about 45 minutes." Nora explained to him how long that would be. Boris then flew off, all excited.

Andre asked, "Can't Boris tell time?"

She said to him, "We have been in hiding for almost two centuries. Where we live, there is no need for time."

Andre was puzzled, "What do you mean, no need for time?"

Nora told him, "Back in the forest, you got up and did what you had to do. You never needed to be somewhere at a certain time."

Andre smiled, "Life must be great! Oh, the simple life! No stress, no meetings—sounds like retirement."

Nora snapped him out of it by saying one word: "Boring."

Andre asked, "Have your people really been hiding for two centuries?"

Nora took offence to being called people. She told him, "My group of fairies broke off from the clan that lived in Northern California. We flew up here, flying for days over the ocean, so the blues couldn't follow. I have lived most of my life up there."

Andre asked, "Most of your life! My God, how old are you?"

She said, "I was just a child when we moved up there."

Boris flew up, "She is at least 350 if she's a day."

"Oh! Don't believe anything he says," Nora said blushing.

Boris said, "I remember you being born, your dad flew all the way to Bora Bora for an exotic orchid for the punch. Your folks were great. I spent many hours flying to Russia, Asia and the jungles of the world, picking roots and flowers to fill the pantry and trade with other colonies."

A light flashed on the console, Nora flew to it and hovered. Then she turned to Andre and asked, "Are we low on fuel?"

"That's fine," Andre ensured her, "I knew we were going to cut it close, just not this close. You had better tell your friend that we will be landing in about 37 minutes." With that, Andre flipped some switches and pulled on a few knobs. This time, he didn't explain anything to Nora as she sat on the co-pilot's head rest. She could sense that Andre's stress level had increased by about three times. He turned and looked at her with a blank face.

Nora flew back to Boris and told him, "It is time to wake him; we will be landing soon." Then she flew right back to Andre and listened to him speak to the tower. He was told to come straight in for a landing.

When he had stopped talking for a couple of minutes, Nora asked him: "Is everything all right?" He started to fill her in on about the runway, how many degrees he had to bank and how they were going to glide.

Boris flew up and interrupted, "Nora, you're needed back here," he turned and was gone.

Nora shrugged her shoulders and flew to the back of the plane; she landed on a headrest in front of Jack and asked, "What is the problem?"

Boris said, "The problem is that Jack won't snap out of it."

Nora grabbed Jack by the hand, lifted it straight up and let it drop on his chest. "Oh my God!" she stammered, "I told you he was too old."

Andre turned in the seat, looked at Jack and asked, "Is he all right?"

Boris flew to the back rest of a seat next to him and asked, "Does he look all right? I have never tried to rejuvenate someone this old this fast. He might be out for a week."

Andre quickly stepped back and felt Jack's face, then gave him a good slap. The old man slowly opened his eyes, then closed them again. Nora gave a scream, "Nobody's flying!"

Andre shook his head, "We're on auto-pilot. Oh yeah, that means the computer is flying. A lot has happened in the last fifty years."

Andre was shuffling around in the overhead compartments and came out with a first-aid kit. He set it on the seat and opened it. He walked over to Jack with a small white thing and smiled, "Well, I hope this works." With that he snapped a thing and held it under his nose.

Jack's eyes opened wide. He tried to pull away from the smelling salts, but Andre held them tight to his nose. Andre said, "Well, he's awake. We'll be landing in a few minutes." Jack pulled his seat to an upright position and sat there rubbing his nose.

Nora flew to him and asked, "How do you feel?"

Jack said, "I feel fine; I heard everything that was going on, but I just could not wake up. For a while, I thought I was dead."

Boris flew up with a small pouch and started to bark out orders, "Jack, put this under your tongue. Nora, keep him drinking, I don't want to see him without a bottle in his hand. Do you understand?"

Nora said back to him, "Yeah I was scared too, I thought he—"

The speakers came to life. "This is your captain speaking. You're going to have to put your seat belts on and store anything that's not secure.

Jack told Boris, "You should get into my breast pocket. Where is the other one—Nora?"

Boris said, "She's up talking with that fly-boy." Nora sat right on Andre's shoulder; he was speaking to the tower. When he was finished speaking, Nora asked if two hundred pounds was a lot of fuel.

Andre said, "I have never ran it down this low before. And you should climb into my pocket, because this is going to be a rough one." Of course Nora wanted to know why. Andre said, "Let's start with I don't know how many tyres have air, and we're coming in fast."

Andre started to flip switches. The engines came to life with a loud roar as he reversed the engines, then the flaps came down. Andre made the sign of the cross, reached over and rubbed a small statue of Mary that was stuck to the dash. When the tyres touched down, there was a squeal, followed by a loud thudding, then the plane just shook, coming to a slow taxi. The tower came on, telling him he had lost his port side tyre.

Andre said, "That's steaks for the deck crew." He looked down to Nora, who was half sticking out of his pocket and said, "This is going to be an expensive flight." He taxied up to a limo parked in front of a hangar. As he slowed, the shaking of the plane got worse.

The jet came to a stop and a man about Andre's age came jogging up. Andre opened the door and dropped the stairs. Jack was standing—well, hunched over, because you couldn't stand in the small jet, getting his bags out of the overhead compartments. Andre said, "Pickupski will get that."

Jack said, "Well, if you will take that bag, we will have it all," and he headed for the door. Andre grabbed Jack's large suitcase that was strapped into a seat.

Nora crawled up his shirt and told him, "Don't forget Jack's cane." Jack was on the blacktop staring at this man, who was checking the plane over. As soon as the man noticed Jack, he walked over.

Andre introduced him as he walked down the stairs. "Jack, this is Ivan Pickupski, and Pickup, this is Jack Robinson. That was a flight that we won't forget soon."

Ivan shook Jack's hand and asked, "What in the hell did my brother do to the plane?"

Andre stepped in, "Not in front of a client."

Ivan yelled: "Client, hell! Marvin's picking this up, wait until he gets this bill." Ivan stood there shaking his head, "What the hell did you do?"

Andre said, "I'll give you the quick rundown. First that dizzy broad you married told me the runway in Oregon was three thousand feet longer then it was, then I had to suck half the fuel in a suicide take-off. You just do me a favour, put tyres on this thing, give it a good check, pay off the tower with drinks. And steaks for the deck crew—and be generous. Oh yeah, she's sucking fumes. Gas her up."

Andre grabbed Jack by the arm and handed him his cane. He leaned into Jack and whispered, "Really act it out."

Jack hunched over and used his cane. He moved slowly, dragging one foot every third step. He stopped and said loudly in an old man's voice, "I have to piss." Pickupski grabbed Jack's suitcase and headed for the limo.

Andre whispered, "Good, keep it up."

Jack said, "I'm going to piss my pants if you don't get me to a crapper."

Andre yelled to Ivan: "I'm going to take him into the hangar." Jack started to walk faster.

Andre said, "Slow down, be needier, Ivan hates that."

Jack turned to him and said, "You listen here, young man, if I don't get to a bathroom right now, you're going to clean me up."

Andre said, "Drop your bags, I'll run for a wheel chair, but don't walk any faster." He turned and jogged off to the hangar that was only fifty yards away and came out with a wheelchair, jogging behind it.

Jack went into a coughing fit. He leaned onto his cane, then slowly sank to his knees. Ivan started toward him. Andre picked up his pace. He reached Jack first. By this time, Jack was on all fours. Then he threw up, a violent heave. He just retched, throwing up black bile.

Ivan reached the two and commented, "That's sick." Then he asked, "Is he going to be all right?" Jack reached up and wiped his mouth with his sleeve and shook his head.

Andre turned to Ivan, "Help me get him in the chair." This was more a command than a request. The two men gently took Jack by the arms and got him back to his feet, then sat him in the chair.

Ivan said to Andre, "I think you should stop by the hospital on the way to the castle."

Andre looked at Jack and asked, "Are you going to be all right?"

Jack waved his cane at him, "Listen here sonny! If you don't get me to the bathroom, I'm going to piss my pants."

Ivan said, "You're not going to put him in the limo, are you? I mean—he smells nasty."

Andre never answered. He just took off on a fast jog, pushing the wheelchair toward the hangar. He stopped in front of the bathroom. "Are you going to be all right?"

"Just get me out of this damn chair," grumbled Jack. Andre kneeled down in front of Jack's chair and folded plates up from under his feet, then reached for his hands. Jack said loudly, "You big dummy, lock the wheels. Come on, I have to go!"

Andre reached down and pulled the levers on the wheels, locking them in place. Jack grabbed onto the armrests and pulled himself to his feet. Andre reached for the bathroom door. Jack said weakly, "I am quite able to go to the bathroom by myself."

Andre stood outside the bathroom door, waiting. Jack was in no hurry, he did his business talking to Nora and Boris. Jack told Boris, "It felt like I was going to hack up a lung."

The little fairy flew down to the sink and started to mix another potion. She asked, "How do you feel?"

Jack asked her, "How do you think I feel? I never slept at all last night, I puked like ten times today, I'm dizzy, dry-mouthed and my whole body aches."

Boris flew up to Jack's shoulder and rubbed some stuff on the base of Jack's neck. He asked, "Really Jack, how do you feel?"

Jack said "I feel like I have more energy than I've had in a long time."

Boris told him, "We had better get going.

Nora asked, "You're not going to put him to sleep again, are you?"

Jack said, "Hey, that's right! I took a nap on the plane."

Boris told Jack, "Drink as much water as you can."

Jack said loudly, "Of course there are no frickin' glasses in here." He splashed some water on his face, then he put his head in the sink and drank from it.

Andre and Ivan stood outside the door, listening to Jack ramble on. Ivan asked, "Are you sure about this guy? I think he's a bit off his rocker. I mean, he holds a pretty good conversation with himself."

Jack finished drinking and took some paper towels to wipe his face and it came back slimy. "What the hell is going on?"

Boris flew up. "It's all the poison coming out of your skin; we should get you into a waterfall."

Nora corrected him, "That would be into a shower—because you are getting a bit ripe."

Jack washed his hands all the way to his elbows; the brown goo just washed off. You could see a line where he stopped. The two fairies climbed into Jack's pocket and Jack looked up into the mirror, "Wow, I need a shave and a haircut." He walked out the door using the cane.

Andre said, "Finally! I thought you died in there."

Ivan said, "We knew you were alive, we could hear you talking."

Andre started to help Jack into the chair when he got a whiff of Jack. "Wow, that will make your eyes water!" They started toward the limo, Andre told Ivan, "I can take care of the plane and you can drive Jack."

Ivan kept in front of the two and said, "No. It has already been decided that you will drive Jack to the castle." Then he asked, "Would you like to ride up front, Jack?"

Jack of course said, "Yes, please." Ivan jogged around the car and opened the boot, producing a blanket; he then opened the passenger door and proceeded to tuck the blanket around the seat.

Andre pulled up with Jack. This time, he locked the chair's wheels. Ivan said, "Just throw the blanket out when you get there."

Jack said, "I can't smell that bad."

Ivan said, "Oh, I've never smelled anything like it. You two have a nice ride," as he turned and walked toward the plane.

Before Andre slid behind the wheel, he said, "Charge everything to Marvin. And thanks for putting Jack up front." First thing he did was roll the windows down.

Nora crawled out of Jack's pocket and across the back of the seats, to Andre. She was all excited. "We're going to Hollywood," she screeched.

Andre asked if Jack was all right. Jack said, "I feel really strange."

Boris asked, "Do we have any water in the car?" Andre pushed a button. The screen between the driver and the riders went down. He told Nora there should be a few bottles in the fridge. She flew back there. In a couple of minutes, she came back and flew up to Jack with a bottle. He just laid there in the seat with his head almost out the window.

She asked Boris, "Is he going to be all right?"

Boris nodded his head, then said, "He'll be just fine." Nora put her hand over her mouth and flew straight out the window. In a minute she flew back in and rested on Andre's shoulder.

She told him, "I needed some fresh air, or car exhaust, anything smells better then Jack."

Andre said, "Just a couple more miles." He jumped off the main road and started to weave through some back streets, bypassing all the stoplights. There it was, the Magic Castle. It didn't look like a castle, but a mansion with a small hotel. Andre called on his phone and told Marvin, "We are five minutes out, coming in the back."

Andre parked in the rear of the place; Nora climbed into Andre's pocket, Boris flew over and did the same. Andre asked, "Is he supposed to smell like that?"

Boris said, "I never smelled anything that bad."

Chapter Six
The Magic Castle

They all took a big breath of air when Andre stepped from the car. Jack fumbled with the latch. Andre jogged around the car, opened Jack's door and pulled his head back, "Wow, are you ripe!" Then he asked Jack if he could walk.

Jack of course took offence to this. "Of course I can walk!" Andre helped him get his legs out the car door, then got him to his feet. Jack asked himself, "Can I walk? God, I feel strange." Then he asked for his cane and slowly walked to the building. "Why the hell did you park here? There's no door!"

Andre chuckled, "You're at the Magic Castle; have faith. And don't always believe your eyes."

They slowly headed toward the building. When they stood right in front of it, Andre tapped the wall three times, then said, "Open sesame," and a part of the wall slid apart. A dark lift awaited them.

Andre helped Jack into the rather large lift. Jack leaned up against the wall. Andre let go of him and asked him if he would be all right for a minute. Jack nodded and slid to the corner. Andre started to gag. He stepped out, took a couple of deep breaths, then ran to the limo and opened the back door, reached in and grabbed Jack's suitcase. Then he headed back to the lift. Just before he stepped in, he took a deep breath and held it.

Andre quickly stepped inside and pushed the floor he wanted. He grabbed onto Jack and told him to hold on. The lift almost pushed him to the floor as it leapt the four stories and came to a stop in a couple of minutes. That was enough. Jack started to sway, he grabbed his stomach and started to retch. Andre pulled him out, into the kitchen, down the hall and to the bathroom.

Jack got down on his knees and hugged the toilet. Andre quickly ran back to the kitchen and held his head over the sink, just spitting saliva, when a voice came from behind him. "So that is our saviour." A pause. Then, "What is that smell?"

Andre lifted his head and asked the old man, "How are you doing?"

Marvin asked, "Is he going to be all right? Oh that smell, it burns my eyes! Did you get the powder, did you bring it?"

The old man looked wild-eyed as tears filled his eyes. His knuckles were pure white, gripping the back of a chair. Andre was wiping his face with a towel. He smelled his hands and went right to work washing them. He said, "Calm down, Marvin, I have the two small bags. God, this stuff stinks," as he shot some more soap into his hands.

The old man walked up behind him and put his hand on Andre's shoulder. "Listen here, Dropoff, did you bring the powder? Oh man, you stink!"

Andre asked, "Are we safe?"

Marvin assured him, "We are the only ones in the house."

Andre said, "OK, you can come out now."

The two fairies crawled out of his pocket. Marvin became all misty-eyed. He put his hand over his mouth and said to himself, "It's true."

Boris flew up to Marvin, "Greetings, Marvin the Magnificent! Where's Jack?"

Marvin said, "That must be Jack in the bathroom."

Boris flew off to find Jack hugging the toilet with his head resting on the bowl. He turned and shot a red streak to Andre, "You must get him into the shower now."

Andre calmly said, "In a minute."

Nora grabbed him by the back of his shirt and pulled him almost off balance. "When Boris uses that voice, it is serious."

Andre started for the bathroom. It was just down the hall. When he stepped into the bathroom, there was a lifeless body of an old man lying on the bowl of the toilet. Boris flew up to him, "His skin is plugged with poison and it can't breathe. You must scrub every inch of him." He flew to Nora who was hovering in the doorway, "You must watch him. Make sure he scrubs every part of him."

Nora just nodded and flew to Andre. She asked if she could help. Andre had Jack sitting up. Jack's eyes opened, then sunk to mere slits. Andre pleaded with him to get up. Nora did the same. She landed on his shoulder, grabbed him by the ear and yelled into it. She pulled back and barfed, looking at her hands. They were covered in the brown stinky goo that covered Jack's skin.

"Man, we need a better exhaust system in here," Andre exclaimed, as he reached down, grabbed Jack by the arm and started to lift. Nora, even though two inches tall, grabbed Jack by the front of the shirt and almost lifted him herself. "Wow! I almost forgot how strong fairies can be," Andre said, as they got him to his feet.

Nora said, "Take off his pants."

Andre muttered, "I can't believe I'm doing this." He unsnapped Jack's pants and pulled them down to his knees. You could see streak marks on his legs where the pants slid down. Andre turned his head and took a breath, then pulled them down to his ankles. He stopped again, turned his head, took a breath and lifted Jack's feet out of the pants. Jack was standing on his own, with one hand on the wall. Nora said his underwear had to go too.

"Not until we get him into the shower," Andre said sternly.

Jack looked weak, but he was standing on his own. He said, "I feel like crap."

Andre reached in and started the water. Nora said, "Scrub every inch of him."

Andre turned to the fairy and asked if she would shut the door, which she did. He got Jack's shirt off and him into the shower. The brown goo seemed to wash right off, it was like a spray tan that washed off and swirled at his feet.

Jack shook Andre's grasp and turned to him, "I can shower myself."

Andre turned to the sink and started to wash himself, when Nora came up with a toilet brush. "Here," she said.

Andre looked at her and said, "You can't use that on a person! It would take the skin right off." She dropped it, flew out the door and out into the kitchen, rummaging through the drawers and under the sink. She came out with a scrub brush. She flew right by the bathroom, looking in the other rooms, until she came to Juliet's room.

Marvin stood at the side of an old woman who was hooked up to oxygen, IV bags hanging by her side and a monitor with her pulse running. Boris was sitting on the bridge of her nose. Nora flew up and asked, "Can I use this brush? Is it okay to scrub Jack with this?"

Boris threw up his arms and started to rant, "Look at this, they have wires stuck to her and hoses with God only knows what pumping into her! There are even hoses running down her nose! Her life force is so weak that it will take all the powder we brought just to get her healthy. That's not why we are here. Marvin is the one who is here for that. Our people's lives are at stake here, our existence is at stake here. What am I supposed to do? Tell me, damn you!"

Nora looked at him and asked again, "Will this brush do? Didn't you hear me?"

Boris looked lost, he shook his head and mumbled to himself, "This is something that we need to figure out in time. He is a very smart guy and will do the right thing when the time comes."

Nora flew up to Marvin and asked if the brush she was holding could be used to scrub Jack. Marvin smiled at her, "I don't care what happens to me, I just want my Juliet to be okay. He can regenerate her, can't he?" Marvin asked.

Nora smiled and told him, "Boris is the best I know, and I have seen him regenerate many humans in the past. But we are here for you." With that she flew off, toward the bathroom. There she saw Andre in front of the shower, naked, washing Jack. She flew in and said, "Here, use this brush that I'm holding."

He looked at her, shook his head and told her that he was done. "Do it again," she ordered, "I have to watch, every part of him has to be scrubbed."

Andre told her, "I have scrubbed every square inch of him." Nora dropped the brush on the floor, flew into the shower and ran her hand behind Jack's ear. She flew back out holding a hand full of brown slime. Andre said, "Well, you're helping."

He reached down and grabbed the brush. With every stroke he made, you could see Jack's skin lighten. A bell rang. Marvin walked by. A couple of minutes went by, then Ivan Pickupski (Andre's partner) popped his head in and said loudly, "Man, it smells like someone died in here! Boy, did I make the right decision to stay with the plane! Yes, I think I did." With that, he let out a laugh that thundered though the room.

A wash rag came flying at him, he ducked and splat! It hit the old man behind him and let me tell you, Marvin didn't look happy. Marvin told the two men, "Stop horsing around." Then he asked, "How long is it going to take to clean Jack up?"

Andre said, "We're just about finished; we just have to wash his hair again." The shower head was a hose type. Nora sprayed as Andre scrubbed. Marvin and Ivan walked in closer.

Ivan chuckled, "This is a sight, two naked old guys taking a shower." They stood there, Ivan holding Marvin by the arm. The floor was soaked. Andre rubbed some shampoo into Jack's hair and it turned into a brownish colour.

"Aw, nuts!" Andre said with disgust.

Ivan started to chuckle again. "Well, looks like you're not quite finished yet. Don't forget behind his ears!" Ivan led Marvin by the arm out the door. As soon as he was in the kitchen he started to laugh and Marvin joined in.

Jack just sat there, leaning against the wall of the shower, as Andre finished his fourth shampoo. This time the suds stayed white. Nora hovered over Jack with the shower head. Andre shouted to the kitchen: "Pickup, get your ass in here."

Ivan came strolling in, "Boy, it stinks in here."

Andre asked him, "Would you wipe up the floor and hand me a towel?"

Ivan handed Andre the towel and started to wipe up the floor. With his foot on a towel, he started to push Jack's clothes. "Oh, I found out what stinks. It's his clothes!"

Andre helped Jack dry off, standing outside the shower. Marvin stood in the doorway with a dressing gown. Boris flew over, took the dressing gown and held it behind Jack. Nora spread out one side, Jack lifted one arm and slid it in, then the other. He looked like a fragile old white guy again.

Andre guided him out of the bathroom. Marvin stepped into the bathroom and told Ivan, "Clean this up. Throw away the clothes, except Jack's pants. Put those in a plastic bag, please." Ivan raised a hand, then dropped it without saying a word. He knew he had to do it.

Jack was out of the bathroom and in the kitchen, sitting at the table. He said one word, "Coffee."

Boris flew to Nora, who was sitting against the salt shaker. The two fairies stood there chatting for a minute. Nora flew to Andre's shoulder and talked into his ear, telling him that Jack had to drink as much water as he could. Andre turned and put the coffee pot back in the coffee maker.

"Hey!" boomed Jack, "What's going on here? I asked for coffee!"

Andre went to the water cooler, filled a glass and sat it in front of him. "Doctor's orders."

Jack said, half under his breath, "I've been up all night, and no coffee!" Boris flew up, looked into Jack's eyes, and flew into Juliet's room.

Marvin was talking to Jack, but Jack was in a different world. Jack finally said, "Marvin, I haven't slept at all last night. I think I saw a unicorn. And fairies! Hell, I think I've lost my mind."

Marvin reached over the table and took Jack by the hand. "We'll get you to bed and we will talk later."

Boris flew up. "Lean forward, Jack." As he did, Boris flew around him and smeared some cream on the back of his neck, then on his temples. Boris flew to Andre, who was watching Ivan, trying to pull Jack's wallet out of his pants without touching them. Boris landed on Andre's shoulder and told him that he would have to put Jack to bed.

Andre told Ivan, "Don't forget to wash your hands." He turned and headed back to the kitchen.

Marvin said, "You can keep the clothes when you're done with them." Andre wasn't going to put the stinky clothes back on, so he stole some of Marvin's, which of course were three inches short in the sleeves and the pants were too tight to button.

Andre took Jack by the arm and headed him down a hall. Marvin said, "It is the third door on the left."

"Now," the old man said, with a fist hitting the table to strengthen the point, "What are you doing to save my Juliet?"

Boris walked over to Nora and whispered something. Nora lowered her head and shook it slowly as she walked across the table to Marvin. She started to speak. Marvin laid his hand down in front of her, palm up, and she fluttered onto it. Marvin raised it up to his ear and she began again. "Marvin, I am truly sorry, Boris promised to protect Jack with his life. There just isn't enough powder."

A tear rolled down Marvin's face. He asked, "Then why did you come?"

Nora told him, "Ivan the unicorn sent us and said you would help Jack learn how to defeat the blues."

Andre came back to the table, "So what did I miss?"

Marvin shot him a look and slammed his fist on the table again. "They're not going to help Juliet, that's what you missed." Boris flew in from the other room and smeared a paste on the back of Marvin's neck and on his temples lightning-fast. Marvin yelled, "What the hell?"

Nora flew to Andre's shoulder and spoke into his ear, "We were sent here for Marvin, not his wife."

Andre said, "Oh, that's not going to work. He loves her more than himself."

Ivan finally came out of the bathroom and asked, "Where is Jack?"

Said, "Guest bedroom."

Ivan asked, "Did you put down a plastic sheet? Because if you didn't, the mattress will be shot; you'll never get the smell out of it."

Marvin pointed down the hall. "There should be a roll in the wardrobe's bottom shelf."

Andre got up and told Ivan, "Come on." They got the plastic. Sure enough, it was on the bottom shelf, behind a pile of stuff. Ivan said, "The old man probably hasn't used it in twenty years. He is still pretty sharp."

Andre said, "Yeah, his brain is there, but his body is taking a toll." They stepped into the guest room to the snoring of Jack. Nora was napping on the nightstand, she awoke as soon as they stepped in. The two men rolled out the plastic to the length of the bed.

"Damn!" Andre said, then he asked, "Did you bring scissors?"

Nora spoke: "I got it." With that, she shot out the door and down the hall. Ivan started to bend over to place the roll on the bed and Nora came back with the scissors. He thanked her and took them from her. Ivan cut the plastic and asked how they were going to do this.

Nora flew down and grabbed the covers by Jack's head and lifted them to the ceiling, toward the foot of the bed. The two men unfolded the plastic and laid it next to Jack. They rolled Jack on his side and slid the plastic sheet up to him again. Then they walked around the bed, rolled him to his other side and pulled the sheet over the rest of the bed.

Ivan said, "He's starting to smell again."

Andre smelled his hands, "Yeah." They both went into the bathroom and washed their hands.

Boris was in Juliet's room, with Marvin. He was explaining again what the IVs and the monitor were for. Boris asked when the last time was that she had spoken. Marvin got all misty-eyed and said, "When she was put in coma 13 years ago."

Boris stood there shaking his head, wrenching his hands; then he spoke. Marvin asked, "What did you say?"

Nora flew to Marvin's shoulder, grabbed him by the ear excitedly and shouted: "He's going to see what he can do, this is great!"

Andre and Ivan walked into the room to see Marvin with tears running down his face and a red fairy on his shoulders. Andre spoke first, asking, "What is going on?"

Nora flew right to him and told him, "Boris is going to save Juliet."

Ivan spoke up, "Wait a second, ten minutes ago you didn't have the stuff!"

Boris said, "Yes, you're right. I don't have the stuff to regenerate Marvin and Juliet, but there might be enough to make them healthy."

Nora asked, "And Jack?"

Boris said, "My plans for Jack haven't changed. He will be regenerated to thirty-five years old or so."

The sound of the toilet flush brought everyone back to Jack. Boris asked, "How is Jack, anyway?"

Nora said, "He was in a deep sleep when we left him five minutes ago."

Andre added, "He is starting to smell again."

Boris told Nora, "You need to get Jack to drink as much water as you can; I don't want to see him without a bottle in his hand. And get him to eat some raw meat every three hours."

Nora said, "Boris, the sense of time is coming back to you!"

Andre asked, "Feed him every three hours?"

Boris said, "Yes, yes, I said raw meat every three hours."

Nora asked nervously, "Where am I going to find raw meat in Hollywood?"

Andre smiled, "One filet mignon tartare coming up, I'm taking orders."

Ivan said, "Great! I'll have the filet medium."

You could hear Jack in the bathroom hack up a lung or something. Nora flew out the room.

Marvin asked, "Why is Jack having such a hard time with the regeneration?"

Boris said, "That would be the unicorn horn he held. He handled the powder, he got too much into his system at once." Boris asked Marvin, "How do you feel? Taste anything strange?"

"Now that you mention it, almonds! I taste almonds!" Marvin smacked his lips.

Boris said, "I have to see what the boys are up to." He flew through the house. Andre was on the phone ordering lunch, Ivan and Nora were in the bathroom with Jack.

Boris flew in and landed on Jack's shoulder. He asked Jack, "How do you feel?"

Jack told him, "This is the worst I have ever felt, I keep hacking up tar and I am sick to my stomach. Every bone and muscle hurts. I can hardly stand."

Boris flew off to Juliet's room, where Marvin was starting to doze off in a chair. He flew in, hovered six inches in front of him and yelled, "Now this is the way it's going to be! You tell me everything! Don't hide anything!"

Marvin's eyes opened. He looked drugged and sleepily said, "What do you want to know?"

Boris asked, "Where are the fairies that have been keeping Juliet alive?"

Marvin said, "What? Oh, up in the tower. There is a secret room. Andre will take you." With that, his eyes closed.

Boris flew to Andre, who was sitting by the phone. "I need you to take me to the tower to meet the other fairies that live here."

Andre stood, "We have to be quick. Or could we wait until after the food gets here."

Boris hovered, "Get going, this is no game!"

Nora flew in from Jack's room and announced, "Jack is sleeping."

"You're coming with us," Boris ordered.

Andre took the two fairies behind the table to the wall of the kitchen. "This is it!" Andre said dramatically. "Open sesame!" He waved his arms. A panel in the wall slid open to reveal a small lift. They all went inside.

Andre hit the button, saying more to himself, "I hope this thing still works. It hasn't been used in years." When they reached the top, the door slid open. There were large windows all painted a light grey that left just enough light in to see.

Andre stepped out and pulled a string that hung from a light. This lit the room with an eerie light. Up two flights of stairs, there was a small village of doll houses, all covered in dust.

"Rupert!" Andre shouted.

Nora flew to a large Victorian doll house. She landed on the porch and walked up to the door. She knocked and the door opened.

A frail old red fairy came to the door. His eyes came to life when he saw her. He asked, "Can I help you?"

Nora said, "Yes, I hope you can." She waved to Boris.

He shot right down to them. "Rupert, I presume." Boris held out his hand.

Rupert asked, "What brought you to the castle?"

Boris said, "Ivan, a unicorn from Oregon, sent us here. To regenerate Marvin."

Nora spoke, "Don't forget Jack!"

Boris cut her off, "Let's get down to why we are here. Do you have any agave root?"

The old fairy said, "There might be some in the pantry. Marvin has to be here to open it."

Andre asked where the panty was; he was sure he could open it. The old fairy could hardly walk. He held onto the railing, pointed to the back of the room and spoke. Boris flew up to Andre and told him, "Rupert said behind the bookcase."

Andre looked at the bookcase. It went from floor to ceiling. "Oh, boy!" he muttered, then he started over there.

Nora stepped close to Rupert and gave him a big hug. She glowed a bright red glow, bright enough to light up the room.

Boris shook his head, "Nora, you're weak as it is! Why give your power away?"

She said in a weak voice, "It had to be done."

Boris grabbed Rupert and flew him to Andre, who was saying all kinds of different magical phrases. He was pulling books and running his hands around the edge of the case. Finally, he pulled out his mobile phone and called Ivan. He said into the phone, "Hey, Pickupski, do you know how to open this bookcase up here? Then ask Marvin." There was a pause, then Andre said, "They're on the way up, it will be a few minutes. Rupert, it's been a long time."

Andre asked, "Try to remember where Marvin stood when he opened the case."

Rupert said, "It is so nice to see someone again!"

Andre asked, "How long has it been?"

Rupert said, "At least two seasons. Marvin is really slowing down." Just as he said that, a bell chimed twice and the lift door opened.

Marvin climbed the stairs and walked right up to Andre. He gave him a slap on the back and chuckled, "Can't open it, can you?"

Boris and Rupert were holding on tightly to Andre shirt. Boris yelled, "You damn fool, watch what you're doing!"

Marvin looked. Both red fairies were sitting on Andre's shoulder. "Oh, I am so sorry Rupert! I just couldn't make the stairs, and I have been so depressed watching Juliet slowly fade away."

Boris yelled at the top of his lungs, "Well, that has changed! Open the door!"

Marvin waved a hand over a line of books, chanting a magic spell. Then he reached over to another shelf and started swaying as he chanted. Then he turned to Andre and said, "I don't know, Dropoff, let's try open sesame." He stepped forward and the case slid back and to the side, leaving a dark hole.

Marvin smiled, "Just like that."

Ivan said, "I'm going downstairs to check on the food and on Jack."

Marvin walked into the dark room, cutting a hole through the cobwebs with his arm. He did this slowly. "It might need a dusting. Ah, there it is," he said to himself as a light turned on, illuminating the room in a soft light.

Andre let out a soft, "Wow."

Boris said to Andre, "What are you waiting for? Get us in there. Rupert, you tell him where to go."

Rupert held onto Andre's ear and talked into it. Andre could tell the old fairy had just about had it for the day.

Marvin was picking up bottles, wiping off dust so he could read them. Andre was doing the same thing when Marvin said, "This must be it."

Boris flew from Andre's shoulder, "Let me see that." The fairy landed right on Marvin's wrist. Boris said with excitement in his voice, "This will do, get me back to Jack."

Marvin put the jar in his dressing gown pocket and walked to the far wall. He started to chant and sway from side to side. A small panel in the wall opened; he reached in and pulled out a large book. Boris flew back to Marvin, landing on his shoulder. He spoke into his ear, telling him that they didn't have time.

Marvin slowly wiped off a light layer of dust to reveal gold letters, *Albrich's Book of Magic*. He spoke lightly, "This was giving to me by my teacher many years ago. It might come in handy." Andre told Marvin that he would take it, but the old man held it tight to his chest. "Go!" he commanded, "I will shut the door."

Andre started for the lift, stopped and turned around. He told Marvin, "We don't need you breaking a hip."

Marvin said, "Done," as the book case slid back in place, "You don't need to know all my tricks."

Andre told him, "I wasn't watching, but you have the root and Boris doesn't want to leave without it."

Marvin shook his head and said, "If you're making what I think you're making, it's going to take at least an hour."

They all got into the lift at once. Andre asked, "So when is the last time you had this thing serviced?"

Marvin said, "You never change. Always thinking of safety."

Boris flew to Marvin and spoke into his ear. Marvin replied, "I thought Nora was your helper and Rupert was a very good doctor."

Boris told him, "Nora gave Rupert most of her energy and they both need as much rest as they can get." The lift came to a stop and the two stepped out. Andre helped guide Marvin. Boris asked, "Why don't you have the lift go to your floor? Marvin told him that it was much cheaper this way.

The two stepped back into Marvin's place. The smell of food filled the kitchen. Andre said, "Food's here."

Marvin quickly stepped out, finding Jack and Ivan in the bathroom. Jack was curled up in a ball lying on the floor. Ivan said, "He is in a lot of pain right now, just keeps coughing and puking. There is nothing to throw up any more.

Jack lifted his head, "Let me die."

Boris told Marvin, "We have to get to work," and into the kitchen they went. Boris instructed Marvin to get some water to a boil, then he flew off. When he came back he was holding the two bags that Jack brought from the forest, as well as his own little bag. He took a pinch of powder to Nora and Rupert, "Here, eat this."

Rupert took it and nodded his head. Nora just shook her head, "I'll be fine."

Boris held it out, "You do as I say." She sheepishly took it. "You will be no help if you are sick. I need you healthy." With that, he turned and flew back to Marvin, who had his book and the jar opened. The root was ground into a powder. The unicorn horn powder was just a couple of grains in a teaspoon.

Marvin spoke in a loud commanding voice, "Pickup!"

Ivan got up from the table, wiping his mouth, "What?"

Marvin stood there looking in the huge book and said, "Run up to the pantry and get a jar called Dragon Fire."

Boris said to Marvin that he was the only one who knew how to open the bookcase.

Andre asked, "Can I finish eating?" One look from the old man and he knew he wanted it now. Marvin told him it would be in the fourth row, from the top right hand side half way down, and to be quick about it.

Then he asked Boris how Jack was. Boris asked Marvin, "What the hell are you doing?" Marvin pointed to a potion on the page and asked if that was what he wanted.

Boris fluttered down to the book and walked up on it, reading it on the way down. It was in a different language. He said to himself, "This is good."

Marvin said, "It's centuries old, given to me by the best sorceress ever."

Jack came staggering out of the bathroom. Ivan popped up from his meal and quickly jogged to him. He wrapped his arm around his waist. "It's back to bed for you."

Boris flew over to him. "You have to get him to drink."

Ivan reminded him, "Jack has been up over 24 hours now."

Boris told him, "Get him to drink, then in an hour he can sleep. Dropoff can open that bookcase." Just then, light footsteps came from behind the wall and Andre appeared, with a small jar in his hand.

He walked up to Marvin, handed him the jar and said, "Boy, is there a lot of stuff with dragon on it! I hope this is what you wanted."

Marvin turned the jar to read what was painted on it. Sure enough, it said Dragon Fire. He held it up to the light. Boris flew up and landed on his wrist, inspecting the crystallised fluid. Marvin said, "I have never used it in this form, it must be decades old. We have to get some fresh stuff."

Boris said, "Pour some potion in the jar. Let it sit for five minutes, then shake."

Marvin's eyebrows raised, "You want to use it all?"

Boris asked, "How else are you going to get it out?"

Marvin gave in, "OK, whatever you say." He dipped a measuring cup into the pan and filled the jar half-full of hot liquid, then set it on the counter top.

"So what's this for?" Andre asked.

Boris questioned himself, "I don't know, just shake and pour the whole thing back into the pot."

Marvin put the glass stopper back into the jar, gave it a quick shake and poured into the pot. The pot shuttered and an eerie blue-green fog flowed out of it. Marvin said a quick prayer, "God, I hope this works."

Boris flew to Marvin's shoulder, "Stir and don't stop."

Marvin started to stir. While stirring, he looked over his shoulder and said, "This is for you, Dropoff, enjoy."

Andre said with disgust in his voice, "I'm not drinking that crap."

Marvin chuckled, "No, this is for Jack. It should put him at ease and help his body regenerate. The Dragon Breath is a bacterium. If mixed right, it will speed up the process."

Andre questioned him, "If it isn't mixed right, what will happen? Who knows how old it is?"

Marvin said, "In the worst case, the bacteria will eat him alive."

Boris walked down Marvin's arm and looked into the pot. He flew back to Marvin's shoulder and spoke into his ear, telling him that it was ready. Jack got up from the table and staggered to the bathroom, holding his chest. Boris said, "Cool it down and get him to drink it."

Marvin questioned Boris, "You know these herbs haven't been used in decades—centuries, or longer. Maybe we can just knock him out with morphine. I have some in the other room."

Boris told him, "I am in charge here. Do as I say."

Marvin set the pot into the freezer. Boris asked him what it was.

Marvin asked him if he had been around when they had ice boxes. Boris told him, "I came over before the white man and I have heard of them. A man would go up and down the street delivering ice to the houses."

Marvin told him it was like that without the ice, everything was electric now. Boris said, "Ah yes, the lines on the pylons. You can feel the power flowing through them."

Marvin took the pot out of the freezer and stirred it, felt the bottom and put it back in. Boris flew back to the counter top and started to weave one of the small bags closed.

Marvin told him that he could get a pill bottle for him to put that in, so he wouldn't have to do that. Boris told him to do that later. He flew off with the bag into Juliet's room, then flew back holding something in his hands.

Marvin watched as Boris flew down into the sink and took a drop of water. He mixed it in with the stuff he had in the piece of leather. Marvin asked, "So what are you making?"

Boris yelled up to him, "It's just something to calm Jack, so he can keep the potion down." Boris flew up and out of the sink, to the bathroom, where Jack was hugging the toilet. He landed on Jack's neck, reached down and smeared the green paste on Jack's jugular, then on the other side.

Jack asked, "How long am I going to be this way?"

Boris told him, "It shouldn't take that long, this should calm you down. It will either cure you or kill you."

Marvin looked at Andre and said, "I wish he wouldn't say that."

Jack lifted his head, turned to Andre and said, "Boy, do I feel like crap!"

Boris hovered in front of Andre and told him, "Don't let Jack rub off the salamander slime."

Marvin said as Boris flew by, "I'm impressed! Salamander slime—that is the poisoned orange spot—should work nicely."

Then he asked if he was going to have Jack drink the potion. Boris asked, "Is it cool enough to drink?"

Marvin pulled it out of the freezer and stirred it with his finger, "Yeah this will work." He put his finger to his lips.

"I wouldn't do that if I were you," Andre said as he walked by with Jack. Marvin stopped and looked at his finger, gave a little "hmm", then told him to put it at the table. Marvin pulled a funnel out of a cupboard and placed it into a glass.

Andre let go of Jack to grab the funnel. Marvin wasn't the sturdiest guy. Marvin raised his voice and gave him a sharp command, "Just hold the thing still." Marvin poured the bluish potion into the glass.

"Good," Andre said.

Marvin said, "The other one too."

Andre put the funnel into the glass that Marvin had put out and they filled that one too. Andre looked at Marvin when they were through and asked him if it was going to work. Marvin nodded and told him that it should if the Dragon Breath was still good. Then he told him to put the glasses in front of Jack.

Boris was already in front of Jack, talking to him. Jack asked, "Where is Nora?" On that cue, Nora flew down off the fridge. She looked beat. Jack asked her, "Is this what you want me to do?"

Nora told him, "I promised with my life to keep you safe, and yes, this is what you have to do. There is no one better, I have all the faith in Boris. In all my years, I have only seen him kill a few people, out of the many he has helped."

Jack said, "You could have left that part out."

Jack reached out and grabbed the glass, smelled it and pulled away. His eyes were running. He shouted, "Oh, I can't drink this! My nose is burning, my eyes sting like hell!" Nora flew to him with a towel off the stove. Jack took it and wiped his eyes, "That is the worst-smelling stuff I have ever smelled," he said, trying to catch his breath.

Marvin asked Boris if he had to drink both glasses. Boris shook his head, then looked to the table, shaking his head. Marvin stepped behind Jack, reached around him and grabbed the glass with less in it. He put it to his lips and slammed it. "See? It's not that bad." He slammed the glass to the table.

Jack stood slowly, holding onto the table for balance for a couple of seconds. He picked up the glass and drank it in a few swallows. He held the empty glass up to show that he had drunk it. Marvin let out a long breath and reached out for Andre, who caught him as his legs gave out.

"Get me to a chair," he said, catching his breath. Nora slid a kitchen chair up behind him. Andre slowly sat him down. Boris was holding Jack by the collar of his shirt as he sat at the table.

Boris flew up and landed on Andre's shoulder. He told him, "Put Jack back to bed quickly, he should sleep through the night." Andre started to help Jack to his feet when Jack's legs gave out.

Andre took Jack's arm, wrapped it around his neck and said, "Now hold on and try to walk." He almost dragged Jack to the bedroom.

Boris walked over to Nora, who was sitting on the table. He cleared his throat. "I think he is going to need some help."

She got up, shot him a look and took off, grabbing Jack's sleeve. She lifted as much as the shirt would allow.

Andre said, "I have this." He lifted Jack and dragged him down the hall.

Ivan asked, "Need help?"

While they were taking him to the guest bedroom, Boris went to Juliet's room. He flew back with a small bag which he dropped on the table. Next, he flew to the cupboard and took out a saucer. He flew to the sink and turned the faucet on, then off, after catching a couple of droplets in the saucer. He flew back to the table.

He stood in front of Marvin and said, "You are a stupid, stupid man."

Boris opened the small bag. Inside it were smaller bags. He took and poured the contents into the saucer and washed the inside of the bag. He turned it inside out, trying to get every bit of the grey powder. Then he took a handful of crystals out of another bag, mumbling, "Stupid, stupid, human."

Boris was on his hands and knees mixing this together, when Andre came in with Nora in the palm of his hand. "What do want done with Marv?" Andre asked.

Rupert flew down from the fridge, walked up, looked at what Boris was making and said, "That is way to strong! It will put him in shock, or kill him."

Boris told the old fairy, "Piss off."

Rupert started to complain, but he was so weak it was useless. He threw his arms up in the air and said to Marvin, "Nice knowing you, Master."

Boris said, "Don't listen to him," as he scooped some of the mixture out using the bag and rubbed it on the almost unconscious Marvin.

Nora fluttered to Andre's shoulder and said into his ear, "I have never seen him use anything but his hands to apply a potion. This must be strong."

After Boris applied the cream on Marvin, he flew down to the table, slowly walking to Andre. Andre asked, "Is Marvin going to be all right?"

Boris replied, "I have never seen a man drink Dragon's Breath and live without being treated with the poison of the Dart Frog. Put him to bed. We will see if he wakes up in the morning."

Rupert stepped toward Boris and tried to talk him into trying something else. He suggested, "We could use the Orchid of Tibet to slow the potion that is running though his body."

Boris told him, "This is all I can do. If we slow down the potion, it would be slowing down the Dragon's Breath. It might eat his flesh." Then he said, "To hell with it all! Andre, put him to bed! And everyone else too!"

Boris flew off to Juliet's room, Rupert followed. Andre grabbed Marvin by the arm and slung him over his shoulder. Then he wrapped his arm around his waist and lifted. Nora flew to his shoulder and asked him what she could do. Andre had Marvin up and was carrying him toward Juliet's room. He told Nora, "The second door on the left is Marvin's; it would be nice if you would open the door."

Nora flew to the door knob and tried to open it. The knob was just too big for her to get a grip on. Andre got to the door and leaned Marvin against the wall so he could open it. Nora flew in and turned on the lights. She said, "Wow!" as she looked at all the magic awards and the props. There were posters covering the walls with a much younger Marvin holding onto a beautiful girl.

Andre said, "Yes, that is Marvin and Juliet in their prime. Hopefully they will be again."

He sat Marvin down on the bed. Nora flew to him. She told Andre to lift him back up.

"OK." He lifted Marvin and Nora pulled back the covers. Andre sat Marvin back down, put his head on the pillow and swung his legs up onto the bed. Just then, his phone rang; it was Pickupski,

"Hey Ivan, where the hell are you?"

Ivan said, "I am on my way to the airport, a quick flight to Chicago. Your plane is grounded for a couple of days."

Andre said, "What? You were just here, when did you leave?"

Ivan said "I told you we are booked for about three weeks out. I will get the repairs on the plane going. I should be back in a week or so."

Andre looked at Nora and asked, "Did Pickupski tell me he was leaving?"

Nora said, "Yeah, and he will be gone for—I think it was three weeks."

Andre said, "Well, I am not working until they get this straightened out. Flying was becoming a drag."

Andre looked around for Nora but she was nowhere to be found. He covered Marvin and tucked him in. As he walked down the hall, he looked in on Juliet. She lay there peacefully and had some colour coming back. The monitors were running numbers. He said softly, "Soon you will be your old self," to the sounds of pumps running. He noticed Boris was sleeping on the tissue box.

From there he stopped and checked on Jack. There he was, his face just wet with sweat. Nora was sleeping on the covers next to him. Andre looked at his watch and said aloud, "Great."

Nora looked up, "What?"

Andre turned on the lights. "It's time for his three-hour feeding." He walked out of the room to the kitchen and straight to the fridge.

Nora flew up and landed on his shoulder. She said, "He is drugged. He can't eat now!"

Andre said, "He has to eat every three to four hours. Go wake him up." He pulled out a filet from the fridge and started to cut it into bite-size pieces. Then he nuked it for 35 seconds; he wanted it just warm and still rare. He went back to the fridge and pulled out a Styrofoam container, reached in and took a little bit of spinach and put it on the plate. He then set the table, poured a glass of water and even lit a candle.

He started for Jack's room, paused and turned the dimmer switch so the candle lit the table. When he reached the guest room, he saw Nora wiping Jack's face with a tissue. The white paper turned into a brown slime with one stroke.

"Great," Andre sighed. "Let's get him fed, then we'll clean him up." He pulled back the covers. "Oh," he gagged as the smell hit him. He had to walk away. He leaned against the doorway and said to himself, "Where the hell is Pickupski when you need him?"

He turned and walked out the door to the bathroom. Nora flew in to check on him. She landed on his shoulder and asked if he was all right. "Boy, does he stink!"

Andre said, "I guess we will have to clean him up first."

Andre pulled three towels out of the cabinet. He then walked back into Jack's room and undressed him. Jack was snoring up a storm. You could see the brown imprint on the once-white sheets. Andre shook Jack, then looked at his hand. It was covered in brown ooze and you could see a smear mark on Jack. "Damn, this isn't going to be any fun," Andre said as he sat Jack up, "Maybe we could just give him a sponge bath."

Nora asked, "Then how are you going to feed him?"

Jack's eyes opened. He blinked several times. There were yellow crystals crusted on his eye lashes. Andre asked excitedly, "How are you, old boy?" he sounded English, not Russian.

Jack said, "I feel really weird."

Andre asked, "Can you walk?" Jack shrugged his shoulders.

Andre let go of Jack's back and swung his feet out of the bed onto the floor. He wiped his hands on the sheets, making long brown streaks. "Let's try this." He helped Jack to his feet.

Jack said, "Stop! The floor is slippery."

Andre sat Jack back down on the bed and wiped his feet with a towel, then got him back to his feet. He asked, "How are you doing?"

Jack rubbed his eyes, looked at Andre and asked, "What the hell is going on here?" Both men stood there naked, looking at each other, just for a few seconds, which felt like half an hour.

Jack told Andre, "I have been showering by myself for eighty years."

Andre said, "Just don't fall."

Jack said, "Just get the hell out of the way!" as he tried to pull from Andre's grip.

Andre said, "I am going to put you into the shower. We cannot afford you falling and breaking a hip. Are you sure you are all right? You took some really heavy drugs."

Both men started for the door. Andre reached over and opened the shower door. "Be careful. And quick."

Jack shot him a look with bloodshot eyes. Andre started the water running and said, "I will come back in a few minutes to wash your back." He helped Jack into the shower.

Nora said, "Make sure Jack washes all the brown goo off."

Andre told her, "That is your job," scooped her off his head and sat her on the shower door. Jack was just standing there. He looked up and said, "Hell, this isn't a dream—this shit is disgusting. What the hell?"

Nora sat there looking at Jack, an old guy in his eighties, naked in a shower, with brown water swirling at his feet. She hopped off the shower door and shouted in his ear, "Wash up, all this brown stuff has to come off."

Jack wiped his arm and a pool of brown formed at his feet. He took a handful of shower gel and scrubbed his face. The suds turned into a dark brown. Nora flew back in and told him, "Start with washing your hair."

Jack's hair was solid brown in the back from lying on it in bed, and had brown roots in the front. He poured shampoo into his hand. The suds turned brown and oozed down his back, the whole floor of the shower turned brown.

The water started to back up. Jack looked down and rubbed the drain with his foot and it started again. He rinsed and grabbed a flannel.

Nora flew in again and told him to wash his hair again. This happened three times. Andre came in to check on the progress twice. The third time, he was carrying a glass of red wine, dressed in a pyjama bottoms, with a dressing gown hanging over one arm. He opened the door, looked in and said, "Well it doesn't look like we're going to get any sleep tonight."

He started for the door. Nora flew right to his shoulder and told him, "If you would have helped, Jack would have been clean already." Andre swirled the wine in his glass, then put it to his lips and downed it, pretending not to hear. He set the glass down on the sink, put the cover down over the toilet and draped the dressing gown over it. He stepped out of his pyjamas. Then he grabbed the spray from the sink and sprayed the room.

Nora was standing on the top of the shower, watching Jack, when Andre opened the door and asked Jack how things were going. Jack looked at him and told him that he was almost done.

Andre told him that Nora wanted him to scrub his back. Jack turned and Andre could see a huge section of brownish goo that Jack couldn't reach. He put one foot in and leaned toward Jack. One swipe, the wash cloth was covered, he held it under the shower head and wrung it out. This continued until his back was all one colour again. Andre announced that they were done. Nora flew down and inspected Jack. She pointed out a few areas that they missed, like the back of his legs, and had them wash Jack's hair one more time.

Jack got out of the shower. He asked, "How long is this going to happen?"

Andre told him, "It is all the toxins leaching out of your skin. And I don't think there can be much more."

Jack dried off, Andre held out a comb, they traded. Andre wiped a spot on Jack's back, and hung the towel that had streaks of brown on it from spots they missed. Jack commented, "I have never had a beard or shoulder-length hair. Do you think we could run to a barber tomorrow?"

Andre said, 'Right now we have to get some food in you, then get some sleep. Tomorrow is going to be a big day." Andre took Jack by the arm, guided him to the kitchen table and sat him down. He said, "Drink the glass of water first, then the steak."

Jack didn't say a word. In five minutes his head started to bob—he was falling asleep. Andre said, "Oh no, you don't."

Nora flew to Jack's head and spoke to Andre, "You have to get him to drink as much water as you can. And feed him." Andre just shook his head.

He went to the cupboard and pulled out a glass. He went to the water cooler in the corner and filled it.

He held it out for Jack. "Drink it all," he said.

Jack looked like he was tired, dead tired. He put the glass to his lips and slammed it back. Andre walked over and got another, and then another. He filled his third glass and walked over to the table. Andre asked Jack, "Are you all right? You look like crap."

Jack rolled his head and said, "I am so damn tired, I just want to go to bed," as he put his elbows on the table and cradled his head.

Nora walked over to him and said, "It's been a long night." Andre sat a plate in front of Jack. There was filet mignon sliced nicely, with a spinach salad, shaved carrots on top and a piece of parsley.

"I'll take that for you." He took Jack's half-drunk water and filled it. "I'll be back." He left down the hall, then came back again with a spray from the bathroom. Jack ate everything on the plate. Andre filled his glass again.

Boris popped his head into the kitchen and asked how everything was going. Jack told him, "The steak was delicious. I have eaten and I'm really tired."

Andre told him, "We have to get you back to bed." He took him to his room and said, "You take a piss, I need to find a garbage bag for your pillow. I threw the one you were sleeping on out, as well as the sheets. Then we will get you back to bed."

Andre had the bed already made. He just had to put the pillow into a bag, then put the pillowcase on it. Jack came out of the bathroom like a zombie. He was dead on his feet. As soon as he hit the bed, he was out. Andre said, "Next feeding is in the morning, I'm not getting up in three hours. It has been one long day."

Then he headed down the hall and passed Juliet's room. He turned on the light and stopped. "Oh my God!" he said. "Her eyes, she opened her eyes!"

Boris told him, "Go back to sleep."

Andre said, "No, really! She opened her eyes." Andre took Juliet by the hand and looked into her eyes. She blinked, and a tear ran down her cheek.

Andre said in a hoarse voice, "Everything is going to be all right. Just give it a little time." He walked down the hall to the living room and had just curled up on the recliner when Marvin stepped in after going to the bathroom.

"Dropoff, hey! Are you sleeping?" Marvin said in a not-so-quiet whisper.

Andre said with a yawn, "Not anymore." He brought the chair to a sitting position.

Marvin walked up in front of him and said, "Isn't this great?"

Andre said, "Marvin, now get some sleep. By the way, why did you drink that potion? You could have died?"

Marvin said, "I know what I'm doing. If I hadn't, Jack might not have. It worked."

Andre told Marvin, "Never do that again, or I will have to kill you myself. Now get to bed, old man. By the way, Juliet opened her eyes."

Marvin said, "You're kidding me."

Andre said, "Ten minutes ago. It's going to be like old times."

Marvin said, "Get some sleep."

Boris flew in and said, "What the hell is going on here? You should be sleeping for a couple of days. We need some fresh herbs."

Marvin asked, "Did you know Juliet opened her eyes?"

Boris said, "Yes, it just happened. Get back to bed."

Andre said, "Seriously, get out of here. I need some shut-eye." Marvin smiled as he left the room. Andre said, "Boris, follow him. He is going to Juliet's room. He needs sleep."

The sun came up and Jack was up to greet it. He got up, showered and used scissors to cut as much of his beard off as he could. Then he put some water in a shaving cup and whipped it into a foam. He put it on his face and shaved.

Nora flew in and asked him how he felt. Jack said, "I still feel weird. And can you believe I grew a six-inch beard overnight? Isn't that weird?"

He started to shave, pulling the shaver an inch at a time. He opened the razor so water ran through it. Nora said, "Why don't you put a new one in it?" she opened the medicine cabinet.

Jack reached in and took out a pack of blades and slipped out a new one. As he was replacing the blade, he asked, "How did you know the mirror opened?"

Nora said shyly, "I know a lot more about you than you know about me. I know you use the shaving gel that turns into foam and a smaller plastic razor."

Jack stared at her for a moment in the mirror. She was lying on his left shoulder, talking in his ear, "You shave every morning, before coffee."

He asked, "Have you been spying on me?"

She laughed a sweet little laugh. "No, Jack, I have been studying the humans for years, from their horse and buggy days."

Jack, still shaving, asked, "Have you learned anything?"

She yawned, "Yeah, there are so many different types of people. Most of them will do anything for money. Surprisingly, you're not that type. You were sheriff, you helped people. All that work gardening, just to give it away."

Jack stopped and smiled. "That was Emma. She canned and froze hundreds of pounds of food a year and gave it to the food pantry." Jack finished up. He had like six pieces of toilet paper stuck to nicks on his face. He pulled one off. To his surprise, there was no nick. He pulled off another: same thing.

Nora said, "Your body is healing. That would be the powder of the unicorn."

Jack then washed his face and started for the kitchen. Before he got there, he let out a sigh. "Oh, coffee."

There was Andre sitting at the table with a cup of coffee, chatting with Boris. He looked up and asked with his Russian accent, "How are you, my comrade?"

Jack walked in and asked, "Didn't you have an English accent last night?"

Andre shook his head, "When I am really tired my English comes back. You'll probably be Russian too—the paperwork is so much easier."

Jack told him, "I don't know what you're talking about."

Andre said, "When the time comes, we will handle that. I asked you how you were feeling."

Jack said, "I feel fine, a little strange. All my muscles tingled last night, and I was never so sick in my life. And whatever I threw up was like tar. That was the worst. I thought I was going to cough up a lung." He poured a cup of coffee, then poured a shot of water out of the water cooler onto it. He pulled up a chair.

Andre sleepily looked at him and asked, "You were saying?"

Jack asked Boris, "What was that brown goo I was washing off myself?"

Boris walked over to his coffee cup and told him, "They were the toxins that have been building in your body for years. And the tingling in your muscles was just cleaning up your body. In a couple of days, you will be healthier then you have ever been in your life."

Jack asked, "Why is my hair growing so fast?"

Boris lifted his arms and shook his head, "I have no idea; you handled a lot of power. I had never seen someone handle so much dust from the horn of a unicorn."

Andre said, "Ah, don't believe everything he says. He said you would be asleep for at least a day."

Jack asked, "So what is for breakfast? I'm starved."

Andre said, "Well, I think there is one more steak in the fridge." He got up.

Jack said, "Sit, I can feed myself."

Andre told Jack, "No, you're a guest, I can do it. And I am getting paid to do it anyway. Boy, I sure hope I'm getting paid."

He went on, "Washing slime off an old guy isn't my cup of tea. Cleaning up vomit—just the smell of you—oh my God, that was the worst!" He went to the fridge and pulled out the last filet mignon. He popped it in the microwave and asked, "How long?" then set it for two minutes.

Jack stood in front of the fridge with the door open. He turned to the table and said, "We need to go to the grocery store. Hell, there isn't even milk or eggs."

Rupert, the fairy, said, "You do know that Marvin has been a little down these last few years." His voice grew with a little excitement, "Speaking of Marvin, is he still alive?"

Jack said, "I checked on him right after my shower this morning and he was still breathing."

Boris walked over to Rupert, who was chatting with Jack, and said, "You should check on Marvin and make sure."

Jack asked, "Andre, what is going on today?"

Andre looked up from his cup of coffee, "Let me tell you, I'm taking a nap. And not in that recliner!"

Jack asked, "Can we take a walk after we go to the store?"

Andre got up from the table and told Jack, "I am going to see what the two old bugs are up to. I couldn't believe the old man drank that potion! He could have died!"

Jack put the fork to his steak and in a couple minutes, it was gone. He got up and stood in front of the fridge, looking at dates on things. He looked in the freezer and it was full. Jack pulled out some chicken that was white on the outside. He said, "Freezer burnt," and put it right back in and closed the door.

He headed down the hall to Marvin's room, there was Andre holding Marvin in a sitting position. Jack asked, "How is he?"

Andre said, "He is running a fever. Boris is making some paste thing to put on him."

Nora flew up to Jack's shoulder and asked, "How do you feel?"

Jack smiled, "Much better, thank you."

The walls of Marvin's room were plastered with posters. Some from were made of cloth, others were new and brightly coloured, but all were of magicians and their assistants. Nora flew over to one, it was dated 1985. She pointed to the man, then flew back. She spoke into Jack's ear, "That is the last time I had seen Marvin."

Jack looked at the poster and said, "He was younger."

Andre told him, "All the posters are Marvin and Juliet."

Jack looked closely at a black and white one, then at Andre. "This is you," Jack said pointing to the poster.

Andre said, "Yeah, that was me. I've been with him for a long time."

Boris flew in with Rupert right on his side. Boris was holding a penny with a cream coloured paste on the top of it. They both landed on Marvin's head. Boris handed the penny to Rupert, took a handful and fluttered to Marvin's shoulder. He walked up and rubbed it on Marvin's jugular and then repeated it on the other side.

Rupert flew down to watch. They had a discussion about where to put the rest. Boris wanted to put it on the base of the neck. Rupert didn't want to use any more. He yelled, "Slowly!"

Boris took the rest that was on the penny and flew to Marvin's back. He yelled to Andre: "Tilt Marvin's head forward!"

Andre slowly tilted Marvin's head with care and supported it. Boris reached into his hairline, right to the base of the skull, and applied the paste. Boris flew inches away from Andre's face and told him, "Lay Marvin down again."

The penny Rupert was holding flew across the room, hitting one of the posters. Rupert left the room slowly. Andre was the first to talk, "OK then! He didn't look happy."

Boris flew over, looking into Marvin's eyes. He said with his face blushing, "I'm in charge here, we do things my way. Do you understand?"

Jack looked at the two-inch bug that was talking to him. Then he looked at Andre, who got up to listen. Andre spoke, telling Boris, "Rupert has been with Marvin for hundreds of years."

Boris, hovering, turned to face him, "What don't you understand? I am in charge here, you will do as I say!" He then turned to Jack, "Tell me how you feel."

Jack told him, "I feel fine."

Boris told him, "That isn't what I asked you."

Nora told Jack, "Boris wants to know if there is any numbness. Do you taste anything weird, any pain?"

Andre said, "Do this—stand on one foot." Andre stood on one foot, balancing.

Jack said, "This is how I feel: you treat Rupert like crap and it will stop! You forget I am in charge here. Without me, your people will starve. There is a green fairy on the way here! You will work together, do you understand?"

Then Jack stood on one foot; he wobbled for a second. "Boy, I haven't done this in years," he said.

Andre put his foot down and said, "Stick out your tongue."

Boris flew in to inspect his tongue. He said, "Jack looks fine. His new teeth are going to give him some trouble."

Jack asked, "I'm getting teeth? How painful is that going to be?"

Boris told him, "Sometimes they all come in at once, and other times one at a time. You're probably not going to be that lucky—you have had such a large dose of horn powder. All I can do is keep you comfortable."

Jack looked at the floor, shook his head and said, "Great!" to himself.

Nora asked, "How is Marvin doing?"

Andre butted in and said, "I need coffee. Let's let Marvin rest and carry on this conversation in the kitchen." Andre turned and looked at Boris buzzing around Marvin's head, then down to his arms. Marvin lay there hardly even breathing, but there was some colour to his face and he looked peaceful.

Andre said in a forceful manner, "Boris, you will consult Rupert before you do anything with Marvin, do you hear? If you hurt him in any way, I will personally crush you. Do you understand?" Boris looked up at Andre, stared at him for a few seconds and then flew out of the room.

Jack was the closest to the door, so he was the first one out. He walked down the hall to the kitchen and poured coffee, one for himself and one for Andre. He asked, "How is Marvin?" with concern in his voice.

Boris told him, "Marvin is resting and should rest for at least a couple of days."

Andre said, "He was fine last night! What did you do to him? He talked with me after I saw Juliet open her eyes. He was all excited. I told you to follow him!"

Boris pointed and said, "He is to stay in bed. Get him up every three to four hours to feed him and take him to the bathroom."

Nora butted in and said, "This could take a couple of weeks."

Jack got up and poured a little water in his coffee so he could drink it. He asked, "What about me?"

Boris shook his head and said, "There isn't much I can do, you shouldn't be awake. Whatever is in your system has to work its way through."

Jack asked, "Can I go for a walk outside?" He walked over to the window. "You know, Andre, I've never been to Hollywood, how about a grand tour?"

Andre said, "We could head down to the Dolby theatre, hit a Starbucks, take a walk and look at the stars on the Walk of Fame."

Nora flew in and landed on Jack's shoulder as he looked out the window. She asked, "Don't you have to call someone? You will be missed."

Jack asked, "Ah, where is that stupid mobile phone?" he rubbed his pyjama's—well technically they were Marvin's, he had gone through the two pair he had brought *and* he had thrown out three pairs of sheets.

Nora came flying in with his mobile phone. It slipped out of her hands and crashed to the floor. Jack walked over and picked it up. When he stood, there was a look of awe on his face. Nora stood on the table, apologising, saying, "There is nowhere to grab onto and it is so slippery."

Jack asked, "Did you see? I picked it up! I bent over and picked it right off the floor!" He stood straight—shoulders back—you could hear the vertebrae snapping into place.

Boris came running to the edge of the table, "Yes, straighten! Stand tall. You can't let them set in the wrong position. Nora, make sure he stands straight and keep him moving."

Rupert flew up, yelling like a wild man, "Shut the drapes! Who opened them? I'll kick your ass!"

Andre lowered his head and took a drink. His eyes looked up and there was Rupert, right in front of him, glowing red.

Nora said, "Someone pissed him off, and it looks like Andre is the one." Jack pulled the shade down, slowly looking at the road outside.

Andre sat his cup down, "OK, I forgot. Sorry, no harm done!"

Rupert, still pissed said, "No harm done? You say no harm done? How do you know that every blue guardian isn't on its way here now?"

Andre told Jack, "The shades have been closed for over twenty years. The house is being watched by the blue fairies. Marvin has only gone out during the day ever since the attack."

Jack asked, "What attack?"

Andre said as he walked out of the room, "I will tell you later. I am going to the bathroom. Then I will take you out for a walk to Starbucks and get a good cup of Joe."

Jack opened his mobile phone. He turned it on. There were nine messages on it. Nora, who was sitting on his shoulder, asked him, "How does this little phone know how many people called?"

Jack hit a button. A list of names came up. "See that's John, my son, he called three times. That's Mary, my daughter, she called five times. And that one is a neighbour."

He clicked on the neighbours name and it highlighted. Then he called. Nora was amazed at the technology the phone had. Jack started to speak on the phone. He got into his cranky old-man voice, "No, I didn't fire my gun the other night. It must have been a car backfiring." He held out the phone and pushed the stop button.

Nora said, "He was still talking."

Jack said, "So?" He pushed his son's number and started talking, just small talk. He asked how the wife and kids were. Then he said everything was fine and he was in California, visiting an old army buddy, and that he had to tell Mary. There was a long pause—then, in a pissed off voice, "No, I didn't fire my weapon last night. Must have been a backfire. I have to go, talk to you later. Call your sister!" He held out the phone and pushed the cancel button.

Nora said, "He was still talking too."

Jack smiled, "He would have talked all day. Besides, the less information you give them, the better."

Jack's phone rang. He looked at it and his son's name came up, "Ah, hell!" he said. He pushed the cancel button till the light went out.

Nora asked, "Why did you do that? He wanted to talk to you."

Jack told her, "He just wanted details, which I wasn't going to give him anyway." Jack started to look though the cupboards one more time, "There just isn't anything to eat here!"

Andre popped his head in and told him, "I'll be ready in five to ten minutes."

The two fairies came flying in. Boris said, "We need some water."

Jack asked how much. Rupert opened a cupboard door and pointed to a saucer. Jack said, "That will be easy enough."

Boris said, "We need a candle."

Rupert said, "That needs to be taken to the room upstairs."

Jack walked to the wall and asked, "How do you get this damn lift to open?

Andre walked up behind him and said, "I will take Rupert up, you should get dressed."

Jack stepped away from the wall and told Andre, "We have to go grocery shopping."

Andre told him, "We will as soon as we get back. And do not forget, we have to go to Target to pick up three sets of sheets."

Jack stood there watching Andre, waiting for him to open the lift. Andre stepped closer to the wall, waved one hand and said, "Open sesame." The door opened.

"What the hell?" Jack said, and turned and headed to the guest room.

Andre stepped into the lift with the two fairies sitting on one shoulder, talking. Andre asked, "What's going on?"

Boris told him, "We were debating if they had enough potions to regenerate Juliet. Rupert said we have to. She is in such a state! And this process will take weeks, if not a couple of months." Andre took them to Rupert's room and did what they asked of him; he opened the pantry door.

Jack went to his luggage, which was lying on the floor. He bent over and sorted through it, pulling out socks, jeans and a shirt. He sat on the bed and started to put on his socks. He stopped, thinking about what he had just been doing. He finished pulling on the socks and started to sing an old song to himself, smiling. He finished getting dressed.

The house was quiet except for the pumps and monitors in Juliet's room. Then the sound of the lift hummed. Jack hurried out to watch it open. The wall just slid back and there was Andre.

Jack asked, "How did you open the wall?"

Andre smiled and said in a happy tone, "Magic."

Jack shook his head. "I'm going to shave and get ready."

Boris flew off Andre's shoulder to Jack's and asked, "How many glasses of water have you drunk this morning?"

Nora flew up and said, "Five, and three cups of coffee."

"Not enough," Boris said. "And make sure he eats."

Jack said, "I'll drink more when I get out of the bathroom. Right now I have to take a piss, all right?"

Boris flew back to Andre, who was putting a box on the worktop next to the sink. Jack went into the bathroom and washed his face. He asked, "When am I going to stop sweating this brown slime?"

Nora said, "I have no idea, I have never seen anyone do that before." She explained, "Usually regeneration takes weeks, or months."

Jack asked, "How long do you think it will take for me?"

She shook her head and said, "I don't have a clue, you're special. But I think it will be sooner than most."

Jack took scissors to his beard and cut as much as he could, then smeared shaving cream on and started to shave.

Nora said, "You know, you look really different with a beard."

Jack said, "I have never had a beard in 82 years. I'm not starting now."

He combed his hair, which was past shoulder-length. He asked Nora, "When is my hair going to stop growing?" Jack walked out to the kitchen, to the sink and poured a glass of water. Andre was placing poker chips under a frame that held a small cauldron over a tea candle. He turned and asked if Jack was ready to go.

Jack told him, "Yes, and I need some pyjamas and a good razor."

Andre told him, "It looks like you could use one. There are little pieces of toilet paper with dried blood on them stuck to your face." Andre motioned to his face.

Jack wiped the tissues off his face, there were no marks—just a little dried blood. He drank the glass and set it close to the sink. Then he told Andre to hurry up. Jack went back to the bathroom, stepped in and took another pee.

Jack walked into Marvin's room. He was lying there hardly moving. Jack had to watch for his chest to move to make sure he was alive. Nora said, "This is the way you start a regeneration. Slowly."

Boris flew in and yelled at her, "Wrong! He should have never drank that potion! I had to slow down his heart rate to damn-near death. You don't know what you're talking about!" The old fairy flew down to his nose, lifted his eyelid; then he flew back to the kitchen.

Chapter Seven
Jack Gets His First Look at Hollywood

Andre came to the room and asked Jack, "Are you ready?"

Jack nodded, "Finally! What the hell have you been doing in there?"

Andre slipped on his jacket and grabbed his hat. He told Jack to follow him. Andre stopped in front of a wall in the kitchen and said, "Open sesame." He waved his arms, took a step forward close to the wall and the wall opened to the lift. He waved Jack in and said, "Your chauffeur will pull the car around."

They hit the button and down they went. On the ride down, Jack asked, "Is Marvin all right?"

Andre told him that he had never seen him so pale and that in the middle of the night, they had talked. "I don't know what they did to him."

Nora popped out of Jack's pocket. She told the two, "Boris is the best. If anyone can save him, Boris can."

Andre asked Jack, "Are you going to take your fairy along?"

Nora flew out of Jack's pocket and right into Andre's face, "I don't belong to anyone. I promised to keep Jack safe with my life. Where he goes, I go." The lift slowed to a stop and Nora got back into Jack's pocket.

Andre pointed his finger right at her and spoke loudly, "You stay out of sight, do you hear me?"

Jack said, "Wow, first it was Boris giving you the business, now him! Don't worry about it."

Nora said, "Yeah, nobody got a lot of sleep yesterday."

Andre pulled up with an older Lincoln town car. He got out and opened the door for Jack. Jack said, "If you don't mind, I would rather ride up front."

Andre stepped forward and opened the passenger's side door. "I picked this car so you would feel more at home."

Jack ran his hand along the bonnet. "Yeah, mine looked like this in its day."

Andre walked around the car and slid in. He asked, "Jack, what's the first stop?"

Jack replied with one word, "Starbucks."

Andre headed right down the road and asked him, "What do you want?"

Jack said, "A triple shot mocha." A kicking came from his shirt and he added a large water.

They got their coffee, went to a store and picked up four sheet sets. Andre wanted to buy the 1300 thread count but Jack said, "We are just going to throw them out anyway. 300 are just fine."

Andre threw a cane in the trolley. Jack told him, "I don't need that stupid cane! No one knows me here."

Andre told him, "You are an old man, and you should start acting your age."

An older woman came up and told Andre, "You should show more respect for your father."

Andre told her, "If he doesn't start to shower more often, you can wash him."

She looked at Jack, then his odour took her over; she put her hand over her mouth and said into it, "Oh my God," and turned and walked briskly in the other direction.

Jack noticed everyone was giving them a wide birth. Even the check-out girl held her hand over her mouth and pinched her nose. As the two walked across the car park, Jack asked Andre, "Do I smell as bad as people think?"

Andre fished the cane out of the trolley and handed it to him. "Now use it! You're 82 years old, you're walking like a twenty-year old!"

They started to get close to the car. There was a group of young men hanging around a convertible. Andre told Jack, "Walk over and ask the time."

Jack said, "You are wearing a watch."

Andre smiled, "Just do it."

Jack slowly walked to the car and asked the guys, "May I ask what time it is?"

One of the men asked, "Do you smell that?" The whole conversation turned to how bad Jack smelled. They started to yell at him, telling him to get away from them.

Jack leaned on his cane, "Do I smell that bad?"

One guy yelled: "You smell like a rotting corpse! Get the hell out of here!"

Jack quickly walked to the town car, where Andre had already thrown the bags in the boot. Jack got into the car and waited for Andre. Andre slid behind the wheel, saying the next stop was the grocery store. Jack told Andre that he didn't get within twenty feet of those guys and they had smelled him.

Andre rolled down all the windows and said, "Maybe we should head back to the castle." Jack gazed over staring straight ahead, not saying anything.

When they pulled up to the back of the place, Andre got out and walked to the rear of the car. Nora climbed out of Jack's pocket and talked right in his ear, saying, "We are back at the castle."

Jack turned his head, looking at the car park. "Come on, Jack, get out of the car!" Andre shouted.

Jack started to unbuckle his seatbelt and Nora scooted back in his breast pocket. Andre came up, opened his door and asked him, "Are you all right?"

The old man got out holding onto the door. "I think I'm going to be sick."

"Great," Andre said as he walked to the back of the place.

This time he didn't say any magic words to open the lift. He took two loads from the boot of the car to the lift. He walked up to Jack, who was still hanging onto the door. He asked him, "Are you OK? Do you need a minute before heading upstairs?"

Jack said slowly, "I just feel like crap."

Andre put his arms around Jack's waist. He rolled his eyes, "Oh my God, do you reek!" Andre told Jack, "You need a shower bad."

They got into the lift and Andre announced, "It's just us, back from shopping." He helped Jack to the bathroom and sat him on the toilet. Nora crawled out and flew out of the room.

Andre took a finger and ran it across Jack's face. It dripped with thick brown slime. Andre asked if Jack needed some help getting in the shower. Jack hung his head in the toilet and barfed.

Marvin popped his head in and said, "Dropoff, I think that was your answer."

Andre took a couple of quick steps to the door and told Marvin, "Taking care of Jack wasn't in my job description."

Marvin smiled and said, "Well, it is now. Get him in the shower." Andre knew that this was just something that had to be done but he let Marvin know how much he hated it.

Boris and Rupert flew in from Juliet's bedroom. They landed on Andre's shoulder. Andre turned his head and looked at them, then asked, "How long is Jack going to be this way?"

The two of them sat and talked on his shoulder. They had Andre to ask Jack to stick out his tongue. Jack rolled his eyes and opened his mouth a long drool formed as he stuck out his tongue. Andre asked them again, "How long is Jack going to be like this?"

Boris said, "Until he feels better." The two old fairies laughed together.

Nora flew up and asked, "Why isn't Jack in the shower yet? His skin is suffocating; it needs to breath."

Andre helped Jack get back on the toilet, then took off with his shoes and socks. The socks just oozed brown goo. He said, "Dustbin, please."

Nora flew in with a garbage bag and handed it to Andre, who dropped the socks in. Andre wiped the soles of Jack's feet with a towel and added that to the bag.

Marvin stuck his head into the room again. His face turned pale white and his hand went up to cover his mouth. He pinched his nose.

Andre got Jack into the shower. Halfway through, Jack told him, "Dammit, I can shower myself!"

Andre went out to the kitchen where Marvin and Nora were speaking. He told them he was going out to the grocery store. Marvin told him, "You should take a shower and put on a clean set of clothes.

Andre told him, "I don't smell that bad," and left.

Boris flew out and joined in on the conversation, telling Nora, "Jack isn't ready to leave for any amount of time. He needs more water and sleep." He flew off and the door to the bathroom opened.

Jack stepped out. He looked like he was a three-day drunk. Nora flew to him and told him, "Sit down at the table," which he did. She flew to the water cooler five times, setting cups in front of him. "Now drink," she said with a stern voice.

Boris flew in with a leaf in his hand. He rubbed it on Jack's temples, saying, "This will help you sleep."

Jack looked right into Marvin's eyes and told him, "There is so much running though my head! I have visions of places and people that I have never seen before."

Marvin told him, "You'll get that when you touch a unicorn. He knows more about you than you know about him."

Jack said, "You saved him during the First World War. You brought him to this country."

Marvin's eyes lit up, "Well, maybe you know more than I think."

Jack told him, "It comes and goes when it wants to."

Marvin took him by the hand and looked right into his eyes. Jack could feel Marvin probe his mind and then he heard Marvin speaking. "Stop me, Jack. Kick me out of your head!"

Jack just stared at him. He told him that he didn't know how. Marvin told him, "Shielding your mind from others is something you have to learn."

Jack yawned. Nora flew up, saying, "Finish your two glasses. Then off to bed with you."

Boris told Nora, "Every three hours—more water. And get him to eat as much as you can, raw meat."

Nora asked, "How long will he sleep?"

Boris said, "I said, wake him up every three hours."

Jack was staring out into space. Marvin put his hand on his shoulder and told him, "OK, it's time for you to take a nap."

Jack looked Marvin in the eye and said, "Try me, search my mind."

Marvin looked him in the eye and froze, not saying a word. Jack smiled, "You are as old as the hills and you love Juliet more than anything."

Marvin said, "Don't ever do that again."

Jack chuckled to himself, then told Marvin, "That is one of the things Ivan taught me."

Nora said, "Come on, it's time for Jack to sleep—Boris's orders."

Jack turned and swayed, rocking back and forth. Marvin grabbed him by the arm. "This way, Jack. I think that potion is taking effect."

The two walked down the hall, Jack putting his weight on Marvin for support. Rupert pointed at Boris, saying, "I told you! You made the potion too strong."

Boris came back with, "He's going to sleep, isn't he?"

Marvin got him to the bedroom and put him down on the bed. Nora said, "We have to get him into his pyjamas."

Marvin waved her off, "He's sleeping already, let him be."

Jack was out like a light, snoring to beat the band. Marvin headed to the kitchen. Boris and Ivan were having a heated discussion there. Marvin poured himself a cup of coffee and sat down, listening.

Boris turned to Marvin, "You are a great sorcerer. Should we put Jack into a deep sleep?"

Marvin took a sip and started to speak, but Rupert cut him off. "The best thing to do is to slow his heart down and let his body heal itself," Rupert preached.

Boris chimed in, "That is the worst thing to do! His body is throwing off so much toxin that if he doesn't eat or drink, he will die."

Marvin cut him off, "Not only that, he has to clean that brown goo off. I think you, Boris, have to figure out how to slow it."

Rupert walked up to him and asked, "How long have we been friends?"

Marvin raised his hands, "Damn near forever."

Rupert asked, "So why don't you trust me?"

Marvin told him, "It's not about trust, it is about how much Jack handled Ivan. Touching a unicorn takes a toll on the body. Not only that—he is such an old man!"

Nora landed on the table and walked up into the conversation. She held up her hand. "The deep sleep you are talking about is a coma. You will not put Jack into a coma."

Boris told her, "Woman, you should not even be here. Keep quiet!"

Nora walked up to Marvin and told him, "I promised Ivan that I would keep Jack safe. There will be no deep sleep. He might not wake up." She turned to Boris and Rupert. "Do you promise with your life that you will not put Jack into a deep sleep?"

The two male fairies promised not to put Jack into a coma. Then she said, "From now on, everything that is done to Jack gets my approval," and she flew off.

Boris said, "She will never be the same. I was there when Ivan made her stake her life on keeping Jack safe."

Marvin started to talk when Rupert cut him off. "I think it is time for you to get some sleep."

Marvin stood at the table, both hands on it, staring down at the two, "Now listen here! You're not telling me what to do! I am Marvin the Magnificent, and if I wasn't so damn tired I wouldn't be taking a nap." With that, he turned and walked to his room and slammed the door.

Rupert turned to Boris, "When Marvin regenerates, you'll see a great man."

Boris said, "I have met Marvin in the forest, many years ago."

In about two hours, Andre walked out of the lift. Marvin met him, "It's about time you got back."

Marvin reached out for a bag he was carrying. Andre asked, "How's Jack doing?"

Rupert flew to Marvin's shoulder and told him, "You have to unplug that buzzer, it woke you from your nap."

Marvin told him, "No way am I going to unplug that! It tells me when someone is using the lift, or if someone is coming up the stairs."

Rupert told Marvin, "You need more sleep."

Marvin looked at him, then told him, "Go check on Juliet, make sure she's all right. Then check on Jack."

Andre finished unloading the lift, piling everything on the kitchen table. Nora flew in and asked if she could help. Marvin told her it was time for Jack to eat, so if she would wake him that would be nice. Nora flew off.

Andre started to stack things in the fridge and in the cupboards. Marvin asked him, "Did you get angels' trumpets or moon flowers? They are the same."

Andre told him, "They were not in season and were hard to get. So I got six bunches of cut flowers."

Marvin started to pull the flowers out of the bags. He went to a cupboard and took out six vases. Boris and Rupert flew in and helped him place the flowers in them. Then the two picked which bunch they wanted and crawled right in, scooping out the pollen from the flowers and licking it off their hands.

Marvin smiled, "Well, that should keep them out of our hair for a while." The two men stood there watching the fairies eat.

Jack came staggering in. The old man looked like he was plastered. Andre stepped to his side and took him by the arm, steering him to the table. Boris flew out of his vase of flowers to land on Andre. Andre asked him, "What did you give Jack?"

Boris said, "Just a mild potion of salamander slime, snake venom and something else."

Andre told him, "Jack looks like he is stoned off his ass."

Marvin poured Jack a glass of water and ran his finger across Jack's forehead. He looked at it, then rubbed it with his thumb.

Andre said, "Don't tell me he needs a shower."

Marvin chuckled, "No, not this time."

Jack tried to speak, but it was like his tongue was too big for his mouth. Rupert flew to the table and walked up to Jack, "See, you mixed it too strong!"

Boris flew down to him and told him, "It's just right. Jack will eat, pee, and go right back to sleep."

Andre cut up a steak and popped it into the microwave, started a side salad and shaved some carrot on top. He arranged everything on the plate and set it in front of Jack.

Jack looked up and saw everyone was staring at him. He just went to work on eating. Andre asked, "Is there anything I could get you?"

"A cup of coffee," Jack slurred. Boris shook his head. Andre got him a cup of juice instead and set it in front of him.

Jack looked up at him with a disgusted ten-second stare and went back to eating his steak. He drank, then wiped his face with a napkin. Marvin put his hand on his shoulder and asked, "How are you doing?"

Jack looked up at him and told him, "I have to take a leak, then go back to bed."

Boris sat and talked with Rupert. He would point at him and Rupert would throw his arms up in the air and pace back and forth. Nora walked over to Andre and said, "I think someone is getting a good ass-chewing."

Andre smiled, "At least it isn't me."

He got up from the table and shook Jack, who had his head on the table, sleeping. "Come on old man, to the bathroom and back for a nap."

Jack lifted his head. He looked as if he had no idea where he was, then nodded his head and said, "OK."

Andre took him by the elbow and led him off. About five minutes later, Andre and Nora came back into the room. Marvin was sitting at the table, drinking his coffee and talking to the two old fairies. Andre grabbed a beer out of the fridge and asked, "What was all the yelling about?"

Marvin looked over to him and said, "They were just discussing what went wrong with Jack."

Andre chuckled, "You mean he isn't supposed to be stoned? Let me tell you, that old dude in there doesn't know if he is on foot or on horseback!"

Marvin asked, "How is he?"

Nora flew to his shoulder and told him, "He was asleep before he hit the bed."

Boris yelled, "Tell all of us!"

Andre turned his head, listening to Boris. Even a yell from a two-inch fairy wasn't loud. He said to them, "Jack is sleeping soundly." Then he asked, "Do we have to wake him in three hours?"

The two started to talk between themselves, Boris waving his arms around. Marvin spoke with a deep voice, "You will wake him at 5:00."

Boris flew up and asked, "How long is that?"

Andre said, "About five hours."

Marvin added, "At nine, you will give him a dose of sleeping potion for the night." He got up and said to Andre, "Follow."

They walked down the hall to Marvin's room. Andre asked as soon as the door was closed, "What's going on?"

Marvin smiled, "Those two have had their own way for decades. All they are going to do is argue. Someone has to take charge."

Andre smiled and nodded his head, "Marv, it's great to have you back. Good times are coming, aren't they?"

Marvin said, "I don't know. Something is going on and I just can't put my finger on it. Like where this Jack guy came from, why the blues didn't kill him, and why Ivan sent him here. God, he's still alive!"

Andre put his hand on Marvin's shoulder and turned him to look into his face. "Hey, this is a sign! Or maybe he just lucked out with that wasp spray, I don't know. Just have faith, Ivan knows what he is doing."

Marvin shook his head, "I haven't been up there in nearly 25 years."

Andre suggested, "Marvin, you should take a nap."

He agreed, "Yes, that sounds good. But promise you will wake me if anything happens!"

Boris and Rupert were arguing about what to do with Marvin. Andre listened for a moment. Then he said sternly, "You will do whatever Marvin tells you—end of story."

The two fairies then started to talk about Juliet. Andre leaned over the two with both his hands on the table, looking straight down at them. He said with his teeth clenched, "Now listen here! You two touch her without Marvin's blessing and I'll squash you like bugs! Do you understand?"

Boris and Rupert just stood there, looked up at him and nodded their heads. Nora flew into the room and landed on the table with the boys. Then she flew to Andre, who was trying to catch a nap on the La-Z-Boy. She told him, "Boris thinks you're overtired."

Andre opened his eyes and told her, "He's right, and thank you for being here. You have brought hope back into the house."

After getting Jack up at 5:00, Andre fed him and bathed him. Jack talked about the wild dreams he was having.

Marvin asked, "What are they were about?"

Jack said, "I have never dreamed like this before. I was in a trench war fighting. Then I flew into the woods where I caught a unicorn that had been hit by a mortar."

Marvin said, "That was the middle of World War I. I stopped fighting and worked on rescuing unicorns. That is where I met Ivan, he was the first. I flew him over to America, to the big woods of Canada."

Jack asked, "How did I get your memories?"

Marvin said, "They are not mine, they are Ivan's. You are seeing what the unicorn saw."

Marvin told the two fairies to get the sleeping potion ready. Boris complained, "He needs to eat to keep up his strength."

Marvin said, "Make enough for the two of us." So Boris drugged both the two old guys.

Jack slept through the night, got up and showered, stripped the bed and put the sheets in a garbage bag, along with another set of pyjamas. Nora flew around the room trying to stay out of the way. Jack told her, "I am going to get some coffee." He went to the kitchen and there was a pot brewing already.

Andre pointed to a cupboard. Jack walked over to it, took down a cup and filled it, then topped off Andre's. He sat next to him at the table. Nora flew to the table, walked over to Jack and told him, "We have been here for two days. The green fairy is going to find us soon. What are we going to do?"

He could detect worry in her voice. He told her, "We will cross that bridge when we get to it."

Andre asked Jack "So how do you feel?"

Jack took a sip of coffee; you could see him thinking. Then he said, "You know, I feel better than I have in thirty years."

Andre said, "That is good, I don't have to shower you anymore."

Jack told him, "The brown slime is almost gone and I don't have that weird feeling of bugs crawling under my skin."

Andre asked Nora, "So why do you think a green fairy is chasing you?" She started to tell him the story of how Jack met Elizabeth when Andre cut her off. "I know that part, why do you think she is chasing you?"

Rupert flew onto the table, "I haven't heard the story."

Nora looked at him, then started the story again quickly. "Jack was in his garden when a green fairy flew up, chased by a hundred blue fairies. He sprayed them with some kind of wasp spray and killed them all. The green fairy—whose name is Elizabeth—pulled him into the blue power from the dying fairies and he didn't die. So she took him into the forest to bring him in front of the red fairy council.

"A unicorn was stuck in a mud hole, wedged between two trees. We figured since Jack was so big, he could get him out, and he did. That's where Ivan—you know, the old unicorn Marvin visited—took Jack to his cave. He had Jack call Marvin and Boris stole the winter supply of fairy dust."

Rupert stuck his head into Jack's coffee cup and inhaled. "Wow, is that strong!" he said. Then he asked, "Was there a lot of blue power?"

"Yes, there was. A green fairy can use straight power, so can Jack." Nora told him, "She did this twice, the first time there were only a dozen or so blues, but the second time there were a hundred or so. The power floated up but then swirled and entered Jack, lifting him off the ground."

Marvin said from the doorway, "You never told us that."

Andre said, "You still haven't told us why you think this green fairy is chasing you."

Jack said, "Well, in the first place, we tricked her. But we're miles away, she will never find us here."

Nora told him, "Ivan will tell her where we are, he will not lie. The first night they drugged her. She was so tired she probably didn't notice. The second night she had to stay for a ceremony. It would have been rude for her to leave. Tonight, she will be here and there will be hell to pay."

Jack asked, "Do you think she is that dangerous?"

Andre nodded his head as Marvin said, "I have seen a green fairy going on a rampage, killing a dozen men just because they had seen her. They can shoot power right into your brain and kill you instantly."

Jack said, "No shit? I wonder why she didn't."

Andre said, "Not to change the subject, but what's for breakfast?"

Jack got up, "I got this." He walked over to the refrigerator, opened the door and said, "Bacon and eggs coming right up."

Marvin sat at the table while Jack poured him a cup of coffee and topped off Andre's. Jack said to the table, "So do you really think Elizabeth tried to kill me?"

Everyone looked up at him. Andre raised his cup and said, "Yeah."

Jack exclaimed, "No kidding!" He turned from the table and put the coffee pot back in the maker and started to fry the bacon and eggs. He made toast, buttered them and fixed three plates so they could eat together. He sat them in front of Marvin and Andre, then sat down himself.

Marvin said, "Hey, you buttered the toast! They don't do that here."

Jack said, "Really? Isn't it dry if you don't?"

Andre said, "It is dry but for some reason they don't butter it for you."

Marvin and Andre chatted about the plane and the business while Jack cooked breakfast. Jack floated the eggs in bacon grease, slid them onto the three plates and laid the bacon on the side. Jack asked, "So what's the next move?"

Marvin pointed to Boris, who was talking with Rupert and Nora. "Boris," Marvin said with a deep commanding voice, "get over here."

Boris flew over, landed in front of Marvin and asked, "What do you want?"

Marvin asked, "Is Jack through the cleansing part of the regeneration?"

Boris walked across the table and wiped his hand across the back of Jack's hand, looked at it, smelled it, then licked it.

He flew up onto Jack's shoulder and looked him in the eye. Jack asked, "So what do you think?"

Boris told him, "Just wait a minute." He flew across the room to talk to Rupert.

The men started to eat breakfast. Marvin asked Jack, "Where did you learn to cook eggs like that?"

Jack said, "Those are old-school eggs, like those before bacon was said to be bad for you. They will stick to your ribs."

Marvin said, "They don't make them this way around here."

Andre smiled, "Yeah, these are like southern fried eggs. All we need are some grits."

Boris flew back and gave them a doctor's report. "Jack should be healthy enough to wander around. He must keep eating every three hours and drink lots of water. His body is still full of blue power. Although he is consuming it slowly, we think that is why it has gone so fast."

Andre asked, "Is Jack done with the sweating brown goo and puking black tar?"

Boris fluttered to him and said, "I think Jack should be just fine. Just make sure he eats every three hours and takes as many naps as possible."

Jack sat there with his cup raised to his lips, staring into space with a blank look. Marvin looked at him, then asked Boris, "How is Juliet doing?"

Boris told him, "Juliet is lying there comfortably; we gave her a potion to keep her in peace. There just isn't enough dust to bring her back right now. Even if there was, all the herbs, roots and stuff are so old, we don't know how they will work."

Jack got up and cleared the table, loading everything into the dishwasher. He grabbed the pot and made another round of coffee, filling everyone's cup.

Marvin asked Jack, "How is everything going on the home front? Do your kids know where you are?"

Jack told him, "I took care of everything just before I left. I stopped the paper and a neighbour is going to get the mail."

Marvin said again, "Your kids, are they out looking for you? We don't need the cops showing up at the door."

Jack said, "I'll go and call them." He walked to the spare room and got his mobile phone. He called his son and he answered. "Damn," he said into the phone.

His son, on the other end, said, "Dad, is that you?"

Jack answered, saying, "I hoped I could have just left a message." Then he said, "What do you want? You left twelve messages."

His son said, "I wanted to know why you just up and flew to California."

Jack said, "If I wanted to go to Timbuktu, that's my business."

Nora landed on his shoulder and spoke into his ear, telling him, "You don't sound as old as you did."

Jack calmed down and spoke in an old man's voice, telling him, "I met up with my old army buddy. His wife isn't doing well. Cancer, late stages. The doctors give her a couple of weeks. We are going through funeral homes, getting everything ready for the day she goes. This will be a lot better than when your mother died."

His son asked, "Where are you?"

Jack knew that he was trying to get information from him. He told him, "I am with a friend. Don't worry about me, everything is fine. Tell the wife and grandkids that gramps loves them. Oh, and don't forget to call you sister. Tell her everything is fine and that I love her. And tell her I will call her soon. You know her, I'll be on the phone for an hour if I call her. You call her," and hit the cancel button.

Jack walked out of his room and into the kitchen and said, "Done. And they still don't know where I am." He put his hand on Andre's shoulder. "Just remind me to check in every day or so."

He reached up for his glasses, he wasn't wearing them. "I need a pair of glasses without a prescription." He asked, "Can they pop out the old glass and put in new ones? I need them for driving, and to match my passport. I have worn glasses for damn near sixty years. Now I can't see a damn thing with them."

Marvin told Jack, "We have been planning what to do when Elizabeth gets here."

Jack asked, "Are we going to fight her?"

Marvin said, "That would be useless. We're not that strong."

Jack said, "How about wasp spray? That sure killed the blues."

Andre said, "I'll add that to my list, that's a very good idea."

Marvin said, "We don't want to kill her, she's on our side. I mean, all we have to do is convince her that Jack is no threat to the fairies, and that he will go in front of the red council in no time."

Nora flew down to the table and said, "Blame me for talking Jack into running."

Boris raised a hand. He told Marvin, "In no way are they to blame Nora! If you need to blame someone, blame me."

Nora walked over to him and told him, "You are needed here. You must help Jack regenerate."

Boris put his arm around her and told her, "Things have changed. Rupert can handle things. We are not going to use you as scapegoat."

Jack looked down at them and said, "Isn't this nice? Hey, where is my coffee?"

Andre got up, "I'll pour you a new one."

"Thanks," said Jack. "Now where was I? Oh yeah, no one dies. If it comes down to it, we shall all go down with the ship. I just can't believe that a two-inch little fairy is that much of a threat."

Marvin told them a story about a green fairy he used to know in the old days. This fairy would have given his life for him. This fairy was his eyes in a war. He would fly into the enemy's camp at night and get the plans of attack, troop strength, who the leaders were and what they looked like. "I had him take out the leader in a few battles that really turned the tables—heart attacks in their sleep, no one caught on."

Jack asked, "So you were a general?"

Marvin said, "At one time."

Andre told Jack, "When Marvin married Juliet, his days of leading armies came to a close."

Marvin stared into his coffee for a second and said, "That was a good thing. I have seen more death then anyone needs to see."

Jack said, "Amen to that. I was in the Korean War and saw my share of death. Well, Andre, since you're the driver, why don't we go into town and get me that pair of glasses."

Marvin added, "And a haircut."

Jack ran his fingers through his hair, "Wow!" he said, "I have never had hair this long before." Jack's hair was shoulder length, snow-white and he was sporting a three-inch beard. Jack said to himself as he stroked his beard, "I had better shave."

"Not to worry," Andre said. "A haircut and shave coming up. I'll show you around Hollywood for an hour or so. Places don't open until ten o'clock around these parts."

Nora flew up to Jack's shoulder so she didn't have to yell. She spoke into his ear. Jack shrugged his shoulders and asked, "Can I get a pen and paper?" Andre stood and grabbed one from by the phone and slid it across the table. Jack started a list: bed sheets, pyjamas, fresh-cut flowers, a razor and towels.

Andre said, "We might be gone for a while, so figure out the next move."

Marvin said, "When buying the flowers, make sure there is some angels' trumpets in it, some lilies. And get a couple of large bouquets. Rupert and Boris have been working hard."

Jack set the pen down and started to fold the paper when Nora climbed down from his shoulder and into his breast pocket. You could see that Jack had something in his pocket. He picked up his pen and wrote shirts with big pockets. Below that he wrote sporting goods.

Marvin stood and told them to wait for a minute. He went into his room and came out with a small velvet bag. He said, "I hope this is the one." He pulled the strings on top, opened the bag and poured the contents out onto the table.

Andre said, "Good idea." Jack looked at a few small electronic parts.

Marvin picked up a disc half the size of a dime, it was flesh coloured like the rest of the parts. He pulled out a plastic strip that was over the batteries, then handed it to Jack, "Put this in with Nora."

Jack smiled, "A microphone." He took the disc and slid it into his pocket.

Marvin took a small wire with two small discs on the ends. He told Jack to sit still. He peeled off the paper backing and placed it behind Jack's ear and ran the wire around the backside of the ear. It stuck to his skin. Marvin then asked Nora to speak.

Jack said, "Marvin you're a genius! I can hear her very well. She said her job was to protect me, so she wants to be with me 24/7."

Andre asked, "Are you ready?"

Jack said, "I will be right behind you." He picked up the list from the table.

Andre told him, "You can wait outside for about five minutes. I will pull the car around."

Jack asked, "What do I need my cane for? It's not like anybody knows me here. Who cares?"

Jack was staring at the floor talking. Marvin shook his head. He told Jack, "You look like a loon, don't talk to her, she will talk to you. And Dropoff, pick up some groceries. Jack pretty much emptied the fridge."

Jack put his arm around Andre's neck, "You know, I feel great."

Marvin walked behind them and said, "Dropoff, don't let him out of your sight."

They stepped into the lift. Jack turned and asked Marvin, "You coming with?"

Marvin told them, "Someone has to watch Boris and Rupert. They could try something stupid."

The door closed. Andre told Jack, "Marvin hasn't been out of the castle for at least eight years, just after Juliet became paralysed."

Jack asked, "How did that happen again?"

Andre gave a short answer, "A blue guardian was stronger than they thought. If it wasn't for Marvin's quick escape, she would have killed them both."

Jack asked, "So what happened to the blue guardian?"

The door opened and the two men stepped out. Jack said, "OK," and picked up his cane, bent over. Andre looked at him and cocked his head.

Jack said, "I'm an old man, I have to look the part. I sure don't feel old."

Andre said, "Well, the blue fairies have watched this place ever since."

Jack said, "I don't feel anything."

He stopped and leaned on his cane, looking up into a tree. "I don't see anything," Jack said, standing there.

Andre put his hand on Jack's shoulder. "Are you talking to the voices in your head?"

Jack turned to him and asked, "Do you see anything or feel anything?"

Andre stood for a minute and said, "Nope, nothing. What am I looking for?"

Jack said, "A blue fairy in that tree."

Andre looked again, staring up. Finally he said, "Boy, would it be hard to see if one was in there!"

Chapter Eight
Jack Explores L.A.

The two of them walked across the car park to the Lincoln. Andre held the back door open. Jack told him, "You will have to get used to me riding in front," as he walked around the car and got in the passenger side.

Andre said, "OK, where to? Should we go and pick you up some clothes?"

Jack said, "How about we get something to eat?"

Andre said in amazement, "Wow! You just polished off a half dozen eggs, four pieces of toast, a plate of bacon, an orange and crème brûlée with five cups of coffee!"

Jack said, "Yeah, I know. I just feel hungry. No, I'm not just going to eat raw meat."

Andre asked, "Are you talking to your pocket again?" Nora popped her head out of Jack's pocket, squeezed out and flew to the dash. She sat and looked out the window.

Jack asked, "What is that Baja Fresh?"

Andre told him that it was a place where you could get salads and wraps, and that they were closed. "Let's go to a Target store and you can pick up some clothes." He pulled onto the 405.

Nora said, "There are so many lanes and cars! How do you know where to go?"

Andre kicked the old Lincoln. He passed a few cars and made four lane changes.

Jack said, "I'm glad I'm not driving in this mess."

Andre told him, "You'll get used to it quick enough." He told Nora, "Remind me to stop at an eye-care centre so Jack can get his glasses changed."

Nora turned around to face him and asked, "Why am I the one to remember all this stuff?" She ran across the dash and said to Jack, "Call your kids."

Jack said, "Once a day is enough, I just hope Johnny called Mary, boy can that girl talk, I will just call and make sure he called her."

Jack unbuckled the seat belt, pulled his mobile phone from his pocket and told Andre that they were pretty handy at times. Andre reminded him, "Do not give too much information."

Jack smiled, "I was a cop for many years." He called his son. "Hey, Johnny, old boy, how you doing? Did you call your sister? No, I'm fine. California, as long as it takes."

Nora flew to his shoulder and talked into his ear. Jack's voice lowered and sounded more like him as an old man. Now he talked instead of listening. "Now listen, I have a job to do. My friend's wife is going to die in a couple of days, if not sooner. There is a lot to do. So if I don't call, it is because I'm busy. Call your sister Mary and tell her everything is fine."

He pulled the phone away from his ear, looked for the cancel button and pushed it. Nora yelled: "Jack, he was still talking!"

Jack said, "The longer you talk, the more he will get out of you. He knows I'm in California. That's all he needs to know. And that Mary! She's left ten messages on the phone since yesterday."

Andre told him, "You should call her. And when you do, sound old and sickly."

Jack asked, "Now why would I do that?"

Andre said, "Well, you're going to be regenerated soon."

Jack asked, "What is this regenerate stuff? I've heard it mentioned a couple of times."

Andre said, "It takes about a month to two, if it's done right. You'll be 20–25 years old. Now the paperwork is the tricky part, that's why I am Russian. Pickupski and I regenerated at the same time. We were 55 last time."

Jack commented, "Pickup and Dropoff! I get it!"

Andre told Jack, "I have been with Marvin since way back in the Viking days, back in the old country." There was a pause as Andre weaved through the traffic to an exit ramp.

"Why would I get regenerated and not Juliet?"

Nora turned around on the dash and yelled, "Because we don't have enough dust and herbs."

Andre said, "She's right. I talked with Rupert, he said there is enough fairy dust to cure Marvin and Juliet, just not enough to regenerate the both of them."

Andre pulled the Lincoln into Target's car park. Nora jumped from the dash to Jack's shoulder, then crawled into his pocket.

He said, "Yes, I have the list." A pause, then, "OK, shirts with bigger pockets."

Andre said, "It's fine to talk to her when you're in the car, but try not to in public." He pulled up in front of the store and told Jack to wait for him there.

Jack opened the door and said, "All right, I'll get my stupid cane." He opened the back door, reached in and grabbed his cane. Andre pulled away and parked.

About an hour later, they came out of the store pushing a full shopping trolley. Andre told Jack to wait for him at the door. Jack protested, "I can walk just as well as you can, let me push the trolley."

When he got to the car, Jack started to rummage through the bags, then grabbed one and headed for the passenger door, leaving Andre to unload the trolley into the boot. When he returned to the car, he saw Jack had already eaten half a bag of biscuits and was drinking a Coke. Jack asked if he wanted any.

Andre said, "Next stop will be real food." He drove across the car park to a Denny's.

Jack got excited, "I like Denny's! It's been a few years since I've been in one, though."

Andre pulled up to the door, got out and opened Jack's door. Jack looked up at him and scolded him. "Don't you think I can open my own door?"

Andre rolled his eyes. "It's my job, Jack."

"Oh yeah," Jack muttered as he got out, "I'll order coffee."

Jack hunched over and used his cane. A girl came and asked, "Would you like a table for one?"

Jack looked at her, "Didn't you see my driver? Get me coffee and a table for four. There are only two of us but those tables for two are too damn small. If you want a tip you had better be quick about it.

"That's what's wrong with people. Everyone tips, even for bad service. That's what makes the service bad."

Andre walked in and a gal greeted him at the door. She asked, "Just one?"

He shook his head, "No, I'm with the grumpy old guy, shooting off his mouth. I think I can find him." Andre walked into the dining area and right over to Jack. He pulled up a chair across from him.

A waitress came with two cups of coffee and asked for their order. Jack said, "I'll have eggs and bacon over medium. Oh yeah, and a steak, medium rare."

Andre ordered the fruit plate with a crescent roll. He then asked Jack, "What's your problem?"

Jack held up his coffee cup, then said, "I am just getting a bit tired, I could use a nap."

Andre said, "And a shower."

Jack took his napkin, wiped it across the back of his hand and looked at the brown smudge, then smelled it.

Andre sipped the coffee while Jack was talking to himself, explaining what was on the table. He finally said, "Jack, stop talking to Nora. People are going to think you're crazy."

The food came and they hadn't even finished their first cup of coffee. Jack said, "Did you notice how many people were here before us, but we were served before them?"

Andre stopped with his fork in his hand, pondering this question. "You're right. There were at least four tables ahead of us. And they're staring at us they now."

Jack smiled. "Our waitress deserves a nice tip. Twenty percent, I think."

The waitress came by and filled everyone's coffee and Jack asked for the bill right away. They finished their meal and went back to the car. Jack asked over the car, "Do I smell that bad?"

Andre opened the door and said, "Next stop, grocery store. Then back to the castle."

Jack asked if he had a list. Andre told Jack that Marvin had just told him to pick up some food. They pulled back onto the 405. This time it was a sea of cars as far as you could see, thousands of them. Jack let out a "Wow" in amazement. Nora flew to the dash to see what Jack was awed by. Andre slowly merged into the traffic and said, "Welcome to L.A."

Jack said, "This is going to take forever."

Andre smiled and said, "It will add a half hour, maybe a little more. Close your eyes."

Jack was asleep in less than five minutes. Nora flew to Andre's shoulder and talked and talked. Andre learned all about Jack, his wife and kids; he was surprised that Nora had been studying him for years. Andre finally took an exit and dropped down into the city to a grocery store. As soon as the car came to a stop, Jack woke up. Andre told him that he could stay in the car if he wanted.

Jack asked him, "Do you know what I eat?"

Nora climbed into Jack's pocket. Jack stepped out of the car and said, "No, this isn't going to be fun. It's a grocery store."

Andre said, "I don't know maybe you'll enjoy yourself."

Jack told him, "Nora has never been in a grocery store."

Andre chuckled lightly, "I keep forgetting you're talking to Nora."

The two took a trolley and started to fill it. "Whatever looks good, throw it in. Marvin's buying," Andre said with a great big smile.

They walked down every aisle. In the bread aisle Jack grabbed a bag of hotdog buns.

Andre asked, "Who eats hotdogs? And you do know we live above a supper club?"

Jack put the buns back and grabbed a loaf of whole wheat bread. The two quickly went down the aisles.

Jack told Andre, "The only thing we really need is eggs, butter and milk."

Andre asked Jack, "Are you going to make it?"

Jack said, "I am just so tired all of a sudden."

Andre said, "OK, to the meat department, then dairy."

Jack told him, "We have to pick up some flowers for Boris."

When they got to the meat department, Andre ordered ten pounds of filet mignon, five pounds of porterhouse and ten pounds of ground chuck. Jack commented that that was a lot of meat. Andre said, "You, by yourself, ate almost ten pounds yesterday. Think. Every three hours, you have been eating a 16-ounce fillet."

The old man looked at Andre. "This is just unbelievable. I just eat constantly and never gain weight."

They walked into the dairy aisle and Jack said, "No, I'm not going to get ten gallons. It gets old."

Andre asked, "Ten gallons of what?"

Jack said, "Nora told me to get ten gallons of milk. I mean really? And where are we going to put ten gallons? Does she even know what size a gallon is?"

Andre said, "The fridge is going to be full."

The next stop was the flower section for the flowers. Nora told Jack which ones to buy. Then they were back to the car. Andre told Jack, "You sit and rest."

Jack grabbed a pack of biscuits off the top of one of the bags and a gallon of milk. When Andre had packed the groceries in the boot, he opened the door to find Jack had eaten half the pack of biscuits and was more than half done with the milk. Andre asked, "A little hungry?"

Jack said, "I can't believe it cost almost 400 dollars for groceries." They drove through town to the castle.

Chapter Nine
Jack Meets the All-Knowing John

Andre said, "Go inside and get a drink, I can handle putting the groceries away."

Nora climbed out of Jack's pocket and hopped to Andre's shoulder. Jack realised that they had forgotten to get his glasses changed. He told Andre so.

Andre told him, "Don't worry, they won't card you."

Jack said, "Very funny. I can't drive without them. And I sure as hell can't see with them."

Andre said, "Don't worry, while you take your nap I'll have them changed over."

Jack leaned back into the car and told him, "Don't forget the photo—grey tint." Jack walked over to the front door of the club. He walked in and up to the desk. A woman asked him if he had a reservation.

Jack said, "No, I'm here for a drink."

She said, "Walk over to the bookcase and say the magic word."

He walked over to an eight-foot bookcase. The shelves were full of books. He noticed that they were just the bindings. Jack stood there with his cane, hunched over, looking at the case, then said, "Open". Nothing happened. He said, "Please"—still nothing.

Jack raised his cane and said loudly, in an old man's voice, "Open this damn door!"

The girl who was doing paperwork said loudly, "Open sesame."

The bookcase opened into a classy bar. A waitress asked if he wanted a table.

Jack said, "I would like to sit at the bar and have a drink."

She took him by the arm and led him to the bar. To her surprise, Jack hopped right up on the bar stool. The waitress told him, "The bartender's name is Tony."

The bartender came up and asked him what he would like. Jack said, "A Manhattan whiskey, Crown Royal." He threw a ten on the bar and scanned the room with cop eyes, taking in all the details. He noticed a man in his fifties, nicely dressed, casually walking around, scoping out the place, looking at people.

Tony came with his drink and said, "Nine fifty."

Jack slid the ten out to him but didn't take his fingers off it, "So tell me about the guy in the suit."

Tony told him, "Now that is The All-Knowing Jonathan, a hypnotist who works here."

Jack turned back to the bar, took a long swig and said to himself, "Ah, Crown Royal." Then Jack noticed the John guy working his way down the bar towards him. He didn't look up, just stared at his drink. He had figured out what the hypnotist was doing. He was looking for someone for tonight's performance.

Jack put his drink down. As soon as John spoke, Jack turned and reached out his hand. John looked into Jack's eyes to see if he could use him in his show, but Jack's eyes peered deeply into his, fixing him in a trance-like state. The two were locked in a staring contest for at least five minutes.

Jack finally said, "I am not the one. Move along and forget you ever talked to me." The old man picked up his glass and downed it in one drink, slammed the glass on the bar and said loudly, "Another."

Tony stopped what he was doing; the tone of Jack's request meant now.

Jack sat, his eyes fixed on the empty glass. You couldn't even see him breathe, so deep was his concentration.

Tony came up with Jack's drink. He started to say, "I haven't seen John stare that long before."

Jack looked up and cut him off with a stare, then said, "You've never seen John talk to me. He skipped right over me. And this drink is on the house."

Tony stood thinking. He cocked his head and said, "This one is on the house." He sat the drink down in front of Jack and took the empty glass. Jack never even lifted the drink, just sat staring at it with his mouth open.

About 15 minutes later, Andre walked in though the back and up the bar. He waved Tony over and asked, "How long has the old guy at the end of the bar been drooling?"

Tony said excitedly, "Dropoff, scotch?"

Andre held up his hand. Tony pointed to Jack, "That guy over there, he hasn't moved in a quite a while, I mean moved at all."

Andre told him, "I'll take care of him," and walked over to Jack. Andre said softy, "Oh, Jack! Are you in there?"

There was no answer. Andre reached out and shook him gently, cooing, "Jack, time to go."

Jack reached up and wiped drool from his chin, still not looking up. He took a long pull from his Manhattan. He slowly looked up at Andre, shook his head and rolled his eyes. He got off the barstool standing straight; he was a good six foot one.

Andre grabbed Jack's cane and told him, "Follow."

Jack turned and stayed right behind Andre. They walked through the dining room toward the kitchen. Andre stopped in the narrow hall and said, "This door will slide open just for a second. Step in and wait for me." He said "Open sesame", put his arm on Jack's back and pushed him toward the wall. It slid open, then shut. Andre then popped in. There just was enough room for the two of them. He hit the button on the wall, "This will bring us up to the third floor. We will have to climb the stairs to the fourth."

Jack said, "I get it! The door opening and closing so fast: you can appear and disappear in the hall."

Andre said, "A little flash powder helps the illusion work."

The lift opened and they were on the third floor. Andre asked Jack, "Are you all right?"

Jack told him, "We have to get to Marvin. Shit's going to hit the fan."

Andre started up the stairs. Jack was right behind him, telling him, "Get the lead out your ass and get going. We're in deep shit."

When they reached the top of the stairs, Andre told Jack, "You have to take a shower because it smells like something died in here."

They entered the flat though a different door. Andre told Jack that this was Marvin's prop room. It was huge. There were boxes and mirrors; there was even a guillotine sitting in the corner with a head in it.

Jack stopped and lifted a sheet that was over rows of clothes—they were mostly women's clothes. "Ah," he said. "This must be Juliet's."

Andre told him that they had been a team for centuries. They came to a door with a bunch of cables and pulleys attached to it. Andre lifted a latch that set everything in motion. The door slid out of the way, stopping about three quarters of the way open. He said, "This door hasn't been opened in years, I'll get Pickupski up here with some WD-40."

Jack was in a trance-like state, staring at the door. Andre had to go back though the door and take him by the shoulders; he gave Jack a little shake, telling him, "Snap out of it!"

All of a sudden, Jack's eyes snapped open and his mouth dropped open. He said nervously, "We have to go."

Andre asked, "Where?"

Jack told him, "Hurry and just get me to Marvin."

The two walked through the door which came out in a hall in the flat. They walked past Marvin's room. Andre popped his head in. "Not here," he said.

Jack didn't say a word—it was like he was deep in thought. They walked to the next door—Juliet's room. There was Marvin, on his knees next to the bed, with her hand in his. There was a woman in there with him.

Andre cleared his throat. He introduced Jack to the lady, telling him, "This is Juliet's nurse."

Marvin told her, "This is Jack. He is the friend that is going to help with the funeral."

Jack cleared his throat and asked, "When are we going to let her go?"

The nurse said calmly, "I will contact hospice and her doctor, there should be no problem. She has been in a vegetative state for years. There is little hope that she will ever come out of this coma with any brain activity."

Jack said, "Not yet. There is so much to do. We want a green funeral, no embalming—just a showing and cremation."

Marvin got to his feet very slowly. Andre stepped to Marvin's side and put his hand on his shoulder and said, "It is time. She has been in a coma for years. It is time to let her go."

Jack asked, "How long is the nurse going to be?"

She told him, "All I have to do is change the sheets." She told Marvin, "Juliet's colour is a lot better and her pulse is much stronger."

Jack told her, "Juliet knows we are going to pull the plug. She's probably happy it will be over soon."

The nurse signed a chart and turned to leave. Jack reached out for her hand, he looked into her eyes and said, "Juliet looks just like she did last week. You will not see anything out of the ordinary in this flat. It is like it always was. Juliet is dying. You will watch her monitors and mark her charts showing her getting a little weaker every visit. And you will not remember this conversation. Now go."

The nurse let go of Jack's hand and walked to the lift. Marvin and Andre stood looking at Jack.

Jack said one word, "Coffee."

The three filed out of Juliet's room and to the kitchen. Jack walked to the coffee maker, took his cup off the cupboard and filled it. Marvin got just a splash.

He turned to Andre and told him, "Add some coffee to it next time."

Jack sat at the table with Marvin and said, "OK, this is what happened." He turned and saw Andre take a green can of coffee out of the cupboard. Jack stood and quietly stepped behind Andre, looking over his shoulder. He asked, "What are you doing?"

Andre snapped his head around, "Making coffee. What does it look like?"

Jack said, "No wonder! It's decaf! Do you have a coffee grinder and real coffee?"

Andre put the green one back and pulled out a red can and poured the coffee in the filter so it was a little over half full. He said to himself, "That ought to do it."

Jack sat back down at the table and asked, "Where was I? Ah yes, I met the All-Knowing Jonathan. He tried to hypnotise me but I got him first. He is a traitor, a spy. He has been telling a blue guardian every move that is made in the castle."

Marvin said, "John was hired about five years ago. I have only seen his show."

Jack said, "OK, so this John guy got his power of hypnotism from a broad, a blue guardian. She is the one that attacked you. She is called Margaret. He brings her fairy dust once a month. I took a lot of information from him that I have to think about. He is slipping out after the five o'clock show."

Marvin asked, "What do you want to do?"

Jack said, "Well, I need a shower, then a nap."

Andre and Marvin both agreed that Jack needed a shower. Boris flew over to Jack's shoulder and smelled his neck, then ran a finger across it. He pulled it away with brown goo dripping off it. He said to Jack, "After the shower, we have to talk."

Jack walked into the bathroom and stripped. There was a knock on the door. He opened it a crack and Andre's arm pushed through with a garbage bag. Jack took it and said, "Thanks." He picked up the clothes, took out his wallet and mobile phone and stuffed the clothes into the bag. He opened the phone, turned it on and said, "Ah, shit." There were six messages from his daughter.

He hit off and a voice said, "You have to call her."

Jack turned to see where the voice was coming from. There, sitting on the towel rack, was Nora. He asked, "Could I get some privacy?"

Nora told him, "My job is to watch and make sure you scrub every inch, remember?" She added, "Mary must be mad as hell—you talking to your son and not her."

Jack told her, "She would want every detail, and that's a lot of lies to keep straight. The less they know, the better. Now John is content with what

I'm doing fine. And not to worry, he knows I don't like to be on the phone long."

He reached in, turned on the shower and stood looking at the stream, not moving, just staring. Nora flew up and said, "Jack, you have to get in."

Jack turned to her with a blank look on his face. Nora ordered him, "Get into the shower."

Jack stepped in and started to wash. There was a little brown swirling around his feet. Five minutes passed and Nora flew in and Jack was just standing there in the steaming water. She yelled at Jack with no answer. She flew into the shower, grabbed onto his ear and yelled into it, "You have to get out of the shower!"

Jack looked at her with that blank expression on his face, but he reached over and turned the shower off. Nora opened the cabinet door and grabbed a towel with her feet and flew it to Jack. He dried himself, leaving brown streaks on the towel. He looked at himself in the mirror. His beard had grown an inch or two, and his hair was back to shoulder length, still white as snow, but thickening.

He opened the medicine cabinet, pulled out scissors and trimmed his beard. He combed his hair, brushed his teeth and put on antiperspirant. He asked Nora, "Would get me my dressing gown?" Nora flew up and hovered by the door. Jack stepped over and opened it and she flew out.

Boris zipped down the hall to fly right next to her. He asked, "So what's going on?"

When they got to the guest bedroom, Nora landed and talked to Boris, telling him, "I have never seen Jack like this. It's like he is so deep in thought that he forgets where he is, or what he's doing. Have someone pour him a cup of coffee," and she flew off with Jack's new dressing gown.

Jack was just standing there, staring at the wall. Nora flew in and laid the dressing gown on his shoulder. He just grunted and took it, letting the towel fall to the floor. He put it on without taking his eyes off the spot on the wall. Nora flew to his shoulder and told him, "They are waiting for you in the kitchen. Come on, your coffee is waiting."

Jack headed out the door and down the hall. He stepped into the kitchen, telling Marvin, "I have met the castle's hypnotist, The All-Knowing Jonathan. You should never meet him face to face. He has been placed here by some broad called Margaret. Does the name mean anything to anyone?"

He went on, saying, "Jonathan is a spy and he has been telling her everything that has been going on here for years."

Marvin said, "You told us this already."

Jack took a sip of his coffee and asked, "Who made this?"

Andre told Jack, "I went down to the restaurant and stole some freshly ground Hawaiian coffee."

Jack told him, "This is much better." He reached across the table and put his hand on Marvin's wrist and looked him in the eyes. The room went silent. Marvin's face froze as he stared into Jack's.

Marvin pulled his arm away and yelled, "You are never to do that again!"

Jack just sat there, staring into space. Andre asked Marvin, "What just happened?"

Marvin said with amazement, "He just read my mind."

Jack let out a "Wow". He picked up his cup and took a long drink this time.

Marvin asked, "Where did you learn that? And never do it again!"

Jack told him, "I felt John's power and remembered what Ivan had said. John opened his mind to read my mind. I got in and hypnotised him first. You have a much stronger mind than his. He was not ready for me to search his. I owe a lot to Nora. If she hadn't shown me how to hide my power, John would have used me to kill you all."

He got serious; his voice lowered to a deep, low tone and he spoke into his coffee cup. "This man is downright evil. He has killed many. He owes his soul to a broad named Margaret. She is a blue guardian, and he is like her hitman."

Jack lifted his eyes to look over his cup. "He works here to keep an eye on you and report back to her. John is going out after his show. We are going to follow him."

Nora flew to Jack's shoulder and told him that he had to take a nap. Jack put the cup to his lips and took a long swig and asked Marvin, "How old are you?"

Marvin asked, "How deep did you see?"

Jack shrugged his shoulders and said, "I need a nap." He got up from the table and headed to the bathroom.

Andre asked, "What's wrong with Jack? He keeps on saying the same thing about Margaret. Is he going to be OK? One thing I know is, he's never to be trusted again."

Marvin cocked his head and asked, "Why is that?"

Andre told, "I have never trusted a hypnotist; there're creepy. I have watched Jonathan and he does just as Jack said. He will walk through the bar, talk to a few people and search their minds for something for the show or will blackmail them. The All-Knowing John is quite rich, you know."

Boris asked, "What's a hypnotist?"

Marvin explained, "A hypnotist is someone who can get into your mind and make you do stuff that you wouldn't do, like cluck like a chicken. But a real hypnotist can search your mind."

Boris said, "Jack must be a real hypnotist."

Marvin took a drink and said, "Ivan has thought of everything. Luckily, Jack was one step in front of Jonathan. People underestimate us old guys."

Nora flew in and asked Boris if he had anything to make Jack sleep. Marvin spoke, "You will not drug him! Leave him to think."

Andre said, "Ivan might have taught him, but it was you who practised with him."

Boris said, "I need to go out and get some fresh herbs and stuff."

Marvin told him, "As long as Juliet needs your care, you don't leave the house."

Rupert laughed and walked over to him. "Looks like I have company for a while."

Jack got out of bed; he walked into the kitchen and asked, "What's to eat around here? I'm starved." Andre pulled a filet mignon out of the fridge and started to prepare a meal for Jack.

Marvin walked in and asked, "What's for dinner?" Andre, without saying a word, walked to the fridge and pulled out two more filets. He put them on a roaster and then slid them into the oven.

Marvin topped Jack's coffee off and asked, "How did you sleep?"

Jack replied, "I didn't sleep."

Marvin smiled because he knew Jack wouldn't have slept. He asked, "So what about Jonathan?" He took a sip of coffee and said, "Now, this is strong."

Jack said, "Yeah, I made that pot. Is it too strong?"

"It is OK," Marvin said.

Jack started to tell Marvin and Andre about Jonathan, "This woman Margaret, she gave him his power and she has used him ever since. He is her personal assassin; he has been a slave for years. She had him get the job here. He is looking forward to killing you. That is his job now. But he doesn't know how strong you and Juliet are. No one downstairs has seen you in five years."

Marvin asked Andre, "Has it been that long?"

Andre stood and thought for a second, "It will be 13 years in October. That's when the attack was."

Jack said, "I lay in bed and thought of the attack. It seems so fresh in your memory. You and Juliet, standing side by side, combining your powers. She was just too strong for you. That disappearing trick saved both your lives."

Marvin said, "I had never seen someone that strong; there was nothing I could do."

Jack said, "We have surprise on our side. I will handle Margaret, and Jonathan I already have under control. You just get Margaret's attention." The old man wrung his hands and let out an evil laugh. "I lay there thinking about the information I got from our encounter at the bar. Amazingly, John is at least a hundred years old, and he doesn't look over fifty."

Andre slid a plate in front of Jack, then Marvin. Then he sat down with his own plate. He asked, "So when do we have to follow John's car? I could put a tracker on it so we don't lose him."

Jack said, "Not to worry. We are going to Long Beach, to the Queen Mary."

Marvin asked, "Why the Queen Mary? Shouldn't we face him here?"

Jack, in between bites, said, "This is the way it has to be done and this is the way I'm going to do it."

Jack had finished half his plate and the other two were just starting. Andre sat a large glass of orange juice down in front of him. He grabbed it, held it up with a grunt, put it to his lips and sucked half of it down. He told Nora, "Don't forget to remind me to bring those pieces of quartz with us. We probably won't use them but they might come in handy."

She flew off to the cupboard where a couple of cloth bags sat, folded. She landed on one, grabbed it with her feet and flew off to Jack's room. Jack pulled out his phone and asked Andre, "Have you entered Marvin's number in it?"

Andre held out his hand. He took the phone, looked at it for a minute, then told him, "It is already entered in and his cell number is also there." He asked, "Did you know that your daughter Mary has called you ten times since yesterday?"

Jack said with disgust in his voice, "She'll keep hounding me till I call. And if I call she'll try to pry out information that I don't want to give."

Nora said, "You have to call her, Jack. She's probably worried sick about you," as she fluttered down, holding the sack of rocks.

Marvin nodded his head. He was standing across the kitchen. Andre said, "That's amazing! You heard her!"

Jack looked at Nora and said, "You know, what's amazing is how much a fairy can lift. Those rocks have to be ten pounds."

Boris flew to the table, followed by Rupert. Nora stood tall, crossed her arms and stared at him. You could feel the tension in the room as she walked over to him. She asked, "Did you use the whole winter supply of dust? You were only supposed to regenerate Jack."

Boris sheepishly said, "I didn't use it all. Marvin was too frail to teach Jack. And for Juliet, we have only been using herbs and potions that were in Rupert's cupboard."

Jack butted in, "Not to worry. If everything works according to plan today, things will be better."

Nora turned. She put her hands on her hips, "When the green fairy gets here, there will hell to pay."

Jack smiled, "I will handle her when the time comes."

Andre shook his head, then said, "You don't know green fairies. If they lose their temper, they can suck the energy right out of your brain and kill you damn-near instantly. I know. I've seen it."

Marvin laughed, "I'll take care of the green thing."

Andre defended his position. "You were there in Florida, Spain, and elsewhere. Oh yeah, remember Russia?"

Marvin walked up, put his arm around Andre's shoulder and spoke gently. "I've talked my way out of many conflicts with the green ones." Then he whispered to Andre, "Don't frighten him, we'll deal with her later."

Jack laughed. "I don't know how, but I heard you guys whisper. And don't worry, I'm not afraid of dying," he said calmly, as he raised his cup to his lips.

Marvin asked, "What was her name?"

Jack said, "I'll tell you in the car." He got up from the table, opened the fridge and pulled out a couple of apples. He put one in his pocket and took a bite out of one. He looked at the table and said, "This is the way this is going down: I'm in charge; let's move it," sounding more like a drill sergeant.

Andre pulled the car around. "Marvin, you're sitting with me in the back. There is a lot I need to know."

Andre was headed to the door. Jack yelled, "Stop! First I want you to find out what time the All-Knowing Jonathan will be done with his performance. Don't let anyone know that you asked."

Andre said, "No problem, I'll ask the receptionist."

Jack took three quick steps toward Andre and watched him open the panel that hid the lift. Andre waved his hand and said, "Open sesame." He moved his foot and the door slid open. Andre stepped in and turned, saying that he needed five minutes.

"Damn!" Jack said, as he slid his hands along the wall.

Marvin laughed, "You are not watching properly, Andre is no magician." He ran his hands across the wall, then said, "Open sesame."

The panel slid open. Marvin asked, "Did you see?"

Jack said, "No, I didn't see you push anything."

Marvin smiled, "This time, stand to the side of me." Marvin slid his hands across, reached up with his right and stopped waving his left. He pushed a knot in the woodwork, then said, "Open sesame." He pushed a small button that stuck out with his shoe and the panel slid open. He turned to Jack and said, "You try."

Jack walked up and pushed the knot on the wall. He watched the button come out next to the floor and pushed it with his foot; the panel slid open.

Marvin shook his head, "Ah, that was a poor performance. You're no illusionist. Don't open it when anybody else's around."

Jack said, "Marvin, let's go. Nora, are you coming with?"

Boris flew up and asked, "Can I come along?"

Jack said, "You are needed to watch over Juliet and the place." Boris started to argue. Jack lifted a finger and looked Boris in the eye.

Boris just said, "I'll stay here."

Jack stepped into the lift. Nora flew to his shoulder and Marvin stepped in. They went down in silence.

Chapter Ten
To the Queen Mary

The lift opened to a warm and sunny day. There stood Andre, next to the Lincoln. He opened the door. Marvin grabbed Jack by the arm and pulled, "Let's go quickly."

Once they were in the car, Jack asked, "What that was about?"

Marvin said, "If anyone saw me, they would know that something was up."

Andre turned and asked, "What has it been—five years—since you came down?"

Marvin said, "Five years—almost to the day."

Andre asked, "Where to?"

Jack said, "That depends on when Jonathan is getting off."

Andre started the car and pulled around to the front of the castle. He turned around and told them, "Wait here. I'll be right back."

Jack told Marvin, "We are going to get a month's worth of dust from Jonathan."

Marvin said, "He isn't going to just hand it over!"

Jack looked Marvin in the eyes; Marvin shook his head and said, "Don't do that to me."

Jack told Marvin, "I have seen what is in Jonathan's head and it isn't pretty. He is a hitman and has killed many."

Marvin's face drained of what colour it had, then he said, "That's why he wanted to see me so bad."

Jack said, "No, he was just there to keep an eye on you, not to kill you—yet."

Andre got back behind the wheel and said, "Jonathan is done at 5:00 today."

Jack asked, "How long will it take to get to Long Beach? The Queen Mary?"

Andre said, "A good hour or so."

Marvin started questioning Jack about Jonathan. "What is he up to? How much have you learned from him? Does he suspect anything?"

Jack told Marvin, "He works for the bitch who put Juliet in a coma. He is going to pick up some dust that the enslaved red fairies have collected. I don't know when we are going to confront him."

Marvin asked again, "What have you learned from the hypnotist?"

Jack said, "I still haven't sorted everything out. There was so much information!" He raised his voice and asked, "Could we stop for a bite?"

Andre said, "As soon as we get off—at the freeway we can find some kind of fast food place."

Nora, who crawled out of Jack's pocket as soon as she got in the car, was sitting on Andre's shoulder asking, "How can you drive in so much traffic? And which lane are you supposed to be in?"

He told her, "We are going a long way, so we would get into the car pool lane—which is a lane for cars with more than two people in them."

Jack commented, "Now that is a river of cars—eight lanes going one way and eight going the other." Then he asked, "How can a cop pull you over in this mess?"

Andre chuckled, "Oh, you'd be surprised! Sometimes they will pull over twenty at a time."

Marvin and Jack talked, getting to know each other, Jack could tell Marvin was very selective with what he told him. Jack asked Marvin, "How old are you?"

Marvin said, "The same answer—85."

Jack asked, "What about the posters that were in your room?"

Marvin let out a long "Ahh."

"Who told you about the posters?"

Andre shook his head and said, "Sorry, boss—wasn't thinking at the time."

Marvin blurted, "Dummkopf, I am 85 in this life. This is the oldest I have ever been."

Jack said, "You were in the room when I asked. How old are you really?"

Marvin said, "It doesn't matter right now. We have to focus on the job at hand."

Andre pulled off the highway and asked, "Will Baja Fresh work?"

Jack said, "OK, let's try Baja Fresh. It's fast food, good tacos—so I hear."

Marvin said, "That would be great."

Andre pulled the big black car into the car park, next to a bunch of kids. He muttered, "Great", got out and opened the door for Marvin. Jack got out from the other side. A kid of about 16 walked up to him and told Jack, "Hey, old man, you owe me fifty bucks."

Jack lifted his head to look the kid in the eye, then told him, "You will keep an eye on the car and you will make sure nothing happens to it."

The kid stepped close to the car and started to shoo the others away from it, guarding it. Jack asked Andre, "Hey, are you coming?"

He shook his head, saying, "I will stay with the car."

Another kid stepped in front of Jack, "Old man," he said.

Jack looked him in the eye and put his hand on his shoulder. He said, "From now on, you will respect your elders."

The kid excused himself, standing dazed. Jack and Marvin were only inside for 15 minutes. When they came out, the kid was standing behind the car, protecting it. Jack pulled out a twenty and handed it to the kid, "Thank you; now find yourself a job. And call your mother and get off drugs."

He snapped his fingers and the kid stood there in a daze. He started to yell at the car, "Twenty bucks? Is that all?"

Andre pulled out of the car park and asked, "Queen Mary, right?"

Jack asked, "Have you been to it?"

Andre told him, "I am not just a pilot; I was a chauffeur. I have been here a dozen times at least." There were signs showing the way. Andre leaned back and said, "15 minutes."

Marvin told Jack, "I can give you the tour. I have sailed the old girl three or four times."

They pulled into the car park. Nora said, "I'm coming with." She climbed into Jack's pocket. Andre drove right up to the entrance. He got out, opened the door and let Marvin out.

Jack got out his door and walked around to the two, "OK, this is what I want you to do. Park where you can see the entrance, then call when Jonathan comes."

Then he asked Marvin, "Do you have your phone?"

Marvin shook his head, "I left it at home, didn't think I would need it."

Jack pulled out his phone, shaking his head. "I hope the kids don't call." His phone made a chirping noise, telling him that he had messages. He told Andre, "Call as soon as you park. To make sure you have the right number."

The two old gents bought tickets for the tour of the ship. They were headed up the gang plank—well, it was cement. The ship was permanently moored there as a tourist attraction. Marvin said, "I would like to go through the Marilyn Monroe exhibit if we have time. One day I will tell you the story about her coming backstage at a show I was in."

They slowly walked through the ship. Marvin told him, "In the old days, this was a huge ship. The best luxury liner in the world."

Jack said, "The new ships are big like a city. They hold thousands of people. A few years ago, I took a cruise with my wife Emma. The main pool was on the 16th floor."

Jack's phone rang. He quickly opened it and excitedly answered, "Yeah, I'm on the Queen Mary, can't talk now. I'll call you tonight. Yes, I promise."

He closed the phone and put it back in his pocket, "Now where was I? Oh yes, the cruise."

He told Marvin about the shows and the food and what islands they had stopped at. Marvin ran his hands over the handles of the door leading into a large room. He started to tell Jack about the dances they had had in here and what his Juliet had been wearing when Jack's phone went off again.

Jack pulled the phone out, opened it, and looked at the number. He put it to his ear and asked, "Is he here?" He slid the phone in his pocket and grabbed Marvin by the arm. He said excitedly, "Let's go! We have to catch him before he gets into the spook house."

The two old men were walking really fast. Jack grabbed one of the crew and said one word, "Lift." The man didn't even answer.

Jack turned and shouted to Marvin, "This way."

By luck, the lift was just being unloaded. The two got in and a young lady reached in to stop the doors from closing. Jack yelled, "You can wait!" It felt like the lift was taking forever. Jack kept muttering, "Come on, come on!"

Marvin said, "Be patient, this thing is old."

Jack said, "Let's get going."

The two were out in the car park and there was The All-Knowing Jonathan walking across the car park to the entrance in the back half of the ship. Marvin grabbed Jack by the shoulder and said between gasps, "Wait—he will see us!"

Jack said, "I have taken care of that already. We just have to catch up."

They reached the tour, it was one of the haunted ones. Marvin walked up and purchased two tickets. Jack stood right behind him, they had ten minutes to wait till the next tour. Marvin asked Jack, "What was the big rush?"

Jonathan stood 25 feet from them, not even noticing them there. Marvin whispered to Jack, "Did you hypnotise him?"

Jack said, "Yes, I did. He won't see us."

Marvin asked, "Can he hear us?"

Jack looked a little confused, "I don't know, maybe he can."

The two old guys walked out to look at the Russian submarine that was moored close to the ship. It was large and old. Marvin asked, "Are you going to kill him?"

A large man in a suit stepped out and waved the two elderly gentlemen towards the tour. Jack mumbled, "Damn it all!"

They walked up to the tour and stood in the back. The tour guide said, "You two, come closer to the front so you can hear."

Marvin did a disappearing act, surprising Jack. He looked and there was Marvin—standing right in front of the tour. Jack circled and people made room for him to step up front. He held out his hand, shook the big guy's mitt and said softly, "In five minutes, you will have two less people in your tour and you will not see the two old guys."

Jack then motioned to Marvin. The two of them worked to the back of the queue. He touched Jonathan, looked into his eyes and said, "When this tour is done, you will think everything went as planned. Nothing out of the ordinary happened."

The tour started and Marvin and Jack took up the rear of the tour, following Jonathan. The tour guide was funny, telling the tale of the ship and its ghosts. The lights flickered and sounds of groans echoed in the large empty belly of the ship. They reached the engine room. There, Jonathan held back. The two old guys stopped, a hand reached out and touched Jack's shoulder. A man wearing all black said, "Move on."

Jack turned and looked at the guy and said, "You will move on. We will catch up with the tour. Think nothing of it."

The man turned and disappeared into the darkness. Marvin told Jack that Jonathan had heard them. Jack walked up to Jonathan, touched his hand and said, "Nothing is wrong, everything is going smoothly."

Jonathan looked around and stepped around the roped-off section. He walked across an I-beam and opened a small steel door. He reached in and pulled out a bag, which he put into his waistcoat pocket. Jonathan then closed the door and headed toward the tour. Marvin asked, "Aren't you going to take the fairy dust? Why are we here?"

Jack walked around the rope and opened the door. He stuck his hand in the darkness. The darkness lit up with a bright blue light which spilled out onto the whole ship. There was a high-pitched noise, then a noise like a thousand kernels of popcorn popping at the same time, and then the moan of the ship as power flowed through its walls. The lights grew bright for a second. You could still hear a few pops.

Jack pulled out a piece of quartz he had in his pocket. The light disappeared into the quartz and he grunted loudly. The blue light disappeared and the rest of the lights on the ship dimmed. Jack put the quartz back in his pocket and closed the door. He held out his hand and shed a little red light to see the I-beam to cross. He got to the other side and stood there with a blank look on his face. Marvin grabbed him by the shoulder and pulled him toward the tour, which had stopped just twenty yards down the grated pathway. They passed the man wearing black and stepped into the back of the line. The tour guy finished making a small speech. Nora asked, "Did you see how much fairy dust was in that bag? There is enough for years to live on! And for Juliet!"

Marvin put his finger to his lips and hushed her. He told Jack that they would talk about this in the car.

Jack asked Marvin, "Have you ever been in this part of the ship?"

Marvin said, "This is the pool. Of course I have been here with Juliet, many times. It looked so much brighter then."

The tour guide painted a much darker story about the fog that flowed in there. Soon the empty pool had fog flowing in its bottom and flashes of blue lights. Sounds of ghostly groans floated through the ship as the guide spoke ghoulishly. The tour ended and Jonathan walked swiftly to his car. Jack started to follow, then he slowed. Marvin stepped to his side, "Remember you're 82, act that way."

Jack said, "Nora just told me that I don't need a cane. I know where The All-Knowing Jonathan is going—Brentwood."

Andre pulled up and stood there with the door open. Marvin told Jack to get in. By the time Jack had slid in, Marvin yelled over the car at Andre, "Hurry up!" and was sitting in the car next to him.

Jack asked, "What is the rush?"

Marvin replied, "Brentwood is a gated community. The house is gated too—most of them are."

Andre said, "Then I shall follow him at a distance."

Jack said, "No need. You can tailgate him and he won't see the black Lincoln."

Andre shook his head, "If he can't see black Lincolns, we will be lucky to make it there alive."

Jack left out a groan, "There so much you have to think of when you screw with someone's head."

Nora asked Marvin, "Hey, did you see the bag of fairy dust Jonathan had?"

Marvin nodded his head and said, "Yes, I saw it. There was about a quarter of a bag."

Nora asked Jack, "Why didn't you take it? There was enough to replace the dust we stole from the clan."

Jack said, "We were there to take out the fairies."

Andre said, "I saw a blue light shoot straight out of the stack of the Queen, then disappear."

Marvin said, "Yeah, that was Jack."

Nora then told them, "We lost the element of surprise. They will feel us coming."

Jack took out the bag he had brought and took out a film bag. He slipped the piece of quartz into it and sealed it. Nora flew down and put her hands out, "I don't feel anything."

Marvin smiled, "An aeroplane film bag, lead lined. Ingenious."

Jack handed it to Marvin, "Take it. You'll need it."

"I don't like the sound of this, and it is blue power I can't use it" Marvin protested.

Jack said, as he put his hand in the bag a red glow came from it, "There now, listen closely. This is how we are going to attack her." Jack closed his eyes and described the house and garden. "This is how Jonathan will make the exchange: it is usually a tea party out on the gazebo."

Marvin asked, "A tea party? You must be joking!"

Andre said, "This is tricky," as he pulled up to the gate leading into Brentwood. He said, "We are with Mr Marcourt, to see Miss Margaret." The attendant opened the gate and let them through.

Jack said, "Hey, that worked very well!"

Andre stepped on the gas and said, "This is the tricky part. We have to sneak in right behind him to get through the gate to the house." He almost kissed Jonathan's bumper as they went through the gate.

Chapter Eleven
Meeting Margaret

The big old town car just made it through the gate. Jack was going over the plan once more. Nora crawled into Jack's pocket and told him to keep his power deep inside himself. Andre parked about a hundred yards behind Jonathan, in the shadows of a tree.

Jack told Andre, "Stay with the car. And here," he handed him a can of wasp spray. "I don't think there will be any trouble, but who knows? This is all new to me. Hell, we might all die."

Marvin asked, "How many cans do you have?"

Jack pulled out two more cans and held them out to Marvin. "I hope you don't have to use them, just get her attention. That's all I ask."

They watched Jonathan walk through the grass around the house, toward the garden. Jack said, "See? He's going to have tea in a gazebo in the garden."

Jack got out, so did Andre. He stepped back and opened the door for Marvin and said, "Good luck, sir," tipping his hat, playing the part of the chauffeur.

Jack said, over the roof of the car, "Give me a couple of minutes and remember you're an old man. We need that element of surprise to pull this off." With that, he was off striding down the driveway across the grass to the other side of the house.

Marvin said, "If I'm an old man, drive me up to the house."

Andre closed Marvin's door and pulled up behind Jonathan's car, he then got out and opened Marvin's door. Marvin got out. He adjusted the film bag in his jacket pocket and put one can of wasp spray in his rear pocket.

Andre said to him nervously, "Be careful," as he wiped a tear from his eye.

Marvin said, "Remember what Jack said. If it doesn't look like it's going well, get out." He turned and started to walk swiftly toward the house.

Andre jogged up to him and said, "Remember! You're a frail old man." Andre walked back to the car, took the can of wasp spray from off the seat, leaned in and took a pistol out from under the dash. Then he stood sentry by the car, wiping it with a rag.

Jack told Nora, "Fly out ahead and look for trouble. We can't afford being seen."

She flew ahead and was back again as soon as she reached the corner of the mansion. Excitedly, she said, "There are blues in the cedar hedge watching the house. I don't think they saw me."

Jack told her, "I want to get close to them. Show me."

Nora told him, "I can feel your power."

Jack stopped and concentrated on hiding the power within himself. Nora whispered in his ear, "I'm scared. I don't feel your power now."

Jack walked casually toward the cedar hedge. He raised one hand and a blue spark popped in the hedge. A flash came to Jack's hand. He asked his pocket, "Are there any more?"

Nora climbed out and asked Jack, "If you want, I could fly ahead?" She came flying back with a blue on her tail. Jack raised his hand and the blue fairy just vanished with a spark. Nora yelled wildly, "That tree is full of them!"

Jack started to jog to the tree. He spread his arms out with palms facing the tree and smiled. Then the whole tree lit up with a soft blue light and its light streamed to Jack's palms. It was a deep blue, then it lightened and faded, all within a minute.

Nora said, "That's amazing!"

Jack turned to her, almost knocking her off his shoulder. He asked, "How do I feel?"

Nora asked him, "Can't you feel the energy you're putting out?"

Jack reached into the bag he was carrying and pulled out a piece of quartz. He brought it to life with the blue fairies' energy, reached down and placed it on the ground. "There! The energy they were putting out will still be here."

Jonathan was just reaching the gazebo, a middle aged woman took his hand, and they stood chatting.

Jack said, "I can't wait. Marvin must already in the backyard."

Jack started to jog. He was already around the backside of the house, peering around the corner of a gardener's shed, waiting. Marvin didn't hide one bit, he slowly walked across the lawn toward the gazebo. He heard Margaret say in amazement, "Look, is that Marvin? By God, it *is* Marvin the Magnificent!"

She stepped out of the gazebo onto the grass. She was wearing a blue dress with a large quartz necklace. Marvin kept walking slowly towards her.

Jack, looking for the advantage, sprinted across the open back lawn to some shrubs. He slowly walked to get behind the gazebo. Margaret laughed an evil laugh. "This must mean your beloved Juliet has finally died!"

When Marvin got within fifty yards, he put his hands together, formed a small ball of red power and threw it at Margaret. She lifted one hand and batted it away, "You're a fool, old man! And you have made yourself weak!" She raised one hand and a ball of blinding blue light formed around it.

While this was happening, Jack reached the gazebo without being noticed. He stealthily walked up behind Jonathan, put his hand on his shoulder and spun him around. He said one word, "Sleep," and Jonathan's head nodded forward.

Jack stepped around him and Nora climbed out of his pocket to his ear. Meanwhile, Marvin ripped open the film bag and held the piece of quartz in front of him. It came alive with a brilliant red glow. Margaret shot the ball of blue light toward Marvin, knocking him off his feet. The light came within five feet of him.

Margaret yelled, "See, old man? Your power is weak!" She threw a duller ball of light at Marvin, who was on his knees, knocking him down to the grass.

Marvin slowly got back to his knees and another ball hit him. This time it knocked the stone from his hand. Margaret raised her hand and a bright ball of blue power formed again.

Jack flew in at full speed, grabbed the necklace that was around Margaret's neck that glowed and held it in one hand. The other hand was on Margaret's neck, forcing her to the ground. The necklace in his hand glowed brighter. He dropped it to the ground and pulled out a piece of quartz that he had brought from the car. It started to glow till it got to a blinding blue light, it almost like he was holding a star. He dropped it and pulled another stone out from the bag that was by his feet. This stone started to glow too, but not as fast.

He kneeled next to Margaret, who was lying on the ground now. His eyes glowed. Bright white, his hair flowed around him. It was like he was in a trance. A shot rang out and Jack snapped out of his trance and looked up to see three blue balls, about three feet in diameter, hovering in front of Marvin. Jack raised one hand and grunted; the balls slowly came toward him. You could see the blue stream of power pulling them. Then it stopped. A ball of white power formed around his raised hand and he threw it. It exploded the first blue ball. Almost instantly, he threw a second one, blowing up the second blue ball. As for the third ball, the blue fairies unlinked their arms and scattered.

Jack exhaled loudly and started to pull. The blue fairies started to pop like popcorn as he pulled their power from them. Jack let go of Margaret. He picked up the quartz that he had dropped and started to fill it with the power from the fairies. When he had finished draining the blue fairies of their power, he stood and started to walk over to Marvin, who was trying to stand. He ended up just sitting on the grass. Marvin croaked out, "Check on Andre."

Behind Marvin, Andre lay sprawled out on the grass, quivering. His hair was still smoking a bit. Jack kneeled next to him. There was a hole burnt in his chauffeur's uniform. Jack put his hand on Andre's forehead and whispered, begging, "Come on, you can do this!"

Andre's eyes opened and Jack's closed. He slowly swayed back and forth. He announced, "That's all I can do."

He stood. To his surprise, Andre raised his arm. Jack grabbed it and helped him to his feet. He asked, "How do you feel?"

Andre just pulled him into a hug and said, "Thanks, how's Marvin?"

Twenty feet away was Marvin, sitting on the grass and looking away from them. Jack and Andre jogged up to him. Marvin said, "She is still alive."

Jack asked, "Did you think I was going to kill her?"

Marvin turned his head and gave him a look of contempt. He uttered one word, "Yes."

Jack, not even moving his legs, flew standing upright, just a couple of inches from the ground, to Margaret. He noticed that he had left the quartz stones scattered by her and she was feeding off them. He said, "Maggie, we have a problem here. You're dangerous. You could ruin the whole plan unless you work with me. And if you don't, you will be destroyed."

Jack reached down and picked up the bag and put the stones and necklace inside. He then reached down, took Margret's hand and helped her to her to her feet. He pulled power from her as he held her hand. "I'm sorry. I can't let you be a threat to my friends." He turned her and looked into her eyes, then said, "Now go into the house. We will meet you there."

Margaret walked to the house. Jack floated back to Marvin and Andre. Jack asked, "How is he?"

Marvin said, "He is very weak. We are going to need an ambulance."

Jack reached down and put his hand on Andre's shoulder. He closed his eyes and mumbled, "Come on, come on, you can do it!"

He stood for a minute, then said, "So Margaret was the one who put Juliet into a coma."

Marvin got to his feet and begged Jack, "Do not trust her!"

Jack asked, "How do you feel?"

Marvin looked at Andre, then back to Jack, "OK. So what are you going to do with Jonathan?"

Jack said, "I forgot about him." He walked across the lawn to the gazebo where Jonathan stood, fast asleep. He put his hand on his cheek and told him to open his eyes. Jack stood gazing into Jonathan's eyes. After a minute or two Jack said, "Go take the 405."

Jack walked back to Andre and Marvin. "Let's go. There is a lot to do."

Jonathan walked across the lawn, toward the car, holding his left arm. He started to stagger a bit. Andre told Jack, "You're making a huge mistake, trusting Jonathan."

Jack smiled, "Don't worry, he will never make the castle alive."

Then he told him, "Pull the car around to the back entrance. And Marvin, follow me." The two walked toward the mansion's back door. As they walked, Jack said, "Margaret won't stay hypnotised for long. You must play along. Make the illusion that we're going to do something dastardly."

Marvin asked, "What are you up to?"

"First thing is to get everything that has to do with fairies removed from this place. We have to wipe it clean." Jack stopped at the steps to the patio, "Marvin, this is important. We need Margaret. I feel the hate you have for her."

Marvin looked up at Jack and said, "I am Merlin the Great. I am older then you could imagine. I have killed thousands of people, I have toppled kingdoms. Yes, I can play your game."

Jack's jaw dropped as he thought about it. He knew Marvin spoke the truth. The two went in the back door, to a sitting room where Margaret was waiting for them. Jack spoke loudly, "Maggie, this is the plan: I am going to have you join us."

She looked up and asked, "Why would I join the likes of you two? For God's sake, Marvin is weak; he is a Red."

Jack replied, "Because I let you live. My job was to kill you. Are you in or are you out?"

Margret's face drained of all colour and she said meekly, "Well, I guess I don't have a choice. I'm in."

She started to ask questions, Jack raised a finger, then said, "You will do as I tell you. This place must be wiped clean of anything to do with fairies." Jack's hair was almost to the bottom of his shoulder blades and he sported a six inch scraggly beard. He said, "Margaret, this is the deal. I was going to kill you, take what I wanted, then burn the place to the ground. If you don't get moving, I could still do it."

Andre walked in, "So where is the stuff?"

Jack raised his hand. "This way." Jack led Margaret, Marvin and Andre through the house down into the basement, then to a sub-basement.

Marvin and Andre hung at the wine cellar door for just a minute, Marvin whispered to Andre, "Do whatever Jack asks, no questions."

Jack walked up to the rear of the cellar, which had wine racks from the floor to the ceiling. He reached into a hole where a rock had fallen out of the wall and pushed a small section of the wine rack; it slid back along with a piece of the wall. This revealed a small, pitch-dark room with an overpowering stench. Jack reached in and turned on the light. There were cages stacked upon cages, with a hundred or so blues watching over at least five hundred red fairies. Margaret said in a screech that no one could understand, "Don't trust them."

Jack spoke with a very low whisper, "She is no longer your master, you answer to me." Margaret's eyes popped wide open and her jaw dropped. Jack put his hand in the air, "It is *you* that can't be trusted." Small streams of blue power whisked to his hand and a light popping noise could be heard of the blue fairies expelling their last power. He turned to Margaret and asked, "Can I trust you?"

She dropped to her knees and begged him, "Trust me! I will do whatever you want."

Jack looked over her to Marvin and Andre. "Everything in this room must go. There can't be even one trace that the fairies were here." He reached down and stroked Margaret's hair. She looked up and Jack said calmly, "Now take a cage and carry it to the car." Margaret stepped over to the wall, where Andre handed her a cage in which a hundred or so red fairies stood watching her.

Jack walked in, reached into a cage and took out a green fairy who couldn't even stand. He held it in his hands and spoke softly to it, "Someone has been looking for you." He was putting it in his shirt pocket when Nora said, "No way!"

Jack had forgotten the fairy in his pocket. He told Nora, "You have to be quiet and take care of the green one." Jack then dropped the fairy into his pocket and took a cage of red fairies. Marvin and Andre did the same. They all walked down the hall. Margaret turned and exited out a side entrance that was much closer to the outside.

Andre started to set the cage down but Marvin cleared his throat and shook his head. Jack said, "Tell your driver to pull the car around." Margaret stepped up to the men and dropped her cage in the grass. Andre set the cage down and jogged to the back of the house. Jack sat his cage on Andre's and told Marvin that the room must be cleared within the hour.

He turned to Margaret and told her, "We are going into the house to your room to clear out the safe." Jack followed Margaret into the house, up the lift to the third floor, to a room that had paintings, a suit of armour and pictures of random men. Jack stood looking at a picture and said to Margaret, "This is your 23rd husband. You killed him by giving him a massive heart attack."

He stepped up to Margaret and asked her, "What are you waiting for? Open it." Margaret walked around a display case. Jack shouted: "Wait!" He waved her over to him, reached over to her and lifted her head by her chin. Then he looked deeply into her eyes. "You can't be trusted. You were going to shoot me, weren't you?"

Margaret started to cry, tears streaming down her face. Jack said one word: "Sleep," and Maggie's head slumped forward. Jack then said, "When I tell you to awake, you will do whatever I say, or you will die the worst death that you can imagine. You will believe that I am just using Marvin and when I am done with him, I will kill him. You are going to enjoy the power that you will have with me in the new order."

Jack stepped away from Margaret and gave a quick scan of the room. "Trophy room—this room must have cost a pretty penny," he said, then turned to the back of the display case, slid a panel open and punched in a code on a number pad. Then he walked over to the wall that was five feet away and pushed one corner. It swung open.

There was a large walk-in wardrobe, shelving from floor to ceiling on one side and boxes piled chest-high across the back and down the other side. Jack reached in, turned on the light and brought out a pistol. He inspected the gun and said quietly to himself, "A 1911, .45—nice gun." He pulled the magazine out of the handle and inspected it, pushing down on the top bullet, "You should never leave your magazine full, it weakens the spring." Jack pulled out his mobile phone and rang Andre as he looked though the stuff on the shelves. Andre answered; Jack asked, "So, how are you doing?"

Andre said, "Oh, much better! We went to the kitchen and borrowed a couple of trolleys. Oh, the smell!"

Jack asked, "How much longer?"

Andre told him, "This was the last load, we packed the boot."

Jack said excitedly, "Good! Get your ass up here. Take the lift to the fourth floor, I'll stand in the hall. Oh yeah, bring your trolleys." Jack took a long purple velvet case off a shelf. He opened it to find the horn of a unicorn. He stroked it, feeling the power that it still contained. There were diamonds in one case, in another there were Russian Easter eggs encrusted with diamonds, rubies and all kinds of gems. He opened a box on the floor—it was filled with quart freezer bags of fairy dust. This took his breath away. He put the bag back in the box and exclaimed: "Oh my God!" as he quickly walked out of the room to the hall. There stood Andre. He waved him over but Andre raised one hand, signalling Jack to wait. The lift opened and Andre helped Marvin get his trolley out. They both pushed their trolley down to Jack, who met them half way.

Marvin asked Jack, "So, what's with the gun?"

Jack looked down to his waist, there was the .45, stuck in his pants, "Oh, Margaret was going to shoot me, but that's not the big news. I have to show you something." Jack spun on his heels and took off towards the room. Andre was stride for stride, but Marvin took his time. The two men stood and waited for Marvin to get there before entering the secret room.

Marvin said, "Great! More stuff to move."

Jack said, "You just wait." He brought out a bag and showed it to Marvin."

Marvin said, "So she likes cocaine."

Andre said, "It's not coke, it's fairy dust."

Marvin's eyes watered up, a tear sliding down his cheek, "There's enough to regenerate all of us and more."

Andre looked at Margaret as she stood sleeping in the middle of the aisle, then he spoke, "She going to be in the way."

Jack stepped out of the wardrobe and up to Margaret. He snapped his fingers but she didn't awake. He told her to come along, that didn't work. Jack stood there looking at her and finally said, "What the hell! Why don't you wake up?" Margaret's head lifted. Jack asked her if anyone was coming to the mansion this evening.

Margaret said, "The staff has every other Tuesday off, they will be back at eight o'clock."

Jack asked, "Is there anything else that has to do with the fairies?" Margaret said there was some jewellery and some fairy dust in her room. Jack followed Margaret to the lift and down to the second floor. Then they walked down a hall to her room. There in her bedroom hung a huge Rembrandt. There was a large four-post bed but no dressers and a large-screen TV hung on the wall.

Jack asked, "OK, where are your dressers?" Margaret opened a door to a huge walk-in wardrobe, it was a small room but not that small. Jack walked in and looked at the wall of shoes—the whole wall had shelves. Jack said, "There must be a thousand shoes here."

Margaret said, "I have never counted them." She walked over to a picture hanging on the wall and pulled it open, revealing a wall safe. She started to open it.

Jack stepped in close, put his hand on hers and said, "I'll do it, you have a .32 calibre derringer in there." Jack spun the dial back and forth, then grabbed the handle. He turned his head and told Margaret to please step back. He cracked it open and pulled out a small pillbox and a small jewellery box. He stood there looking at it and asked her, "Did you really make earrings out of fairies?"

Margaret said with a smile, "It takes high pressure. A Swiss diamond-maker made them. There are a thousand fairies per earring." Jack opened the case and it glowed bright. He shut the case and walked over to a display case of purses, where he took down a brown leather and put the two cases in it.

Jack noticed Margaret was slowly moving to the safe; he raised up an inch or so from the floor and slid to the safe in a whoosh. Margaret gave him a dirty look. Jack, smiling, said, "I forgot my gun, didn't I?" He reached in and took out a shiny double-barrel derringer.

He asked as he took stuff out of the safe, "What do we have in here? A stack of hundred-dollar bills, a ring and gold coins. I'll just take the cash. Let's get a cup of coffee and chat." The two headed to the kitchen. Jack sat at the table and told Margaret to pour him a cup. He called Andre with his mobile phone and asked how everything was going. Andre was very excited, telling Jack all the stuff that Margaret had. Jack said, "That's nice. When you are done, call me."

Margaret came to the table with a silver platter filled with coffee cups, creamer and sugar. She sat them on the table and went back to get the coffee. Jack sat back and admired her elegance as she set everything in its place and poured the coffee.

Jack told Margaret to sit down and listen. She pulled out a chair across from Jack. He asked, "Now, what are we going to do to keep you alive?" Jack picked up his cup and blew on his coffee, looking over the cup at Margaret.

She wiped a tear from her cheek and asked Jack, "What are you planning?"

Jack smiled, "What I am supposed to do is eliminate you, take all that is fairy and destroy all the evidence. However, I like you and think you would make a good partner."

Margaret pleaded, "I will do whatever you say, no questions asked. If not, you could kill me later. I could be such an asset!"

Jack sat his coffee down and looked across the table. "Look into my eyes, damn you!" Margaret lifted her head and opened her eyes wide open. Jack felt her hiding a part of her mind. They sat for a minute, then Jack spoke. "OK, then you will regenerate. Set up an appointment with your attorney tomorrow." He sipped his coffee and said, "You will keep your word. There is nowhere in the world that you can hide from me."

He stood and pulled power from Margaret. She tried to fight it but there was no use. "I will call you tomorrow. Get everything in motion and when you fire your staff, be generous."

Jack pulled his phone out of his pocket and dialled Andre's number, then he asked, "Are you done yet?" Andre must have told him that they were. So he started down the hall, when he felt a movement on his chest. It was Nora crawling out of his pocket to his shoulder. Jack stopped and said, "The coast is clear."

Nora screamed, "Are you nuts? Her a partner! She tried to shoot you twice! She can't be trusted!"

Jack said mildly, "You must have faith, trust me."

Nora yelled: "She's evil! The fairies can take care of her if you get her weak enough."

Jack shook his head, "She would feed off your power. Just trust this old man and get back in my pocket." Jack walked to the lift and hit the button for the ground floor. As soon as he exited, he met a young girl of around 25, very pretty. She wore a short black dress with four-inch heels. Jack spoke to her in a calm voice, "Hello, Linda."

She stopped and asked, "Do I know you?"

Jack said with a sly voice, "No, but I know you." He looked her right in the eye and hypnotised her, searching her brain for information. Jack waved his hand in front of her and said, "Take me to the side door." With that, Linda started down a hall to the very end, then down a stairwell to the service entrance.

Jack walked out to find Marvin leaning against the Lincoln. Marvin asked, "Who is this lovely creature?"

Jack said, "This is Margaret's right hand gal. Linda, tell Marvin how long you have been with Margaret."

Linda spoke with a soft seductive voice, "I have been with Maggie for 105 years now, give or take a few."

Andre walked up, pushing a dolly with four cases of wine on it, "You look pretty good for being over a hundred."

Jack said, "Margaret likes her to be young, so she never gets over 30."

Andre parked the trolley next to the side door of the limo, put his arm around Marvin and said, "Those were the days, hey, mate?"

Marvin looked at Linda and asked, "How can you trust her?"

Jack said, "Linda, bark like a dog for me." Linda started to bark. Jack then said, "Bark like a big dog." Linda lowered her voice and started to bark in a lower tone.

Marvin spoke loudly, "We don't have time for tomfoolery."

Jack told Linda, "Go into the house and help Margaret get everything in place. The mansion is to be sold, Margaret is to regenerate, and the two of you are going to move. She is to be a leader in the new order." With that, Linda went back into the house. Andre loaded the cases of wine into the back seat of the car.

Chapter Twelve
Back to the Castle

Marvin asked, "Do we have everything that has to do with fairies?"

Jack handed him the purse. "Here, there are some dust and weird earrings inside." The men got in the front of the car, Marvin got stuck riding in the middle. Jack commented, "You're lucky this is an older model, since all the new cars have bucket seats."

Marvin slid in and asked, "What is this crap? You should have killed that bitch."

Andre started the car, looked over to Jack and said, "You know, he's right. She can't be trusted, she will be on the phone with all the other blue guardians. Next time, you'll be fighting more than one."

Marvin then remarked, "You didn't have to kill her. We could have just fried her brain or turned her into a vegetable."

Nora flew out of Jack's pocket and landed on the dash. She yelled to be heard: "Now listen here, Jack has to be trusted. He is the chosen one; he has the power. We could regenerate Margaret to a child. It would take ever so long to break down all those bones and they usually die anyway." She pointed to Jack, "Why didn't you wipe her brain? She could have been a stammering idiot for the rest of her life."

Jack sat back in the seat and said, "She has so much money and information. If we are going to fight this war, we need resources."

Nora asked, "Do you feel that? Don't speak. I think there is a blue spy in or on the car. Jack, take me out and let's search the car." The two walked around the car, checking it slowly. Nora said, "Do you feel that in the back?" Jack raised his hand and a blue flash sparked under the bumper.

He asked, "Any more?"

They walked around the car. Nora said, "I don't think so," So they got back into the car.

Jack said, "Boy, the car is full and it stinks! Let's get going."

Marvin then asked, "What are we going to do with all those red fairies? There must be around a thousand."

Jack said, "We feed them, nurse them to good health and release them."

Marvin asked "Dropoff, where the hell are you going?"

Andre said, "There was an accident on the 405. I'm cutting down along Highway One."

Jack shook his head slowly, "I have to tell you that it's my fault. The All-knowing Jonathan had an aneurism on his way back to the castle."

Marvin asked, "Did he die?"

Jack smiled, "I kind of hope that he did."

Andre croaked, "I have to crack a window. It smells really bad in here." The two other men agreed, so the windows went all the way down.

Jack said, "Car exhaust would smell a lot better than those fairies. Don't they ever wash?"

Nora flew to his shoulder and yelled: "They were prisoners for years and years! I don't think the blue guardians cared."

They drove in silence for a while, then Andre asked, "How much money?"

Jack replied, "Margaret is incredibly rich. I'm talking four million in the bank, another 24 in stocks and bonds, plus the house and all the art. She figures four to seven hundred million."

Andre whistled, "Ah yeah, that is a lot of cash!"

Jack smiled, "Well, tomorrow we will see if we can keep it."

Marvin shook his head in disgust, "Anyway, Margaret is too much of a threat. She has to be eliminated and it could be harder than you think. We found unicorn blood in the upstairs safe. That would make her immortal so she can't die."

Jack put his hands on his head, "I know, I know already! She can be destroyed! Just let me think."

The car went silent again. Jack asked Nora, who was sitting on the dash watching the traffic and taking in the sights, "How is the green fairy?"

Nora stood and turned, facing Jack, "She has been abused for years. She was used as a battery. They fed her, let her build power up, then they drained her over and over again. I don't think she will ever be the same."

Jack asked, "Will she live?"

Nora yelled, "Didn't you listen to me? She might be insane!"

Jack said softy, "As long as she lives." He gave out a long yawn, then asked how much longer.

Andre told him with the traffic, less than an hour.

Marvin said, "I'm beat. Give me a couple of minutes of shut-eye."

Jack chimed in, "Sounds good!" He hung his head to his chest and within three minutes, the two old guys were out.

Nora flew to Andre's shoulder and asked all kinds of questions about driving edicts, the car, roads and buildings; she didn't stop talking until they were a block away from the castle.

Andre spoke loudly, "We have arrived. Time to wake up!"

Marvin shook Jack, "Come on Jack, there's a lot to be done tonight! Juliet can start regenerating." You could hear the excitement rise in his voice.

Jack rolled his head on his shoulders, "Oh, my neck," he said, stretching. He rubbed his eyes, "I could have slept for a week."

Andre pulled up behind the Magic Castle and said, "We will empty the car. I will stay down here and load the lift; you two empty it."

Nora flew off Andre's shoulder to the dash of the car and started pacing back and forth. She stopped and cried out, "What are we going to do? The green fairy is here!"

Jack shrugged his shoulders and said, "We'll just have to deal with her."

Nora said, "You don't understand! She will kill us all!" with tears streaming down her face.

Jack said, "You know, you're overreacting! She's on our side."

Marvin shook his head, "She isn't; green fairies are very strong. You don't want to get them mad."

Jack opened the car door and got out. He stretched, cracked his neck, then leaned down into the car and asked, "Andre, are you coming up to meet this green bitch? Might be fun! Well, let's get this over with."

Andre stepped out and came around to help Marvin out. He took Marvin by the hand and helped him out. Nora caught a ride out of the car with Marvin; she then fluttered to Jack. Marvin straightened out, you could hear the vertebrae snap into place. "God, that feels good!"

Nora crawled close to Jack's ear and said, "Do you feel that?"

Jack asked, "What, the green fairy?"

Nora stammered, "Ah, yeah, that too. But we are being watched. There are blues in that tree."

Jack raised his hand and cooed, "Come to daddy," and a wisp of blue light came streaming out of the tree. He asked, "Do you feel any more?"

Nora stood on Jack's shoulder and said, "That was amazing!"

Jack said, "Do you or do you not feel any more of those blue suckers?"

Nora sat for a second and told him, "The coast is clear, whatever that means."

Marvin put his arm on Jack's shoulders and said, "You know, this might be all right."

Jack looked over at Marvin and said, "You California people are kind of touchy, aren't you?"

They stepped to the back wall of the place. Jack asked, "Why don't you teach me how to open this stupid door?"

Andre stepped up, "This is the Magic Castle. Don't always believe your eyes." He stepped to the wall and said, "Open sesame," and the wall slid in six inches and out of the way, revealing a lift door.

Marvin said, "Sleight of hand."

All three stepped into the freight lift. Marvin said, "I hope this goes well."

Jack chuckled, "She can't be that mad! She flew like eight hundred miles; she should have cooled off by now."

The doors slid open. There wasn't a sound. Andre said, under his breath, "This isn't good."

Jack pushed by him. He called out, "Boris, it's me, Jack." There was an eerie silence all of a sudden. A streak of green slammed into him, throwing him into the wall. Then his feet rose off the floor.

Marvin jumped out of the lift and started toward the two. Jack waved him off and smiled. Elizabeth was giving him a royal chewing out. She screamed, "You made a fool of me! No one does that! Now I'm going to kill you."

Jack, still with a smile on his face, said, "Now how are you going to do that? There are witnesses."

Elizabeth screamed, "I don't care—I'll kill you all."

Jack slowly sank to his feet. "So, Lizard Breath, how are you going to energise my heart into a heart attack when you have no energy?"

She shouted, "What the hell? What is going on here?" She was losing her colour. She let go of Jack and started to fly away, but Jack raised his hand and a bright green stream of energy came into it.

Jack turned to Marvin and asked, "Do you have a piece of quartz here?" Marvin jogged to the other room and came back with a crystal ball and floated it to Jack. As soon as Jack's fingers touched it, the ball came alive, with bright green light flowing into it.

Nora flew to Jack. "Don't kill her!"

Jack stopped pulling energy from her and she fell toward the floor. Nora streaked to her, catching her five inches from the floor. She flew up to the counter top, asking her, "Are you all right?"

Jack was looking at the crystal ball Marvin gave him. "This worked, but I can feel the power leaking out of it."

Marvin said, "I know where some quartz is.' He left the room and walked down the hall. Rupert flew to him and spoke to him. Marvin came sliding into the kitchen and grabbed a sugar bowl off the table. He shouted, "Be alive!" as he dumped the contents on the table. There was Boris's lifeless body—lying in a pile of sugar.

Jack handed Andre the crystal ball. He took it and dropped it on a chair. Jack cupped his hand around Boris and a warm red glow formed. Nora flew to Boris; she hovered over the top of Jack's hands because she was too short to see over them.

Rupert flew in, landing on Marvin's shoulder and told him, "Jack has to stop for now."

Marvin said to Jack, "That's enough for now."

Boris was starting to move. Jack took his hands away from him and Nora flew in and gave him a great big hug. She was crying, "I thought you were dead!" Boris tried to talk but failed; he leaned into Nora.

"Dammit!" yelled Marvin, "Dropoff, here, now!"

Marvin took off in a dead run to Juliet's room. Andre was right behind him. Marvin ripped the covers off Juliet, unsnapped the IVs and ripped the wires off her from the monitors. "We have to get her in the shower. That stupid fairy poured all the fairy dust on her, trying to get her to talk."

The two had her out of bed and on her way down the hall before Jack even got there. He asked, "What is going on here?"

Marvin just yelled, "Get the hell out of the way!" Jack stepped into an open doorway and the two walked by, carrying Juliet. You could tell she hadn't walked in years. Her legs were just skin and bones and big knobby knees.

Jack followed them into the bathroom. Andre shouted to Marvin, "Hold her!" Marvin held her close, talking gently into her ear as Andre turned on the shower. Juliet's eyes opened and she tried to lift her arm; a half smile came to her face.

Andre said one word, "Good", and Marvin carried Juliet into the shower. She probably weighed sixty pounds. Her hair was thin and draped over her shoulder blades. You could see the bone structure, but there was a metallic shimmer to her—almost a glow.

Andre stepped into the shower. He took Juliet under her arms and pulled her hospital garb off. Marvin took the shower head and started to rinse her off. Jack stepped up and asked for his wallet. Marvin handed him his and Andre's. Jack then stood and watched. Marvin washed her hair twice and kept rinsing.

He yelled, "Wash rag!" Jack pulled a wash cloth off a rack near the sink and handed it to him. Marvin soaped her up, rinsed and started all over again.

Nora flew onto Jack shoulder and asked, "How is she doing?"

Jack said, "She looks like she is coming out of it."

Nora sobbed, "Ah, shit!"

Jack turned his head to look at her, then put his hand out for her to step onto. He held her out in front of him. Jack walked out of the room and asked, "Why is that a bad thing?'

Nora had marks where streams of tears ran down her face. She sobbed, "Juliet, she—" She started to cry.

Jack walked to the kitchen and sat Nora down next to Boris. Then he said, "Boris, you have to tell me what happened! Nora is useless."

The old fairy struggled to his feet. Nora flew up and landed on Jack's nose, yelling hysterically, "Jack, you have no compassion! She will never be the same!"

Jack spoke loudly, "We will do whatever can be done for Juliet. But for now, get off!" Jack put his hands down near Boris. His hands glowed red and the fairy stood and turned.

Rupert flew up and landed on his shoulder, "That's enough, Jack. Just a little at a time."

Jack lifted his hands and the light went out. He asked, "Where the hell have you been?"

Rupert flew off his shoulder and hovered in front of him. He said with authority, "Put out your hand!"

Jack put out his hand and Rupert landed in his palm. He raised it so Rupert was a foot from his face. The old fairy said, "This is what happened."

Nora flew up to Jack's shoulder to hear. "The green fairy came. She was full of rage. Boris went to talk to her. That didn't work. The first thing she did was to suck the life out of him; she kept on asking where you were. He wouldn't say, so she started to slam him into the wall. Soon, he couldn't even stand. She picked him up and put him in the sugar bowl."

Jack said, "What the hell? He didn't know where we were!" He stepped over to the other side of the sink where Elizabeth was lying. He lifted his other hand and pulled power from her and said in amazement, "My God! She has been powering up from that crystal ball!"

Nora asked Jack, "What happened to Juliet?"

Jack sat Rupert down on the counter top and said, "First, we must get this ball out of here." Jack stepped over to where Andre had dropped it, on a chair.

Nora jumped off and fluttered to Boris. She picked up his head and rested it on her lap, talking to him as she stroked his head. Jack picked up the crystal ball and carried it into the other room. When he got back, he heard the shower turn off and the men talking in the bathroom. Jack hurried to the kitchen. He put his hand down in front of Rupert and ordered, "Get on."

Rupert did as he was told. Nora rested Boris's head on a flannel and flew to Jack's shoulder. Jack asked, "Now what did that green thing do to Juliet?"

Rupert cleared his throat, "OK. After she interrogated Boris, she started to search the house. The only one she found was Juliet, and she wasn't talking. She found the dust and poured the whole thing on her, trying to get her to talk. She just didn't know how far Juliet was gone. That's when you guys came home."

There was movement in the hall. The guys were taking Juliet back to her room. Boris stood, wavering. Nora flew down to him, then grasped his shoulders with her feet and flew him to Jack's shoulder. Rupert helped him sit. Jack started down the hall, then he stopped.

Nora asked, "Why did you stop?"

Jack smiled and said, "I had forgotten to do something." He turned around and walked back to where Elizabeth was lying on the counter-top. He pulled open his shirt pocket. Jack looked inside and said, "Come on out! Don't be afraid?"

Nora spoke into his ear, "I think she is insane."

The green fairy poked her head out of the pocket. Jack said, "Do you see? I even found your cousin."

Elizabeth struggled to her feet and stared at the fairy. "That's not Aurora," she said, as she slowly sat down. The fairy in his pocket looked up at him and said, "I am Shelia, thank you so ever much! I owe you my life. I will be your servant, if you will have me."

Jack put his finger at the top of his pocket and said, "Hold on." She did, and Jack pulled her from his pocket and turned his wrist so she was lying on his palm. He then sat her down next to Elizabeth.

Jack said, "This is your first job. Watch her." He turned and started to walk down the hall toward Juliet's bedroom.

Nora spoke, "Don't worry, Jack. Green fairies are trustworthy."

Rupert held Boris on Jack's shoulder as they walked down the hall. Jack stopped right before entering the room and said, "Ah, shit!" Both men in the bedroom turned to look at him.

Jack said, "I brought Boris to help." He reached up with his palm flat to his shoulder. Nora stepped over and helped Rupert get Boris to his feet and onto Jack's palm. He then stepped into the room and placed them on the dresser.

Jack asked, "How is she?"

Marvin said, "She'll be all right. We need to get the oxygen hooked up. She needs air—ah, nuts! The nurse!" Marvin's eyes watered up, then he choked up, "She has to be!"

Andre had hooked up the IVs and was placing the electrodes on her. Boris started to take charge; he would say something to Rupert, then the fairy would fly down and tell it to Andre.

Jack walked over to Marvin and put his arm around his shoulders. He gave him a quick hug. "She'll be fine; I'm going to unload the car." Jack stepped away from the bed and loudly said, "Nora, let's go."

Marvin stood and cocked his head, "Dropoff, you go with them. Jack will never figure out the lift door."

Andre said, "Oh yeah," and he headed toward the door. Marvin stepped excitedly to the dresser, telling Boris what they had found at Margaret's house.

Jack and Andre walked through the kitchen to a wall with a picture hanging on it. Andre said, "Open sesame", and waved his hand; the wall slid open.

Jack looked at him, then said, "I'm going to be using this thing. Show me how to open it!"

Andre said, "See, I push this outlet on the wall with my foot and push this knot in the wood work." The two of them stepped into the lift and Andre said, "Juliet isn't that good. She'll live, but it's not going to be a good regeneration. Hopefully she will not be disfigured."

Jack shook his head, "That damn fairy!"

Nora said, "That is in the past. We have to look to the future. If anyone can help Juliet, it's Boris."

The lift door opened, Andre stepped out and said that he would pull the car closer to the lift. Jack got out, looked at the palm trees and said, "What have I got myself into?"

Andre swung the big Lincoln around and backed up to the lift. Jack motioned him to come back farther, then waved him off. The boot popped open to reveal small cages stacked tight. Jack said, "I'll get in the lift; you hand them to me.

Andre started handing him cages and the two worked fast. In five minutes, the boot was empty and the lift side wall was stacked two cages deep to the ceiling.

Andre stepped in and said, "That worked pretty well. We will do the same thing upstairs." Then he started to gag, "Oh my God, does it stink in here!"

Jack grimaced, "Kind of takes your breath away, doesn't it?"

When the doors opened, Andre stepped out with his hand over his mouth and pinched his nose. He had tears running down his face. Jack stepped out and commented, "It's not that bad!"

Andre headed right for the sink. He hung his head over it like he was going to puke. Jack walked up and told him, "Hey! You don't look so good." He then pulled a chair from the table and asked him if he would like to sit down. Andre did sit and Jack poured him a glass of water, "Here, have a drink." Andre took it and Jack said, "Just sit here, I can unload the fairies."

Jack stepped over to the lift and took a cage off the top row. When he turned to step out, Marvin was standing there. Jack asked, "How's Juliet?"

Marvin took the cage, looked Jack deep in the eyes and said, "She'll be fine."

Jack felt the pain in Marvin's eyes and knew Juliet wasn't fine. He asked, "How long before we know?"

Marvin said, "A day or two. Let's just get this thing unloaded." Marvin stacked the cages right outside the lift door. He stood shaking his head, "Boy, do they smell!"

Andre stepped in and sprayed a bathroom spray, trying to cover the smell. Jack walked over and cracked the window. Marvin stood and looked at him like he had done something wrong. Jack asked, "What?"

Marvin said, "It's just—well, a window hasn't been opened in here for close to ten years."

Andre said, "It's about time."

Jack walked over to the sink where Andre had a cutting board in the sink and was fixing the sprayer above it. He had a rubber band on the sprayer. Andre said, "It's a fairy wash."

Jack reached behind the sink and took a bar of soap and placed it on the board. Nora, who was sitting on Jack's shoulder, said, "This is a great idea." She flew off and flew back with a cage, holding it with her feet. She sat it down on the countertop.

Andre opened it; there were about a hundred fairies all talking at once. Andre turned on the water and adjusted the heat and the spray. "OK, this is what we are going to do."

The fairies were still chatting among themselves; none of them where listening. Andre slammed his fist on the counter-top: "Listen up!" He stepped over to the other cages. "I'm only telling you once, this is how you're going to do it: You walk into the shower, take a handful of soap, suds up and rinse off. And then step out, one at a time."

Marvin came out of the bathroom with a hair dryer. He hung it over the other side of the sink and put a baking tray over the sink, then put a couple of flannels over it. Andre waited for Marvin. As soon as he was done, Andre told a red fairy who was standing outside the cage to do it.

The little fairy walked onto the cutting board and rubbed the soap bar with his hand. Jack reached around Andre and pushed the soap into the stream of the sprayer. "Try that," he said.

With that, the little fairy soaped herself and rinsed off all at once. He walked through and went under the hair dryer to the other side. Then he flew up and thanked Andre.

Andre looked at Jack and said, "Nora, you're in charge here. If one is too weak, have two of them walk him through." He stepped over to the cages and pointed, "Everyone takes a shower, got that?"

Jack walked into the other room and came out with the crystal ball, still with a little green fog on it. He held it and closed his eyes for a second. It turned to a blood red. He sat it on the kitchen table. He looked to the far corner of the counter-top and said with a commanding voice, "Is this safe?"

Shelia, the second green fairy, flew up and said, "Jack, I owe you my life. I will do anything for you."

Nora flew up, "I got this. I don't need any help."

Jack said, "This is Nora's job. You do what she asks."

The green fairy bowed and said, "Yes, master."

Marvin said, "Now, I would have never thought I'd see that."

Jack said quietly to Marvin, "That's not the one I'm worried about."

Nora stood next to the cage, telling the fairies to get in queue and start. Marvin walked into the house and returned with Andre. "You two, finish unloading the car. I'll supervise this production."

Andre grabbed the bathroom spray and sprayed half the can in the lift. "OK, let's go."

Jack followed him into the lift and said, "You know, I'm tired as hell. I haven't slept in over 14 hours."

The two exited the lift to the car still backed up to the building. Andre said, "I think I can squeeze it in here." He walked up, climbed behind the wheel and he pulled up alongside the building. Jack opened the back door, almost hitting the building. It was stacked full from floor to ceiling.

Andre stepped behind Jack and asked, "Hey, would you like me to hand you the stuff?" Andre started to dig his way into the car. There were bags, boxes and crates. Soon the lift was full.

The two rode it up. When the door slid open, the stench hit them. Andre yelled, "Quiet down!" The room came to a mumbling. There were fairies all over and half the cages were still full.

Marvin disappeared, then reappeared with Boris and Rupert on his shoulder. Jack started to hand things out to Andre; soon the two unloaded the lift. Marvin would take the ones he wanted.

Andre walked over to see how things were going in the fairy wash. Nora was standing there, bossing the fairies around. Andre asked, "How's it going?"

Nora flew up to Andre. He put out his hand and she landed on his palm. She said, "Everything is working out quite well. We had to put a dish cloth on the cutting board because it was getting slippery from the soap. Other than that, everything is going to plan."

Jack said, "They get five minutes on the table next to the power, then I don't care." He put his hand on Andre's shoulder, "Let's empty the car."

Andre held up one finger. He quickly stepped into the bathroom and sprayed all the way to the lift. They turned to find all the empty cages were piled in the lift. Nora said, "Oh yeah, I had Shelia stack the empties in the lift. They really stink."

Andre grabbed the other can of bathroom spray. "Great", he said, as he sprayed the cages that were in the lift.

Jack said, "What are we going to do with all these cages?"

Andre said, "I guess I'll take them to the airport, I have a dumpster there. No, not the airport. They will think I'm smuggling animals."

Jack asked if they could just pile them next to the building for now, so they did. Jack told Andre, "I will crawl in this time." Jack started to hand out cases and cases of wine like champagne, then boxes and bags of all sorts.

Finally Andre said, "That's it, the lift is full." The two stepped in and Jack said, "There's a lot of weight in here, with all that wine."

Andre asked Jack, "Do you know a lot about wine? Most of that is over a thousand dollars a bottle."

Jack looked at him and said, "No way!"

Andre smiled, "Oh yeah. We're going to have a bottle of 1962 Bollinger to celebrate."

They rode the lift to the room and the doors slid open. This time it was pretty quiet, but now there were fairies all over, shoulder to shoulder, waiting to get into the shower. Marvin must have sensed that they were back, because all of a sudden he was right there with the two fairies. "Well, about time! Did you get it all?"

Jack stepped out, "Pretty close."

Andre started to hand Jack boxes and bags. Marvin was hand picking what he wanted right away. As soon as the unicorn skin came out, Boris grabbed it and flew off. Shelia was flying back and forth with cages, almost dumping them out. She flew up to the lift with a cage, piled it next to the lift with the rest and said, "As soon as you gentlemen are done, I will load the cages."

Jack said, "Thank you. When you are done with the cages, get in queue and take a shower." Then he stepped over to the sink where Nora was watching the group form a queue to shower.

Jack asked, "So how many?"

Nora asked nervously, "Was I supposed to count them? I could have counted. Ah, nuts, do you want me to count them?"

Jack said, "Just guess."

Nora said, "About three thousand. And I didn't put the fairy dust on the saucers. That was Marvin's doing."

Andre said, "Let's go find Marvin. And I think that was a good idea, they have to be strong."

The two walked down the hall to Juliet's room. There was Marvin, unpacking and reading the labels for Boris.

"How's everything going?" Andre asked.

Boris flew to within six inches of his face with his whole head glowing red. He yelled, "Get out!"

Marvin said, "She's doing better."

Jack walked in and looked at Juliet and all the bottles and jars. It looked like a mad scientist's laboratory. Boris was fit to be tied. He paced on the dresser. "I told you to get out! We have a lot of work to do."

Jack turned toward the door and told Andre, "Let's get out of here."

They walked back to the kitchen where it was a sea of red fairies all over. Elizabeth flew up to Jack and he held out his palm. She landed in it and said, "I have killed every blue that is within half a mile."

Jack said, "Well, I can see you're feeling better!"

She asked, "What should I do now?"

Jack said, "Nora's in charge. Do as she tells you."

Elizabeth told him, "I'm not taking orders from a red piece of garbage like her!"

Jack just said, "Yes you are. Andre let's get that lift empty so I can get some shut-eye."

The two started to unload the lift. Andre was inside and Jack was stacking more onto the pile, against the wall. The cages were stacked three high. Jack climbed into the limo and started to hand boxes and bags to Andre, who stacked them in the lift. It was mostly loose stuff; soon the limo was empty.

They went upstairs and started to unload the last of it; Jack stood outside. Elizabeth started to fly small bags and boxes to Marvin. Soon, they had it empty.

Jack commented, "That car can hold a lot of stuff."

There was a box with about ten pounds of fairy dust. Jack picked it up and carried it to Marvin himself. When he entered the room, there was a flash of red. Boris was right in his face. Jack told Boris, "I'm only delivering this box of dust."

Marvin was holding Juliet's hand as Rupert applied some paste to Juliet's temples. He got up and stepped over to Jack with open arms. "You finally got to it."

Jack handed it to him and told him, "I am taking one bag for the fairies back home."

Marvin said excitedly, "Yes, yes you do that," and turned back to Juliet.

Marvin spoke to her in a gentle voice, "Look, my love! More fairy dust than you or I have seen in our lives."

Boris apologised, "I'm sorry, Master Jack, there is so much work to do!"

Jack cut him off, "Just do it right, and get some sleep."

Boris cocked his head and shouted, "Sleep, yes, sleep. How could I have missed that? I need the venom of a king cobra."

Jack did a 180 and yelled down the hall, "Elizabeth, come here!"

Meanwhile, Jack stepped into the room, this time walking right up to the bed to look at Juliet. One could see she wasn't doing well; her white skin had blotches of colour. There were chunks of hair that were falling out.

Elizabeth came flying into the room, landing on Jack's shoulder, "What can I do for you?"

Jack held out his hand, palm up, and she jumped into it. He said, "It's not what you can do for me, it's what you can do for Boris."

Elizabeth put her hands on her hips, "Now, what the hell do you want me to do?" she asked with a sharp tone.

Jack asked Marvin, "Where would one find a king cobra around here?"

Marvin said, "Oh I see, I'll look for exotic pets in the yellow pages."

Andre, who was standing in the doorway, said, "Hey, green thing over there! There are three within ten miles. Look at the GPS map, there is one five blocks from here."

He pushed the call button and rang a number. He spoke into the phone, "Yeah, I want a king cobra." There was a pause, then, "How about five grand?"

Andre said, "He has one, but won't sell it unless we have the right papers."

Jack said, "Tell him we'll be right there."

Andre said, "He's not going to sell it to us."

Marvin walked into his room and came out with a pile of cash in his hand. Jack smiled, "I'll buy it for one dollar over cost." He took the money, folded it and pushed into his back pocket.

Boris, who was watching Rupert page through the big spell book, flew over and yelled excitedly, "Hurry! We are going to put her back in a coma."

The two started down the hall. Boris flew up to them; he asked all nice and calm, "Can you leave the green fairy?"

Jack said in a forceful voice, "Lizard Breath, you are to do whatever Boris tells you. You got that?"

The green fairy didn't say a word. Her head glowed a light green; that was enough to know she was pissed. There was an alarm that went off in the bedroom. Jack turned to see the charts were going wild above Juliet.

Jack grabbed Andre by the arm and ran down the hall, "Let's move!" The two got into the lift and went on their way.

Nora was interviewing the red fairies and getting them moved around so they were in groups from where they came from. There were about 150 that came from the castle.

Marvin came into the kitchen and said, "This is not good. What happens if someone stops by? Where are you going to hide all of these guys?"

Nora flew to him and landed on the shelf he was getting a glass from. "Who would stop over?"

Marvin took down a glass and walked over to a calendar. He said, "Oh shit! The nurse will be here at ten o'clock tomorrow morning!"

Nora asked, "Can we put them upstairs?"

Marvin poured a glass of water. He looked plain tuckered out. "Do what you have to."

The old man really looked his age now; he started to shuffle down the hall. Nora flew to his shoulder and spoke into his ear, "Step into the living room." Marvin did. There were fairies sprawled out everywhere. She said, "Look at the ones on the couch." Marvin stepped over to the couch and a cheer filled the room.

Fairies jumped into the air, all floating around Marvin, screaming and hollering his name. Marvin put his hand over his mouth and tears welled up in his eyes. "My God! You're alive! Come, come and see your Queen."

He led them into Juliet's room where she was tossing and turning; the charts were going mad. Boris and Rupert tied her to the bed. Nora flew in front of him and yelled, "There is nothing you can do! Get out."

All the red fairies became silent, not a word was said. Marvin kneeled alongside the bed. He looked into the terrible pain in the eyes of his wife. He reached down and lifted her head ever so slightly, "Look! The fairies have come home." The charts stopped spiking so much. Her legs started to shake.

Meanwhile, five blocks from the castle, there was a house with a small sign in the window saying "Exotic Pets". A man greeted Andre and Jack at the door. They stepped in. He asked, "Are you affiliated with the police? Or animal control?"

Jack looked into his eyes and said, "You have seen our papers. Bag up that cobra so we can get going."

The man led them into a small bedroom upstairs, where there were aquariums stacked all over, most of them empty. He took a box out from under a large 55 gallon aquarium. He took a long steel pole from a corner and slid it under the lid, pinning the cobra's head to the floor of the containment. Then he slipped his arm under the lid, grabbed the snake by the back of the head and took it out. It was about two inches around and five feet long.

Andre put his hand on Jack's shoulder and said nervously, "We only need the venom. Can we milk it?"

Jack asked, "Can we milk it?" as the proprietor was trying to fit the snake into a small box.

He looked up and said, "Sure, there is a glass behind the rattlesnake cage."

Andre brought the glass. It had cling film wrapped over the top and handed it to the man. He took the snake and worked the fangs into the plastic and a shot of venom streamed into the glass. He looked up and asked, "How much do you need?"

Jack said, "I haven't a clue."

The man worked and another stream oozed down the side of the glass.

Andre said, "That should be enough." He reached out and took the glass from the man. Jack lifted the lid of the tank and helped lift the snake into it.

Jack asked, "How much do we owe you?"

The man said, "A grand would do."

Jack looked into his eyes and said, "In five minutes you won't even remember talking to us." He peeled off a hundred dollar bill. "You found this on the street."

With that, the two headed out to the car and were on their way back to the castle. When they got back to the castle, the whole top floor was lit. Andre commented, "It's been a long time since I saw that many lights on upstairs."

They pulled up to the back of the building and went to the lift. Jack stepped out of the lift and said, "Wow, the place is clean!"

Andre pushed by and said, "It doesn't smell as bad either." He broke into a jog down the hall.

Boris met him at the door. "Where is the snake?" he snapped.

Andre pulled the glass out of his pocket. "Here is the venom, not 15 minutes old."

Boris said, "I didn't ask for venom, I asked for the snake."

Andre asked, "Isn't that what you needed?"

Rupert had Andre pour a little venom in a small cup, then worked it into the potion. Boris went to work with him, then applied it to the inside of her eyelids. Her vital signs started to drop instantly. Within three minutes, she was flat lining. They started to flush her eyes out. Boris started to bark out commands and they got her stable.

Jack was standing in the doorway, his face dripping with sweat. He stepped to the foot of the bed and let out a gasp. He said, "I thought you killed her."

Marvin said with disgust, "If she could have died, she would have. I thought Boris was supposed to be the best."

Nora flew up to him and said, "I have never met a more knowledgeable wizard."

Andre said, "Look! The skin tone is blending. Everything looks like it has slowed down."

Marvin raised her head and clumps of hair fell out; there was new hair filling in the bald spots. Jack said, "That's impressive! She's growing new hair."

Boris flew up, Jack held out his hand and he landed in it. "I don't know if there is any permanent damage. Let's leave her in a coma for a few days and let her slowly burn some of this energy."

Marvin stopped stroking her arm and stood slowly, "I'll find a hat for her and we'll powder her face. Hell, her whole body!"

Jack asked, "Why?"

Marvin told him, "Tomorrow, the nurse comes. Every other day she will be here."

Jack smiled, "Make sure I'm here. I've been pretty persuasive lately."

Andre said, "Great! We can start on the funeral."

Marvin chuckled, "The paperwork has been done years ago. I'll contact a solicitor and make sure it still legal."

Jack blurted out, "What the hell? I thought she was going to be all right!"

Marvin put his hand on Jack's shoulder, "We all have to die, have a funeral and be reborn. So start thinking about yours."

Andre said, "Juliet's is going to be great. I have to see who is still alive on the list."

Marvin shook his head and said, "Not this time. She has been out of the act for so long that people won't remember her. The same with me."

Andre seemed disappointed. He said, "When this is over, I'll show you what a funeral can be. We had acts from around the world and full orchestras. In the old days we would bring in a three-ring circus and have magic acts. We'd party for a week."

Nora flew up and said, "I'm putting all the fairies upstairs. Marvin, your group is hosting. Now Boris, you get some sleep."

Jack added, "I've been up for more than 24 hours. Boy, I can't keep doing this. I will get sick."

Marvin told Jack, "Follow me. I will show you to your room."

The two walked down the hall to another hall. It was a wing in itself. Marvin turned into a room and Jack's luggage was there. The bed was turned down, a pitcher of water was on the night stand and his pyjamas were laid out on the bed.

Jack was impressed, "This is nice! Why aren't I staying in the guest room?"

Marvin smiled, "This wing hasn't been opened for years. This is your room now. Stay as long as you would like. You're not a guest, you're family. I just told Nora to get your room ready. She brought the fairies in, they dusted and the works. I wonder if she did my room. Well, sleep in. You've had a long day."

Jack said, "I just can't believe this is happening to me. My God, am I going insane?"

Marvin said as he pulled the door closed, "No, you're not going insane. You're going to war."

Jack looked over to Nora, who was standing on the head board, "I'm no saviour, just in the right place at the right time." He started to undress and put his pyjamas on. He asked, "Is there a reason? I mean, really. Why me? I am not a hero or a great warrior."

Nora flew to him and landed in his palm. He lifted her so she was looking him in the eye. She said, "I promised Ivan the unicorn that I would look after you and Boris."

Jack smiled, "I hate to tell, but it looks like Boris is in charge."

She smiled as she flew up with his pyjama bottoms, "Don't you worry about Boris. I've known him for more than a hundred years. Everything is under control. But I do wish you had killed that green thing."

Jack looked at her and his jaw dropped, "I can't believe you said that! Kill Elizabeth? Why would I do that?"

Nora said, shaking her fist, "You can't trust her! She would have killed you if she could have. And why the hell didn't you kill Margaret? You killed that Jonathan guy."

Jack lowered his hand to the pillow and she stepped off. "It's OK if you sleep in here."

Nora hopped over to the other pillow and curled up to go to sleep. Jack sat on the bed, pulled on his bottoms and slid into bed. He lay there for a minute and said, "Why me?"

Nora said, "You were in the right place at the right time. Now be quiet and get some sleep."

Jack lay there for another minute, then asked, "Why did Elizabeth fly a thousand miles to bring me back?"

Nora sat up. "She had to. If a human sees us, they are brought in front of the council, or killed."

Jack opened his blood shot eyes, "She flew a thousand miles to kill me. That didn't work. So why didn't she kill me right in the garden?"

Nora said, "She tried. You wouldn't die. I told her she had to take you to the council."

Jack closed his eyes and whispered, "So why can't you trust her, if she keeps her word?"

Nora just lay back down and said, "Good night." Jack was already snoring.

Jack rose to the sound of the shade rolling up. He looked over and Nora was hovering in front of it. She grabbed onto it, pulled it down and let go and it started to wind right back up again. She flew up, grabbed it and flew back down, this time past the window. This time it stayed.

Jack said in a quiet voice, "Tricky, aren't they?"

Nora flew to Jack, who turned his wrist so she could land on his palm. She said, "Good morning, Jack."

He smiled, "You know, I thought this was just a dream. But I guess it's real." He got up and said, "It's going to be a sunny day." He paused, then said, "Of course it's going to be sunny. We are in California."

He pulled down the shade and let it roll up slowly. He looked outside and said with a yawn, "Hollywood." He stood and stretched, his vertebrae popping as he reached to the ceiling. Then he rolled his neck and small cracking noises filled the room. He twisted and turned; he even dropped down and did some squat thrusts.

Andre peeked around the open door to Jack's room to find him doing a set of push-ups. He said, "I see you're feeling better."

Jack stood, his white hair lying on his shoulders, with a three-inch shaggy beard and moustache covering his mouth. "Do I ever! I still have this strange feeling running though my bones."

Andre smiled, "Well, there is coffee in the kitchen when you feel like it."

Jack ran his fingers down his arm. He left streaks with his fingers, "Hmm. I guess I should take a shower before anything. Hey, by the way, could I use your laptop? I want to research something."

Andre said, "Sure, don't be looking at your email or anything else that can be tracked. And don't be looking at porn. I don't need a virus."

Nora flew up, "You might want to change the sheets again."

Jack walked and looked over to the bed. You could clearly see the top sheet had a large brown spot on it and the bottom was even darker. Jack took the top sheet and wiped his hands and forearms. The white sheet turned a coffee colour. He pulled the sheets off and rolled them into a ball and set them in the bathroom. Then he took off his pyjamas and placed them on the pile of sheets.

Jack stood in front of the mirror naked and ran his fingers across his chest. He could see the finger marks in the light layer of brown gunk that covered his body. He said to himself, "Why is this happening to me?" He stepped into the shower stroking his beard. He asked himself, "What the hell is going on and how did I become involved in?"

Marvin stepped in and talked to Nora. She told him, "Yes, Jack is still oozing brown goo, but not as bad as he was."

He told her, "I will be in the kitchen with Andre."

She flew up to him and landed on his shoulder. She walked up to his neck and ran her hand down it. She spoke into his ear, "Marvin, you need a shower."

The old man looked at his hand and there was a clean spot where his pyjamas rubbed his wrists. "Ah, I'm having my coffee first."

He stepped out into the hall. She could hear him yell, "Hey Dropoff, the regeneration is starting!"

Nora flew in to listen to the conversation. Andre had Marvin's coffee sitting on the table waiting for him. Marvin stepped into the room. Andre said, "You're not ready."

Marvin growled, "No shit! I have to take care of Juliet first and there are hundreds of details that have to be worked out."

Andre sipped his coffee, "Yeah, it's not like the old days, when you could just change your name."

Marvin asked, "What time is it in Wisconsin?"

Andre told him it was in the Central Time Zone. That would make it two hours earlier. Then it came to him, "Ah, the circus museum."

Marvin took a couple of quick steps down the hall. Nora flew to the table and landed right in front of Andre. Andre smiled, took a sip from his coffee, sat it down and cheerfully asked, "And how are you this fine morning?"

Nora said, "This has been such an adventure! If I died tomorrow, I would die happy."

Marvin came into the room with a telephone book. He put it on the table. Andre said, "We humans have a paper trail. It starts with a birth certificate. Vaccinations, baptism, school, taxes, licence—all kinds of crap to make up a new identity. You have a lot of i's to dot and t's to cross."

Nora asked, "So why the circus?"

Marvin, holding his finger on a name in the back of the book, said, "Because I am an Illusionist, a man of magic. They are loose with the rules in the circus, very hard to track. Jack will have been home-schooled, paid very little taxes, and never stayed in one place."

Andre smiled and said, "That is why I am Russian. My childhood records were bought for ten thousand roubles."

Marvin joked, "Andre bought his pilot's licence too."

There was silence as Marvin dialled the phone and said to himself, "Be there, come on, please." Then, in an excited voice, "Suckolofski, is that you? It's Marvin the Magnificent, out here in California. Yes, I am still alive. A favour. No, first a forty-year old man. When? OK. Juliet? She's in bad shape. Very soon. I'll send him out. Sure, great, tons. Fifty? No problem. See you soon."

He took the phone from his ear and said, "He's still alive."

Andre asked, "Boy, he has to be getting up there in age, like eighty! Can he still pull it off with computers nowadays?"

Marvin cut him off, "He has been waiting for years for that phone call. Everything is in place."

Jack got out of the shower, cut his hair and shaved again. When he stepped out of the bathroom, Andre's laptop was there. Jack dressed, sat down and typed in Merlin. Then he clicked on timeless myths and sat and read it. He picked up the laptop and carried it to the kitchen.

He said, "Marvin, you were Merlin, Myrddin Emrys, Merlin Ambrosius and Merlin Calidonius. From the 9th century to the 15th Century, you had nine books written about you. You were a wizard, a sorcerer, a prophet, a bard, a tutor and an advisor. You were with many kings. There are poems from the sixth century about you.

Marvin said, "Oh, so you're researching me? Don't believe half of it. The lady of the lake didn't give me the sword. My teacher gave me the sword called Excalibur. Well, in fact, it never had a name. It is just a sword. And Camelot? King Arthur was an idiot. I saved him and his castle and the power still went to his head. And flying dragons? They could never fly. They were just big lizards, thirty feet long or so and travelled in packs. They would destroy towns, eat everything—horses, cows and people."

Jack said, "The first mention of you is in Welsh; you were a mad man running wild in the forest."

Andre said, "See? Not everything you read is true. Juliet has been with him longer than that. I was with him when we moved to the island."

Jack said, "This was 573 AD."

Andre said, "And your point is?"

Jack looked at Marvin and asked, "How old are you."

Marvin asked him, "How are you feeling?"

Jack sat his coffee down and a great big smile came over his face. "I feel twenty years younger—look younger too. But I still have this weird feeling all over. It's like something is crawling under my skin."

Rupert came fluttering down from the fridge. He walked up to Jack and asked, "Does it feel like a buzzing under your skin or a burning sensation?"

Jack looked at him, cocked his head and said, "It does feel like a light buzzing under my skin."

Rupert told him, "That is normal. You should be drinking lots of water. And eat." He said to Nora pointedly, "Lots of water!"

Boris looked around, "Hey, where are all the fairies?"

Marvin told Rupert, "Show Boris how to get upstairs to the fairy village." Marvin took a long stare at the clock and said, "This is the plan: after the nurse leaves, Andre, you take me to the bank. I need to get fifty grand out of the safety deposit. Then you need to get a flight plan for Wisconsin."

Jack said, "Wait a minute! I can't go anywhere! I have a lot going on here that has to be taking care of. I have a meeting with Margaret and her solicitor. I have to go and take fairy dust up to the woods and clear my name and Elizabeth's. Oh yeah, and there's a couple thousand fairies that have to be dispersed."

Andre got up and grabbed the pot of coffee. He refilled Marvin's, then Jack's and his own. As he was doing this, he said, "That's not all you have to plan. Three deaths and funerals. Jack, yours shouldn't be so bad. But Marvin, the last time it took you almost a year. And you were on the road with your troop!"

Marvin laughed. "My old army buddy is here to help plan Juliet's funeral. We will get all the paperwork ready. Maybe we can pull the plug tonight."

Andre sat back down. He looked Marvin in the eyes and said, "Marv, think about it."

Marvin asked with a tear rolling down his cheek, "Have you looked at her? She is so peaceful. Her colour is coming back and her hair is about a half inch long. I miss her so very much."

Andre shook his head, then blurted, "Ah, shit! That nurse is going to plug in her computer and it's going to show the monitors going nuts when that stupid green fairy dumped the dust on her."

Marvin turned and looked at Jack. Then he told him, "You're not going anywhere till she is dead and buried."

Jack said, "OK, It's a deal. I told my kids that's what I was doing down here anyway. So let me get this straight: I am not going anywhere. You want me to hypnotise the nurse so she thinks Juliet is on her deathbed and convince her into getting the paperwork ready to pull the plug."

Marvin smiled, "You have been listening. There is a lot to do. We pull the plug. Then Andre or you need you to find a funeral director you can control."

Andre cleared his throat, "The sooner the better. You're going to kill off Margaret anyway, and there will be no showing. Pickupski knows a doctor that does this sort of thing. All we have to do is pay a small fee and he will give a death certificate."

Marvin shook his head, "No, I have faith in Jack. He can talk Juliet's doctor into believing that he saw her dead."

Rupert flew into the room to the wall leading into the secret passageway. He moved a piece of moulding and slipped inside. Marvin got up and stretched; his back cracked like three times, "Oh that felt good. There must be something wrong. I wish I could just regenerate and get it over with."

Rupert wouldn't leave Juliet's side. He walked over and did his hand wave thing in front of the wall. Jack watched as Marvin pushed a spot with his foot and the wall swung back to reveal the staircase. Marvin started up the stairs at a pretty good rate. He slowed by the time he reached the top. Jack was right behind him and Andre was falling behind.

When they reached the top to the small village, all the lights in the small doll houses where on. The small river that ran though was running and a huge sun lamp was shining. There wasn't a spot of dust in sight. Everywhere you looked, there were fairies, just lying around, talking in groups and chilling. Marvin stepped in. The whole village stopped what they were doing and looked.

He said one word, "Rupert." The small fairy came flying out of a larger house and all the other houses windows and doors opened to see Marvin.

Rupert flew up to Marvin and said, "Juliet's waking up. We have to find a different potion."

Marvin said, in a voice he hadn't used in years, a very strong and demanding voice, "You will tell me everything you do to her. And you will ask permission, do you understand?"

Nora landed on Jack's shoulder. She asked, "What is this about?"

Boris landed right next to her and said, "You remember saying don't piss off Jack? Well, it looks like the old Marvin is back. And you don't want to piss off Marvin. He always ran a tight ship. I met him back in the '20s. The fairies feared him."

Marvin boomed, "Downstairs, Juliet's room, now!"

Andre had just stepped into the room. "Great." He turned around and started back down. All three of them clomped down the stairs to the kitchen, not saying a word. Andre opened the door, walked in and stood. Jack walked to the counter-top where the coffee pot was. Marvin stepped out and stormed through the house to Juliet's room, not saying a word.

Marvin stepped into Juliet's room, where the monitors blinked and buzzed. Juliet turned her head and opened her eyes. Marvin reached down and told her, "Don't try to speak."

Andre peered over Marvin shoulder, "I am here too. Everything will be all right. As Marv says, the game is afoot."

She blinked and stared at them but didn't move. Her mouth hung open. Boris flew off to the nightstand and took out a bottle of powder. "Where the hell is that cobra venom?"

Rupert flew to the kitchen and came back with the small jar. Boris flew to Marvin and hovered in front of him. "This time, she must drink it." He flew down to Rupert on the nightstand and they talked together.

Rupert flew to Andre. "Dropoff, we're going to need a small amount of Dragon's Breath."

He asked, "From upstairs?"

Boris flew over and told him, "That will do for now. But we will need fresh stuff for the regeneration."

Jack looked at them and said, "I hate to tell you, but there aren't too many dragons walking around nowadays."

Marvin looked up from Juliet and said, "We have been using Komodo dragon saliva for years. It's the same bacteria the big dragons had."

Jack chuckled, "I'll keep my eyes open for a Komodo dragon walking down the street."

Marvin asked Andre to help prop up the bed so Juliet was sitting in the upright position. They did that and Nora flew in with half a cup of water. She struggled, holding it by the handle with her feet. Jack stepped over and put his hand on Juliet's arm. He closed his eyes and mumbled something. Marvin looked over to him. Jack said, "She's ready. Give her a drink. She will try to swallow it. She is so weak, but so awake."

Marvin put the glass to her lips and she tried to swallow. She got a little down. Andre said, "We have to take out the feeding tube."

Marvin said, "She swallowed, that is enough."

Boris flew to Jack and told him, "The potion is ready."

Jack walked over to the nightstand and picked up the shot glass that stood there, half full of brown liquid, and handed it to Marvin. Marvin cooed to Juliet, "OK baby, you have to drink this."

He poured it slowly into her mouth and she struggled to swallow it. Then Marvin gave her a small splash of water; she swallowed that also. Jack asked, "Is that all we can do?"

Boris said, "That will take a few minutes. Then she should rest. She still has a lot to go through."

Jack said, "I'm starving! What's for breakfast?"

Andre looked at him and asked, "You have to be kidding me! Juliet's life is hanging by a thread here and you think about food!"

Jack put his hand on Marvin's back and asked, "What can we do for her?"

Boris landed right on Juliet's forehead. He looked up at the two men and said, "This is what you're going to do: lay her almost flat. Then get out. We will handle her regeneration."

Marvin's hand started to shake. His lips tightened till they turned a purplish hue. His eyes welled up and a tear slid down his cheek. "Damn it all! You will not touch a hair on her head without talking to me first! You will get my permission to do anything, do you understand?"

Boris stood there, then nodded his head and gave him a "Yes, sir."

Jack then asked, "How long will she be in a coma this time?"

Boris shook his head, "If she hadn't had that dose of dust, she would be out for a week."

Jack asked, "How long will the regeneration take?"

Boris flew to him. Jack held out his hand and the room fell silent. All you could hear were the oxygen pumps and the monitors running. Boris cradled his chin with his hand and hummed, searching for an answer. Then he spoke, "At least a month. We are going to go so slowly. She is so old. And the damage that Elizabeth has done—I don't know how deeply that will go.

Rupert says that was a good shock to the system and a great way to start a regeneration. I myself have never done it this way."

Jack asked, "So, there is nothing we can do? So let's eat."

Andre put his arm around the old man, gave him a hug and said, "You know, there's lots to be done. It's time to plan her death and funeral."

Jack said, "Didn't you listen? She's going to be fine."

Marvin said with a commanding voice, "Stop." He grabbed Jack by the shoulder and spun him around. Jack could see the fear in his eyes, "You can talk to her. Tell her what is going on; assure her that we are doing our best."

Jack looked back into Marvin's eyes. He could feel the love, sadness, caring, pain and the deep hate. "Of course, I could try." He turned to Andre and called out, "Pour me some coffee. And see if there a steak in the fridge."

Jack followed Marvin slowly down the hall back to the room. When they entered, the two red fairies where paging through a huge book; the pages were yellowed and brittle. Jack closed his eyes and stood for a second too long. Everyone was staring at him when he opened them.

He stepped over to the fairies and asked them to move. He put his hand on the book and a greenish light penetrated the book. The pages whitened. "There! The book should be as good as new."

Boris flew in Jack's face. "Do you know how old that book is? What if something had gone wrong?"

Jack cut him off, "There is another one just like it upstairs with Margaret's stuff." He stepped over to Juliet's side and placed his hand on her forehead. The room went silent again. Jack took his hand off her forehead and said, "Marvin, she's fine. She told me to tell you that whatever happens, she loves you. And however long it takes, she isn't going anywhere."

Jack turned and exited the room, heading for the kitchen. There, Andre had a steak sitting on a plate. Jack sat down and picked up his coffee and took a sip. Andre asked, "Well?"

Jack smiled. "She does love him. You know she was more interested in how he was holding up?"

Marvin walked into the room and Jack said, "Oh my God! Do you stink!"

Andre chimed in, "Is that what I have been smelling?"

Marvin ran his fingers down his arm and left streaks. "OK, I'll take a shower."

Jack excitedly said, "Wait, the nurse should be here any minute, right? You stay next to her so she smells the smell of death."

With that said, a buzzer went off. Marvin said, "There she is, right on time."

Jack said, "You have to be kidding me, right?" He picked up the steak and put it on the counter, opened the cupboard door, took out some seasoning salt and sprinkled it on the steak.

Andre said, "Come on." Jack grabbed a couple of biscuits and sat back down at the table.

Andre told Marvin to wait in Juliet's room. An older, grey-haired lady came up the stairwell, carrying a medical bag. She stood for a moment, catching her breath. Andre introduced them. He told her, "This is Jack, Marvin's old army buddy. He just lost his wife."

Jack held out his hand. She took it and said, "Nice to meet you again." She looked into his eyes. That was all it took, and she stood there with a blank look.

Jack said in a flat voice, "Mary, you will see that Juliet is in a bad state. She is dying and you are going to suggest that Marvin should pull the plug."

The nurse asked, "How is Juliet doing?"

Andre looked puzzled. Jack said, "Oh, she doesn't look good. Her condition is getting worse by the hour."

The nurse said, "We'll see about that."

Andre looked at Jack with a puzzled look. She turned and headed down the hallway. Andre whispered to Jack, "What's going on? She doesn't seem hypnotised."

Jack smiled, "Have faith."

The nurse entered Juliet's room. The first thing she did was to put her hand over her nose, a "Whoa!" slipped out. Jack motioned to Marvin to stay put. Marvin looked up from Juliet's side; he stood and stretched out his hand and she took it. Mary asked, "So how is Juliet doing? Her vital signs seem weak."

Marvin shook his head, "Oh, this is the worst I've ever seen her."

The nurse held his hand. A tear welled up in her eyes. As she held back the tears she managed to choke out, "I'm so very sorry! She doesn't look like she's going to make it too much longer. I'll call the doctor."

She stepped back from the bed, pulled out her mobile phone and called the doctor. She said into the phone, "I'm at the Magic Castle and Juliet, your patient, an 83-year old woman, is on her death bed. They're talking about pulling the plug."

The nurse stepped back to Marvin and said, "The doctor will be here at four o'clock. He is rescheduling a meeting and he is going to be here for dinner." She stepped in and stroked Juliet's hair, "She looks so peaceful. I'm going to inject some morphine in her IV; that will keep her calm."

She filled a syringe, Jack stepped up and said, "You already gave the morphine." He took the syringe, shot it onto the floor and handed it back to her.

Marvin asked, "How is she?"

The nurse gave a long sigh, then said, "I'm sorry Marvin, but it looks like the time has come. I don't think she will make it through the day."

Marvin looked her in the eye. A tear streamed down his face. "Are you sure?"

She put her hand on his shoulder and told him, "Her vital signs are down. She is slipping away as we speak. It's time. All we can do is try to keep her comfortable."

Jack let out a sigh in the background. Andre stood there sniffling and wiping his nose. Jack stepped up and talked to the nurse, "You will come back at 4:00 and assist the doctor. Have your husband meet you downstairs for dinner at five o'clock. Marvin will pick up the tab."

Jack turned to Marvin and Marvin said, "What the hell did you say to her? We are not ready for this! She can't die today!"

Andre stepped up, shaking his head. "There is so much that has to be done! The death certificate is easy. But the funeral, the storing of her body—all the paperwork!"

Jack put his arm around Andre's shoulders and told him, "You have to have faith. This is coming together a little fast, but we can pull it off." He gave him a little hug and asked Marvin, "Are you going to be all right?"

Marvin, who was sitting on the chair next to Juliet, looked up and said, "The game's afoot." He stood and caressed Juliet's face, which left a streak of brown.

Boris flew over and told Marvin, "There is nothing you can do here. Please leave!"

Marvin objected, "Juliet's pores are all going to clog up. She needs a shower."

The little fairy hovered right in front of Marvin's face. "I am trying to slow her regeneration down, let me do my job. You do yours. Now, out!" Boris pointed at the door.

Marvin turned and said, "He's right. There is so much that has to be done."

Jack said, "Like breakfast." He led the way, striding down the hall.

Nora flew up, landed on his shoulder and asked, "What should I do?"

Jack whispered, "Come into the kitchen. Then sneak back to Juliet's room and find out what Boris really thinks. Marvin, she needs a blanket bath. After breakfast, give her a quick wipe down."

Jack walked into the kitchen and right up to the stove, where he had put the steak before the nurse came in. He turned the oven on broil and started to look for a grill pan. He came up with a baking tray. He went back to the refrigerator and found two more steaks hidden in the back; he threw those on with his. Jack sat the table and poured more coffee and started another pot. Then he asked, "What the hell is taking them so long?"

Andre appeared, his hair was wet and he had changed. He commented on the clothes he was wearing. "These damn things must have shrunk in the wardrobe." He explained that Pickupski and he had a wardrobe at the castle just in case. And you never knew where you might need another chauffeur costume.

Jack said, "I take it Marvin is doing the same."

Andre chuckled, "Yeah, Boris has Rupert supervising, making sure every nook and cranny is scrubbed."

Jack smiled and shook his head, "Been there and done that."

Andre left the room and came back with a small note book. He sat down and asked, "Where do we start?"

Jack looked at him and said, "With Juliet. Marvin is going to have a heart attack, he is so stressed out."

Andre sat down his pen and picked up the coffee. "Now, what do you have to do today?"

Nora flew up and landed on Jack's shoulder. She walked up and spoke right in his ear. She told him, "Boris thinks Juliet out of the woods. He will keep her in a coma for at least a week, maybe two. She would regenerate too fast if she isn't. And the steaks are on fire."

Jack's eyes snapped open and he was at the oven in a second. He grabbed the oven gloves, pulled the baking tray out of the oven and sat it on top of the stove. The smoke swirled into the vent. Jack took a fork and flipped the steaks and put them back in the oven.

Andre was at the fridge, pulling out juice. He took some avocados and a cutting board back to the table, cut them in half and started to scoop out the meat. Jack popped bread into the toaster and asked, "Why don't you people butter your toast? Yesterday everything was dry."

Andre asked, "What did Nora tell you when she came sneaking back down the hall from Juliet's room? And it took longer, then there your steaks are on fire."

Jack nodded, "I thought there was more Boris knew and wasn't saying, so I sent Nora back to get the scoop on Juliet. And she will be just fine. It will take up to two weeks."

Marvin, who was standing in the doorway wearing a dressing gown, spoke in a low voice, "That's bullshit, it takes up to two months. And when you're this old, it will take longer."

Jack said, "Maybe, but he said she would be in a coma for a week or two."

Andre butted in, "She's strong, and Boris seems to know what he's doing."

Marvin said as he sat down, "The morning is shot. What have you two got going?"

Andre looked at his note book. It was blank. Jack said, "What do you mean? We have to get our ducks in a row. Well, let's figure this out."

Andre put the pen to the paper and said, "Let's see. You have to go to Margaret's this morning. The rest is still open."

Marvin asked Jack, "So why do you have to see Margaret?"

Jack paused as he took a bite of steak, then said, "There is much to do before Margaret bites the dust."

Marvin shook his head, "Don't trust her. She is one evil broad."

Jack looked up from his juice glass. His voice went flat, "You don't have to tell me. I've been inside her head. She has done stuff you wouldn't believe."

Andre asked, "When are we leaving?"

Marvin blurted out, "That damn nurse! Was she going to have the doctor come this afternoon?"

Jack got up from the table and went to the fridge. He spoke into the fridge. "Give the nurse a call and ask her." He came out with a banana and a slice of cheese. As he sat down, he told Andre, "We have to go and do some grocery shopping again."

Marvin stood next to the phone and spoke loudly into it, "No, there is no change. Around 5:00? That will be fine. She doesn't seem to be in pain. Good, yes, yes, almost flat lined. Good bye."

Andre asked, "Well?"

Marvin said, "She doesn't think Juliet will make the day, so that's good."

Boris flew in and landed on the table. Rupert just appeared there sneakily. Boris walked up to Jack and said, "We need you to pick up a few things."

Jack looked down at the small red fairy. "Sure, whatever you need."

Rupert fluttered to Andre and read off a small piece of paper: "Pine pitch fresh from a Norwegian pine, eye of newt—about thirty, fresh Dragon's Breath—about half a jigger."

Boris said, "Oh yes, please don't forget the leeches!"

Rupert added, "About twenty large blood suckers."

Jack sat his coffee down and stared at Marvin. Marvin finally said, "What?"

Jack asked, "Andre, did you write all that stuff down? Where are we supposed to get the sap out of a pine tree, and where can we find all this?"

Marvin got up from the table, grabbed his coffee cup and said, "Pine pitch is easy, put a cut in a tree and heat the tree, it will bleed. Just be back here by 4:00," and he headed back down the hall to Juliet's room, followed by the two fairies.

Andre looked at his list and questioned himself aloud, "Dragon's Breath! Where the hell are we going to find a dragon?"

Jack answered him, "Bali! They have a national park, north of Australia. It's called, oh some big lizard thing. Komodo, that's it!"

Andre said, "OK. Halfway around the world, then."

Jack asked, "Don't they have big zoos down here?"

Andre smiled, "The zoo *should* have them. And I know who we can send."

Jack said, "They're not just going to give you dragon slobber! Anyway, those things are supposed to be dangerous as hell."

Andre said, "Not to green fairies, they're not."

Jack gave an order, "Nora, go upstairs and bring Elizabeth here."

The little red fairy flew to the panel in the wall and she was gone. Jack told Andre, "That is a good idea."

Andre said, "Eye of newt, that one's easy—a pet store. But Norway pine and leeches—where the hell?"

Jack said, "The leeches are the easy part, any bait shop will have those. But pine sap that will be tricky."

Jack got up and started to clean the table. Nora came and two fairies followed her. They landed on the counter-top next to the sink. Jack said, "Good morning, Lizard Breath."

Elizabeth crossed her arms and stared at him. The other fluttered up to Jack. He held out his hand palm up and she landed on it. She bowed to him and said, "Jack I am here to serve you, whatever you ask."

Jack said, "Isn't that nice?" He looked at the other green fairy and said, "Dog breath, get up here."

Elizabeth hopped to Jack's hand, pointed her finger at him and shouted, "Stop calling me names!"

Jack cracked a small smile and said, "What I need the two of you to do is go out and get some Dragon's Breath."

Andre walked over and held out his iPhone, which had a picture of a Komodo dragon on it. Elizabeth said, "Now where are we going to find one of those?"

Andre tapped his screen, held it out and showed it to the girls. Elizabeth said, "In a cage, you would figure."

Andre placed his finger on the screen and it zoomed out, showing the zoo, then the state, all the way out to seeing the whole country. Shelia said, "Wow! That is amazing!"

Andre smiled and said, "Google earth." He asked, "How long were you prisoner?"

She said, "I think about thirty years."

Andre smiled, "Well, you're going to be amazed at the technology nowadays."

Jack, who was sitting across the table, commented, "We shouldn't send them. They have to be brought up-to-speed on the surveillance. There are cameras everywhere."

Andre asked, "Did you hear us talking from all the way over there?"

Jack cocked his head, took a few steps over to them and said, "Well, I guess I did. I'll have to call the grandkids. Those little bastards have that high squeaky voice and I couldn't ever hear them at all."

Andre asked, "So, what do you want to do with the green ones?"

Jack threw up his arms and asked, "Can we send them halfway around the world—to wherever that place is, Bali?"

Nora said, "The blue fairies will chase and capture them. They will risk everything for a green fairy."

Jack slowly shook his head. "Oh what the hell!" Andre, show them the new cameras, electric eyes; see if you can get a virtual picture of the zoo."

Andre stood, "OK girls—a crash course on spying." Andre headed down the hall, followed by the two fairies who were hovering and talking right behind him.

Nora asked, "What are we going to do?"

Jack got up from the table and said, "I am going to take a dump. You are going to find something for the girls to carry that live bacteria in."

Nora flew up. Jack raised his hand palm up and Nora landed in it. Jack asked, "Now what?"

Nora shyly asked, "What is live bacteria?"

Jack asked, "Haven't you been listening at all? The Dragon's Breath is from the saliva of the Komodo dragon. It has bacteria in it. Once bitten, the infection kills quickly. Emma used to love watching animal shows. Anyhow, you need to find bags or something they can fly with."

Jack left the room, walking slowly down the hall and mumbling to himself. He came out of the bathroom cleanly shaved. He went right for the coffee pot and grabbed a handful of grapes that were on the counter. He started down the hall and stepped into Juliet's room, where Marvin was giving her a blanket bath. He had his pyjamas sleeves rolled up to the elbows and a brown stain on his hands.

Jack let out a breath and everyone turned towards him. He said, "Wow, does it reek of death in here!" Then he paused and said, "That's what it smells like."

Marvin dropped a rag in a pail of brownish water and stood. He put his hand on his back as he straightened, "What are you still doing here?"

Jack asked, "How is she?"

Marvin raised his hand, pointed a finger and said, "Now you listen here, there will be no lollygagging. The game is afoot, you must keep going."

Jack was going to comment, but a wad of a hundred-dollar bills appeared in Marvin's pointing hand. Jack asked, "What's this?"

Marvin replied, "Just some getting-around money."

Andre said from the door, "That was good, boy! I haven't seen you pull anything out of the air like that in years!"

Jack said, "You just had your hands in a bucket of water! And the money wasn't even up your sleeve. That was amazing!"

Marvin said, "No, what is amazing in you. Yesterday, I could hardly pour a cup of coffee. Today, I'm free. Just like the fairies, you freed us all."

Andre walked into the room and looked at Juliet, "Boy, does she look better!"

Rupert flew up and landed on Andre's shoulder, "Put this on your list—more of that saline solution. That stuff is great; she is well hydrated."

Andre pulled out his day planner and a pen and asked, "How many?"

Marvin looked over and said, "The page is pretty full. You're into tomorrow already. Maybe you should get going."

Jack said, "Yeah we could sit and yak all day and nothing would get done." He looked at Juliet.

Marvin said, "Four o'clock—be here." Then he turned to Andre, "Write it down—four o'clock." With that, they headed to the lift.

Chapter Thirteen
Dealing with Margaret

Nora told Jack he had better take his cane. Jack said bluntly, "What the hell for?"

Andre smiled, "Jack, you're an old man. You have to look it and act it."

Jack broke out into a smile that went from ear to ear and said, "You know, this is the best I've felt in thirty years."

Andre said, "That's nice. You are not to touch any fairy dust. You're looking younger all the time. Soon, you won't even resemble your driving licence or passport."

Jack asked Nora, "OK, smarty pants, where did I leave my cane?"

Nora said, "It's in your room, by the bed."

Jack broke off in a jog down the hall. He was back in a minute, maybe two. Andre said, "When we get to the bottom, I will pull the car around."

Jack told him, "That is stupid, it's a waste of time. I'll come with you."

Andre asked, "Are you telling me how to do my job? You're an old man, act like it."

Jack reached in his pocket, put an earpiece in his ear and asked, "Nora, would you turn on the microphone?"

She told him, "I already did. And don't talk to me unless you absolutely have to. Even then, be smart about it or people will notice."

Jack chuckled. He put his hand over his mouth and said, "I'm an old man; I'm supposed to talk to myself."

The lift hit the bottom floor. Andre stepped out and turned to Jack. "I'll be back in five."

Jack bent over and hobbled out into the car park with the cane for support. He was talking to Nora all the way. Andre pulled up with the Lincoln. He got out and stepped back to open the back door. Jack raised his cane and said loudly, "If you think I'm riding in the back, you're nuts. If it wasn't such a zoo around here, I would be driving." Jack walked around the nose of the car and told Andre, "I am quite capable of opening my own door."

He got into the car, pulled his phone out of his pocket and turned it on. He said with desperation, "God, I hope this works! I fed Margaret a bunch of lies. I hope she bought it." His phone lit and he checked his messages.

Nora said, "Wow, your daughter called you 12 times, and your son just once!" Jack started to delete them, one after another.

Andre asked, "Aren't you going to listen to any of them?"

Jack said, "I'll call my son." He went to contacts, pushed on John's name and then called him.

Nora was amazed. "Wow, that is neat! Can I call next time?"

Jack said, "Yes, you can." Then, "Johnny, what the hell is up with your sister? She's called a dozen times! Tell her to get a life, a hobby or something! No, I'll go home when I'm good and ready. The address? Not in your life! You take care of your family, I'll take care of myself."

Nora climbed up to his shoulder and yelled in his other ear, "Act like your old self."

Jack let out a "Damn it, don't yell in my ear!" He changed his voice to a much older Jack. He said, "You tell your sister that when I get new batteries for my hearing aid, I will call her. And tell her I love her and the kids." He pushed the end button.

Nora said, "You did it again, you hung up before you said goodbye! He was still talking."

Jack said, "If they found out where I was, my son would be on a plane here just to check out what is going on. I don't think he believes the helping Marvin with the funeral thing."

Nora fluttered to the dash so she was facing Jack. She said, "Maybe if you told him how Juliet was doing? And that you were planning to pull the plug today?"

Jack said, "Too much information. See, you tell them what you want them to hear. It's a cop thing."

Andre said, "You know, she's right. They are worried about you. If you would tell them about others' troubles they wouldn't worry about you."

They pulled out onto Highway Two. There was traffic like Jack had never seen. He turned to Andre, "Boy, I'm glad you're driving!"

Andre smiled, "This isn't bad."

Jack asked how long it was going to take. Andre told him, "About twenty–thirty."

Jack punched in Margaret's number, Linda answered. Jack told her to get Maggie on the phone. There was a pause then, "Yes, Margaret. Did you make the appointment with your solicitor? 11 o'clock? Yeah, that should be fine.

An hour. Do you have coffee on?" He turned off his phone and blankly stared out the window.

Andre asked, "Well? Do you think she is still hypnotised?"

Jack looked over to him and said in a sleepy voice, "Oh yeah, she's on the hook. You have to give me a couple of minutes, I'm trying to remember what I told her." The rest of the drive was almost in silence; Nora sat on the dash asking about the rules of the road.

They were about a block from Margaret's mansion. Jack opened his eyes to see that they were back in Brentwood, a gated community, with long driveways and huge houses. Jack said a little prayer, "God, I hope this works!"

Andre pulled up to the gate and said to the security gaurd, "Margaret Webster, she is expecting us," Jack Robinson, 30 seconds later the gate slid open. Andre pulled up to her driveway and rolled the window down and pushed a button on a pad, "Hello, this is Jack Robinson. You are waiting for us." The gate swung open. There was activity up by the house—U-Haul trucks and a pickup loaded with bags.

Andre asked what is going on there. Jack said, "The mansion is for sale. She fired all her staff except Linda. She is a blue fairy guardian." The Lincoln came to a stop right in front of the place. Jack said, "This shouldn't take more than a couple of hours. In fact, I think the meeting with the solicitor will have to wait. I'll give you a call in a couple of minutes. You have that list of crap you have to get for Boris."

Andre nodded his head, "Yeah, I'll find out the closest place to pick the stuff up. But were not going to find a medical supply store in Brentwood or Beverly Hills."

Jack opened the door and Nora spoke to Andre. Andre grabbed Jack's cane and said, "Here. You're an 82-year old man, act like one."

Jack grabbed the cane and leaned back in the car. "I don't have the time to act like an old man." He hung the cane on his arm and swiftly headed to the door, then he bent over and used the cane, dropping back into an old man.

An older lady going out the door with a box walked by him. He called out to stop her. Jack walked up to her and told her, "Put the box down and tell me what is going on here."

Her eyes met Jack's and she did as he said. She put the box on the pavement, then she said, "All the staff had been let go. And they are clearing out their stuff."

Jack then asked, "What kind of severance package did she give?"

The lady said without blinking, "Five thousand for a year of service."

Jack asked, "Where is Margaret?" The lady said she was in the upstairs study. Jack waved his cane at her and told her to carry on with her business. He turned and headed into the house. He walked in. The marble floors shone. There were two staircases wrapped around a huge water fountain. He headed past the stairs to an old-looking door and pushed a button on the wall. A lift opened up. He stepped in and pushed his floor. There were only three in this section of the place. When the door opened, the place looked like it had just been spit-shined. Jack cupped his hand to his mouth and said loudly, "Linda! Get me coffee!"

Then he slowly started to the study. It was down the hall and to the right, a couple of doors down and through a music room that had two baby grands along with a host of other instruments. Finally, he came to a door, opened it and Margaret and Linda were there, sitting at a long table with a pile of papers on it. There was a small old lady sitting on the other side of the table. Linda stepped up behind the little old lady. She put her hand on her shoulder and said, "Lucy, you have been with Margaret the longest—16 years. There is nothing out of the ordinary here. Margaret has had a couple of cosmetic surgeries. She *does* look older now than when you started."

Margaret then said, "Thank you so very much for your services. You may go now." The little old lady picked up a pile of wrapped hundred-dollar bills and walked out the door.

Jack said, "She did like her job, you know. A letter of recommendation would have been nice."

Margaret scoffed, "She's been with me for 16 years. She's an illegal anyway, I picked her up in Poland."

Jack asked, "Was she the last one?"

Margaret was sitting there sipping her coffee, dressed to impress. She had a low-cut dress on with a diamond necklace like no other Jack had ever seen, matching earrings and a watch. Linda, not to outdo her boss, was wearing a suit. She was the one who was pushing the paperwork. She asked Jack, "Do you think five thousand for a year of service was enough?"

Jack smiled and looked at her. He could feel the contempt she had for him. "Five thousand is generous. And don't you worry about our plan. There will be a place for you, a place of power."

Margaret asked, "Now, when is this going to take place?"

Jack walked around the table to get close to her. He put his hand on her and looked into her eyes. "As soon as we kill you off. What name would you like in your new life?"

Margaret said, as if she was in a daze, "Lisa."

The old man shook his head, "No, no, not Lisa. Jaclyn. That is going to be your name. Now get going."

Jack stepped over to Linda and put his old hand on her shoulder as she sat. He started with: "You are a beautiful girl. Now, you have been though Margaret's regeneration before. Do whatever she needs. The house has to go up for sale. The solicitors have to change her will over to the new Jaclyn. I will have the new paperwork written up. Just keep things rolling."

Margaret asked, "What's the big hurry? These things take time."

Jack said, "I was sent here to take you out of the game and harvest all that was fairy from your house. You will now be a player in the war of all wars. This is bigger than you would have ever thought."

He said, "I will be back tomorrow. Things had better be in place. Tell your solicitor you're changing your will and are going to give everything to a long-lost child of yours. Make a meeting for tomorrow."

Chapter Fourteen
Finding a Birth Certificate

Jack turned and walked out of the room, as he did so, he pulled his phone from his pocket and dialled Andre's number. "Pick me up now, in front." He was speed-walking though the mansion and then he ran down the stairs.

Andre pulled the car up to the front door and got out. He walked around to the passenger side. Jack busted out the door, ran up to the car and yelled: "Get in! We have a lot to do." Andre left the door open and walked to the driver's side and slipped behind the wheel. Jack jumped in and slammed the door.

Andre asked, "Didn't go too well, I take it?"

Jack said, "The game's afoot, whatever the hell that means!"

Andre laughed, "It's English. It means the game is in play."

Jack said, "Whatever. This is going to take a while. Drive."

Andre asked, "Where?" as he put the car in gear and started down the driveway.

Jack asked, "Where is the list? Saline for Juliet's IV. Is that next to a hospital?"

Andre asked, "You want to go to a hospital?"

Jack said, "I need a birth certificate for tomorrow and a copy."

Andre said, "Call Marvin. Suckolofski will make one and air it to you the next day."

Jack said, "Just get me to the hospital; I'll see what I can do."

Andre said, "You can't trust Margaret."

Jack interrupted him, "It's for me, you idiot! She is a cruel, evil bitch."

Andre said, "You know, it would have been a lot easier to just kill her."

Jack said, "Just get me to the hospital." Andre pushed a couple of buttons on his GPS and a map came up, showing him the way.

Nora jumped down to his lap and watched the screen. Andre said, "It talks too." He touched the screen and increased the volume, a British speaking woman came on, telling him he had to turn right. Andre chuckled, "I don't need a broad telling me where to go, so I leave the voice off."

Twenty minutes later, they pulled into a hospital. A valet came out to the car. Andre told Jack, "We are here." Then he reached over to Jack, who was in some kind of a trance, shook him and yelled, "Hey, we're at the hospital!"

Jack shook the cobwebs loose. "OK. I'll call you when I need a pickup."

The valet tapped on the window. Andre powered the window down and said, "I am just dropping off the old man."

Jack leaned over and asked, "Do you deliver babies here?"

The young man said, "I don't, but the doctors do."

Jack mumbled, "For Christ's sake, everyone's a frickin' comic." Then he told Andre, "This should take about an hour." He opened the door and stepped out; his cane fell out the door. Jack turned back with a dirty look.

Andre said, "Use it, old man." The valet told Jack he would get it for him. He reached down and picked up the cane for Jack and took him by the arm.

Jack stopped, pulled his arm away from the valet and spoke in a demanding voice, "Get the hell away from me! Do I look like I need help?"

The valet looked stunned, then he smelled his hands. Andre said, "Now there's an old man with an attitude!" He pulled out of the car park and drove down the road.

Jack walked up to the desk and asked where the record room was. The gal that was there pointed him to a different building in the complex. Then she said that they could wheel him over there. Jack smiled and thanked her. A young man came up and helped him into the chair. Jack said, "I'll give you five bucks if you hurry."

The young black man said, "Let's see the five bucks."

Jack reached in his pocket, pulled out his wallet and handed him the five. The young guy turned and went to a lift. Jack yelled: "Hey, I want to go to that building across the complex!"

The young guy smiled wide, put his hand on Jack's shoulder and said, "Don't sweat it, old dude." The lift opened and he hit basement two.

Jack said, "What the hell? Am I going to get robbed? If you're going to rob me, I have one hell of a surprise for you."

The young guy said to Jack, "Shut the hell up. I jog in these tunnels every morning."

The lift door opened and he pushed Jack though the basement at a good pace. As soon as they went through a set of doors, the guy opened up to a full sprint. The floor was like glass. In a few minutes, they were there. The young man ran right up to a lift and inside, he pushed the lobby button. Jack pulled out his wallet while his pusher was catching his breath, handed him a ten and asked, "What floor would records be?"

The guy said, "This whole building is records, mostly computer data storage. It has its own separate electrical grid and backup generators." They pulled up to the main desk and Jack got helped out of the chair.

He walked with his cane, all bent over; his white hair hung past his shoulders. He walked up to the front desk and asked, "Where do I have to go for a birth certificate?"

The young lady looked up at him and asked, "Were you born here? I should be able to do that for you right here, sir."

Jack stammered, "I would like to see someone who could help me. I don't know if this is the right hospital."

The young girl said, "Go up one floor and three doors to the right. I'll call her and tell her you're on your way." Jack started for the lift. He raised his cane toward the young man that ran him to the building and the man gave him a polite wave back. Jack reached the lift and went up to the floor.

Jack took his time walking to the office. His mobile phone rang. Jack figured it was Dropoff, so he just answered it. It was his daughter Mary. Jack talked loudly into the phone, "No, I haven't been screening your calls. In a minute or so, my batteries are dying. I can hardly hear you, I'll call you back."

Jack held the phone out in front of him and pressed the end button with a big smile on his face. He walked a few feet, then entered an office. He walked up to a woman who was sitting at a desk. She stood, introduced herself and held out her hand. Jack took it and asked if she could look up a birth certificate. She asked loudly, "When were you born?"

Jack said, "You don't have to yell. I'm old, not deaf. I tell you, people nowadays! It's not for me. It's for a man of about forty."

The lady blushed and said, "I heard you out in the hall say that your batteries were running low in your hearing aids."

Jack smiled, "Yeah, you wouldn't believe how many times I've used that excuse. This is taking too long." He reached across the desk and touched her arm. She looked at him. That was enough: she was entranced. Jack said, "You will tell me how to make up a fake birth certificate for my son."

She told Jack that she couldn't do it. She could pull up a file from the archives but she couldn't change anything. Jack asked, "Then how could I make a fake birth certificate look real?"

She said, "I have heard there is an old abbey fifty miles up the coast where they still have everything on paper. You wouldn't leave an electronic footprint."

Jack told her, "You tell me about this abbey."

She said, "I have done some work there. They take in young pregnant women and keep it a secret."

Jack said, "I'll go there. Thank you. Oh yeah, you will remember looking for a certificate and not being able to find it." Jack took his hand off her and slowly headed to the door. He fished out his mobile phone from his pocket and turned it on. He called Andre to pick him up. Jack stepped out the door, looking across the complex. He grumbled, "Ah, crap!" He was a full block away from the car park Andre had dropped him off at.

He picked his route, walking down in front of a row of buildings. It was a warm sunny day. Jack was taking his time, slowly making his way, when a young girl, around six or seven, grabbed him by the hand. Jack looked down. She was staring up at him. The little girl said, "You have to help my brother!"

Jack didn't said a word. He could feel her pain and knew what she wanted and where she was going. He let her lead him into a huge glass building; she was dragging him toward the lift.

Jack said, "Wait." He walked over to the front desk and said, "You will announce over the loudspeakers in ten minutes that Julie Backstir is in her brother's room."

The little girl grabbed Jack by the hand and started to drag him to the lift. They stood waiting for the lift. Jack told her, "Wait here for me." He stepped into the gift shop and took all the quartz rosaries off a display. He fished in his pocket, pulled a fifty off his money clip and dropped it on the counter. He got back right at the time the doors were opening and stepped in.

The little girl pushed basement one, then looked up at him, tears streaming down her face. "You have to help him! He is sick."

Jack put his hand on her head and said, "I know he is and I will see what I can do."

She said, "You can help him. I just know it."

The doors opened and she grabbed him by the hand and started to pull. This time Jack broke into a jog. The girl let go of him and started to run. She stopped in front of a door. It looked more like a prison then a hospital. Jack bent over and acted like he was catching his breath. An orderly walked over and asked if they could use some help. Jack told him, "I would like to have a talk with this young man."

The orderly said, "That is impossible. He is violent. You have to have the parents' permission, and the doctors'."

Jack cut him off. He raised his hand and looked him in the eye. "You will open the door now."

The orderly slid his key though the card reader and the light turned green. There was an announcement over the intercom: "Julie Backstir is safe and is in her brother's room."

Jack knew there was no time to waste. He pulled the door open and stepped in. A young boy, about 12 years old, jumped in front of him. He reached out to grab Jack. Jack raised his hand and powered up. The kid screamed, holding his head. Jack calmly said, "Darron, take it easy." He stepped towards him. Jack's voice flattened and lowered, "Look at me, damn you! We don't have much time."

The boy sheepishly looked up. As soon as his eyes came in contact with Jack's, his face went blank. Jack stepped to the boy, not noticing that the whole floor sounded like a zoo. A lot of the patients were screaming and yelling. Jack spoke in a calming voice. He put his hand on the boy's head and said, "You will leave this boy." He held a piece of quartz in his hand and it had just a slight glow for a second.

Jack reached into his pocket and held the rosaries in his hand. They glowed a bright white light. He then took one and put it around the boy's neck. Jack turned and walked out of the room where the girl stood. Jack put his hand on her head and said, "Make sure he goes to church until his faith is strong enough. Then he can take off the rosary. Darron is back and his demon is gone."

Jack started down the hall. The screams echoed through the halls. In some rooms, the patient was up against the door to see what was happening. Others were cowering in the corners: those are the ones that were possessed. He got to the lift. When it opened, a couple that was quite upset came bursting out. They saw Julie standing there with Darron in the hall. The man made a mad dash for the kids.

Jack watched from the lift door. There were lights flashing; the intercom was calling for people. Doctors and interns were running from room to room trying to get the noise level down. In the middle was a boy hugging his parents and a little girl standing, wiping her tears.

The door closed and Jack was on his way again. He pulled the phone out of his pocket again and turned it on; there was a missed call. People were running around, all heading for the lifts. Jack checked his phone with a sigh of relief—it was Andre, not his daughter. Jack went into contacts and called. He asked where the car was parked and told him, "Pull up a map and find St Catherine on the coast. It should be about fifty miles away."

Jack didn't look like an old man making his way. He looked more like a man on a mission, powerwalking down the pavement. Andre pulled up to the end of the walk. He got out and held the door open on the passenger side. When Jack got within twenty feet of the car, he yelled: "Drive!"

Andre quickly stepped around the nose of the car and slid behind the wheel. He fired up the car and as soon as Jack jumped in, the car was moving. Jack questioned Andre, "How long will it take to get there?"

Andre said it would take at least an hour. Jack let out a "Damn." Then he asked, "Do we have time? We have to be back at 4:00 for Juliet."

Andre asked, "Why are we going to an abbey? And how long are you going to spend there?"

Jack turned his head quickly to see Nora gently climbing up his arm to his shoulder. He told Andre the story about all the files being on computer now and that the gal there couldn't make a birth certificate. He told him the abbey's office had made bogus papers in the past.

Andre pulled off the 405 and headed for the coast. The GPS on the dash didn't agree with him. A sweet English girl was telling him to turn around. He reached up, pushed a button and she went silent. He turned to Jack with a smile on his face, "Don't you wish you could do that with all women?"

Nora flattened herself against Jack's neck and asked, "What happened at the hospital?"

Jack turned his head but couldn't see her. He held out his hand and she flew into his palm. She sat there looking at him, so he told her, "Look at that car over there." Jack pointed at a Jag. "Do you see inside the car? The windows are tinted. They can see out but you can't see in. Nobody can see you."

She stood up, looking Jack in the eye. Jack told her about removing the demon spirit from the child. Then he asked, "How did the child know I could help her? She walked right up and took my hand."

Nora said, "Children are the hardest to hide from. They search you out like they can feel you."

Andre was pressing the pedal down, weaving in and out of traffic like a pro. The next thing you knew they were on Highway One and heading up the coast. Jack said, "Boy, it's beautiful up here! How much further?"

Andre smiled, "Just on the other side of Malibu, in a hidden valley. I never knew it was there. The church owns a large chunk of land right on the coast."

They pulled up to a stop light. Jack sighed "There's an IHOP. Too bad we don't have time."

Nora asked, "What's an IHOP?"

Andre answered, "Jack doesn't take you out often. That would be the International House of Pancakes; they serve breakfast all day."

Jack added, "And they have great coffee."

Andre pulled onto a narrow drive that twisted down the hill, then back up to a 90 degree turn and then a 60 percent grade down to a series of buildings. The church was the highest—if it was the one with the cross on the top.

They got closer. There were signs. The chapel was up the hill, and offices, dorms and halls were all downhill. Jack said, "Wow, this is a big place!"

Andre followed the signs to the office. They pulled in. They were the only car in the car park. Jack said, "I hope someone is home."

Andre said, "Turn on your phone. We're going for a walk to the beach."

Jack headed for the office. Once he entered, he saw a nun sitting behind a huge front desk made of redwood. She turned and peered over her glasses at him.

She asked with a cheerful old voice, "Can I help you?"

Jack knew he didn't have time for chit chat, so he hypnotised her right off the bat. "You will tell me who can make a birth certificate."

The old nun said, "I can do that. Do you have the information?"

Jack looked at her kind of strangely. The old nun asked again, "Do you have the information or not?"

Jack stammered, "Yes, of course I do. It is for my son. He was born here 45 years ago."

The old nun stepped away from the computer and said, "In that case, he's not in the computer database." She walked around the desk. She looked to be around seventy or so. She looked up at Jack and told him, "Come on, gramps, we haven't got all day."

They stepped through a door into a huge room filled with shelves. Jack put his hand on her shoulder and turned her towards him. He looked deeply in her eyes. "This is going to take forever. Can't we just print up a new one?"

This time Jack could tell she was under his power. He gave his new name: Jack Johnson, and the date of birth—all the info she needed. The old gal got right to work. She took a box from under a table, then pulled out two old forms out of the box. She filled one out by hand and signed it, dated it, then changed hands and signed the doctor's name with a small comment on the side, wishing a happy life.

She turned to Jack and said the mother must sign it. Jack took the pen from her and sat down to read it. He looked around, put the pen to the paper and signed Margaret's name just as she would have signed it. Jack said, "Make another copy."

Then they walked up to the front desk and Jack said, "You will remember finding the file right away and that is all." He asked, "How much do I owe you?"

The nun said, "I need to give you a copy. You can't have an original."

Jack waved his hand in front of her and said, "You must make another copy." They went back in the file room. She made up another certificate and filed it in a shelf marked 1965–75. The dates started at 1880; there must have been 600 files on that shelf.

Jack asked, "Are these all unwed pregnancies?"

The nun said blankly, "Yes, mostly." They walked up to the front and she pulled out a stamp that said "Copy" and stamped a clean sheet of paper. It was a bright red "Copy"—shiny and wet.

The old nun stamped the paper ten more times. Then she pulled a pad out from the bottom drawer and stamped a different paper. This time, it came out dull reddish brown. She stamped the paper twice more, then the two copies of the birth certificate.

She looked up and said, "That should do it."

Jack looked at her and could tell she was coming out of the hypnotic state. He waved his hand and said, "You will forget ever seeing me as soon as I walk out the door." He took his phone from his pocket, called Andre and told him to meet him at the car. Then he took the two papers and walked to the car. He opened the back door to lay the papers on the back seat. He turned to see a queue of girls, all in their last months of pregnancy, walk between the buildings.

Andre called out, "Riding in back?" He was about fifty feet of the car.

Jack called back, "Come on! Marvin left two messages on my phone."

Andre said, "The doc is going to be late, between 6:00 and 6:30. He is meeting his golf partner downstairs for a meal and show first."

Jack said, "Hey, that's great! Can we stop and get something to eat?"

Andre said, "Marvin bought us the time; it's hard to turn down a free meal and a show."

Nora waited till they were on the highway before peeking out of Andre's suit pocket. She crawled out and flew to the dash in front of Jack. He smiled and asked, "Did you have fun?"

Nora, all excited: "Did I ever! I found a group of red fairies. They live close to the church. I think they have a red guardian here, but they wouldn't say."

Andre then asked, "How was your mission?"

Jack smiled, "Everything went quite well, actually. The old nun had done this before and was pretty good at it. I have the certificates drying in the back seat."

Andre pulled the car up to cruising speed and said, "We had better get straight to the castle. Marvin will need that information for Suckolofski. He is working on getting you the papers and tax statements. There's just a whole pile of stuff he does."

Jack asked "Don't I have a say in what my life will be?"

Andre said, "This will take months, if not more than a year."

Jack shook his head, "It has to be done this week."

Andre turned, looked Jack in the eye and said, "Good luck!"

They drove down the coast, Nora talked about all the pregnant women they saw and the priests that were on holiday. She couldn't believe that most of them didn't talk while they were there; it was a silent retreat. Andre pulled into a Starbucks when they got to Malibu. He said, "Boy, did your eyes light up when I pulled into the car park!"

Jack said, "Let's go inside, I have to take a leak." Nora asked if she could come along. Andre held his suit jacket open and she shot right in.

Andre said, "Stay hidden."

Jack walked up and ordered, "A ventimocha with two extra shots of espresso. And could you ice it down so it doesn't burn my lips off?" He pointed to a piece of carrot cake, an apple turnover and two biscuits and then he disappeared into the men's lavatory. He came out, rubbing his hands together. He strolled right up, took a sip and then paid for his and Andre's, leaving a ten-dollar tip.

When they got into the car, Andre thanked him and asked, "Do you always pay a third for the tip?"

Jack said, "No, sometimes I don't leave anything. Depends on the service. This is an excellent cup of Joe, she cooled it down to about a 105—just the perfect temperature. And she was courteous."

They drove down the coast. Nora tried some of the coffee. She didn't like Jack's at all—way too bitter. But she liked the chocolate chips in the biscuits. When they finally pulled up to the castle, the car park was half full. Jack said, "Great, the kitchen is open."

Andre pulled up to the back of the place to the hidden lift. Jack said, "OK, I'll meet you upstairs."

Andre popped the boot, got out and pointed Jack's cane at him. "You're forgetting something."

Jack turned and rolled his eyes. "Oh! That stupid thing!" He took it and pushed the button on the bottom of the siding.

Andre said, "That's not the way it's done." He waved his hands and said, "Open sesame." He said in a demanding voice, "Never let anyone see how it is done." The lift doors opened. Jack walked to the boot, picked up a bag of supplies and stepped to the side.

Andre brought two cases of saline solution and sat them in the lift. He said, "I will park the car and be right up. Wait for me to order lunch." The door closed, the lift disappeared and it was just a blank wall again.

Jack stepped out of the lift with the bag. He walked to the kitchen table and set it there. Boris flew up. "Where the hell have you been?"

Jack said, "It takes time to do get around this place, it's not a small city."

The little fairy flew into the bag and started to take inventory. Jack walked to the lift and retrieved the two cases of the saline. Rupert asked, "Did you get more cobra venom?"

Jack looked at him, shook his head and told him, "That wasn't on the list." He went to the fridge and pulled out a pudding. He grabbed a spoon and devoured it. Boris was in the bag, checking everything out.

Jack said, "Here, let me help." He reached in, started to pull things out and set them out on the table. He stopped, closed his eyes and muttered "Damn!"

Marvin said, "What?"

Jack looked up to see the old man standing there in the doorway. "I forgot some papers in the car." He reached in and pulled out his mobile phone.

The lift snapped open and closed. Andre was standing there. He walked up and said, "Hey Marv, we have to oil that thing. It made a noise. Takes all the fun out of just popping in."

Jack said, "I'm sorry, you're going to have to go back to the car and get those certificates."

Andre handed Jack a vanilla envelope, "They're dry now."

Jack reached out and took the package. He stepped toward Marvin and handed it to him. "Here, call this in. I need these two. I want you to look at them. I had to jump through some hoops to get them, the original is in a file at an abbey fifty miles north off Highway One."

Andre walked up to the two and told Jack, "After we order lunch, I'll scan it and send it off."

Jack asked, "Can we order dinner now? I'm starved."

Marvin said, "Tonight, the special is tenderloin and shrimp."

Andre asked, "Did you order?"

Marvin said, "Yes I did, about half an hour ago. I called down and asked if they had filled the All-Knowing Jonathan's act."

Andre said, "You're not performing and that's that."

Marvin waved his hands in a big sweeping motion and poof! A small smoke cloud appeared and there was a glass of champagne in his outstretched hand. Jack's eyes widened, he reached out and took the glass from Marvin. "That was great!"

Andre said, "No, and that's final."

Marvin said, "Yes, yes, I know we have a lot to do and not much time to do it. We must strike while the iron is hot."

Jack said, "Enough of this chit chat! Andre, order the food. Marvin, call that circus guy and tell him Andre will email him the birth certificate. As for me, I am going to take a leak, then check on Juliet." Jack went back to the fridge and stood with the door open, staring inside. Marvin took a box off the counter and held it open to him. Jack reached in and took a couple of biscuits.

Marvin said, "Try a couple of strawberries. It brings out the flavour of the champagne."

Jack reached into the fridge, took out a couple of berries and sat them on the table next to his champagne. Marvin picked up the envelope and pulled out the birth certificate. He held it up and smiled, nodding his head, "These are done very nicely. The paper is old and the ink looks faded."

Jack said, with a mouth full of strawberry, "Those nuns know their stuff. They refuse to change to the computer completely."

Andre said, "OK, I checked on dinner. It will be twenty minutes, they're all coming up together. Marvin, you call Suckolofski, give him our email address and have him shoot us a letter. Then I'll send him the scan." He then walked over to the fridge and pulled out the bottle of champagne. He held it up and studied it, took out two glasses, filled them and stepped to Jack. He tipped the bottle and said, "This is the good stuff."

Jack said, raising his glass, "This is the best I've ever tasted."

Andre said, "Let me tell you, this bottle costs a hell of a lot more than your town car."

Jack's eyes popped open as he looked at the glass. He said, "You have to be kidding!"

Andre chuckled, "Well, maybe not a new town car, but I would think 15, 20 thousand, complements of Margaret." He held up his glass as a toast. He went on to tell Jack, "There is at least a quarter of a million in wine in that cellar."

Jack said, "You had better start sending that to Wisconsin." He strolled to Juliet's room, eating biscuits and sipping champagne. As he got closer to her room, he could smell it: the smell of death. There, in the room, the fairies were tending to her. She looked so peaceful. The monitors blinked on and her heart rate was super low. She was almost flatlining. Jack pointed that out rather loudly, "What the hell! She's almost dead!"

Boris flew up to him, Jack held out his hand palm up, Boris landed. "Elizabeth got the fresh Dragon's Breath and we used the rest of the cobra venom. Everything is going quite well."

Jack asked, "When is the doctor getting here?"

Rupert flew up and landed next to Boris. "He should be here around 6:00–6:30."

Jack looked at his watch. "Crap, we have to get the show on the road here first. You, Nora, fly to the kitchen and get Andre to get you some flour. We want to cover that blond that is coming out on her. There must be a good two inches of growth." He looked around. "He's going to be here anytime. Make sure there's nothing out of the ordinary. That would mean you too! Get ready to hide."

Andre quickly stepped into the room and started to powder Juliet with stage makeup. Marvin stepped into the room. "He's sending the email now, so go do your thing." He took the makeup from Andre and finished Juliet's face and hair. He powdered her arms and hands, then took out some blue powder and mixed it, giving her a grey look. Then he added a little yellow for around the eyes and asked, "What do you think?"

Nora flew to his shoulder, "She looks dead."

Rupert flew up and said, "Her fingernails are too bright. They should be almost purple."

Marvin walked out of the room and to the study, almost knocking Andre from the desk chair. "I need a purple marker now." Marvin got what he needed and ran back to Juliet. He took one of her hands and started to colour her fingernails. He had rubbed them to a dull purple, almost black, when a small beeping sound sounded.

Andre popped his head in the room. "I'll get it." He walked down the hall and came back with a waiter. They walked by Juliet's room to the kitchen where Jack was sitting eating strawberries. After setting out the meal, Andre pulled out his wallet and handed the waiter a twenty. Jack cut into the steak and started eating before Andre and the waiter had even left the room.

The beeping started again about a minute after the waiter had started down the stairs. Andre, who was just getting to the table, grumbled under his breath, "Ah shit, what did he forget?" He walked down the hall quickly and turned a picture on its side. You could see a blue light softly light up his face. He straightened the frame and ran to Juliet's room.

Chapter Fifteen
The Death of Juliet

Andre burst into the room, yelling excitedly, "Mayday, mayday! The doc is on his way up!" He sprinted down the hall to where Jack was getting up from the table; he was chewing a mouthful.

Jack said, "OK. We don't want him here long, so don't ask questions." Jack walked down the hall to Juliet's room. He stepped inside and looked at the monitors. "Hell, she's flatlined."

Juliet's doctor followed Andre to her room. Jack heard Andre tell him, "She is weak and really pale."

Jack looked around the room. Everything looked good, but the heart monitor didn't beep. It just ran a straight line. The doctor introduced himself to Jack, he said, "I am sorry for your loss, Marvin. We all knew this day was coming. How is she?"

Marvin said, "Sorry about calling you at the last minute. Did the nurse tell you?"

The doc took a breath and asked, "How long has she been dead?"

Marvin took his hand. "Glad to see you, doc. Juliet has been taking a turn for the worse."

The doctor studied the monitor, then looked at Juliet lying peacefully on the bed. He reached down and took her hand. He placed it on her chest, then took the other hand and laid it over the first. He turned to Marvin and said, "I'm sorry, she has passed. It seems she went peacefully into a good night."

Jack put his hand on the doctor's neck and closed his eyes. In a second, he opened them to hear Marvin say, "She can't be dead!" Tears welled up in his eyes and he grabbed his chest.

The old doctor turned to Andre, put his hand on his shoulders and spoke gently, "Help him to a chair and get him some water."

Andre slipped his arm around Marvin and helped him to a chair, comforting him, saying, "Her time had come. You knew for years that it was coming."

Jack came back into the room holding a glass of water; he gave it to Marvin. Jack stepped to the doc and looked him in the eye. "She's dead." He and asked the doctor, "Who would you recommend for the undertaker? They would have to have a crematorium on site."

The doctor gave his recommendation. Jack took the doctor's arm and headed him for the stairway. Jack turned him and told him, "The first thing you need to do is to make out the death certificate. Then we are going to need ten copies. For some reason, I ended up using six and my wife wasn't a star. You checked the monitors. Time of death was 4:20."

Andre stepped in with the nurse, he told her, "The doctor said she has passed."

The nurse asked the doctor, "Is your office going to take care of the paper work?"

The doctor said, "They are going to need death certificates tonight."

The doctor repeated what he was going to do back to him. Jack turned his head and listened, then told him, "Don't worry about the body, we have everything under control." The doctor walked down the stairs and Jack turned and walked back to the kitchen. He walked right to the fridge and pulled out the bottle of champagne.

This time he walked down to the bar in the front room and took out some champagne glasses. When he walked into Juliet's room, the three fairies were examining her. Marvin looked like she really had died. Jack poured three glasses and held two out. Marvin looked up and took one. He had tears running down his cheek. Andre reached out and took his. Jack raised his glass and said, "That went well. What's next?"

Nora flew to Jack and landed on his shoulder. She walked up to his ear and said, "We think she really died."

Jack tipped the glass all the way up, slamming the contents. Then he said, "Damn, that's good!" He sat his glass down and put his hand on Juliet's forehead. He closed his eyes, then said, "Sleep, don't worry. Sleep, everything went well. The undertaker will be here soon." He opened his eyes, then said, "Shit, wait! What name do you want?" Jack opened his eyes and asked, "How long are you going to keep her in this state?"

Boris said, "I would like to slowly bring her out—two days, three max."

Rupert flew in. "She's alive, she's alive! Thank you, God, she's alive! I thought we killed her."

Marvin threw his arms around Jack with tears streaming down his face and said, "Thank you! I thought we lost her."

Jack smiled and said, "All I did was unplug the leads to the heart monitor, that's why." He stepped to the head of the bed, plugged in two wires and the line on the monitor got a small bump in it. He said, "See, almost dead. Not quite."

Boris and the other two fairies were having a heated meeting on the monitor. Jack said to Andre, "Well, are you ready to eat now? I'm starving."

Nora flew to Jack. He held out his hand. She landed on it and waved Jack to bend down to hear her. She said, "Boris wants you to get some blankets on Juliet and warm her up. She is too cold."

Jack stepped to Marvin and held out his hand with the fairy standing on his palm. "Here, take her. She wants you to do something. I'm going to eat."

Jack walked back into the kitchen, followed by Andre. Jack took the phone off the charger and a phone book from a drawer. Andre was putting his plate in the microwave. He asked, "What's the book for?"

Jack smiled, "I have to call at least three funeral homes, see if they would pick up and if they need the death certificate for the cremation."

Andre asked, "Aren't you rushing it a bit? I throw a great funeral, but it takes time."

Marvin, who was listening from the doorway, said, "Not this time. She has been out of the limelight for some time now. There won't be a showing. I just want it done and over with. But it has to be done right. Jack, you're in charge. Do what you have to." He turned and headed back to Juliet's room.

Andre said, "We really thought she was dead. The fairies, Marvin and myself."

Jack said, "You guys had me going for a second there, too." The two ate in silence for about two minutes. Jack started to look through the phone book, taking notes and asking how far places were, and if Andre knew where a funeral home was. He had narrowed them down.

Marvin stepped in and asked, "How is everything going?"

Andre said, "I just finished, and we narrowed down the funeral homes to three."

Marvin said, "That's great. Now help me strip the bed and put clean sheets on."

Jack looked up from the telephone book and said, "That's not a good idea. I want the place to smell like death for a couple of more days. Then we'll have it deodorised; it's best to have a professional do it."

Andre asked, "How is Juliet doing?"

Marvin eyes teared up. He reached out and took Andre's chair and leaned on it. "She is still cool to the touch. My God, I thought she was dead!" He put his hand over his eyes and took small gasps of air.

Jack said, "OK, let's get it done." He picked up the phone and called the first funeral home and started to take notes. Andre stood and put his arm around Marvin to comfort him; the two men stood there, sniffling.

Andre kept saying, "She's going to be fine."

Jack sat down the phone and asked, "What the hell was that doctor's name?"

Marvin pulled himself back together. He walked by the table, took a note off the peg board that had the doctor's number on it and handed it to Jack. Jack said, "I need that death certificate. Without it, nobody will do anything. I don't know if he'll do it tonight." He pushed the talk button and asked for the doctor, then his voice changed. "I don't care. I am sending a driver over for that paperwork, it had better be waiting for him."

Andre said, "I'm on my way."

Jack said, "I'll turn on my mobile phone. They will be here to pick up Juliet in about 15 minutes. So you get the death certificate and meet us at O' Mally's funeral home." He scraped the rest of the potatoes off his plate and started to get the dishes together. Then he asked excitedly, "Hey Marvin! Do you have a wheelchair? We could wheel Juliet right out the door."

Marvin told him there was one in the hall wardrobe. Jack pulled his mobile phone out and called Andre, "Hey, would you like to come back up here?"

Marvin blurted out, "Ah, Christ, I had better call down to the restaurant. If the hearse pulls up to the front door, it won't be good for business."

Jack smiled, "You do have a point there."

The lift door opened and Andre stepped out into the kitchen, "OK, what did you guys forget?"

Jack asked, "Would you dig out that wheelchair from the wardrobe and put it into the car? You're going to wheel Marvin in, then we're going to wheel Juliet right out of there."

Marvin walked back into the kitchen wearing a black suit as well as carrying one. As soon as Andre walked back in, Marvin explained, "When we make our exit, we will dress Juliet in my suit. It will look like we just have one more person."

Andre took the suit, "OK, that is the plan."

Jack said, "The hearse should pull up to the back door. Are you using the lift?"

Marvin said, "Certainly not! That is to be a secret. Andre said he would bring them up the back steps." With that, the lift door closed and so did the wall hiding it.

Jack walked around the room and grabbed the pot and poured coffee. Marvin asked, "Do you always drink this much coffee?"

Jack laughed, "Yeah, me and the wife would drink four to five pots a day."

Marvin asked, "How long ago did she die?"

Jack took a sip of coffee and said softly, "She died about a month ago. They say it was a heart attack, but Nora said she was killed by the blue fairies. You know, I remember that night clearly now. She said there were huge lightning bugs in the flowers. They must have been blue fairies watching the red ones. She was stone cold when I reached her."

Marvin put his hand on Jack's shoulder. "That must have been a shocker."

A chime rang and Andre pushed a button. A voice said, "We are from O' Mally's funeral home for a pick-up." A light flashed, 1-2-3, 1-2-3.

Andre said, "Why can't the doc email the death certificate?"

Marvin said, "They're here, someone just stepped on the first step." Marvin walked down the hall and turned a picture sideways on the wall. A screen lit up, showing two men on the stairs carrying a light gurney.

Nora flew onto Jack's shoulder. She asked, "How long will Juliet be gone?"

Jack said, "Hopefully an hour or two—could be three."

She then flew off to report the news. The mortician's assistants finally reached the top of the stairs. Marvin had the door opened and was standing there. He told the guys, "Come in and take a rest. I'm sorry about living on the third floor."

The men were wearing black suits, the uniform for their trade. Jack said, "She is right in here." The fellows followed him to Juliet's room. As soon as they entered the room, you could see the smell get to them. One tried to hold his breath and let out a "Wow."

Juliet was unhooked from all the machines and was ready to go. They gently slid her onto the gurney, covered her and strapped her down. Jack told them to follow him and he led them down the hall to the stairway, then slowly down the stairs.

They reached the bottom of the stairway, where the hearse was parked. Jack asked if he should open the door. One of the assistants said, "The keys are in my pocket."

Marvin brushed by him. To his amazement, Marvin stood there with his keys, pointing them at the car. The rear door popped and opened on its own. Jack stepped in close and worked the buttons for the floor section to roll out.

The two men laid Juliet on the floor and pulled out some straps that were hidden in the floor. They pushed a couple of buttons that tightened the straps.

Marvin said, "Not tight."

The older attendant held out his hand to Marvin and said, "You're still pretty good. My parents took me to one of your shows twenty years ago. Is this the gal that worked with you?"

Marvin slowly nodded, "Yes, this is my wife, my soulmate of many years."

Jack stepped over to them. He took the other attendant to the side of the hearse and told him nothing out of the ordinary had happened on this pick-up, and had him explain how the undertaker worked the cremation. The man told Jack the details, standing straight and never blinking. Jack then asked if they could ride with them. The attendant told him, "No one rides in the hearse. It's a company policy."

Jack said, "Call us a cab then." He walked over to Marvin, who was talking magic with the other guy. Jack stepped in front of the attendant and looked him in the eye. "Nothing out of the ordinary happened on this pick-up. You will wait till the cab gets here, then you will do as I say."

Marvin asked, "Why aren't we riding with them?"

Jack said, "It would throw a red flag; it's against their policy."

A cab pulled up, the two old guys strolled over to it. Marvin said to the driver, "Follow that hearse."

The cabby joked, "One day they will let you ride in the back."

Marvin started to get in. He saw Jack was already in and asked, "Are you going to tell the boys to go now?"

Jack gave him a weird look, then it dawned on him. The two undertaker's assistants were standing there, waiting for their orders. Jack got out of the car and jogged over to them. He said, "When I say go, you will awaken." He jogged back to the car. Then he turned and yelled: "Go!" then slid into the back seat of the cab.

Marvin said to him, "Jack, you have to stop running around. It looks strange to see an eighty-year old guy running around."

Jack smiled and replied, "Nobody knows me here."

Marvin said, "Don't see you with your cane."

Jack rolled his eyes and muttered, "Ah, shit!"

Marvin laughed, "See, you should have let Nora come along. We would act more like our old selves."

The cabby pulled in behind the hearse at the funeral home. Jack said, "I'll get it." He pulled out a fifty and said, "This was a normal pick-up. Nothing out of the ordinary happened. You didn't even hear us talk in the back."

With that, Jack started after Marvin, who was talking to the two guys in black. Jack slowly shuffled his feet and bent over. One of the guys went in through a side door, unlocked it and opened it. The big black Lincoln pulled up, Andre jumped out and ran to the boot. He pulled out the wheelchair, snapped it open and unlocked one of the wheels. He then went back to the driver's door and came out with a vanilla envelope. He came across the car park at full stride.

Jack raised his hand, waved the two gentlemen over from the hearse, then told them, "Wait a minute." They stopped and stood.

Andre quickly walked up behind Marvin. He took the envelopes off the seat and helped Marvin into the chair. He then handed the envelopes to Jack and said, "This is the death certificate, the funeral director makes the copies." He put his hand on Marvin's shoulder. "I'll give you the bill when we get to your place."

Marvin looked up at Jack. "Well? Shall we go? Those guys look silly standing there." The two suited guys stood frozen in the doorway. Jack told the men to start moving and they started through the door, continuing the same conversation they were having before.

One turned and said, "Hey! The old guy is in a wheelchair! Where the hell did that come from?" The two funeral assistants stopped just inside the door and one turned and told them they had to go up to the front office.

Jack said, "You will take Marvin and Andre with you. I will go up to the office." He then told Andre, "Don't let her out of your sight." Jack turned and walked toward the front of the building and up to the front desk and talked with the girl. She told him, "The funeral director is busy at the moment. Would you like to take a seat, sir?"

Jack leaned over the desk, looked into her eyes and said, "You will take me to see the director now."

She said, "I don't think so. You're going to take a seat over there and wait your turn."

Jack cocked his head. He reached over and lightly put his hand on her arm. Her face went blank. "Now, you will take me to the director."

She said flatly, "Yes, I will take you to Mr Smith." She got up and took Jack to the back through several doors and to a large office. There were two suited men sitting and talking. The receptionist said, "This is Jack Robinson, he is representing Juliet and Marvin Remington. These are Mr Smith and Mr Ashland." She then exited the room.

Jack walked in and looked them both in the eyes. "This conversation is over, Mr Ashland. You may call back tomorrow if you need to." With that said, Mr Ashland stood, loaded his briefcase and left the room. "Now, Mr

Smith, let's get down to business," Jack said with total control. He spoke as if he was still in the army.

"Marvin the Magnificent has brought his wife Juliet in. Here is a copy of the death certificate. You will lead me to her and you will slip her into the crematorium. She is to be cremated today."

Mr Smith got off his chair and led Jack through a maze to the embalming room where Andre and Marvin were waiting with the two attendants and Juliet, of course. It was a sanitary room with a table in the middle and lots of stainless steel. Mr Smith entered the room, followed by Jack—this pretty much filled the small room. Jack said, "You two!" he pointed at the assistants, "Step outside till you're needed."

Marvin said, "Step into the hall."

Jack corrected himself, "Step into the hall until you're needed."

Andre said, "They would have stepped outside."

Jack cut him off. "Now, Mr Smith, is a crematorium open?"

The suited man blankly said, "Yes."

Jack told him, "Look at Juliet. See her every time you think of her. This is the face you will remember. Now, walk me though the process of cremating a body."

Mr Smith told them the first thing was to undress the deceased, then to put her on a gurney with a top sheet and to slide her into the crematorium.

Jack asked, "Who do you have undress the body and prep for the cremation?"

Mr Smith said, "Todd and Larry prep and cremate all the clients."

Jack then asked, "Are Todd and Larry the ones out in the hall?"

Mr Smith blankly answered, "Yes."

Jack said, "Andre, get them back in here." He then told Mr Smith, "You will remember telling them to cremate Juliet now. Then you will go back to work and make out the bill. You will remember just how Juliet looked and telling Todd and Larry to cremate her."

The two men came back into the room, Mr Smith told the men to cremate Juliet, then left the room. Jack told the guys, "Undress Juliet and get her ready for cremation. You will not remember anyone else in the room." The men watched Todd and Larry undress Juliet and place her on a clean white sheet, with a white sheet covering her. Jack held up a hand.

Marvin said, "They're hypnotised, you have to speak."

Jack said, "Stop!" The two men froze. Jack then said, "OK, it's time to dress her and sneak her out to the car."

Marvin got up, took out the bag and laid out the suit. It took all three of them to dress her. They then put her in the wheelchair. Jack told Todd and

Larry, "OK. You still see Juliet on the gurney. Let's go and put her in the crematorium."

Jack followed the two to a large room with three golden doors built into the wall. All three of them had a small green light above them. Todd, who was walking backward, let go of the gurney and quickly stepped to a door. He opened it, pushed a few buttons on the keypad that was next to it and a table slid out of the door. Larry pushed the gurney right alongside the door. Todd turned around, grabbed the sheet laid on one side on the table and they pulled it onto the table. Jack said, "Explain to me how this works. Picture it in your mind." A couple of seconds later, he said, "That is good, that is the way you will remember it."

Then he asked, "How much ash do you get from a person and where can we get some?"

Larry said, "About three to nine pounds—a bit less from a woman, and she is a small woman."

Jack asked, "Where can we get some ashes?"

Todd asked, "Should I get you enough ashes to fill an urn?"

Jack said, "Put the ashes on the table like they would look when you cremate a person."

Todd opened a drawer and pulled a plastic box. It looked like an oversized VHS tape box. He walked over to the table and poured it slowly. Halfway down, he poured it quickly down one side, then stopped. He went halfway up and made the other leg. Jack said, "OK then, let's slide her in."

Larry pushed a button and a small light from inside the furnace turned into a bright yellow flame. Todd started to chant lightly and Larry joined in; it was in Latin. Jack put his hand on Larry's neck and asked him, "Think about this afternoon. What do you remember?"

Jack then walked over to Todd, placed his hand on his neck and asked him to do the same. Jack said, "Now, when you scrape the ashes from the crematorium, you will remember opening the door and crushing the bones, just like for any cremation. You will not notice anything different. Now take me to the office."

Todd led the way. He walked slowly so the old man could keep up, Jack noticed it and slowed down. He realised that he had lost another cane. When they got to the office, Mr Smith was sitting at his desk and Juliet's death certificate was laying in front of him.

He looked up and said, "Ah, Mr Robinson, I have a few papers for you to sign. And you have to pick out an urn."

Jack picked up the pen and asked, "When can I pick it up? And I need twelve copies."

Mr Smith said, "Her ashes will be ready by this time tomorrow."

Jack said, "How about this? I'll take the most expensive urn and have it sent to Marvin the Magnificent at the Magic Castle tomorrow."

Mr Smith told Todd, "You heard the man. Make it quick so we can get out of here."

Larry said, "I'll put away the hearse and lock the backdoors."

Mr Smith pulled open a drawer in the desk and a screen glowed. He tapped a few keys and said, "You have made a very good choice, the Cadillac of urns." With that, he picked up the phone and called down to the store room. The phone was answered right away. He said into it: "The golden eagle."

Jack peered over the desk to see a statue of a golden eagle with a plaque engraved on the front. Mr Smith said, "The engraving is free. What would you like it to say?"

Jack pondered for a second, then said, "To my lovely Juliet, whom I shall love for eternity, Marvin the Magnificent."

Mr Smith wrote everything down and asked, "Are you going to pay half now?"

Jack stood, put both hands on the desk and peered down at him, saying, "You will give me the bill and you will trust me that you will be paid on the day of the delivery of the plaque—which I need by next week."

Mr Smith said, "You can pay me after I get the engraved plaque."

Todd walked in, pushing a trolley with a box on it. Jack said with a smile, "OK, lead me to the car; I'll follow you." Jack stepped behind Todd and walked to the side door. As soon as they stepped out on the pavement, Andre pulled up.

Todd stepped over to the car door and Jack blocked his view. "Please give Marvin my deepest regrets."

Jack said, "You popped your head in and told him yourself." He walked around the car and got in the passenger seat. He turned and saw Marvin with Juliet. She was laying with her head on his lap. Andre pulled out onto the road and into the carpool lane.

The car was silent for a long minute, then Marvin asked, "What the hell took so long?"

Jack said, "Well, someone had to sign the papers. And now we are done. One of the boys will come over with the urn. You should have picked it out, I just got the most expensive one they had. I think it is gold plated—it's a big thing." He reached into his breast pocket and pulled out the brochure. He looked at it and whistled, "That has to be one nice urn, a cool fifty grand."

Nora crawled up the seat to Jack's shoulder and said, "Next time, I'm not sitting in the car."

Jack turned his head, "You're going to do as you are told."

She crossed her arms and looked away. Jack told her, "This has to be done right the first time. There is no room for error."

Andre was driving on aggressively: he pulled onto the 405 and said, "Crap, it's rush hour." between his teeth. There were cars as far as the eye could see.

Jack exclaimed, "Wow, I have never seen traffic like this in my life!"

Marvin commented, "The faster we get her home, the better it will be."

Chapter Sixteen
Bring Juliet Back from the Dead

Twenty minutes later, Andre got to the first off ramp. He took it and shot though the city, taking half the GPS directions and half his own. Soon, they were on Hollywood Boulevard.

Jack commented, "Hey, this place has a few cars in the car park!"

Andre said, "The car park will be completely full in an hour or so. We had better get Juliet upstairs."

Jack looked in the back seat to see Marvin stroking Juliet's hair as she lay on his lap. He asked, "How is she?"

Marvin looked up with tear-filled eyes. "She is so cold and stiff! We have been gone a long time."

Nora flew back and said, "Boris will fix her right up. There is no one better."

Marvin sighed, "I used to be one of the best wizards in the world—well, in the top five anyway. I should be able to save her."

Nora flew to his shoulder and said, "You will do as Boris says and everything will be all right."

Andre pulled up to the back, to the blank wall. Jack said, "You open that stupid door and pop the boot," He turned and said, "Stay!" like he was talking to a dog. He was out of the car and at the boot before Andre was halfway to the wall. He pulled out the wheelchair with one hand, closing the boot with the other.

Jack bounced the chair on its wheels and snapped the handles apart. He got down on one knee and locked the chair into position. In three steps, he was at the back door of the Lincoln. He opened it like he was afraid of something falling out. He looked inside and Marvin had Juliet sitting right next to the door.

He looked at Jack and said, "Hold her, I'm coming around."

Jack carefully took Juliet by the shoulders. She was so cold and stiff—she wasn't going to move for anyone. He felt a hand on his shoulder; it was Marvin. Jack said, "I got this. You hold the chair."

Jack slid his hand under Juliet's legs and around her back. He bent at the knees and picked her right up. He said to her, "There, there. Everything is going to be all right." He took a step back and Marvin drove the chair under her. Jack lightly set her into it. He turned back to shut the car door and when he turned, Marvin was at a dead run to catch the lift. Marvin must have taken off as soon as she sat in the chair.

Andre said, "That took just over three hours."

Marvin stroked Juliet's hair, saying to her, "Hold on, my love, just a bit longer."

Jack said, "You know, she is worried about you. She said so when I picked her up. She is so weak." Jack put his hand on Marvin's hand that was stroking her hair and a deep red glow formed around their two hands.

Nora flew within inches of Jack's face and screamed, "Stop it! What are you doing?" The glow disappeared and Jack's eyes focused on Nora, who was lighting up the lift with a red glow. He could tell that she was pissed. She held out her arm, pointing at Jack's nose. "You will do nothing unless Boris says so! Do you understand?"

Jack looked at Marvin, then back to Nora. "I understand. Marvin asked me to do it."

Nora who was cooling down, turned a little redder. "He did not! I was right here! You're such a lair."

Jack said, "Sure he did. He said he wished he could give her a bit of his power. I asked how and he said to run it through his hand and he would adjust the strength of it."

Marvin said, "Huh. I thought that, I didn't say it."

Jack looked to Andre. "Nope, I didn't hear anyone say anything."

The lift stopped and Jack said, "That's weird. I heard your thoughts. Boy, I wonder if I can do it again!"

The doors opened and Andre squeezed to the side. Jack stepped out and Marvin pulled Juliet out. He headed down the hall to Juliet's room. They moved fast, almost running down the hall. The three of them turned and went into the room.

Boris and Rupert came out from behind a chair, both holding an end of a tray with all kinds of stuff on it. They sat it on a bedside table. Then the two of them flew off behind the chair again and came back with the book. It was a huge book, wrapped in leather, and it was propped up on the seat of the chair. The two fairies carefully opened the book to the right page.

Marvin backed the wheelchair next to the bed and told Jack to lift one side of Juliet and Nora to pull out the wheelchair. The two men lifted Juliet and Nora pulled the chair so hard, it slammed into the chest of drawers. Jack slid his arms under Juliet and told Marvin, "I got her. She weighs about sixty pounds, no problem. Get to the other side of the bed."

Marvin scurried to the other side with open arms. He reached over and helped lay her down gently. Boris flew up and started to bark commands to Nora, who told Marvin what to do. "First you need to put in that water thing back into her arm."

Jack asked, "What did you do with the IV solution?"

Marvin said, "In the wardrobe, on the floor."

Jack went for the wardrobe and Marvin started to rummage through the chest of drawers. They both met at Juliet's side. Marvin handed him the end of a clear rubber tube. Jack looked at him.

"I'll do it," Marvin said. He hooked the hose to the bag and ran some saline solution threw the hose, then connected it to a connector that was taped in place on Juliet's arm. Marvin said, "Thank God we left that thing in, or we would have never found the vein."

Nora flew to Jack and told him, "She has to be clean. Most of this stuff soaks in through the skin."

Marvin said, "I'm on it." He turned and went into his room.

Jack asked, "How is she?"

Nora said, "Boris and Rupert have everything ready. We need blankets and we need to start a fire."

Jack asked, "What do they need a fire for?"

She said, "They want to warm her up."

Jack walked over to a thermostat on the wall and turned it up to eighty. He turned to Nora, who was standing on the bed. "You had better watch those two."

Marvin returned with a pan of soapy water and washcloths and towels. He handed it to Jack and told him, "I'll be back with a rinse."

Jack put the pan down on the chair. He went to the foot of the bed and took the wingtip shoes of Marvin's off her. They were so big that he didn't even need to untie them. Next, he slid off her socks.

Marvin came back in the room and asked loudly, "Is that all you've done?" There was a pause, then, "Where the hell is Dropoff?"

Jack looked at him for a second, then asked, "Do you think I'm going to undress your wife when you're not here? And Andre is putting away the car."

Nora told Jack, "They are ready. They need Juliet's face washed. And her neck."

Jack said, "Quick, get her shirt off!"

Marvin whisked his hand and all the buttons came undone. He asked Jack, "Pull her arm out of the sleeve and push it under her." Marvin rolled

Juliet onto her side and they got her shirt off. Then they washed, rinsed and dried in the same manner.

They were working on getting off her pants when Andre walked in. He stepped to the foot of the bed and pulled gently on the pants legs. He asked, "How is she?"

Jack said, "Don't know yet."

Rupert rubbed some bluish gel on her temples. Boris was up to his wrists in a bottle cap, mixing some other concoction. Nora flew down and talked to Rupert. He was rubbing a wide circle on Juliet's temple. Nora then flew to Jack. She landed on his shoulder and talked into his ear, "Next, they want to put a potion on the soles of her feet and they want you to give her some of your power."

Jack looked to Marvin. "You two finish washing her. I'll be back."

Nora flew after Jack, landing on his shoulder again. She spoke into his ear again, "Didn't you hear me? They want you to give her some of your power."

Jack said, "I have to make a call."

Nora yelled, "Who, Jack? Who do you have to call?"

Jack said one word, "Margaret."

Nora stood on Jack's shoulder. She cocked her head, thinking—just standing there, thinking. Jack pulled out his phone and dialled. He asked for Margaret, then he asked how she felt and if everything was in place, if she had called the solicitor. Then he told her he would be there tomorrow. He hung up the phone. Nora wanted to know if she was Jack's new friend. Jack smiled and said, "Yeah. For now. We have to get back." Jack walked back to the room that Juliet was in.

He asked how she was doing. Marvin was just setting her foot down. "She's all clean, head to toe. Now we have to warm her back up to her normal temperature."

Jack asked, "Do you have an electric blanket?"

Marvin stopped, cocked his head and shouted, "Hey, Dropoff! Do I have an electric blanket?"

He stepped back into the room with both wash pans, "You know, that's a great idea. I'll be back in 15 minutes. By the way, I have no idea where these go." He handed the two tubs to Jack and jogged to the lift.

Jack said, "You know, it's probably better to buy a new one. There are more safeguards on them."

Nora flew back from talking with Rupert and Boris. She fluttered in front of Jack and yelled, "It's time."

Boris and Rupert flew to the headboard. Jack's face went pale. "OK, let's do this." He stepped over to the bedside and sat the two wash pans on the chair that was next to him. He stood like he didn't know what to do. He looked at Marvin and asked, "Have you ever done this before?"

Marvin said in a quiet voice, "Yes, but it has been decades. We are talking closer to a century."

Jack's colour came steaming back and he smiled. "So you've done this before. Why don't you do it again?"

Nora flew up in front of Jack and said, "Don't you feel his power? He is weak compared to you. And you are to do as Boris asked, you promised!"

Marvin asked Rupert, "Can he run his power though my hand? That way, I can control the amount he gives her."

Rupert turned to Boris, they talked for 10–15 seconds, then Rupert nodded his head. Marvin looked Jack in the eye and said, "Let's do this. I'll put my hand on Juliet's forehead. You put your hand on mine, then give me a little juice."

Jack said, "Wait." He reached out to Marvin and asked, "Can we try it without Juliet?"

Marvin let out a long breath. "Good idea." He put his hand on the rail of the bed and Jack gently placed his on top of Marvin's and it started to glow. Marvin automatically said, "Slow down, that's way too fast! That's it, a little less. Oh boy, that's perfect!"

Jack chuckled, "OK, we can do this now."

Marvin rested his hand on Juliet's forehead. Jack put his carefully on Marvin's, then he started to transfer some energy to Juliet. Boris hopped down to Juliet's shoulder and Rupert hopped to the other. Jack could feel Marvin taking a lot of the energy and just giving Juliet a trickle, so he slowed the transfer of power. .

Rupert crawled up and across her lips. He sat on Juliet's raised cheekbones and pushed her eyelid up. He sat and peered into her eye. Jack and Marvin stood motionless, feeding Juliet the spark of life. Rupert dropped the eyelid and waved them off with both hands. Nora shot to Jack's ear and yelled into it: "Stop!"

Jack blinked, seeing Rupert frantically waving. The old fairy flew inches from Jack's face, pointed his finger at him and yelled: "You watch what you're doing!"

He flew down to talk with Boris. Marvin said, "We have to get her warmed up. She is still so cold. Her blood must have clotted."

Jack said, "Let me try something." He went to the foot of the bed, took Juliet by the feet and closed his eyes. He was putting energy into her legs. Her legs started to twitch as the nerves got the signal. Boris flew to Nora, who flew to Jack and yelled into his ear, "What are you doing?"

Marvin took Juliet by the hand, closed his eyes and said with a commanding voice, "Leave him!" Marvin pulled down the covers and took Juliet by both hands. There she was—naked. You could see all her bones; she was as grey as a corpse.

Boris and Rupert where having a heated discussion; you couldn't make out what they were saying. This went on for some time. Nora yelled into Jack's ear, trying to find out what was going on. She waved in front of his eyes. It was like he was entranced. Andre walked into the room, carrying a cloth shopping bag. "What's going on?" he asked.

Nora flew to him, speaking fast, "We don't know; they won't talk to us."

Andre stepped closer and commented, "Whatever they're doing, Juliet looks a lot better. She has a little colour now."

The room became silent. Boris and Rupert stood and gazed at Juliet. Andre broke the silence. "Well, I got the electric blanket. This is supposed to be the best they have." He pulled out a cling film-wrapped blanket and started to take it out of the packaging. He unfolded the blanket and looked around Jack's legs and found a socket to plug the thing in. He then looked at the directions. A few minutes went by. Andre asked the room, "How long are they going to stand there like that?"

Nora flew down to Boris and Rupert, then flew to Andre. She landed on his shoulder and said into his ear, "They don't know what Jack and Marvin are doing, or how long it will take."

Ten minutes went by. Andre got up and said, "If they come out of their trance, tell them I went to make a drink." He walked out of the room.

Nora flew after him. She landed on his shoulder and asked him, "What do you think is going on?"

He smiled. "I think the old Marvin is back. He must have figured out a way to help Juliet." Andre poured a small amount of cognac in a sniffer, swirled it and took a small taste. "Not bad." He walked back to the room Juliet was in and asked, "So why isn't Juliet in her room?"

Nora said, "Stick your head in there. It smells bad. I mean like death! Someone is supposed to come tomorrow and deodorise it." The two of them walked down the hall, chatting. Andre wanted to hear the story from the beginning till now. They walked into the room to see Jack and Marvin were still frozen, holding onto Juliet.

Andre walked up to the bed and felt Juliet's forehead. "Huh. She feels warmer, and her colour is back. If she wasn't skin and bones, she would look normal." Rupert shot to Juliet. He put both arms on her neck, feeling for a pulse. Then he shot to Boris, who was reading the old sorceress's book.

Andre stepped over and leaned his head down to hear. Then he asked, "So, how is she?"

Boris said, "She has a pulse and is warming up. Whatever those two are doing, it's helping."

Andre swirled his drink, took a sip next to the bed and said to Nora, "Now tell me more about this green fairy. What was her name? Elizabeth?"

Nora told him about fooling her in the forest with Ivan the unicorn, and how he told them not to go in front of the fairy council. Andre asked, "Why is she still here? Green fairies do whatever they want."

Nora cocked her head, thinking out loud. She said, "You know, I think it's about protection. She's been talking to that other green fairy—the one you guys found at Margaret's. She was caught decades ago and made a slave. I think Elizabeth is scared. She was chased across the country and the blues were wearing her down. If Jack hadn't saved her, she could have been caught."

Andre pondered on this. Then he asked this question: "OK, now she is at full power. There is no way they could catch her. So why doesn't she just fly out into the stars and go back to where she came from."

Nora said, "The way I figure, she is pissed off. Jack is starting a war against the blue fairies and she wants to watch it happen. And she came here to find her cousin."

Andre took a long sip, swirling it in his mouth and let out a little "Yum", then he pointed with his glass. "Did you see that? Marvin moved." Boris and Rupert flew right to the headboard and stared. Then Jack slowly lifted his head and looked at Marvin.

Marvin leaned forward and gently put Juliet's arms at her side. Andre jumped to his feet and stepped to Marvin's side. He put his arm around him. He said quietly, "OK Marvin, let's set you down on this chair right here." Andre guided him to the chair and eased him down. He stepped quickly to Jack's side, who was holding onto the bed rail. "Let's get you to a chair for a minute," and guided Jack to a chair next to Marvin. Andre asked both men, "How do you feel?"

Jack said, "My legs are asleep," as he rubbed them.

Marvin said, "My frickin' back is killing me."

Andre said, "You do know that you guys stood there for over an hour?"

Jack turned his head and you could hear his neck pop. He asked, "How is she?"

Rupert flew down to Marvin and asked, "What did you guys do to her?"

Marvin said, "We heated her and got her blood moving. It was all clotted. Between the two of us, we broke up all the clots and cleaned the arteries. I think she will be all right; her pulse is strong and regular."

Boris flew over and commanded, "Andre, get those covers back on her."

Andre got up and pulled the sheet over her, tucking it in. Then he laid the electric blanket on her. He turned to Marvin and said, "Set it for 98 degrees and keep an eye on it." Andre brushed his hand across Juliet's forehead and said, "Welcome back, Mum." He turned to see what Jack had planned, but both the old men had their heads against the wall and were fast asleep.

Andre stepped over to the bedside table where the two fairies were reading and mixing a new potion. Boris looked up and told him, "You get that green fairy. I need some fresh kelp and a fire."

Andre asked, "How much kelp do you need?"

Boris said, "Just bring me some. I'll use what I need." Andre started down the hall. Nora flew right to his shoulder. "You have to be careful with Elizabeth. She is still dangerous."

Andre said, "It would be quicker if I got it. Would you like to come along?"

Nora cried with delight, "Sure, this will be fun!" She climbed into Andre's chest pocket. He hit the stairs; Nora climbed out and up to his shoulder. "Why didn't you use the lift?"

Andre said, "The lift is a secret. We're using it way too much now. OK, back into hiding." Andre stepped down a passage and popped out in the hall. He walked into the kitchen and asked for a plate with fresh kelp and a butter warmer with a couple of gel packs. A server handed then to him, Andre thanked him and a twenty dollar bill appeared between his fingers. The server thanked him back.

Andre said with a big grin on his face, "It depends on the chef. Sometimes you will get thrown right out of the kitchen." He walked down the hall almost halfway, then stopped, turned toward the wall and stepped into a door. The door snapped open, then closed. When he was inside, he said to Nora, "You have one and a half seconds to walk through the door. And let me tell you, if you're not fast enough, it hurts like hell."

This time he took the lift up to the third floor. He walked right to Juliet's room and sat the plate down on the bedside table along with the butter warmer.

Boris walked over and said, "I didn't need that much." He searched the plate and took a leaf from it. "Now what the hell is that?"

Andre took the butter warmer off the table and placed it on the floor where he stepped on it, compacting it. "There," he said, as he picked it up and put it back on the table. He reached into his pocket and pulled out the gel packs. He put one into the ring. "All you need is a light and you will have your fire."

Boris said, "Well, I need it now."

Andre stepped over to Marvin and shook him ever so lightly. "Hey Marvin, I need a match. Where can I find one?"

Marvin opened his eyes and said sleepily, "God, I'm beat! What do you want?"

Andre told him: "I need a light for Boris and his butter warmer." Marvin got up and walked out of the room. In a minute he was back with a long lighter.

He lit the gel pack and it started right up. He asked, "Where is the ceramic dish that fits in it?" Andre looked around the table and took it out of the pile of gel cups. He then placed it in the holder.

Boris walked up to it. He studied the blue flame that licked the bottom of the dish and flew to Marvin. "Now that's going to be too hot!"

Marvin told Andre, "He thinks it is going to be too hot now. You work with him, I need a nap." With that, he walked over to Juliet and swept a strand of hair off her face. He stared at her face for a few seconds, then told her, "I won't be long, hang in there."

He straightened the blanket and slid his hand under it. He turned and yelled: "Andre, get over here."

Andre, who was working with Boris trying to get the right heat out of the gel packs, took three quick steps to Marvin and asked, "What?"

Marvin said with concern written over his face, "Put your hand under the blanket. Isn't it too hot?"

Andre said, "I bought the one that was programmable and it is set to 98 degrees. Everything should be fine." He put his hand under the blanket and said, "I'll get a thermometer and check it."

Marvin yawned, "No, no, I'll check it. You help Boris." Marvin stepped over to the chest of drawers and pulled one of the drawers open. He rummaged through it and pulled out a thermometer that went into your ear. He took out the little plastic sleeves that went over it, looked at them, then tossed them back into the drawer. He then placed it in his ear, then looked at it and said out loud to nobody particular, "It works." He stepped over to Juliet and put it under the covers. When he pulled it out to read it, Andre stood looking over his shoulders. Marvin said, "You're right. 98 on the head."

Andre asked, "How warm is Juliet?"

Marvin placed the thermometer carefully into her ear and waited a few seconds. Then took it out. He read it, "Ah shit, she is only at 96!"

Andre said, "I don't think you had it in her ear long enough."

Marvin asked him, "Didn't you hear the beep?"

Boris flew up to Marvin. "I heard the beep. What was it for?" Marvin explained the thermometer to him and told him Juliet was still two degrees below normal. Boris asked "What did you expect? She is skin and bones; her organs haven't worked right in years. I have never even tried a regeneration with someone in this condition."

Marvin asked, "You *can* do it, can't you?"

Rupert flew up and said, "She is a very strong-willed woman. We can do this if you would let us do our job."

Marvin said, "I need a nap."

Andre pointed to Jack, who had his head resting on his shoulder and a line of drool hanging off his jaw. "Take him with you."

Marvin stepped over to Jack and gave him a shove. Jack sleepily opened his eyes and yawned, "What time is it?" Marvin looked at the clock on the wall and told him it was 3:30. Jack said loudly, "Crap, Andre get the car. We have places to go."

Jack wiped sleep out of his eyes and pulled his mobile phone out of his pocket. It rang as it powered up. "Ah shit, I have 15 missed calls." He made a call, then started walking down the hall. He said loudly, "Margaret, is that you? Do you want me to pick you up? Fine, I'll be there in an hour."

Marvin was standing right behind him when he powered down the phone. "Don't trust that witch. She is more powerful than you think."

Jack smiled. "Trust me."

Marvin said, "I think this is a huge mistake. She could ruin everything."

Jack opened the fridge, pulled out half of a steak they had had the night before and started to eat it. Nora appeared, coming out of the knot hole in the moulding. She asked, "Where are we going?"

Jack said in between chews, "I'm going, you're staying."

Nora flew up and landed on his shoulder. "I promised Ivan I would look after you. I'm coming, like it or not!"

Jack said, "Fine, get in." He held his breast pocket open. He turned to Marvin. "I'll fill you in on all the details." He went back to the fridge, took out a juice and slid it into his pocket. He hit the stairs and in a couple of minutes he was at the bottom. He stopped and said to Nora, "This is amazing! Three flights of stairs and I never had to rest once."

Nora climbed up and said into his ear, "I think you are ready to regenerate. You look much younger. And I have never seen someone hold so much energy."

Jack asked, "Will I *have* to regenerate? And can you feel my power?"

Nora answered, "You *will* have to regenerate. We can't have an 82-year old man running around like he's twenty. By the way, where is your cane?" Jack held his pocket open. Nora took the hint and crawled back inside.

Chapter Seventeen
Setting Up Margaret

Jack opened the door and stepped out into the car park. Andre had the car parked at the blank wall where the lift was. Jack gave a wave and the Lincoln coasted up to him.

Andre got one foot out the door when Jack slid in the passenger side. Andre turned back into the car and looked at Jack, "You have to let me do my job. And act your age!"

Jack said, stone-faced, "We have to go. It is very important that we get this right the first time."

Andre sat staring at Jack, then he spoke, "Marvin and I were talking. We think it is very dangerous to work with Margaret. It would be easier just to kill her. She is not to be trusted."

Jack turned and said, "Just drive. This can be done."

Andre pulled out of the car park and headed down the road. He turned to Jack and said, "I hope you know what you're doing."

Jack replied, "I hope this works." He closed his eyes and fell asleep within a block. Nora crawled out of his pocket and hopped to the dash. She walked right in front of the steering wheel and sat down, looking at Andre.

Andre smiled and started to chat with her. He asked her where she was born, if she was ever married, and other personal stuff. Nora did the same. By the time they got to Brentwood, they pretty much knew each other. Andre told Nora to hold on and he hit the brakes a little harder than he needed to. That launched Jack into his seatbelt. He shook his head and wiped the sleep out of his eyes.

Andre told him that they were a couple of miles from Margaret's. Jack fished out his phone and hit Margaret's number. He said into the phone: "Hi, we will be there to pick you up in five minutes." He hit the messages and 15 missed calls showed up. He opened it and 14 were from his daughter and one from his son. He went back into contacts and clicked on John.

Nora, who had flown to his shoulder, asked, "Why are you calling your son, when your daughter called so many more times?"

Jack smiled and said, "Watch." Jack spoke into the phone, "Johnny, my boy! Hey, you might want to call your sister and tell her everything is all right. And I'll call her tonight sometime. No, I have some business I have to take care of. She died, funeral next week. Whenever I feel like it. Just call Mary." Jack rolled his eyes and sighed as he shut his phone off and said, "See, that didn't take long. If I had called Mary, she would have been on the phone for an hour."

Andre pulled up to the gate to get into Brentwood. It was a lovely day, sunny, with just a hint of a breeze. He asked Jack, "Do they know we are coming?"

Jack said, "Tell them Margaret Webster is expecting us."

Andre spoke to a golden speaker and the guard opened the gate. Andre said, "Well, we're in. I sure hope you know what you're doing."

Jack shook his head, then pointed to a gate. "That one. And everything should work out as planned. There are a lot of details to work out."

Andre pulled up to another speaker and a young woman's voice came on. He said, "A Mr Jack Robinson, here to see Margaret Webster."

The young woman said, "She will be right out."

Andre pulled up to the front of the mansion, a huge place with huge marble pillars. Margaret strolled down the stairs toward the car. Jack got out and so did Andre, who gave Jack a dirty look, so Jack backed away from the door. Margaret said a polite "Good morning."

Andre said, "Good morning," as he held the door open for her and helped her into the car. The younger woman carried a briefcase and handed it to Andre, who then handed it to Margaret. Andre closed the door and walked around, a little shocked to see Jack standing by the door on the other side. He walked over, opened the door for Jack and helped the old man into the car.

Once he was behind the wheel, he turned on the speaker system and asked, "Where would you like to go?"

Margaret said, "To Edward Woodlawn Law Service, here in town."

Andre punched it up on the on-board computer. A map came up, Andre studied it for a couple of seconds and said to the intercom, "It will be about half an hour, depending on traffic."

Nora crawled out from under the dash. Andre put his finger to his lips as he pulled the car down the drive. He waved to Nora so she would know to stay out of sight. The garden was perfect, all the shrubs were clipped with sharp edges or were rounded. Jack asked Margaret, "Do you have everything taken care of."

She said, "The solicitor is waiting for us."

Jack then asked, "Have you stopped at your safety deposit box and got the birth certificate?" He knew she hadn't.

Margaret pushed the talk button on the intercom and said forcefully, "Driver, turn around, we have to go back to the house." Margaret then pulled out her cell and said into it, "Linda, I need my safety deposit key now. Run it out to the car, we will be waiting for you."

Margaret apologised for not thinking of that before. Andre once more pulled up to the gate. This time there was a pause for a couple of minutes. Margaret said, "It might be a couple of minutes, I downsized my staff."

The young woman's voice came on. "I will meet you at the front."

Andre pulled up, got out and stood next to the passenger's back door. He saw her run down the flight of stairs and jog down the pavement to meet him. She gave him the key. He in turn walked up to the back door and the window powered down. He handed the key to Margaret.

Once they were on their way, the plan started to come together. Jack asked, "Is Linda, your faithful servant, going to be with you in your new life?"

There was a pause. Then she said, "I didn't think I had that option. Yes, I would love to have her at my side."

Jack started to weave a story. He said, "We will go to the bank and take out this birth certificate, go to the solicitor and get everything legal for transfer to your daughter that you had out of wedlock at a nunnery on the coast. Then we will fake your death. You will come back as a young lady, I will return as a younger man and we will go to the ceremony together. And all others will bow before us."

Margaret face was blank as she listened to it. She seemed like she was taking it all in. Andre double-parked in front of a large bank. He got out and opened Jack's door, then Margaret's. He told Jack to call him for a pick-up. Jack quickly caught up with Margaret. Then he hunched over and slowed down. They walked through a metal detector. Margaret went through and it beeped and the lights flashed. She stepped over to the guard. He opened her purse, peeked inside and motioned her in.

Jack slowly made his way through the detector. It beeped and flashed again. He handed the guard the briefcase and stepped back through. This time everything was quiet. Jack walked to the guard and asked rather loudly, "I suppose you want to go through my private papers. And where has Margaret gone to?"

The guard handed Jack back his briefcase and pointed to Margaret standing by a desk. Jack made his way toward her. When he got within ten feet of her, he said loudly, "What the hell is taking so long?"

Margaret turned around and put her finger to her lips. Jack commented, "What do they think, we have all day?"

A bank teller walked over and asked, "May I be of any help, sir?"

Jack pointed to Margaret. Margaret said, "We are here to get something from my safety deposit box."

The teller said that she could help. She opened a drawer and pulled out a form for Margaret to sign, asked if she had her key and what number it was. Then she pulled out a key and asked, "If you would follow me?"

She led them into a vault. Margaret took out her key and handed it to the teller. The young teller looked at it and said, "You have a large one. Would you like to look at it in here, or shall we take it into our viewing room?"

Margaret said, "I only need to get a document out of it."

The teller rolled over a table, then put both keys in the front of the box and turned them both at the same time. She then pulled the box out and slid it on the trolley. Margaret told her that she would only be a minute and then she could put it back.

Margaret opened the box to show stacks of bills, gold coins and stacks of titles. Jack opened his briefcase and told Margaret, "You never saw me touch the box." He rummaged through the papers, there were house titles from around the world, stocks and bonds and contracts. Jack put some of the papers into his briefcase, then took them all out and put them into the box. He then said, "Now what are you waiting for? Grab that damn certificate and let's get out of here."

Margaret looked through a few papers, then handed one to Jack. He put it in his briefcase and said, "Boy, how many properties do you own? OK, let's get going."

Margaret asked, "Don't you think we will need some walking-around money, while I get my fortune changed over?"

Jack smiled and said, "I have money."

Margaret started to hand Jack stacks of banded bills, all hundreds. He stacked them neatly in his brief case.

Margaret said, "That should be a hundred grand. That's my walking around money."

Jack's eyes met hers. He said softly, "Yes, I will count it and write it down. This is your money."

Margaret told Jack that she would get the teller to put the box away. Jack smiled as he said, "You don't want to kill me, I am your ally!" He took a .38 double-barrelled derringer out of his pocket and handed it to her.

Margaret blushed. She took the pistol and put it back in the safety deposit box and shyly said, "I wouldn't kill you. I don't know the odds. You were sent to kill me and rob me. Who sent you?"

Jack said, "All in good time."

Margaret stepped out of the vault and waved the teller in. The small girl swiftly strolled in, lifted the table to the hole and slid the box back into its place. She then took the keys out of the front of the box, handed one to Margaret and said, "That is one heavy box!"

Margaret just said, "Thank you," then tipped her nose in the air and walked out. Jack slowly walked out, hunched over and carrying the briefcase.

Andre had seen them and pulled up with his flashers on. He was standing there with the door open for Margaret. She got in. Jack stopped to take a break. Andre jogged over to him, took the briefcase and his arm and helped him to the car. Jack said, "Do I look like my old self?"

Andre said with a chuckle, "You forgot your cane again."

Jack stopped and looked at him, "Ah nuts! Why don't I remember that stupid thing? I have carried that thing for a year now!"

Andre said, "Come on, I'm double-parked." They rounded the car and Jack got in and got handed the briefcase.

As soon as Andre got behind the wheel, Margaret ordered, "To the solicitors, and be quick about it." Andre told her that the GPS said 15 minutes. He pulled out from the curb and swung a U-turn. Well, almost a U-turn—the Lincoln was a bit too long for that—it turned into a Y-turn.

Jack opened the briefcase and unloaded the case into the bar. Jack was impressed, "Hey, the Champagne is cold!"

Andre answered, "Would you like me to have it uncorked for you, sir, when you return?"

Jack spoke in a sophisticated voice, "Yes, that would be grand. And if you would clean out the bar? It seems like someone has left some garbage in it."

Andre swung the limo in front of the solicitors. He hopped out and walked around to Margaret's side, opened the door and gave her a hand out. Then Jack held out his hand. Andre took it and gave Jack the dirty eye. Jack just raised an eyebrow, then said, "I will call you to pop the bubbly."

He stepped in closer to Margaret so that they were arm-in-arm. Jack stopped and looked her in the eye to feel her out. He exclaimed, "Oh, you have it done every twenty years!"

She then asked, "Why do you wait so long to change?"

Jack said, "A long time ago, I had a very bad experience during a regeneration, so I put it off as long as possible."

Margaret said, "You do know that the longer you wait, the harder it is? I get little upgrades every couple of years; it's better than plastic surgery."

They reached the door to the solicitor. The receptionist came out from behind the desk and escorted them to his office. Margaret went in first. An elderly man stood, came around the desk and exclaimed, "Margaret, it's so nice to see you!" He put out his hand and shook hers, then asked, "And who is this?"

Margaret said, "This is Jack Robinson. He is from Oregon, we'll get to that in a minute. For now, just an old friend—well, a bit more than that."

Jack reached out, took the solicitor's hand and looked him in the eye. He, paused then, "Ah Bill, you will listen to me. You will do as I ask. If not, I will have you disbarred and imprisoned. I know all about your affairs and your drug habits. You're dealing with the Italian mob and most of all, that first wife of yours! A drive-by shooting while you were in the car? How daring! Bill, you go sit in your chair. Margaret, you sit in that chair over there and every time she says Jack, you will hear Jaclyn. And when we refer to our child, you will think it is a she. Now, shall we get started?"

Bill started things out, "And why are you here? Are we selling or buying?" Jack sat the briefcase on the desk, popped it open and handed him the birth certificate. Bill held it up to the light and studied it for a moment. His hand went to his forehead, then he asked, "Margaret, you had a child?"

Margaret said quietly, "Yes, I did. As you see, it was a long time ago."

Bill then asked, "And where is the child? Or should I say the young woman?"

Margaret said, "I have no idea. I sold it to a travelling circus a week after it was born."

Jack jumped in, "And I am the father of this child. Back then I paid her ten grand to keep it quiet. Now, I want to find her and give her an inheritance."

Margaret said, "Yes, I want to do the same. I want to put her in my will as the main recipient."

Bill looked at his computer and said, "OK. What you want to do is change your will to your daughter Jaclyn, from your niece Barbara?"

Margaret nodded, "Yes, that is what I want."

Bill then turned to Jack and a small tick came to his face. "And you, sir. You want me to change your will and you want me to find your son."

Jack said, "*I* will find my son. You contact my solicitor up in Oregon and have him send you my will and change it, leaving everything to my new son. I will straighten everything out with my kids. Hell, I put them through college! And they make more than I ever did."

Margaret said, "One more thing. Linda is still the executor of the will."

Jack stood and said, "That's a great idea," and announced, "That should take care of that, we're leaving."

Bill said, "Wait just a minute." He pushed a button and told his secretary to come in and copy a birth certificate. Bill asked Margaret if she minded.

Margaret said, "You know, that's a good idea. That is the only one I know of, it is stamped copy so it can't be the only one."

Bill smiled and said, "The ink is old, but it is a stamped copy. That does mean there is an original out there somewhere."

Margaret said, "It's been forty years now. I might have given the original to the couple that took the baby." The secretary came in with the copy and handed it to Bill, who handed Margaret hers.

Jack took his mobile phone out of his pocket and called Andre. He said, "We will be at the curb in five minutes."

Bill said, "This will be on the top of my list, sir. Everything should be done tomorrow, if I get your last will and last testament."

When they got to the pavement, Margaret stopped and turned to Jack. "As long as I have dealt with Bill, he has never gave me time. He's good, but he is slow."

Jack said, "He knows that I know what he has done. And let me tell you, that is one sick puppy. And he has some shady dealing with the mob." The two walked arm-in-arm down the pavement, Jack all hunched over and Margaret standing tall, walking in four-inch heels and dressed to the tee.

Andre stood next to the car with the door open. When the two reached the car, Andre took Margaret by the hand, helped her into the car and closed her door. He took Jack by the arm and quietly said, "How did it go? By the way, there was about a hundred grand in the bar. Was that my tip?"

Jack took a few steps with him around the car, slowly looked both ways, then stopped, turned to him and said, "Yes, everything went to plan. Did you uncork the champagne?"

Andre said, "Bollinger '74. A very good year, sir." He opened the car door and Jack slipped inside. Margaret handed him a glass of champagne. He looked into her eyes and could see that she was worried. He looked deeper and asked, "Why are you so worried?"

Margaret was in a trance. "I do not trust you. I am not in control. How do I know you won't just have me killed?"

Jack said, "From now on, you will trust me more than anyone you know. I need you and without you, I can't succeed." Then Jack asked, "Did you put anything in the champagne?"

Margaret said, "No."

Then Jack snapped his fingers. He said, "Awake." Margaret's facial expressions came back. He said, "Now we are toasting to a new world order! We shall rule and you shall be my right hand." He spoke loudly, "Drive to Margaret's. She has to get her affairs in order if we are to pull this off."

He clinked glasses with Margaret and said, "This is the start of a new and powerful alliance."

They took a sip Margaret started to ask question after question. Jack handled it beautifully. She wanted to know why he hadn't regenerated. Jack said to her, "Nobody thinks of an old man as being a threat, and nothing is expected of me. Everyone thinks I am just a tired old coot."

Margaret asked, "Are you going to regenerate?" Jack read her mind. She wanted Jack to be a young and handsome guy, but also she thought that would be her chance of killing him off.

Jack said, "We have some business to take care of in upstate New York. Then I shall regenerate to around 35 or so."

Margaret took a long sip of champagne and said, "That would be nice. We will be the same age."

Jack told her the plan. "I have to take over North America first. I am working with seven other guardians spread throughout the world. We meet once a year and have for ten years now."

Margaret believed every word; she kept nodding. Then she asked, "What is the plan for my regeneration?"

Jack said, "You are going to commit suicide, then you are going to New Orleans for a month—a nice slow regeneration—and do some work there."

She asked, "How am I going to commit suicide?"

Jack smiled. "I will handle the police. You're going to hang yourself from that beautiful staircase of yours. I will pull enough power from you so you will look dead for the police. We took care of the funeral arrangements in your new will. Linda will have a funeral with an urn full of somebody's ashes. She will have a small presentation, pictures—nothing big. A quick send off and you will be there to watch. Won't that be nice?"

Margaret said, "Then we get married and combine our estates."

Jack said, "No, I think we will be partners first. I don't even know you. I don't want to jump into marriage right away. We have a lot of work to do."

They pulled up in front of Margaret's mansion and Jack said, "You have a lot of work to get done and only a few days to do it in."

Chapter Eighteen
Back from the Solicitors

Andre pulled away from the house and down the long drive to the gate. When he got close to it, Jack told him to stop. He got out, jumped into the passenger's side and asked Andre, "Do you think she bought it?"

Andre said, "Some of the stuff was pretty far-fetched—taking over the world? You're not going to try that, are you? I don't know much about the blues."

The ride back to the castle was uneventful. As soon as Andre pulled out of Margaret's drive, Jack asked for a Starbucks. He told Andre, "In Oregon, I drank at least two pots a day."

Andre tapped the GPS. Four of them popped up. There was one four blocks away. Jack filled Andre in about the solicitor and the will. Andre pulled up to the Starbucks and asked him what he wanted. Jack said, "Just a triple shot mocha. And a blueberry scone, a brownie, banana nut bread. And water."

Andre put in Jack's order and said, "I'll get this one, I've fallen into a bit of cash lately."

Jack took a sip of coffee to wash done the scone, then said, "About that. I'm going to give some of that to Marvin for repairs on the plane. Other than that, it's spending cash. Everything you touch nowadays costs money."

Andre said in a mobster's voice, "You know everything works better with a little grease."

Jack shook his head and said, "You know my wife Emma gave 13 percent as a tip where ever she went. Even if it was terrible service."

Andre said, "Well, you're with me now. Did you see me tell the girl at Starbucks to keep the change? She greeted us with a smile and asked if she could do anything for us. Hey, that was worth forty cents!"

Jack asked, "How far is the castle from Brentwood?"

Andre told him, "That depends on what time of day it is."

Jack stared at him for a minute, then said, "That doesn't make any sense."

Andre smiled, "It's a traffic thing. Right now it should take a half hour to 45 minutes. Between 4:00–8:00, it could take two to three hours, depending."

The Magic Castle came into view. Jack said a little prayer, "God, I hope I can pull this off."

Andre dropped Jack off at the back of the castle. Jack walked over to the blank wall and looked for the panel to push to open it. He closed his eyes, then started to wave his hands and chant. He finally said, "Open sesame." He started to wave his hand again. This time, he moved over a couple of feet, looking at the ground. He pushed a small panel on the cement with his foot while he waved his hands, then stepped in close. He put his hand on the siding and the wall slid open.

Andre stepped in behind him and said, "You're getting better at this. But we should use the stairs more. If someone is watching this place, they'll figure it out." They walked to the side of the building. Andre punched in a code and then opened the door.

When they reached the top floor, Jack asked, "When does the restaurant open?"

Andre asked, "How can you eat so much?"

Elizabeth flew over and asked, "Did you kill her?"

Jack said, "No, I didn't kill her! What kind of question is that?"

Marvin walked into the room. "Then we have a problem. Margaret will turn you. She is very strong. While she is in the picture, she is a threat."

Jack stepped over to him and put his hand on his shoulder. Marvin wouldn't look him in the eye. He knew Jack was strong enough to hypnotise him. Jack said, "You just have to trust me."

Then he asked, "How is Juliet doing? Mind if I go and see her?"

When he walked into the room, Boris flew up. "Did you do it? Is she gone?"

Jack didn't answer. He asked, "How is Juliet doing?"

Boris told him, "We are slowly bringing her out of the coma she was in. She is a strong woman, she should be fine. It's just going to take some time." Jack stepped close to her as she lay in the bed. She still had an IV but no monitors. He put his hand on her forehead and closed his eyes.

When he opened them, he saw everyone standing there, waiting for him. Marvin said, "So did you reach her?"

Jack said, "I just told her how everything was going. And Marvin, she told me to give you her love."

A tear ran down Marvin's weathered face. He choked out, "I love you too, my love."

Andre said, "I fixed you a salad and water."

Jack walked back into the kitchen and sat at the table. He looked up and said, "I'd rather have coffee, and what is up with the salad, I thought I was supposed to be eating protein."

Andre said, "Take that up with Nora," who was sitting on Andre's shoulder. Jack picked up his fork and started to eat.

Boris came flying in and landed on the table. He asked Jack, "So when are we going?"

Jack looked at him, finished chewing and then swallowed. He asked, "Going where?"

Boris blushed. "They didn't tell you? We have to go back. You have to stand in front of the council."

Jack sat there with his fork halfway to his mouth and his mouth hung open. He cocked his head, then said, "I have so much to do here! I can't just up and leave!"

Elizabeth flew to the table and looked at him. "You have to do this! It is my duty. I have to bring you in front of the council."

Boris flew to Jack's shoulder. "We have to replace that fairy dust. Without it, my people will starve."

Jack conceded. "OK, when did you want to go?"

Andre spoke, "Well, we have a flight plan and we have to leave here in about a half hour or so. I'll bring the car around and load the fairies."

Jack said, "Wait a minute! You have a fight plan? This was planned all along! And fairies! What fairies?"

Andre calmly said, "We didn't want to stress you out any more than we had to. The green fairy made it perfectly clear that we had to do this. And the fairies—there are about four hundred that need to go to the coast. It's not far out of the way. And a couple hundred to the forest."

Jack gave Elizabeth a stern look and spoke to her with authority, "Now you listen here! I am in charge here, not you! Everything goes my way, OK? Do you hear, Lizard Breath?"

He turned to Andre and said with a look, "OK, I'll go. I do owe the council an apology. But we are not going to use that short runway."

He nodded, then took another bite of salad, washing it down with a long drink of water. He then asked, "When?"

Andre said, "Nora, get the fairies down here. I'll grab a few empty wine cases, that's what they will be travelling in."

Jack got up from the table and poured himself a cup of coffee, then said in an old cranky voice, "I asked you something. How much time do I have before we leave?"

Andre asked, "How long before you get your stinky butt out of the shower?"

Jack grumbled, "For Christ's sake!" He took a sip from his cup and walked toward the bathroom. He popped in Juliet's room and asked Marvin, who was rubbing Juliet's hand, "Did you know about this trip to Oregon?"

Marvin put Juliet's arm under the covers very gently. He turned and said, "I wish I could go with you. The council would listen to me. And yes, I knew about it. The green fairy wants to settle this and get on her way."

Jack said as he walked out the room, "She isn't going anywhere."

Nora flew up and started to apologise. Jack said, "Shut it, I'm taking a shower. And you don't have to watch." He put the cup to his lips and tipped it up. He said, "Here, take this and fill it. Leave it on the table and tell Dropoff 15 minutes. Oh yeah, and set out some clothes out for me." He walked into the bathroom.

Marvin walked into the kitchen and Nora was struggling to handle the coffee pot. Marvin said, "Here, let me help you with that." He reached down, took the pot and filled the cup that was on the table. "Now tell me why Jack is ticked off," Marvin said.

Nora flew up and landed on Marvin's palm. She said, "That would be Elizabeth, making plans for him to stand in front of the fairy council. He thinks he is in charge."

Marvin smiled, "He *is* in charge here. Without him, we all die."

Nora said, "Well, my job is to take care of him and Boris's job is to regenerate you and him."

Marvin said, "What about my Juliet?"

Nora replied, "Ivan wanted you and Jack to wage war and free us all."

Marvin said, "I'm saving Juliet before anything else."

Boris flew up and landed next to Nora. He said, "I will go and speak to the council on Jack's behalf. Rupert is skilled; he can handle Juliet for a couple of days."

Jack stepped out of the shower with a towel wrapped around his waist. He walked into the kitchen and grabbed the coffee, stepped up to Marvin and asked, "What is going on?"

Marvin said, "I should stay here with Juliet. Boris will come and plead your case."

Jack took a sip of his coffee, then said, "No, Boris is staying. Nora, you and Lizard are coming, end of story." He took his coffee and went back into the bathroom."

Marvin asked, "Who is Lizard?"

Boris spoke, "That would be Elizabeth. Lizard Breath, as Jack would call her." The knot hole in the kitchen was opened and a stream of fairies came flying out, one after another. There were hundreds of them. They flew out and landed anywhere they could find room.

Andre said, "I don't think we have enough boxes for all of them."

The green fairy was the last one out. She hovered in the middle of the room and asked Marvin, "I have assembled the fairies that have come from up the coast. What next?"

Marvin asked, "How many are there?"

Elizabeth said, "There are 742, not counting the 76 that are too weak to travel."

Andre asked, "Can we fit a hundred in each case?"

Nora flew to the cases that were stacked by the door. Elizabeth looked at them and said, "Easily."

Andre said, "I'll go down and empty a couple more cases."

Nora flew to his shoulder and said into his ear, "Could you get four more boxes?"

Andre nodded and said, "Yes, I was going to. It would be a really tight fit otherwise. I was thinking maybe 50 per case." Andre then asked, "Do you want to go with?"

Nora said, "If it keeps me away from Elizabeth, then sure!" Andre stepped into the lift, pushed the button and they were gone.

Jack stepped out of the bathroom cleanly shaven. He had cut his hair. It didn't look too bad. He asked, "Now, what's going on?"

Marvin sat at the table talking to a small group of red fairies. He looked up and said, "Elizabeth is organising the fairies according to what colonies they come from. Then she is going to pack them in the wine cases for travel. Your clothes are laid out on your bed by Nora, like you asked."

Jack picked up his cup, took a long swig and apologised, "I'm sorry. I have a lot on my plate right now."

Marvin raised his cup. "I understand. Always keep the high hand with the green one. She has more power than you think."

Jack then asked, "When is the flight?"

Marvin chuckled, "Well, when you own the plane it can be anytime."

Jack pulled up a chair. "God, there are a lot of fairies! You would have though we knew they were here."

Marvin said quietly, "A lot of good people have died to keep their secret."

Jack finished his coffee and said, "Time to suit up. This should be interesting!"

Marvin spoke loudly, "Pack an overnight bag."

Andre stepped out of the lift; the whole back wall was filled with empty wine cases. He sat next to Marvin and said, "Boy, did we ever score at Margaret's! There's got to be a hundred thousand dollars' worth of wine. Boy, there's some good stuff down there. I brought up a 1962 bottle of champagne. I'll put it the fridge for when we get back."

Marvin asked, "Well, what are you waiting for? Start packing them."

Elizabeth flew around and started to bark orders. Fairies flew into the lift and stacked boxes next to the other boxes in the kitchen. They left one row on the floor. Elizabeth flew to a small group on the fridge. You could tell that they were the elders of their colonies.

Marvin said to Nora, "Fly up there and find out what is taking so long."

Nora did as she was told. She fluttered up and asked the group, "They want to know what the holdup is."

Elizabeth said, "OK, if you're so smart, how many fairies go in each box?"

Nora said, "I'll ask Marvin if he has an adding machine." Nora hopped down and told Marvin what they were doing and asked him about an adding machine.

Andre stood and pulled his mobile phone from his pocket and walked to the fridge, "OK. How many fairies are there?" Elizabeth told him there were 742. He tapped his phone, then said, "That will be around 60 per box. Now how many per colony?"

They sat and figured out how many and how to mark the boxes. Soon, there were fairies flying all over. Jack came out of the bedroom with an overnight bag, dressed in a nice shirt, pair of jeans and tennis shoes. He pulled up a chair to the table. Marvin said, "OK now, don't take any shit from the council. They are going to charge you with theft of their dust and a whole lot more. Tell them you will never tell a soul. And tell them I am doing much better; Juliet and I are going through regeneration and should be up next year."

Jack said, "Nora and I have figured out my defence. Which pretty much goes: here is five times the dust I stoled. I'll recharge your stone and I will pledge an allegiance with you. The biggest thing is to get them their dust back so they don't starve."

Andre got up. "I'll pull the car around and start loading the cases." He stepped into the lift, which was half full of boxes. The door closed and he was gone.

Jack and Marvin sat, drank their coffee and talked about Juliet's funeral and funerals they had gone to before. Marvin told him about her last funeral. It had lasted for days. People from around the globe came and they had a three-ring circus. They went into Juliet's room, where Boris and Rupert were applying a pink salve to her feet. Marvin said, "Here," as he waved his hand toward a large circus poster.

It had a line of acts in bold letters: "This show is in remembrance of the greatest showgirl on earth, Madame Joyce of Sweden!"

Jack said, "You threw her a party."

Marvin said, "Hell, *she* planned and hosted it. It was a celebration of her life. She died a star. We had no choice. She missed a trapeze and fell. There was no net. That's why she is still with us—she can't die."

Jack leaned over her bed and placed his hand on her head, closed his eyes and mumbled, "You get better. Marvin will watch over these guys and I'll be back in a couple of days." Jack looked up at Marvin. "She grows stronger all the time."

Marvin's eyes filled with tears. He turned to look at Jack and a huge smile came over his face. He blubbered, "Have you noticed that her skin is no longer grey?"

Jack turned back and he looked at Juliet. This time he studied her. "Her hair is growing and it's blonde. The age spots are disappearing."

Marvin stepped over to him, put his arm around his shoulders and said, "Thank you so very much! I can never repay you. Now get out of here and don't take any crap from the council."

Jack stood and looked Marvin in the eye. "You know I have to go. If Margaret gives you any shit, tell her that you know nothing and I will rule the world of the blues. I know, don't ask—there is a hundred million at stake here. That is why I didn't kill her."

Nora flew to his shoulder. "Jack, it's time to go," she said in his ear.

Jack pointed at Boris and said in a stern voice, "You two, no shortcuts!" He walked out of the room into the kitchen, where Andre was waving to him. There was just enough room for Jack to squeeze in with wine cases piled three high across the floor. Jack asked, "Aren't we overloading the lift?"

Andre said, "Each case weighs about five pounds. The trick is not to raise suspicion loading the jet. We should be in the hangar."

Jack asked, "Are we taking a pickup to the airport?"

Andre chuckled, "You would not believe the room in a limo! There's plenty of room." He said, "You stay here and hand me the cases." Jack handed the cases to Andre. He set them in the back door and they would disappear. In five minutes the lift was empty.

Jack walked out and got into the passage door that Andre was holding. Soon, they were on their way to the airport. Andre called with the hands-free phone that was built into the car. "Hey, Pickupski, how is the plane? She's all gassed up. Did you get my flight plan? See you in half an hour. I'm going to drive right into the hangar to load."

He cancelled the call, then said, "Damn it all! I was hoping he wouldn't be there."

Jack asked, "Why?"

Andre said, "Oh, he got stuck cleaning up my mess. If anything breaks, it breaks when I'm using it." He pulled into the private section of the airport, came to a gate and showed the guard his ID. He asked if he could pull into the hangar. The guard pulled out his walkie-talkie and a gate to the left opened. Andre said, "A lot of people don't want to be seen, so this is common practice." Andre pulled into a large hangar that had half a dozen jets parked in it.

Jack asked, "Is this Marvin's?"

Andre smiled, "No, we own this jet and that six-passenger gull. We rent the hangar like everyone else."

When they pulled up, a tall man who looked like Andre's brother opened Jack's door. Jack got out and thanked the man. He introduced himself, "Hi, I am Ivan. We met on your arrival. I suppose you don't remember me."

Jack shook his head, "I don't remember much of that plane ride—or after."

Ivan said, "You look one hundred percent better than you did then. You looked and smelled like you were dead."

Andre said, "OK, let's start loading this. We have to get out of here." Andre leaned into the back door of the limo and came out with a wine case; he sat it next to the limo. Andre laid out the plan for loading. "Ivan, you take them from the limo, hand them to Jack, who will hand them to me."

Ivan said, "Why the hell do I have to climb in the car?"

Andre said, "Just trust me."

Ivan stepped to the back door. There were three cases sitting in the doorway. He took them and handed them to Jack, who handed them to Andre. He lifted them and slid them into the plane. Ivan stepped back to find three more cases waiting for him. He quickly took them to Jack and jogged back to catch the fairies moving the cases, but they already had them waiting for him. He looked inside and they had the wine cases stacked inside and were pushing three out at a time. He popped his head inside the limo and said, "Thank you very much! And good luck on your travels." He knew they wouldn't show themselves unless they had to.

Andre said, "That went well. Just ten minutes."

Ivan said, "Your flight plans to Oregon are loaded. There will be a Cadillac Escalade in your name. It will pull up to the jet."

Andre said, "I am so sorry about leaving you with such a mess!"

Ivan said, "Everything is good, I hired out the repairs to the plane. I have today off, then 13 days of flying that I couldn't reschedule. We may have lost a couple of clients."

Jack said, "Hey, where is the restroom?"

Andre said, "Use the one on board."

Ivan wished them luck and told Andre he'd tow them out of the hangar. Jack started to climb the stairs when Ivan handed him his cane. "Here, you had better use this when you get home."

Jack took it and scoffed, "That damn thing!" He ducked, sticking his head into the plane. Everything came to a stop; about 30 fairies were adjusting the cases. Jack said, "It's just me. And why don't you strap them in with the seat belts?" He showed them how to use the seat belts, then he dropped the upper compartments. "See, a case can fit in here." The fairies were belting everything. Jack made it back to the bathroom. He opened the door and barked a command, "Get this stuff out of here! How is a guy supposed to piss?"

Andre climbed aboard and pulled up the stairs. He looked in and commented, "Looking good." It took only two fairies to carry a case—one could have done it, but they were hard to handle. They took the three cases out of the bathroom. Jack went in and did his business; he checked the cargo on his way to the cockpit when the plane started to move.

Andre said over the intercom, "Pickup moved the limo. Now he's towing us outside."

Jack slid in the co-pilot's seat. He asked, "Is everything going according to plan?"

Andre, who was checking things off on a clipboard, said, "Everything is on schedule. Wait, I told Boris that you would have water with you at all times."

Nora buzzed off to the back and returned with a bottle of water. She was gripping it by the cap with her feet. Jack reached out and took it. "Thanks," he said.

Andre checked with the tower, fired up the engines and did a pre-flight check. "I have to do a walk-through to make sure everything is secure." He said, "Close enough."

He put his head phones on and talked to the tower; he thanked them for letting him land straight off last week. They taxied right onto a runway Andre turned to Jack. "And off we go!" The jet picked up speed and they slowly lifted off the ground. He pulled it up to cruising speed, set the cruise and talked with the tower for a couple of seconds.

Nora was right up front on the dash; Jack said, "Don't you touch any of those switches!"

Andre said, "Jack, now's a good time for you to take a nap. You have three to four hours, depending on the wind."

Jack took a long swig out of his bottle and said, "I think I'll go in back and talk to some of the fairies."

Jack stepped in back and opened a case; he asked, "What colony are you from?" They all started to talk at once. Elizabeth flew to the case and landed on the edge. Not one word was spoken. Jack said, "OK, let's try this. Has anyone one heard of a green fairy called Aurora?"

Jack looked at Elizabeth and said, "I tried. Now who is going to speak for this box?" Elizabeth hopped over to a group of old fairies. Jack excused himself for a moment and walked back to the cock-pit; he motioned to Nora. She fluttered up to his outstretched hand and landed on his palm. Jack whispered, "Not right away! Give it a couple of minutes. Find out what the green one is up to. And don't let her catch you!" He gave a wink. Then, in a loud voice he asked, "Captain, is everything going well?"

Andre said, "We're making good time; we have a tailwind."

Jack walked back to the box he was talking to. "So do we have a speaker?"

A rusty-red fairy flew to the side of the box. "I guess I am the speaker."

Jack asked, "Where is your colony?"

The fairy said, "We have been a colony for a long time. The last place we lived is up the Rat River. We lived with a powerful guardian. He was killed and most of the fairies where taken as slaves. I don't know if Mary, our guardian's wife, lived. Or if there is anyone from the colony left."

Jack said, "That changes everything! We can't just take you guys up there and let you go! We have to find your colony."

A streak of green light flashed past. Elizabeth was standing on the box. "We do as planned—land. And as soon as it is dark, we release the fairies."

Jack turned and then stated sternly, "That's not the way it's going to happen! I will not allow them to be released unless they are in a safe location."

Elizabeth started to argue but Jack said, "Lizard Breath, this is the way it is going to be." A light green glow could be seen illuminating the plane's interior. Jack held out his hand palm up. "Jump aboard," and the rusty fairy did. He headed back to the cockpit; he slid into the co-pilot's seat and held the fairy up to Andre.

Jack said, "This is Andre Dropoff. He is our pilot and driver. You will have to tell him where your colony is and he will take us there."

Andre asked, "Who will answer my question about the green light boiling back there?"

Jack smiled, "Yeah, Lisa isn't very happy, but we can't send them into a trap. They don't even know if there is a colony left."

Andre said, "Hey, it's your dime! But we have to get you back."

Nora said, "That was boring. They were talking about the world outside earth, where Elizabeth lives. And the old one is saying that the blue fairies were chased off the earth because of eating human flesh—I heard it all before. What I came up here to tell you are that you should call your kids, they're going to be worried."

Jack let out, "Ah nuts, I guess I can call John. He should be on his way home from work now, so he won't talk long." Jack wiggled in his seat, took out his phone and turned it on. He turned to Andre and asked, "Have you ever heard that the blue fairies eat human flesh?"

Andre said, "Yes I have. Marvin described it once. They tear a child apart, slowly, in some ritual. And the white guardians gathered all the blue fairies in the world and banished them to some distant planet that didn't have anyone living there."

Jack looked at his phone. "Wow, 27 messages, most from Mary, a couple from John, and a number I don't know."

Andre said, "Call that one first, it's probably Marvin. He changes phones all the time."

Jack called the number and Marvin answered it. Jack talked for just a minute, then made a sign like he was writing. Andre handed him a notebook with a pen clipped to it. Jack wrote down five things. He then ripped off the page and yelled for Nora. He handed her the paper. "You're in charge of getting this shopping list filled."

She laid the paper out on the console, read it, then asked, "Do we have some small jars, or something to put this in?"

Jack said, "Remind me to pick up some Ziploc bags." He then dialled his son. The conversation was short and to the point. "I am on my way back home to tie up some loose ends. Do not worry. And tell your sister that everything is fine."

He then went into contacts and called Margaret, "Yes Linda, tell Maggie Jack flew out and is pleading their case. Two days max—not to worry. I will take out Marvin, then she will regenerate. Get things in order."

Jack leaned over to Andre. "Hey, remind me that I have to get the title of the town car and sign it over to Earl. It's junk. I guess the fire was hot enough to blister the paint behind the front doors. And let's face it, it was old."

Andre spoke over the intercom, "We will be landing in 35 minutes. Time to get back in your boxes and put on your seat belts!" He turned and said to Jack, "Now is the time to take a leak if you want. And check the overhead storage."

Jack walked back to the restroom and did his business. On his way back, he checked the overhead compartments and clicked seatbelts over the cases. Jack sat down. "I still can't believe blues would eat children!"

Andre said, "Yeah, that's what I heard. And I guess some of them stayed. I have to land this thing. It should be better than my last landing."

Jack asked Nora what she had heard about the blues eating people. Nora said, "A long, long time ago—we are talking thousands of years before Christ—the white guardians came down, gathered all the blues together and shot them up into space. See, blues can't travel though space like the green ones do. Elizabeth can fly off to the stars anytime, but she has to take you to the council."

Jack asked, "What if she just splits? I mean, no one would know."

Elizabeth landed on his shoulder. "I came to find my cousin and my Honour is at stake here."

Nora said, "And you're safe with Jack around."

Elizabeth shot her an 'I'm going to kill you' look, then she scoffed, "You're the one who is using Jack as a shield!"

Andre announced, "Here we go!" A straight shot in—he made a sweeping bank and put it down. All you could hear were the tyres hitting the runway. He taxied halfway back and headed towards a couple of smaller hangars, off to the right.

Jack got up and said, "I'll take a leak now." He headed to the restroom, checking the cases, making sure they hadn't fallen over on the way.

Nora asked Andre, "How do you know where to go?"

He pointed to the tower and said, "Inside my headphones—the guys up there tell me what to do, when I can land, take off, where to park. They run the place."

He pulled into a hangar and parked next to a big black Cadillac Escalade. He walked over, dropped the staircase and walked to the Caddy. He opened the driver's door, lifted the floor mat, picked up the keys and slid in behind the wheel. He manoeuvred the Caddy so it was two feet from the plane's stairs. Jack stepped out and said, "Just like before, let's get this unloaded."

A dozen fairies slowly climbed out of a case, they were looking around out the windows. Nora flew up and said, "Stay away from the open door and stay as close to the ground as you can. I haven't seen anyone, but I'm sure there are cameras."

Jack said, "Where is the crew for inside the truck?"

Andre popped his head in and said, "I'll load this, you can't be seen. Jack, one case at a time, these cases are supposed to be heavy."

Jack took two steps down the stairway so he could still reach into the jet. He took one case and handed it to Andre, who put it in the Caddy. Andre stacked them three high and pushed them in. He had the rear seat pushed up as far as it would go—all 17 cases slid right in there.

Jack said, "That only took twenty minutes. Not bad for a couple of old guys!" He said, "I'm going to double-check, make sure we haven't forgotten anything." He opened all the overhead doors and looked behind all eight seats. On his way from the back of the plane, he saw his suitcase strapped to the wall. He said with disgust in his voice, "Now how the hell did they miss that?"

Jack unstrapped it and took the cane. He walked down the stairs, bent over and pulled his case behind him, passing Andre, who had moved the car. Andre smiled, "Almost forgot your luggage? Hey, I'm going to shove the jet against the wall—ten minutes."

He walked over to a small tugger and walked behind it. He hooked it up to the front landing gear, then he did a quick walk to the plane and raised the stairs. He then positioned the plane into its parking spot. Andre did a half-jog to the Caddy. He got in, out of breath. "Boy, am I glad you're here! I need to regenerate; this is the oldest I've been in three hundred years."

Jack looked at him and said, "No way are you three hundred years old!" Andre shrugged, "More like a thousand—somewhere around there."

Nora popped out of Jack's breast pocket, "I think I remember. You came to the woods with Marvin."

Jack asked, "Do you know where you're going now?"

Andre said, "Let me programme the GPS and we can be on our way. Hopefully we can drop off the fairies before finding a hotel room—which there are just a few to pick from."

Jack told Andre, "Stop fiddling with the GPS and watch the road!"

Chapter Nineteen
To Sara's Place

Andre drove for what felt like forever. Jack asked Elizabeth, "Go out and find a blue to interrogate—better yet, find a red if you can." He opened the sunroof and Elizabeth flew out.

Within five minutes, Andre shouted, "Incoming!"

Jack looked down the road and a streak of green was coming right at them, followed by a dozen blue streaks. She slowed as she got to the Caddy, then shot by in a flash. Jack put his hand out the sunroof and closed his eyes; a small beam of light came from each blue and they followed it right to Jack. There was a popping noise as some of them disappeared. Jack pulled his hand back into the truck. There were two blue fairies suspended in an eerie blue light. You could hear the gasps of five hundred red fairies.

Jack smiled and asked in a friendly voice, "Hi, I was wondering how far your colony is—by road, that is."

The blue fairy just screeched. That one just popped in a spark and was gone. "OK. We can do it the hard way or the easy way."

The other blue started talking—it was just a bunch of snarls, screeches and grunts. Jack said, "Take Highway X for a few miles, then it comes to a crossroads. There is a towering pine you can see from there." Jack then asked, "How many entrances?"

The blue screeched and grunted, then popped a spark and then nothing. Elizabeth, who was sitting on the roof watching, said, "You're not thinking of attacking them?"

Jack smiled, "Well, we are here—and it'll be fun!"

Andre asked, "Are you sure about this?"

Jack said, "We have surprise on our side. Now is the time to do it!"

Andre pulled onto Highway X and started to climb, going into a dark and big forest. Jack said, "OK, Elizabeth, you and Nora plug the back entrance and I will pull all of them out the front."

Jack pulled out a piece of quartz the size of a soft ball. Nora asked, "How many blues are there?"

Jack smiled, "He really didn't say, but I think there are a few."

Andre reached the first crossroads, "Well, here we are!"

Jack got out and said, "I can feel them. They are watching us."

Nora fluttered to him and asked, "Are you sure about this?"

Jack said, "Now is the time. Tell Lizard Breath to get out there and take out the sentries." Jack took a long piss; a shot of green light went flying past, then came a blue spark with a popping noise.

Jack asked, "What is the easiest way of getting in there?"

Elizabeth said, "Full-out attack. Fly in there at full speed."

Nora said, "We can sneak in, watch them and look for weak spots."

Jack walked back to the Caddy, opened the door and slid in. He bent over and took off his shoes. Andre asked him again, "Are you sure about this?"

Jack looked at him and said, "Trust me, we take them out now! Then we won't have to fight them later. Anyway, we're here." He gingerly walked out barefoot. "All right, meet you at the big pine."

He pointed to Nora, "Change of plans. You plug the back entrance and hunt and destroy anyone that tries to get away."

With that, Jack flew off like a shot, leaving a white streak behind him, followed by a green and red. As soon as Jack got to the tree, he spotted the opening. He hovered right in front of it and pulled as much power as he could. A bright blue stream came from the tree. Jack was levitating the piece of quartz a foot from his hands and it glowed.

Elizabeth was out hunting blues at warp speed. All you seen was a beam of green light zipping between trees and sparks of blue. Nora flew right to the back entrance, dove onto a branch and was hammering it in with a rock. Jack flew straight up and shot a bolt into the tree, blowing the top of it right off. He then flew straight down into the tree, then back to the truck. Nora flew back with him. As soon as they landed, Jack took another piss and floated to the passenger door.

Nora landed on his shoulder. She stood there with her arms crossed and barked, "Was that worth it? You risked all our lives for what?"

Jack shot her a look. "There were damn near a thousand blues in that tree! Would you like to have met them when they had the advantage? We are at war. They are the enemy, and we released at least two thousand reds."

Elizabeth flew in the sunroof. "Don't worry about me. I just had to chase a couple down—must have taken twenty miles, but I got them."

Jack put his hand up with his palm up. "Come here."

Elizabeth landed on Jack's palm and a green glow filled the cabin of the truck. Jack said with pride in his voice, "You did good—very good. Now, as long as word doesn't get out, we should be OK."

Andre asked, "OK, now where?"

Jack said, "Back to the highway, to a small town called Cadot. Then follow the river up till you reach the high-tension power lines."

An old red fairy flew up and landed on the dash. He said, "She lives up at the top of that hill in a huge house, with beautiful gardens."

Jack shook his head, "Nope, she lives in a small house next to the power lines. And if we don't save her, she will die tonight."

Nora flew to the back and yelled, "OK now, power down! There is so much energy flowing out of this truck, they'll know we are coming."

Jack asked Andre, "Where is that lead lined photo bag?"

Andre said, "I didn't pack one."

Nora came flying up with it. "Damn it, Jack! You're going to get us all killed."

Jack smiled. "Thanks. And I didn't see you at work, but you must have done a good job plugging that hole."

Nora's face flushed; she was pissed. "You blew that tree in half!"

Jack slid the piece of quartz into the bag and said, "That's better."

Nora flew up to Jack, who just closed his eyes. Andre raised his hand. "Give him a minute; he has to think about what just happened."

Nora flew to the steering wheel, landing on the top. "That's not what I'm worried about; it's what he's planning to do."

Elizabeth landed right next to her and said, "This has to be done; those red guys don't have a chance if we don't take out the blues."

Nora said with a shaky voice, "You don't understand, it's not just blues, its guardians. And who knows how many?"

Jack opened one eye and said, "Three."

Nora stuttered, "Th—th—three? Margaret alone almost killed you and Marvin! What are we doing?"

Jack closed his eyes and said, "Rest. I think it's going to be a long, long night. It would be nice to get a bite to eat and some coffee. And maybe a scone."

Elizabeth looked at Nora and said, "It has to be done," and she flew back to the group of fairies in the back seat.

Nora just stood there, staring at Andre. He finally said, "You know, I think that green fairy is pissed. And it's not at Jack."

Jack opened his eyes. "She is going to be one hell of an asset, but don't tell her that."

Jack said, "This is good! There are the power lines. Let's do a drive-by first." Andre slowed, but not too much. Down to about 45, they passed a small ranch-style house. Jack said excitedly, "That's it! Nora, do you feel anything?"

The red fairy said sadly, "Yes I do. I feel this is one big mistake."

Jack shot her a dirty look, "You know what I mean! If they're going to knock her off, you would think they would be watching the place."

Nora said, "There *are* blues, but the power from the lines mixes in with everything and it just feels like a buzz."

Jack smiled, "That is why Sara moved there. They can't tell her strength." Jack spoke loudly, "I need someone who knows this Sara broad."

A couple of seconds went by and a fairy who was in the group talking to Elizabeth flew up front. He landed on the dash next to Nora, "Hello, I am Eric. I am the elder of Miss Sara's colony."

Jack held open his breast pocket. "Well? Get in! You too, Nora. Now, when we meet, you tell Nora if it's her or not." Jack asked Nora to hand him his earpiece. She climbed down to the bottom of his pocket and held out the earpiece Marvin had given him. Jack placed it in his ear, then asked, "Try your microphone."

Nora asked, "Are we really going to do this?"

Jack smiled, "Yes, it works. And don't worry, it'll be all right."

Andre said, "Remember, Jack, your cane! I will walk you to the door."

Jack said, "OK then, if this is the right place, which it is, you'll have to unload the truck yourself."

Andre said, "Hey, it has to look real! If we lose the element of surprise, we're in trouble."

Andre pulled up to the small house; he got out and helped Jack out of the Caddy. Jack took his cane and started to the porch, slowly looking around at the layout of the garden. He started to mumble to himself. He was talking to Nora in his pocket. She told him there were blues watching the house and there was one in the bush right next to the steps. Jack grabbed onto the railing and pulled himself up the steps. There, standing on the porch was an old lady in her eighties. The red fairy in Jack's pocket yelled, "Yes, she's alive! I mean that's her! She is Sara."

The old lady asked, "Now what is going on here?"

Jack looking up at her said, "Sara, I have something for you." Jack looked into her eyes and started to pull information.

Sara pointed her finger at him and said, "Stop that! I don't know who you are, but there is something strange about you."

Jack said, "Trust me," and he held out his hand. As she took it, they shook. You could see a small red glow form.

Her eyes came to life. She stammered, "Who are you?"

Jack asked, "Do you have some coffee? This is going to take a while."

She told him, "Come inside and bring your driver too." Jack turned and waved to Andre, who got back into the Caddy and backed it right up to the porch steps. Jack took that opportunity to go back down the steps and reach into the bush, pulling out a blue fairy. It was dull while hiding in the bush but now it was bright blue. When Jack put it into his pocket, it was a weak light.

Andre got out and walked to the back of the truck. He opened the back doors and asked over his shoulder, "Hey Jack! What are you doing?"

Jack said, "Be careful, there are sentries all over. I will question this one."

Andre said, "Get in there and find a spot for 17 cases."

Jack slowly climbed the stairs and made it over to the door. Sara was on her way back. She said, "What happened to you?"

Jack smiled and asked, "I need a place to put a bunch of boxes—that would be 17 wine cases."

Sara said, "Just stack them in the living room right here."

Jack shook his head, "A room with fewer windows."

She said, "You'll have to put them in the spare bedroom then."

Jack said, "Show me."

Sara walked across the room and opened the door. Jack followed her and as soon as he stepped into the room, opened his jacket and said, "Fly to her."

Eric shot out of Jack's pocket, hovered in front of Sara and said with tears running down his face, "Sara, it's me, Eric! I have brought back the whole colony. We have enough dust to regenerate you! It's going to be like old times."

Jack said, "The house is being watched; I have to shut the shades." Sara was blubbering with her long-lost Eric. Jack said, "Enough of that, we have to talk."

Andre came in with two cases and asked, "Where do you want them?"

Jack waved to him and said, "Put them in here." Andre sat them on the bed and opened one. Jack said, "Tell them they can come out, but they must stay in this room."

Fairies burst out of the open box. Sara put her hand over her mouth. Jack said, "Nora, out here." Nora flew to his outstretched hand and landed in his palm, "Now you open the boxes. Keep them in this room and send me Lizard Breath. She's going to be in charge."

Jack apologised, "I'm sorry. This is Andre Dropoff, Marvin's chauffeur and pilot."

Andre smiled and said, "You must be Sara."

Jack said, "After the cases are empty, could you pile them up so I can make a quick disappearing act down the basement window. What I was thinking was, when you pick me up later today, I'll slide in on one side of the truck and out the other side, right down the basement."

Andre said, "We'll talk about this later."

Jack held his hand out to Sara, "My name is Jack Robinson, at your service. I guess I'm working to release the red fairies and kill the blue ones. Shall we have some coffee?"

Sara shook Jack's hand lightly and said, "This way." She led him to the kitchen. Jack sat down and Sara started to fill his coffee cup when Andre stepped into the room.

He asked, "Have you looked at the size of that window? It's going to be tight."

Jack got up. "I'll check it out."

Andre sat in Jack's chair, held up his coffee and said, "Thanks."

Jack shot him a dirty look and mumbled, "He probably just wanted my coffee."

Jack walked down the stairs to the basement and started to move stuff around. He leaned an old door against the wall under the window and checked to make sure the window opened. To his surprise, it opened to the inside. It was hinged on the top, which was an ideal slide. He made it back up to the kitchen where Andre sat, eating a piece of pie and drinking his coffee.

Jack pulled up a seat and asked, "That wasn't the last piece of pie, was it?"

Andre said, "You two should get to know each other, I'll unload the Caddy."

Jack said, "Remind Nora I want Elizabeth in here ASAP." His tone left an icy feeling in the room.

Sara asked, "Who is this Elizabeth?"

Jack cut her off, "This is the deal: the blue fairies are going to try to kill you tonight. Oh, do you have a jar with a lid?"

Sara opened up a cupboard door and pulled out a jar half full of peanuts. She unscrewed the lid and dumped the contents in the garbage, then she handed it to him. Jack carefully opened his jacket pocket; a blue fairy jumped out and started to fly. Jack raised his hand. It came right to him and he put it in the jar. Sara said, "Where did you find that thing?"

Jack said, "They are all around the house, watching every move we make. We have to be very careful. You were smart, hiding under the power lines. That has saved you, but then you can't feel them either. They're getting ready to take you out, so we have to set up a surprise for them. Andre will get the weapons."

Sara asked, "When are they going to attack?"

A greenish fairy flew in nice and slow. Jack said loudly, with a bit of anger in his voice, "Finally! What the hell have you been doing?" Before Elizabeth could say anything, Jack introduced her, "Sara, this is Elizabeth. She is the captain of the fairies."

Jack turned and asked, "Are all the boxes unpacked?"

Elizabeth snapped a salute, "Yes, sir."

Jack grabbed the jar off the table and told Sara to follow. He led her to the bedroom where all the fairies were. As soon as he opened the door, he could feel their power. Jack raised the jar with the blue fairy in it and there was a gasp, then a silence. He opened the jar, shook the fairy out and held it by its wings. He growled and snapped his teeth; the fairy did the same. Jack said, "There are fairies around the house watching and they have orders to capture any red fairies that come out. Now I am going to show you what it takes to kill a fairy."

Jack then cut off its hand. A light shot out, but then stopped. Jack said, "Did you see that? It is not a mortal wound."

Jack then cut off his arm, a spark, then a pop and the blue fairy was gone. Jack said, "You must cut off an arm, leg or give it a fatal hit to the head or body. Elizabeth will be getting you spears, bows and arrows, shields, and most of all, wasp spray."

Elizabeth flew to Jack's shoulder. "How am I supposed to do that?"

Jack smiled. "Tell Andre what you need."

Jack looked around and then asked, "OK, what did you do with my suitcase?"

Andre replied, "You never said you needed it." Andre turned back to Elizabeth and said, "Hold that thought, I'll be back in a couple of minutes." He took a couple of empty cases and out the door he went.

Jack gave a small pep talk. "OK, all of you that are in good shape are going to fight. We will make some spider webs out of piano wire. That will cut the blues to shreds. We will set up ambushes. Everything is on our side. They think there might be a hundred fairies to round up here—they are not expecting five hundred warriors. You are to listen to Elizabeth, the green fairy. She is your commander, she will bring us to victory."

After that speech, all the fairies jumped to their feet and screamed. Sara put her arm on his shoulder and whispered in his ear, "Good speech."

Andre came into the room and asked, "Where would you like it?"

Jack said, "Throw it on the bed." Andre gave it a good toss onto the bed. Jack said loudly, "Nora, outside the room—see if you feel anything different."

The small fairy flew out of the room and Andre shut the door. Jack opened the suitcase and pulled out a film bag, then opened it and took out a large piece of quartz. He then walked over to the desk; it started to glow a light blood-red glow. He sat it on the desk. Jack then said, "Let Nora back in."

Andre opened the door. Nora flew in and said, "It will be OK, I could hardly feel the difference with all the power flowing overhead."

Jack smiled, "OK, power up. Tonight is going to be one of the biggest losses the blues have ever had." He zipped up the suitcase and headed to the kitchen, Sara followed. He put the suitcase right on the table and started to open it and then he stopped. Jack looked around and asked, "Hey, can we close some of the shades? Not so many to make them think there's something up."

Sara closed the one in the kitchen and opened the basement door to block them from looking through the living room. Jack opened his suitcase and pulled out another film bag. "This one is for you. Just to protect yourself from their attacks—it's an amulet." He then asked, "Do you know how to shield yourself?"

He reached across the table and put his hand on her arm. Then he closed his eyes and said softy, "That's it, just let me show you how."

After a minute or two, Sara said, "Let me try." She put her arm up, her hand glowed and she threw up a shield which knocked everything off the wall.

Nora came flying out of the bedroom right to Jack. She yelled wildly, "What's going on?"

Jack said, "Just showing Sara how to shield herself from the bad guys."

Nora said, "I think everyone felt that."

Sara said, "I'm sorry. I didn't mean to." Then she teared up. "If I would have known how to do that twenty years ago, I could have saved my husband."

Jack looked in her eyes. He could see the pain and sorrow. Then he turned to Nora and asked, "How's your new leader?"

Nora folded her arms across her chest and told him, "You should have never put her in charge; she's bossing everybody around, making them do all kinds of weird stuff."

Jack said, "You go and ask her if there is anything else she needs Andre to pick up." Jack looked over to Sara and asked, "Did I introduce you to Nora? Her job is to keep me safe and to watch over me."

Sara smiled, "Yes you did, and I think she has one big job in front of her."

Jack smiled and said, "I'll be back to review the troops and look at your plan. I want it on paper." He took Sara by the arm and said, "Let's take a walk out on the front porch." He opened the door for her and said, "Damn it all, I forgot my cane again!"

Sara said, "Let's sit for a minute and you can tell me what you are thinking." Jack turned and walked to a small table and two chairs; he pulled one out for Sara, then sat in the other. Sara then asked, "Why did you pile those empty cases next to the house?"

Jack said, with a sly look on his face, "That is how I am going to get in and out of the house. Andre will pull up to the cases. He will open the back passenger door and I will get in the driver's side, slip right out the other side through the window and into the basement in one smooth shot. I just wished I could have practised."

Sara smiled and said, "Where's Dropoff going?"

Jack said, "Oh, to some hotel, I'm not really sure, but he can't be here." Jack reached over to her and said, "Now, I don't want you to leave the porch when the time comes, do you hear me? That should keep the attackers in front of you."

Sara asked, "Where will you be?"

Jack smiled, "I will be right by your side, just out of sight. You have to lure out the guardians and I will give them a surprise."

Andre stepped onto the porch and said, "I hope there's a hardware store in town. I have a pretty good list. Is there anything you want?"

Jack said, "How about a bottle of wine?"

Andre said, "I have a bottle in the Caddy." He walked to the truck and came back with a bottle in his hand. He said, "I'll put it in the house for you."

Jack slowly got up from the chair, stepped over and helped Sara from her chair. He said to her, "This is very good wine; it's from Margaret's cellar."

Sara asked, "Who is this Margaret?"

Jack smiled, "She's one of the enemy—a blue guardian, an evil woman." He squeezed her arm, "One thing at a time. Are you comfortable with how this is going down? You are the bait to lure out the guardians—that is your only job. Elizabeth will take out the blue fairy army."

They slowly went back into the house. Andre pulled out of the driveway. Sara said, "Let's sit and get to know each other better."

Jack rolled his eyes, grabbed the bottle of wine from the table and said, "OK, let me open this, then take a piss. Then you can pick my brain."

Sara said, "That's fine. I'll be in the spare room." She opened the door and a red glow came from inside. The room came to a stop and everyone turned to see who was coming through the door. Elizabeth flew up and asked, "When is Andre getting back with my supplies?"

Sara said, "He just left, its ten minutes to town and he might not find everything. He might have to run to Wal-Mart—that's another thirty minutes." She stepped over to the stone, which was glowing red. She put both of her hands around it and closed her eyes, absorbing its energy.

Jack opened the door and asked in a loud voice, "What in the hell is going on here? I told you to train these slobs into soldiers! Lizard Breath, front and centre!"

Elizabeth flew to his palm and he asked, "Do you have them separated into groups? Does everyone know their job?"

Elizabeth said, "This isn't going to work. There isn't enough time!"

Jack stared at her, then told her, "This is the way it's going to happen: they're going to send in a thousand fairies to test our strength, you are going to send out a few. You are going to fly out too. That will get the guardians excited."

Sara said, "Yes, if they see a green fairy, it would be a big prize for them."

Jack pointed his finger at Elizabeth and said, "I am counting on you."

Elizabeth said, "Jack, I just saw you take out a thousand blue fairies singlehandedly."

Sara's eyes widened. Jack said, "Lisa, I need you to hold off the blues."

She asked, "What are you going to do?"

He said, "I will handle the guardians." He then stepped over to Sara and whispered to her, "You must learn to hide your power." He turned and spoke one word, "Nora."

The small fairy flew to him. She landed on his shoulder. "Yes, Jack?"

He said, "Take Sara out to the kitchen and teach her how to hide her power."

Nora fluttered to Sara and they both went out to the kitchen. Jack stepped up to the piece of quartz, cupped his hands around it and made it glow even brighter. He then turned around and barked out commands, "I want all the flyers over here," he pointed to the desk.

The room started to move—there were seven hundred fairies lounging around. He then barked, "I want the sick and weak on the bed, the ambushers on the chest of drawers; shooters over there on the chair.

"Lizard Breath, I want you to get a dozen more shooters and have them practise with the bathroom air freshener. Find the fastest of your flyers, they will be the first to go out."

Jack then stood tall. "OK. Your job is to kill as many of those blue animals as you can, without dying. Do you understand? I don't want to lose too many of you." He started for the door and a rusty old fairy flew up to him.

Jack raised his hand and the fairy landed in his palm. "What do you want us that can't fight do?"

Jack said, "Stay in this room. You will be the last defence for the house." Jack reached down and turned the knob. The fairy flew from his other hand. As Jack closed the door, he could see Elizabeth questioning the flyers.

He walked out to the kitchen where Nora was standing on Sara's shoulder talking into her ear. He picked up the coffee pot, refilled his cup and topped off Sara's. He then asked, "So what is the problem here?"

Nora flew to him, "This is going to take some time."

Jack smiled, "Time—we don't have time! Do I have to do everything myself?" He took a sip of coffee and sat down next to Sara. He took her hand and said, "Look into my eyes." She did. Jack said, "Trust me."

Sara's face went blank, then she mumbled, "I understand."

Jack then let go of her hand and said, "Wake up now."

Sara smiled and asked, "Why didn't you do that in the first place?"

Jack took a drink of coffee. "You didn't trust me before. I didn't think you would trust me now."

Sara said, "I have no choice! I have to trust you."

Jack turned to Nora, "Can you feel her?"

Nora flew to Sara's shoulder and asked, "Power up, then down again."

Sara held her hand up and it glowed red for a second, then put her hand back on the table. Nora flew to Jack and landed in his palm. She asked, "What do you think?"

Jack said, "I can't feel her."

Nora said, "I can, but very lightly. I can feel blues surrounding the house. With those power lines, I can't tell how many."

Jack said, "Andre has been gone for over two hours. It's going to get dark soon."

Nora asked, "Why don't you call him?"

Jack smiled, "See? There is a reason I keep you around." Jack pulled out his phone, then he heard a car pull up. He walked to the front door to see Andre coming in with three bags. Jack took the bags and Andre walked back to the Caddy and got more stuff. He just set it at the door and out he went again. This time he brought in three empty wine cases. Jack met him in the living room and asked, "Why the empties?"

Andre said, "Shooting boxes. I bought all the wasp spray I could find—two and a half cases, so we put ten in each box. I even bought a few of these plastic triggers that fit over the cans that might help."

Jack said, "OK, get your butt in there and show them how to make the swords."

Andre went into the bedroom, pulled out a bag with five-minute epoxy glue in it and then showed them how to glue a double edged razor blade to a finishing nail and how to make shields out of poker chips. Elizabeth came flying into the kitchen, landing on the table.

Jack said, "What do you think? The chip will insulate you from the blues' power. Do you think you can swing that razor?"

Elizabeth started to twirl it one-handed. Jack said, "If you left a half inch sticking out the top, you could use it as a spear." The green fairy's eyes popped wide open and off she was, back to her room. Jack said, "You need to insulate the finishing nails or the reds will die from the blues' power."

He then told Sara, "OK, now that you know how to hide your power, you should power up as much as you feel like. I'll help with the training, then I must get out of sight." He asked, "Where is the piano wire?"

Andre reached into a bag and took out four packs of wire. He asked, "What are you going to do with it?" Jack walked over to the window, reached behind the shade and opened it. Then he pulled out the screen, pulled out his pocket knife and cut the screen out.

He told Andre, "Now I will leave one hole for them to fly though, but the blues won't know it. And they will dice themselves." He finished making a crisscross pattern and weaving in a piece of yarn so the fairies could see the hole. He then forced it back into the window.

Andre said, "Jack, it's time to go."

Jack walked toward the door. Sara ran to him. "You can't leave!"

Jack said, "I'll be right back. Walk me to the door, then turn out the lights like you normally would. Act like it's just another night."

Sara followed them to the door. She said goodbye and waved. A tear rolled down her face. Jack said, "Don't you think those wine cases look out of place?"

Andre said, "You wanted them to cover the front garden." He then picked up a wine case and walked to the Caddy's back passenger door.

Jack said under his breath, "I hope this works." He climbed in the back door on the driver's side, shut the door and slid right out the passenger side, next to the wine cases that were stacked there and through the basement window.

Andre shut the back door and said, "Timing."

Sara stepped back into the house, shutting the door. Jack opened the basement door and whispered, "Shut off the kitchen light."

Sara turned to see the door open a crack. She then turned on the TV, walked by the basement door and shut off the light. Jack then opened the door just enough to squeeze out. He stayed low and crawled to the corner. Sara asked, "How did you do that? I am so glad you are here!"

Jack said, "Just do your normal routine; we don't want to spook them."

Sara said, "Well, I'm going to the bathroom. Then I will watch Sherlock on PBS, then to bed." Jack repositioned himself so he could watch TV too.

Just before the end of the show, a car pulled into the driveway with its lights off. Nora came flying slowly out of the bedroom. She flew up to Jack. "They're here; they just pulled into the driveway and parked halfway in."

Jack said, "OK, they're getting a report from the blues. Hang tight!"

Elizabeth flew out, she didn't take her time. "Jack, they're here! What should we do?"

Jack said, "First settle down, stay calm and wait. Second, when they attack, take your first wave and wipe out the sentries around the house, do a fly-by and check their numbers. Make sure they see you."

Sara walked back, "They're here, aren't they? I can feel something has changed."

Jack said, "Let's play this thing just as planned. Just give it a couple of minutes to play out."

Sara screamed, "Here they come!"

Jack crawled out of the kitchen to the living room. Elizabeth took a dozen of the red troops out, there were flashes and pops and streaks of red and green all over. The fairies were running at full charge and were armed. Jack crawled into the spare bedroom and barked out an order, "Go lay your traps." About twenty reds flew out with wire and cans of wasp spray.

Jack motioned to Nora, "Go out and have Lisa come back. Tell her to retreat."

Sara stepped into the room, "What now?"

Jack said, "It's their move. Let's talk to Lizard Breath." Just as he said that, Elizabeth flew into the room, followed by ten red fairies.

She flew to Jack, who had his hand out for her to land in. She quickly asked, "Why did we retreat? The car is still parked halfway down the driveway. There must be a thousand blues just outside the garden!"

Jack asked, "How did you do?"

Elizabeth said, "The sides and back are clear. The front porch is clear, but I lost three trying to clear the front garden."

Jack said, "OK, it's time. Sara, leave the amulet in the film bag until you really need it. Greeny, you, man your troops! This is going to be one hell of a battle."

A dozen red fairies flew in. The leader flew up and landed next to Lisa on Jack's palm. She said, "Repeat this to the room. We have set wire traps with the red yarn holes from the apple tree to the pine tree on the other side from the clothesline to the house. There are fairies on the roof and in the pine with wasp spray."

Jack then repeated that so the whole room could hear. Just then, a red fairy came flying in across the room to Jack. "The car is on the move."

Jack looked at Sara, "You, out on the porch! Let them make the first move and just shield yourself."

Elizabeth, "Take care and God be with you."

Jack looked up. "The blues are to be wiped out. Take no prisoners. Kill them all!" Sara turned and stepped to the door, Jack reached into a film bag and pulled out a small piece of quartz. He held it in his hand and a green glow came from it. He tossed it on the bed. "Lizard, power up! And good hunting!" With that, he turned and went down the steps.

Sara turned on the garden light and stepped out on the front porch. A Cadillac limo pulled up and the back doors opened. Two women stepped out. They stood by the car. Sara yelled to them, you could hear the fear in her voice. "I know who you are, just leave!"

One of the ladies said, "Give us your green fairy and we will leave."

The trees started to move. Sara yelled back in an old lady voice, "You know I can't do that!"

The other woman raised her hand. A blue ball of energy formed in her palm and she threw it. Sara raised her hand and threw up a shield, which stopped it twenty feet from her. The night sky filled with streaks of blue. The blue fairies started their attack.

Jack had slid out the basement window and was hiding behind the empty wine cases, watching. A group of red fairies flew by. He watched them. They flew close to the ground and fast. They swung close to the front porch. When they streaked back, they had a hundred blues on their tail. Jack noticed there were only a few reds. The rest had hid somewhere. They flew back toward the window. The blues were much faster. The red streaks turned into one as they went single file thought the hole in the piano wire. When the blues hit the wire, all the attention went to the side of the house. When they all hit the wire at once, there was a huge spark, then bang! The whole garden lit up in a blinding flash of blue.

The two women walked closer to the front porch, stopping to watch a hundred of their fairies disappear in a flash. They stopped right in front of the porch, then started to throw energy balls at Sara. She held her own. Soon, she was on her knees with both hands up, trying to stop the attack. The energy balls were getting closer. Sara was getting weaker with every block she made. She reached into her dressing gown and pulled out the film bag, ripped it open and stood. The amulet shone bright.

The war with the fairies was raging on. The reds clashed with the blues, just hacking into them. They had no idea the red fairies could even fight. This lot was fighting and were armed. The blues would chase them, fall into the trap and the gunners on the roof would spray the wasp spray. The blues would fall to the ground and flop around till they popped.

The blues started to link into balls and came in to help soften Sara. They came in close to the porch and shot a burst of power at her, which she blocked. Elizabeth came screaming across the garden with a five-pound rock and slammed it into one of the balls. It blew it right apart and a wine case's lid flew opened. Three streams of wasp spray shot out. There were over a hundred blues flopping on the ground. Elizabeth was so fast that she caught the rock she had thrown though the first ball and was on her way to building up enough speed to blow the other ball apart.

Jack noticed that the back door of the limo flew open. A young man jumped out, raised his hand and started towards Sara. Jack stood and threw two balls of nearly white light at the two women, blowing both of them across the garden. All eyes were on Jack and this other guardian. This was the real fight. The man from the limo threw a ball of whitish-blue at Jack, which Jack didn't block. He caught it. With the other hand, he levitated three large dull looking quartz stones which Andre had left.

Jack reached out and started to pull. Any fairies that were between Jack and this new guy were sucked into the stream. The man threw another ball which just went right into the stream that Jack had flowing into the stones floating in front of him.

The two women were back on their feet. They stepped closer to Jack, but Sara threw two shots of energy, knocking them back by ten feet. She then blocked another shot from a ball of blues. Lisa blew that one apart with her rock and the streams of wasp spray took them down. They flopped on the ground, snapping and popping, but this time the power went right to Jack's stream.

A large group of blue fairies seemed to run. They all flew off, then about fifty more shot to the back of the house into the woods. Sara stepped back so her back was to the house and watched Jack as he pulled and pulled, grunting as he did so.

The man from the limo sank to his knees and then fell face-first onto the gravel driveway.

Jack bellowed, "Nora, I need some more quartz!" He raised his hand and shot a blinding white power though the last ball of blue fairies, blowing them apart. He pulled, sucking all the energy from them. It sounded like a popcorn maker. They tried to fly from him, but it was no use. Everything came to a stop when they saw Jack's power. The blues went into full retreat; the two women bowed their heads and stood silent.

Sara handed Jack the amulet. It turned to a bright light pink. He walked over to the two women and took one by the chin. He lifted her head so she looked into his eyes. He said, "Sleep." She closed her eyes.

The other one lifted her head. Jack chuckled, "You didn't think the old lady was going to be any trouble. I guess you were wrong."

Her eyes met his. He said, "Let's see. You are going to clean out your mansion. There will be no trace of fairies in it. You are going to put it all in a U-Haul and have it sent here. No tricks, or you will die." Jack then woke the other woman up and told her the same thing. You could hear popping all around the house as the battle went on. Sara stood with him.

"Now the three of you are going to meet me at a Caribbean island. I will call you and we will become partners. Now sleep."

Jack walked over to the man, reached down and put his hand on the back of his neck. He said, "Oh, good day, Dave Hanson!" The limo started. Jack flew right to the door and pulled it open. The driver pulled a pistol on him. Jack said, "No need for that now." He shot a beam of white light at the driver's hand and it froze.

Jack smiled, "Boy, I'm glad that worked!" He stepped in closer to the chauffeur, looked him in the eyes and said, "Sleep."

He then reached in and took the gun, unloaded it and put it in his lap and turned the car off. He walked back over to Dave and put his hand back on his neck and pulled information. After a couple of minutes, Jack said, "Get up."

Dave stood, shook Jack's hand and said, "OK, the five of us will run from North America."

Jack said, "Sleep," and he walked over to the driver. He reached in and said, "Wake up. Dave and I have made an agreement to work together. We will meet at my island. I will tell you when." He then told the women the same thing. He got them into the car, wished them a safe trip and said that he would get in touch with them within two weeks. And he told them to clean out all the red fairy stuff and send it there in a U-Haul the next day before three.

He walked back to the house where Sara was standing. He looked up to her on the porch and asked in a quiet voice, "Are you OK?" She looked down and started to cry. She nodded her head.

Jack walked up to her and gave her a hug. Sara buried her head in his neck and sobbed, "I never want to do that again!"

Jack said, "That's OK, everything went as planned." They stood silent, holding each other. You could still heard a pop every once and a while. Jack said, "I think we should go in."

He led her back into the house and asked, "Should we have a snack before we call it a night?"

Sara asked, "How could you sleep after all that happened?"

Jack said, "You're right, we should call in the troops and find out the damage. You know, it's weird. You can't have a body count. When the fairies die, they just disappear."

He then let go of Sara's hand and bellowed: "Nora!"

Fairies scattered. They all were looking for Nora. In a minute, Nora flew in up to Jack and landed in his palm. She asked, "What do you want, Jack?" He said, "A report. How many did we lose?"

She said, "That will have to wait until tomorrow; I have people searching the forest for the wounded."

Jack asked, "And Elizabeth?"

Nora said, "You gave the order no prisoners, we must wipe them out. The last I saw her, she was flying like a bat out of hell, on the hunt."

Jack smiled and said, "You're right about one thing. You don't want to piss off a green fairy. Did you see her fight? She would decapitate blues in a hundred-mile-an-hour fly-by."

Nora said, "She saved so many lives and took so many. She was feeding off their energy, like a drug."

Jack then asked Nora, "Do you have everything under control?"

Nora cocked her head, "I'm in charge?"

Jack smiled and added, "When Lisa's not here, yes, you're in charge."

Nora stood straighter, "Well then, if I am in charge, we need that stone recharged in the bedroom. And you need to take a shower and drink as much water as you can. We also need a dish with fairy dust."

Jack looked at his hands, he was rubbing them together. "Yeah, you're right, I need a shower and have to stay away from the fairies."

Sara stepped over to him, took him by the hand and led him back to the house. On the way she asked, "Why don't you want to grow young?"

Jack said, "When I get into the house, I will show you."

They walked up the stairs, Jack said to Sara, "You did a wonderful job. That Dave guy wasn't going to come out of the limo, but you made him."

Sara said, "If you hadn't shown me how to shield myself from their attack, I would be dead right now. And look at this! They burnt the paint right off the wall!" Sara was pointing to a five foot area where you could see the paint blistered from a shot of energy.

Jack said, "You should get the place sided anyhow. Then you don't have to paint every five years. Been there, done that. It's a big expense, but it's worth it in a long run."

They stepped into the house. Jack followed Sara to the guest bedroom. She opened the door and there were fairies all over. She stepped in and they all rose to their feet. Jack said in a loud voice, "At ease."

They all sat back down and resumed what they were doing. Jack said, "Crap, I need a couple of guys to go out and pick up the quartz stones out in front."

A half dozen fairies flew out the window. Jack looked and said, "They can't get them though that hole. I'll be right back." He jogged through the house and out the front door. The fairies were trying to get close to the stones but there was too much energy coming off them. Jack said, "I got it." He raised his hand and the quartz pieces rose and floated to him.

Sara said from right behind him, "Nice trick."

Jack said, "It sure comes in handy sometimes." He stepped back into the house and back to the bedroom. He held each stone, then touched the one that was already there. He said over his shoulder, "I hope the lead-lined film bags shield the power."

Sara said, "Lead-lined for the airport? I was wondering about that."

Jack said, "There! That should do it." The room had a red glow to it. Jack took the stones to the bed where his luggage was. He took out two film bags, slid the quartz into the bags and sealed them. He turned to Sara and asked, "Is that better?"

Sara smiled and asked, "Now are you going to show me why you don't want to grow young?"

Jack reached into the suitcase and pulled out his passport. "This is eight years old."

He then pulled out his driving licence from his wallet. "Here, this is two years old."

She held them up and looked at him. Her eyes kept going from his driving licence to him. "Now I know why. You look ten years younger than your driving licence and a couple years younger than your passport."

Sara then said, "You were clean-shaven when you came here. Now you have a six inch beard with shoulder-length hair."

Jack said, "Now you see. There was so much fairy dust floating around, I have to get into the shower." He reached back into the suitcase and pulled out a Ziploc bag with his deodorant, tooth paste and shaver. Then he handed Sara a two pound bag of fairy dust.

She took it and asked, "This isn't what I think it is?"

Jack rolled his eyes, "It's fairy dust. Do you need it?"

Sara had tears streaming down her face. "I have never seen so much at one time."

Jack looked around. All faces were staring at him holding the bag—hundreds of fairies and not a sound. Jack finally said, "What?"

An old fairy flew to Jack, "That would take us fifty years to make."

Jack said, "Well, I'm off to the shower." He reached into his pocket, took out his mobile phone and handed it to Sara. "Here, call Dropoff. Tell him to call me in the morning. Plans have changed again."

Sara took the phone, then said, "OK, get into the shower. Towels are in the right hand cabinet."

Jack turned and was gone. He undressed and stepped into the shower. Brown swirled on the floor and he muttered, "Ah, nuts!" and started scrubbing the brown from his hair. He washed it three times before it came clean. When he stepped out of the shower, his clothes were gone. A dressing gown sat folded on the toilet. Jack looked around. There was a pair of shears, his razor and shaving mug. He took the shears and started with his beard. He cut it down to about one quarter of an inch. Then he chopped off his hair, right at the neckline—he took a good six inches off. He whipped up some shaving cream in his mug and slowly started to shave. He stepped out to find the door to the spare bedroom open. He walked over to it. Sara saw him and stepped to him, taking him by the elbow and turning him right around and toward the kitchen.

Jack protested, "I have to talk to my commander. About what all happened."

Sara said, "All in good time. Right now, chamomile tea and a good night's rest."

He sat in a chair that was already pulled out. "How can I sleep? Do you know all the stuff that has to be done before tomorrow?"

Sara put her finger to her lips. "Now be quiet. I will tell you the green fairy's report. She said her company spread out a hundred miles in all directions, chasing down rogue fairies and finishing off the wounded. She thinks they got them all. I think there was too much going on and a few might have escaped."

Jack looked up from his tea and said, "I've talked with blues. They stick to orders and fight to the death."

Sara sat down and asked, "Can you really talk to the blues?"

Jack took a long sip of tea, then asked, "How do you think we found out about them attacking you tonight? All you have to do is tear off a few wings and arms and they will talk. Well, not all. I think I questioned three."

Sara sat next to Jack and said, "That is amazing. The only ones that I know can talk to blues are their guardians."

Jack raised his cup and asked, "Aren't you going to have some?"

Sara said, "As soon as I put you to bed and shower."

Jack looked at her and his eyes were glassed over. He slurred, "Boy, this is good stuff."

Sara stood and asked, "Some help here, please."

Nora hopped down from the fridge and a couple of reds flew to her side. Nora barked out commands, "Grab him by the collar and lift gently." The two lifted Jack from the chair, to his feet. Sara slid her arm around his waist and Nora lifted his arm and wrapped it over Sara's neck.

Sara said to Jack, "You will be sleeping in my room tonight."

Jack was done, he was like rubber. Sara sat him on the side of the bed and the fairies took his feet and swung his legs in. Sara bent over and kissed him on the forehead, saying, "Thank you, you are my saviour."

She then walked out the door and asked, "How long will he be out?"

Nora said, "At least until morning. Now you get into the shower."

Sara raised a bony finger. "Don't you try that with me, little girl." Sara walked into the spare bedroom, which looked more like a war room. There were maps of the traps, positions of the wasp spray ambush points and fairies lying all over. Sara raised her hand and said, "I thank you from the bottom of my heart. Now get some sleep."

She turned and started down the hall. Elizabeth flew to her shoulder. Sara stopped and said, "Tomorrow is a big day. You need your rest."

Elizabeth asked, "Are we going to kill the blue guardians tomorrow?"

Sara cocked her head. "I would think so. One thing is for sure. You're going to clean up that spare room." She started on her way to the bathroom. She really didn't want to wash off the fairy dust. She was feeling younger all the time.

She showered and a small voice said, "Do your hair again." Sara looked up. There was Nora, watching her shower. She rolled her eyes, put some more shampoo in her hair and it turned to a light brown. She rinsed it and did it again. This time the suds stayed white and she rewashed her body. When she was done, Nora flew over with the towel and said, "You will shower again in the morning. So will Jack."

Sara asked, "Who do you think you are?"

Nora said, "I thought you knew. I am here to watch out for Jack, so finish drying your hair and I will get you a cup of tea."

Sara said, "I'm not drinking that tea. It's laced with drugs."

Nora flew out, warmed up a cup in the microwave and sat it on the table. There were fairies all over the place. She then flew to the living room where the troops were camped right to Elizabeth.

Lisa asked, "Now what do you want?"

Nora said, "Sara's not listening to me, she won't drink the tea."

Elizabeth stood, stretched, fluttered her wings and she was off down the hall, with Nora in tow. She flew into the bathroom and landed on the sink in front of Sara. She turned a light green and asked not-so-politely, "Now what is this? We agreed both of you would drink the tea and sleep."

Sara snapped, "Well, I don't feel like it."

Elizabeth glowed and said, "You will stick to your word or there will be hell to pay!"

Sara knew she would have to listen to Elizabeth. "Well, OK then, if I said I would do it, then I will do it."

Elizabeth flew within inches of her face and told her, "You will listen to me and you will drink that now."

Sara stood there staring at the fairy. Elizabeth's head just glowed, lighting up the whole room. Sara said, "In a minute, let me finish here."

Elizabeth said, "Damn it, woman! I told you to do it now!" Sara tossed the brush into the sink and walked out the door with Elizabeth and Nora following.

Nora said, "Wouldn't you like to read minds like Jack? I wonder what Sara was thinking when you put her in her place."

Elizabeth said, "That's something I don't want to know. But she knows who's holding the power."

Nora said, "Yeah, so you have to get to Jack before she does." Elizabeth shot her a dirty look.

Sara picked up the tea and felt the cup. Then she blew on it. She took a sip and said, "Jack was right. It tastes good." She walked to her room and took off her slippers, picked up the cup and finished off the tea. She crawled into bed with Jack and within two minutes, she was asleep.

Elizabeth said to Nora, "Fly down and see if Jack is still breathing."

Nora flew down and landed lightly on his nose, then flew back and said, "Wow—that must be some strong stuff. He's barely breathing."

Elizabeth said, "We better get some shut-eye, tomorrow is going to be a busy one."

In the morning, Jack woke up feeling slimy sheets. He looked over and saw Sara in bed. He sat and thought for a minute, then said, "What in the world?"

His feet hit the ground and he almost slipped. He pulled his feet back into the bed and wiped off the bottoms of his feet with the sheet. He tried it again and walked right by the bathroom and into the living room. He asked the first fairy he found, "Where is Nora?"

It said, "Follow." The fairy flew to a bookcase.

Jack said softy "Nora, we have to speak."

She hopped off the shelf right to his shoulder and said, "You're up early!"

Jack said, "You drugged me!"

Nora stammered, "It wasn't my idea! Sara is the one that said we should knock you out. You were so excited, you would never sleep!"

Jack walked back towards the bathroom. He said, "OK, it was Sara's idea. You had nothing to do with it."

Nora's head sank so she was looking down at Jack's feet. "Well, one of the elders brought it up and word got around. But Sara did say it was a good idea."

Jack walked into the bathroom. He said, "This is what I want: make a pot of coffee, tell Lizard Breath I want a presentation about the battle. And I'm not talking tomorrow. I want it when I have my first cup of coffee."

He reached in and turned on the shower. Nora still stood on his shoulder. Jack asked, "Don't you have something better to do?"

Nora took the hint and flew off to the other room. Jack shut the door and stepped slowly into the shower. He put his hand in to check the temperature and his tan washed right off. He stepped in and started to wash his hair three times. He went through the whole thing again and cut his hair straight off at the neckline. This time, it was past his shoulders and he had a four-inch beard by the time he got out of the bathroom. The coffee was done and Elizabeth was sitting there, chewing on a cube of sugar.

Jack walked out with a towel wrapped around his waist. "Nora, I need some clothes please," he bellowed. He walked into the kitchen.

Elizabeth dropped the sugar cube and flew right to him, landing on his shoulder and started to talk. Jack said, "Let me sit down, then you may start." He took a cup from the cupboard, walked to the coffee pot and poured it.

Then he set it on the table. He walked to the phone, looked around it, came up with a pad of paper and a pen and sat at the table.

Jack picked up the cup, took a sip and said, "Now."

Elizabeth hopped off Jack's shoulder and stood on the table, looking him in the eye. She said, "We won, that's all that matters."

Jack asked, "Did you do a head count? How many did we lose?"

The green fairy looked at the table. "We did our best. There were more blues than we thought there would be."

Nora fluttered down. She said, "68, we lost 68. And 112 injured."

Jack wrote that down, then asked, "How about the piano wire? Did that work?"

Elizabeth said, "That was a great idea! That itself must have killed a thousand. When they hit that, it sliced them right apart." She said, "The gunners with the wasp spray, they killed hundreds. The guys on the rooftops killed hundreds more."

Jack said, "I told you that spray would kill any fairy. It was a risk we had to take."

Elizabeth said, "The swords and shields worked really well. I could chop their heads off at full speed. They would chase me and I would turn on them and just hack them apart."

Nora raised her hand. Jack said, "OK Nora, what's your thought?"

Nora said, "The ambush worked really well. The reds would get chased, leading them into a trap where they were hacked to pieces. The red fairies never fought before, because they couldn't win. But with the swords and shields—"

Jack interrupted, "So you're saying is the blues were surprised and weren't expecting a fight."

Elizabeth said, "We're just lucky we stopped on the way and wiped out that colony. Another thousand blues might have turned the war."

Jack wrote that down and made some more notes. Elizabeth said, "OK. If I would have changed anything, I would have trained the gunners better. I would have sent out a clean-up crew and took a division and flanked them. You wouldn't believe the time we had chasing them down when they retreated. I was the only one fast enough to catch them in a straight shot. Oh yeah, and we need a better way to break though the balls! Once they link up, they're pretty safe."

Jack said, "That was a good idea with those rocks, it blew them right apart. Then the spray wiped them out."

Elizabeth said, "I am the only one that could get rock moving that fast."

Jack asked, "Did anyone else drop a rock on it? So we don't know, do we? What you have to do is make the weapons better and see what worked and what didn't. Talk to the rest of the crew, ten at a time. And Nora, you take notes."

Sara walked up behind Jack and asked, "Did you sleep well?"

Jack stood and said quietly, "You drugged me."

She smiled, "It was just a sleepy, no harm done."

Jack said, "If you ever do that again, you tell me what is going on!"

Sara apologised, "I will never do that again, I promise."

Jack said, "Well, that was the best night of sleep I had in a long time." He then put his hand to his nose, "God, you need a shower, big time."

Sara ran her finger down her arm, leaving a streak. Tears ran down her face, washing the brown off and leaving white lines. Jack said, "There's nothing to worry about. It washes off."

Sara cracked a smile ear-to-ear and said, "I didn't think I would ever regenerate again. It's been thirty years now. I have never been this old in two hundred years." She went to throw her arms around Jack, but he raised one arm and put his other hand to his nose.

Jack said, "I'm not kidding. You need a shower, my God! You bring tears to my eyes." Sara turned and started towards the bathroom. Jack said loudly, "Nora, take a couple of fairies and help her to the shower. Make sure she doesn't slip. Then clean up the tracks."

He pointed to the floor. There were brown tracks coming off the carpet into the kitchen. Jack got up and looked into the fridge. It was jam-packed. He started to pull things out and looked at the expiration dates. He opened the freezer. Same thing.

Jack stood and shook his head. He poured himself another cup of coffee, sat it on the table and pulled out his phone. He pulled up contacts, the first call was to Andre. Jack told him, "Eat before you come and take your time. We're not leaving until the afternoon."

Andre asked, "How did it go?"

Jack said, "Well, I think we lost 68, but I think we are going to gain a thousand. It's on a need-to-know basis and you don't need to know right now. See you around two or earlier."

Andre said, "Why don't I go down, eat, then shit, shower and shave. Then I'll be there about eleven o'clock."

Jack said, "The earlier the better. I'll see you then." The next one he called was his son. He told him that he was all right and back in Oregon. He wanted to straighten a few things out and he wanted him to call his sister to tell her everything was fine. He had buried his friend's wife and there were still a few loose ends to straighten up.

Jack then called Marvin. He said into the phone, "Yes, we made it here. Everyone is safe. It will take a day longer to do this, so see you sometime tomorrow, I would suspect."

He then turned off the phone, poured another cup of coffee and returned to stare into the refrigerator. He pulled out the eggs and looked at the date, then sat them on the counter next to the stove and started to make eggs and toast.

Sara walked in. She was clean and wearing a dressing gown. She walked up behind Jack and gave him a hug. She whispered in his ear, "Thank you so very much."

Jack smiled, then asked, "How many eggs do you want?"

She said, "One, maybe two."

Jack said, "I'm frying them hard, they're just past the due date. Sit. I'll pour you a cup." Jack did just that, poured her a cup, topped off his and started another pot. He slid four eggs from the pan and onto a plate. He sat the plate down in front of Sara, then a plate with toast. "Eat. We need to throw everything that is in your fridge out."

Sara looked up at him, "You know how it is, living alone. I just don't cook like I used to."

Jack said, "I lost my wife two months ago, so I don't have much experience living alone."

Jack had the rest of the eggs in the pan and made more toast. He inspected each slice of bread. There was a pile next to the toaster that you could see mold on. He slid the eggs onto a plate and sat with Sara. They discussed what Jack had planned for the blue guardians and the timeline he had for the day.

She noticed the fairies scrubbing the carpeting. "Oh, I left tracks!"

Jack said, "When you get up, wipe off your feet. That slime is slippery."

Sara got up from her chair and ran her fingers through Jack's hair. "Why don't you let me cut it?"

Jack turned and looked up at her. "Ah! That's what's different! You cut your hair. And did a nice job! Would you like to cut mine?"

She said, "Sure, right after I'm done with breakfast."

She said, "I'll get dressed, then I'll be right back."

A half hour later, Sara came into the kitchen. This time she was wearing makeup and was carrying a shaver, cape and shears.

Jack said, "Wow, you've done this before."

Sara smile and said seductively, "I've done a lot of things that would surprise you."

Jack shot her a look. "Well, you're over two hundred years old. Let me see. Did you go parking with a team of horses?"

Sara said, "Many times. Shot myself a few Indians and lost a husband in that fight. He was a good man."

Jack asked, "Really? Were you in an Indian battle?"

She said, "We were in four battles. The wagon train started out with two hundred people. When we made it to California, there were only thirty original people that made it—sickness, cold and the Indians."

Sara started to cut his hair. Jack pulled out his driving licence to show her a picture of how he had it cut. She continued her story, "So when we got to California, I didn't have a husband. I also lost my son and all I had was a team of horses and a wagon. So I sold them and bought a partnership in a saloon, did a little bartending and dancing. I made a pretty good life for myself, got married again. He was shot in the bar, so I sold out of that and moved north.

"That's where I found my next husband; he had the gift of changing fairy dust into power and had himself a colony of about five thousand red fairies. He didn't ask for much from them. He would power up a beautiful stone in the fall that would keep them warm and healthy though the winter. I went through three regenerations with the man. The fairies showed him where there was some gold. He panned it, then sold the rights to the land.

"His last regeneration, he was a salmon fisher and an artist."

Jack asked, "Did you have any kids?"

Sara said, "The first marriage, just the one boy. He died on the wagon train. The next, the marriage wasn't that long. Before he was shot, I told him to never cheat at poker. Shot dead right at the table! Now the last one, the first time, we had four girls and one boy. The second, two boys and two girls. The last regeneration we had a boy and a girl; they're both still alive."

Jack asked, "Do they know about the fairies, or how their dad died?"

Sara sighed, "A massive heart attack, he was 52. If I knew how to throw a shield to block the blues, he would be still alive today."

She combed his hair out one more time and asked, "What do you think?"

Jack said, "It feels short, good enough."

Sara brushed the neckline off and took off the cape.

Jack got up and walked into the bathroom, looked in the mirror and muttered, "Ah, hell."

Sara asked, "Is it too short?"

Jack replied "No, the hair cut is fine. I could use another shave. It's only been two hours since I shaved last."

He said, "While I'm here, I might as well take a leak." He turned to Sara and asked, "Do you mind?"

She finished folding the cape and said, "You know, that was the first time in about thirty years I cut somebody's hair. Not bad, if I say so myself."

Jack said, "You know you did do a pretty good job. Thanks. Now shut the door on your way out."

Jack stepped out of the bathroom to find Sara sitting in the living room with the fairies. Jack stepped in and the room went silent. "OK, what's going on here?"

Sara said, "I was just finding out what happened to my guys after they were captured. They were turned into slaves and traded with other blue guardians."

Jack nodded his head. "Yes, they are a tight-knit bunch. There only a few on the west coast, I'll ask That Dave Hanson guy. Oh and by the way, there are going to be a couple of thousand fairies showing up around three, via U-Haul.

"Sara, Nora and Elizabeth, in the kitchen." Jack turned and walked down the hall. When he reached there, he went straight to the coffee pot and poured himself a cup and topped off Sara's. He then sat down and waited. When Sara strolled in a few minutes later with Nora and Elizabeth, Jack shot them a dirty look.

He took charge, "Now, Andre should be here any minute. You," he pointed to Nora, "I want you to set up a fairy wash, like the one at Marvin's."

Nora snapped to attention and gave him a salute. "Yes, sir."

He then pointed to Elizabeth, "You, Lizard Breath, I want you to get a team going to unload all the fairy stuff and get it in here. We will need security."

Jack then pointed to Sara. "You just stay out of the way and out of sight. We have to be on top of our game. There is a chance this could be bad, so get your troops out there ready to fight."

Jack's phone rang. He pulled it from his pocket and answered it, "No, I haven't made it back home. No, I didn't fire my weapon. When I get there, I'll get there. I have to go, love you."

He held out his phone and called Andre. He put the phone to his ear and asked, "How long?" Then he held out the phone and pushed a button.

Sara asked, "What was that about?"

Jack said, "Andre will be here in ten minutes and my daughter is checking up on me. She has called my next-door neighbours. I shot my .45

while saving the green one. And something is not right. She isn't telling me something."

Sara asked "You saved Lisa?"

Jack gave her a look. "Why do you look so surprised? OK, what did she tell you?"

Sara said, "I understood you were attacked and she flew in and saved you."

Jack chuckled, "Well, I *was* attacked, but not until after she led them to me. The blues had her on the run. I understood they chased her from southern California to my garden in Oregon. She was out of power and they were seconds behind her. Did she save me? Yeah, she probably did, but she brought them to me, then she tried to kill me."

Jack took her by the hand, looked her in the eye and said, "Things are going to get better. You have your fairies back. I hope you have someone to regenerate you. If not, I know a couple of great fairy doctors."

Sara said, "There are a few reds that could do it, but the fairy that did my last two generations is not here."

Jack nodded, "There will be a thousand fairies coming today in a U-Haul, I hope they are early."

Sara's eyes filled with tears. "Another thousand," she sobbed.

Jack looked past Sara and stared into space for a second, deep in thought. Then he muttered, "I'll tie up that loose end somehow. The plan is in the works as we speak."

A fairy flew in and said, "A big black Caddy just pulled in the driveway."

Jack smiled, "Ah Dropoff! I will have Nora tell him the story of the battle."

Sara stood, a thin and fragile little old lady. She walked to the door and opened it. The living room was quiet—you could hear a pin drop. Andre stepped from the Caddy. Sara asked, "Are you alone?"

Andre answered, "Yes, I am." He opened the back door and pulled out a large bunch of flowers and a jar of honey. Both hands were full. Sara held the door open for him and he pushed the flowers through the door.

The fairies gave out a little, "Ahh!" Andre laid the flowers on the couch, then started to separate them, a handful here and there so they were spread out over the room. He then asked for an empty wine case. Jack grabbed one from the kitchen and gave it to Andre, who broke it down and poured the honey over it.

The fairies tore into the flowers. Their faces turned yellow with pollen; others flew down to take handfuls of honey. Nora flew to him and said, "Thank you, so ever much!"

Andre said, "I heard a celebration was in order."

Jack walked up and put his arm around Andre and said, "Everything has to fall into place or this house of cards could come tumbling down. Walk with me, I will tell you my plan." Jack and Andre walked toward the kitchen. Sara followed closely to see what she could hear.

Jack turned to her and said, "The less you know, the better. You too, Nora." Jack filled Andre in on the way he was going to take care of Dave Hanson and crew over another cup of coffee.

A fairy flew in. "A truck pulling up the driveway!"

Jack stood and said, "That must be the U-Haul. Is it a big trailer?"

The fairy said, "It's a big truck, but not as big as a semi."

Andre smiled and asked, "Do you have any of that wasp spray?"

Jack's eyes popped wide open, he asked excitedly, "Do you think this is a trap?"

Andre said, "It could be, they might have not bought your story."

Elizabeth came out of nowhere and started barking orders to an empty room. All the fairies were hiding, to not be seen by the stranger driving the U-Haul.

Fairies started to fly to the spare room where there weapons were. Jack said, "Let me go out and see."

Andre held out his arm, "No, I believe I should do it." He walked to the door and onto the porch, down the stairs to the truck.

Jack walked up to Sara, who was white as a sheet. He took her shoulders from behind, leaned in and whispered in her ear, "It will be all right."

Andre shook the woman's hand and walked to the back of the truck. He opened the back, then pulled out the ramp. Jack said, "It looks safe to me." He turned, looked at Nora and asked, "What do you think?"

Nora said, "It is hard to feel anything with all this power flowing through those lines."

Jack walked out to the truck. Andre was starting to unload boxes. He walked by Jack and said it seemed clear. Jack asked, "Did you check the box? We don't need a Trojan Horse."

Andre sat the boxes on the porch and opened them. He stared inside for just a moment, then back up the stairs where Sara was playing doorman. Jack stepped up and shook the driver's hand, he looked her right in the eye and asked, "Did Dave Hanson load *all* things to do with the fairies? Even the stuff in the safe and in the safety deposit?"

The driver said with a blank face, "Everything that had to do with the fairies was packed. The blue fairies were sent to a colony downstate."

Jack said, "You have done your part. Now you will help unload this truck. Everything is to be stacked in the living room."

The driver said, "Yes, sir." She let go of Jack's hand and started to unload the U-Haul, it was one of the mid-sized ones, about a twenty-footer; you could stand in it. The three got into a rhythm and it unloaded quite quickly. There were boxes and garbage bags and a large trunk which took two people to lift. The living room was filled with stuff.

The driver asked Jack, "Dave and the girls want to know when they are going to meet."

Jack said, "Within two weeks. There might be a couple of players I need to line up. And I have to get the Europeans and Africans. They are on-board already, but to fit everyone's schedule is almost impossible. Just remember: St. Lucia, bring sunscreen and a bathing suit."

The driver said, "OK then, I will see you in a couple of weeks."

Andre walked to the door and watched the U-Haul pull away. Then he turned and asked, "What the hell is this 'I'll see you in a couple of weeks?' Marvin isn't going to want those guys around the castle!"

Jack, who was opening boxes, said, "They don't know where we live. Let me handle it, I do have a plan. Didn't I tell you the plan? Or was that Sara? I have so much shit floating around in my head, I think I'm going to lose my mind."

The fairies lined the bookcase, all in battle gear, watching every box get opened. Jack looked at them and asked, "I see you're not taking any chances."

Elizabeth flew to him, landing in Jack's palm. Andre stepped closer to hear her. She said, "This blue guardian guy, he is not to be trusted. He is very powerful. There is stuff in the boxes that he could have only collected by killing other guardians. Please watch him closely."

Jack said, "You're doing a great job, by the way."

Elizabeth asked, "When are we leaving? We want to get there about dusk. I have to clear a path, set up sentries—you can't be seen."

Nora flew to Jack's shoulder. "When are we leaving? I have so much to tell."

Jack asked Andre, "By what time do we have to leave?"

Andre said, "Oh, about half an hour ago."

Jack said loudly, "Red fairies get out here!" A hundred fairies appeared. Jack said, "Open the boxes and dump the bags. Nora, put somebody in charge of getting them washed. Lizard, you put someone in charge of security. Let's go, people! We need all the fairies that go up north to get washed."

The fairies dove into opening the boxes and dumping the bags. Sara walked in and shouted, "What the hell is going on here?" Everything was opened or dumped on the floor in less than five minutes.

Jack said, "Sorry about the mess, but we have a meeting to catch. You're in charge of the whole operation."

Sara asked, "What meeting? You're leaving?"

Jack said, "I told you we stopped on the way. I have to go on trial for seeing a stupid fairy."

Sara put her hand over her mouth and said quietly, "Don't take this lightly. I had a good friend years ago who went in front of a council and I never saw her again."

Elizabeth said, "Jack is special. I have never seen a human so strong. And he is learning fast. The council will bow to him."

Jack said, "Just do your jobs, there is a lot to be done." He turned and walked swiftly into the kitchen; there were boxes lying all over. He barked, "Nora!"

She hopped from his shoulder to his palm, a foot from his face. He asked, "What the hell is this mess? Have it cleaned up now, I need the head doctor in the living room now and I need the fairies that are going with."

Jack dropped his hand. Nora fluttered to the counter-top where the fairies were lining up to go through the sprayer on the sink. She started shouting and pointing; fairies started to fly around, stacking boxes next to the door. Three started cutting paper towels into smaller pieces for the fairies that were done showering. She then put a girl fairy in charge of keeping everything running smoothly. One old fairy came up and said he was a fairy doctor once, a long, long time ago. Nora grabbed him and said, "Good enough," and yelled, "Come!"

The fairy she had left in charge flew after them. Nora flew to Jack, who was rummaging through the boxes. He stood and held out his hand. Nora said, "Here's your doctor and the one who is now in charge of cleaning the fairies."

Jack said, "You fairy cleaner, report to Sara. She's your boss, tell her to put out a dish of dust and a charged rock."

The fairy flew from Jack's hand and to Sara's. Jack's hand started to glow a deep red. "Now for you. See all these boxes? They have potions and herbs, dust, rocks, all kinds of crap that I have no idea of. You're in charge."

The old fairy asked, "What do you want me to do with the stuff?"

Jack said, "You have to work with it. Make it so you can find it when you need it." Jack yelled: "Andre!"

Andre came in from outside and asked, "What?"

Jack said, "Let's get going, I'll grab my suitcase. You get Nora and the green one."

Jack went to the spare bedroom. When he opened the door, all eyes were on him. He said, "Ah, shit!" He zipped up his suitcase, shook his head, then said, "Who is the eldest from the forest? Come with me." Jack stepped out of the room and yelled, "Nora!" She flew from Sara to him.

Jack said, "We're going to leave now. Is there anything you forgot? Like five hundred fairies maybe?"

Nora's eyes got really wide her hand went to her mouth, "Oh I am so sorry, I'll get them."

Jack said, "You have five minutes. Tell Sara goodbye for now."

Sara said, "Five minutes? There's too many!" Jack looked over to Andre and shrugged his shoulders.

Andre yelled, "Elizabeth, get all the fairies from the forest! It's time to box them up. We should have left an hour ago."

Elizabeth said a few words to the old fairies she was talking to and they all scattered. Jack followed Andre out the door and asked, "How many cases?"

Andre said, "I'll throw the rest in the truck. They can spread out once we are on our way."

Jack picked up three cases, then turned to Andre. "Don't use the two they were shooting wasp spray out of."

Jack walked in to see hundreds of fairies waiting; he sat the cases down and said, "Get in."

The fairies poured in. Jack took the first case out to the truck. He said as he was walking, "Wait for the other two cases, then you can spread out. In fact, once you're all in the Caddy, you don't need to be in the cases."

Andre said, "It's going to be a tight fit. We're two cases short and we have at least three hundred more fairies."

Jack said, as he was putting the case of fairies in the back of the Caddy, "There are two more cases, let's just go." Jack sat the case in gently, opened the top and said, "Stay" like he was talking to a dog.

Sara came out with a case, Jack opened the back door for her. She slid in the case and Jack said over her shoulder, "Stay in the case until we get on the road."

Sara said, "I thought there were too many in there."

Jack said, "It's going to be tight. We lost two cases and gained three hundred fairies."

Andre ran down the steps and asked, "Where do you want them?"

Jack said, "Other side."

Sara turned to Jack, who was still standing right next to her. She was about six inches from him. She leaned in, gave him a kiss on the lips and whispered, "I can't thank you enough."

Chapter Twenty
To the Forest for Trial

Jack reached out and gave her a hug. He said, "I'll call you. We have to go."

The Caddy fired up and started to purr. The fairies poured out of the cases. Jack rolled his eyes and got in the truck. He asked, "OK, how long?"

Andre said, "About two, two and a half hours."

Jack said, "That GPS thing is showing you the shortest route, not the fastest. Take the freeway north and set your cruise five miles over the speed limit."

Andre pulled onto the freeway and the GPS changed to an hour and a forty five. Jack pulled out his phone and called Sara. He said nervously, "Hi, this is Jack. I was wondering, do you need a new birth certificate? I know this place that makes them up."

Andre looked over to him, "So you're kind of sweet on her."

Jack looked at him, "I'm too old for dating. Those days are over."

Andre smiled, "You have your whole life in front of you. Didn't you think your days of battle were behind you?"

Jack sat silent for a minute, then he said, "My head, it is so messed up! I can't hold a thought. There is so much to learn!" He lowered his back rest and closed his eyes. When he opened them, they were pulling into Jack's small town. Jack said, "Slow down. Turn right on the third intersection." Andre did. Jack said, "We can stop at my house."

There was Jack's house, yellow tape across the front door. Jack stared. He muttered, "What the—?"

Andre said, "Windows are black and there's a hole in the roof."

Jack set his jaw and frowned, "Dammit!"

Andre said, "Sorry about that."

Jack said, "Why the hell didn't anyone tell me?"

Jack then told him the way to the forest. Andre turned the Escalade around in Jack's driveway. Jack just stared and shook his head. Then he pulled out his mobile phone and called his neighbour, "Yeah, Pete, what the hell happened to my house?" There was a pause, then, "OK, you take care now."

Jack looked over to Andre, "It burnt the night I left. Electrical, they say."

Elizabeth flew to the front, "Now that means war—to burn someone's house."

Jack said quietly, "Yes, yes it does." He flipped the phone open again.

Nora asked, "Who are you calling now?"

Jack snapped, "My son. This is crap!" He went into contacts, scrolled though and found his son's name, then clicked on it. Nora was on his wrist watching. Jack said, "Next time I call someone, I'll let you do it."

Nora hopped off his wrist and he put it to his ear. Jack growled into the phone, "Why didn't you tell me the house burnt down?" A pause, then, "You know what, you take the kids and clean it up. Do whatever you have to, there's nothing here for me now."

Jack pushed the button and turned off the phone. Andre said, "He will call back within a couple of minutes."

Jack said, "I use the phone to call people. If I had listened to my messages I would have known that my house was on fire that night." Jack pointed out: "There! That is the motel you will be staying at. You know why? Because it's the only motel in town.

"There's a small road behind the tavern, take it slow." The chatter from all the fairies got louder and louder.

Andre turned and yelled, "Be quiet! God! It's like driving a school bus."

Jack said, "You'll go in a couple of hundred yards. Then there is a small car park."

Andre said, "With these ferns and tall trees, it's a bit spooky."

Elizabeth said, "It's dark enough to fly all the way there. It will take a few minutes to get my men stretched out along the way, to make sure we're not seen or followed."

Andre stopped and opened one of the back windows. Fifty or so fairies flew out.

Jack asked Nora, "What do you think?"

She flew out, then back in. "I think it's clean."

Elizabeth ordered a check of a mile around. Another fifty fairies flew out. This time they were wearing shields and carrying swords.

Jack opened his door and stepped out. Andre joined him, shook his hand and said, "Good luck."

Jack said, "Open the back doors. Nora, you're in lead." He kicked off his slip-ons and stuffed them in his shirt.

Elizabeth flew up, "It's not safe; we don't know what's out there!"

Jack said, "Screw it!" Then he said to Andre, "Leave your phone on. You can pick me up here."

Jack said, "Nora, up and over. None of this weaving through the trees stuff." He was off the ground, heading for the tree tops. Nora flew to the lead. There were hundreds of fairies following them. Nora stuck tightly to the treeline. Through the valleys she flew, as fast as she could without glowing. Jack was right behind her. They landed on a rock face. Jack asked, "How far from here?"

Nora said, "A couple of hundred yards. We should walk that way. They know we're coming,"

Jack said, "Screw that, let's fly and get this over with!" He raised off the ground about six feet, just over the tops of the ferns.

Elizabeth flew to him, landing on his back. She walked up and spoke into his ear, "Jack, you just let me do the talking. I put fear in them when I left."

Nora landed. There was a large furry animal lying on its stomach with its arm stuck in a hole. Red fairies were dropping rocks and sticks on him. He just swatted them away. He rolled over with a fairy in his hand and went to put it in his mouth.

Elizabeth shot to him, grabbing his arm and stopping him from eating the fairy. The furry beast laughed, grabbed her and said something, but not in English. He put his head back and started to lift Elizabeth, who was trying to suck the power from the beast. She screamed. Jack floated down to the beast, throwing a shot of white power, hitting him in the shoulder. His arm dropped.

Elizabeth pried his fingers open. She shot over to Jack, landing on a branch. Jack calmly walked over to the beast, who was at least eight feet tall. The beast took three fast steps toward Jack, raising his fist and letting out a loud roar. Jack threw another shot of power, hitting him in the knee. The beast fell flat on his face. It howled as it rolled onto is back, trying to get back to its feet.

Jack raised his hand and everything went still. He said in a booming voice, "I need someone to translate for me. Does anyone know how to speak its language?"

A small furry animal stepped out of the ferns and a loud mumbling came from a distance. The furry animal walked up to Jack, keeping its eyes low to the ground. It stopped and said, "I kind of speak your language."

Jack said, "Now don't be afraid, let me just take your hand." He took her hand and lifted her chin with the other so they were looking eye to eye. He said, "OK." Then he started speaking an old language and really getting into it. He was yelling and pointing to the beast that was sitting on the ground.

Then he yelled at the woods where five huge furry things stood. They all lowered their heads.

Jack turned back to the beast and yelled, "Nora, I'm going to need a large piece of quartz. And get the fairies to clean that spot for that boulder to rest. Someone will have to guide me to set it." Jack then walked right up to the beast and said, "I'm sorry, but this has to be done." Then he said it in that old language.

Jack started to pull the power from the beast. He grunted as he pulled. Nora showed up with the quartz and Jack levitated it between him and the beast. The stone turned a deep red, then pink and a blinding white. The beast's head collapsed, then his body wilted till all that was left was a big rug. There in a large puddle of goo in its place. Jack reached out and took the piece of quartz out of the air and set it on the boulder. He said, "I'll be back."

Jack jumped to where the other beasts were. He spoke in the old language; the beasts nodded as Jack spoke. Then Jack started walking down the hillside. He flew out of the ferns and landed right next to the dead beast. The small beast was talking to some of the fairies. Jack walked up, seeing all these fairies sitting and listening to this small thing—well, maybe not that small, she stood about five foot; she was young.

Nora flew to Jack. "That Yeti that you killed was mentally ill."

Jack said, "He fell on his head two seasons ago and he hasn't been the same since. And do you know why he ate the fairies? It was because they tickled his throat going down."

Then Jack asked, "Are these Yeti? Sasquatch? In other words, he was a Bigfoot."

Jack walked over and asked Nora, "Did you get the seat ready for the boulder?" Jack picked up the quartz stone that he had set there and set it in the hole the Yeti had dug. He then asked, "Will it fit?"

Nora said, "There is a whole cave system ten feet in. Marvin closed it off and moved the stone in front of the entrance."

Jack stepped back and asked, "How did Marvin move that boulder? Maybe if I get the Yeti down here they could do it."

Ivan the unicorn walked up and said, "Jack, I've been waiting for you."

Jack turned around and looked down at the small talking unicorn. He said, "We have to talk."

Ivan said, "Search your brain. You know how to move this rock."

Jack closed his eyes, put his hand on the boulder and the thing came right off the ground. He took three steps, rolled the huge stone in the air and set it down in front of the hole in the hillside. He opened his eyes. "My God, did you see that?" he exclaimed.

Jack asked, "OK, where is this council? I want to get this over as soon as possible."

Ivan looked up at Jack. "You will come with me; the council will be here when you get back."

Jack said, "OK, you lead the way."

The old unicorn streaked thought the woods. Jack was right behind him. In a couple of minutes they had covered at least ten miles. Ivan stopped and Jack landed right next to him. Ivan said, "You have learned much in a week."

Jack said, "Here, let me show you." He reached down and touched the unicorn's horn and closed his eyes. They stood there for a good two minutes, not saying a word. Finally, Jack took his hand off the horn, breaking the link.

Ivan said, "Sit down," as he folded his legs and lay down. The two of them were silent for a good half hour. Ivan said, "That will be enough. You have to go back and tell the council to piss off."

Jack smiled and said with a quiet voice, "Thank you so very much."

Ivan said, "When you get alone, sort all the information in your head and junk the stuff you don't need. You have way too much." Then Ivan asked, "Can you find your way?"

Jack said, "Yes. And I am sorry about your mate. You should find another. And thank you again."

Ivan looked up at him and said, "That was fifty years ago. You should be going. Make me proud, Jack."

Jack was off, flying through the woods, this time not glowing. He was moving right along. It took him about five times longer than when he was chasing Ivan. He landed next to the boulder, some leaves were moved. All the foot prints were gone, the hide of the Bigfoot was gone; it looked like nothing had happened there at all.

A line of old rust-coloured fairies stood on a rock. Nora flew to Jack and landed on his shoulder. She said into his ear, "They are the council."

Jack walked over and picked up his backpack. He stood in front of the fairies, unzipped the pack and took out a gallon Ziploc bag filled with fairy dust. He held it up. The whole forest filled with whispers. The council motioned and some red fairies flew to Jack to take the bag. Jack took out another gallon bag. This one wasn't full, but it was still more than half. They took that also.

One fairy stepped forward and asked, "Jack Robinson, what do you have to say in your defence?"

Jack said, "I have returned your dust. This should feed you for years. I will keep in contact; there is a war going on and I will fight to the death for your cause."

The council huddled in a circle, debating. Elizabeth flew up and landed next to them. She walked right up and pushed her way into the huddle. You could hear her voice. "Now you listen here! You give Jack your blessing and tell him to be on his way."

Nora stepped to Jack's ear. "That should do it. Nobody's going to screw with a green fairy."

Jack said, "You've got to be joking! You mean all I had to do was to send Lizard Breath? I didn't even need to come." The forest became silent, not one noise, not a fairy moved. Ivan nudged Jack with his horn, Jack looked down.

Ivan said, "You had to come. You freed Sara, saved hundreds of fairies, even saved Elizabeth!"

Jack rolled his eyes. "OK, I needed to be here." He looked up and asked, "May I approach the council?"

Elizabeth said, "Step forward."

Jack did and said, "I have done what I can for you, but now I must leave."

One of the fairies said to Jack, "Thank you for taking care of the Yeti, and thank you for the twenty-year supply of food. We were worried." He then turned to Elizabeth, "Thank you so very much! With you bringing Jack here, you have saved us all." He bowed to her.

Jack asked, "One more thing, what did you do with the beast?"

One of the council said, "Tonight, he will be brought to the mountain of fire and dropped in."

Jack said, "I just wanted to make sure you covered the evidence. We don't want anybody finding it."

With that, Jack pulled out his phone. He said, "I'll tell Dropoff to meet us at the car park."

Ivan asked, "Is that Andre Dropoff? I had seen him when he was about twenty. Does he still have that brother, Ivan?"

Jack smiled and said, "Yeah, his last name is Pickupski, so you have Pickup and Dropoff. Both of them are in there sixties. I really have to go." Jack said into the phone, "It's a go, meet you in twenty minutes."

Jack then said to himself, "I hope he got separate rooms. God, I'm tired."

Elizabeth flew up to Jack and asked, "Are you ready?"

Jack reached down and petted Ivan. He said, "I'll be back. The bastards burnt my house down."

Ivan said, "Yes, I know."

Jack said with a flat tone, "Nora." Then he turned to the council. "I am taking Nora, and Boris—well, he's busy. I don't know when he will return."

Nora flew to the council and asked, "May I have permission to stay with Jack?"

Jack lifted from the ground with his shoes still tucked into his belt. He bellowed, "Nora!"

A stream of deep red streaks shot by. Nora flew to Jack and said, "Fly slowly. Let them check the route, we can't be seen."

Jack said, "We are going up and over. I'm tired. None of this weaving through the woods shit." Jack went straight up, just out of the treeline and started to fly down the valley.

Nora's head glowed a deep red. Jack could tell she was pissed. She flew up and said, "Follow me."

Elizabeth flew to Jack, landed on his back and rode him all the way to the landing. Jack was flying nice and slow, letting Nora fly ahead and check for trouble. Nora blinked on and off. Then blinks came from the woods. Nora flew back to Jack. She said excitedly, "They're people in the turn-around with a fire."

Jack said, "Just kids. Let's land up the road farther."

Elizabeth flew off fast, but still not lighting up. She dropped into the wood line. Jack and Nora flew on around where they were going to land. Up the road they flew, seeing the big black Caddy sitting there. Jack landed right next to the passenger side; he opened the door. Andre grabbed his chest and said, "Jesus."

Jack said, "No, it is just me. Do you know where Lisa is?"

Andre said, "She was just here."

Nora, who was sitting on Jack's lap, yelled, "Turn off the light!"

Jack shut the door. The dome light went out, Elizabeth came out of hiding and Nora flew to Jack's shoulder. Jack asked, "How did you know to stop out here?"

Andre asked, "Didn't you send Elizabeth?"

Jack stared at the green fairy, then asked, "What happened to your wings?"

Nora said, "Didn't you notice when that Yeti—Bigfoot, whatever—grabbed her, he crushed her wings. I was surprised it didn't crush her."

Elizabeth said, "Could you believe that stupid thing tried to eat me?"

Andre shook his head. "Damn, I miss all the fun!"

Nora flew over to Elizabeth and said, "Here, let me try to straighten them." Nora took one wing and gently straightened it, taking out the wrinkles, but there was serious damage.

Jack held out his palm and said, "Bring her here."

Nora picked her up and fluttered to Jack's hand. Jack took the little wing between his thumb and forefinger and started to rub. His fingers turned a deep green and the wing straightened right out. He did the other wing as well. Elizabeth opened and closed her wings. She fluttered up and to the headrest.

Andre said, "So you saw a Yeti? I haven't seen one of those in years!"

Nora flew to him. She said all excitedly, "Not only did he see one, he killed one! You should have seen it! A mentally ill Yeti rolled the rock from in front of the cave and was fishing out fairies and eating them. Elizabeth flew in to save a red fairy from being eaten. Then the Yeti grabbed her. Then Jack killed the Yeti and sucked him dry. All there was left was a pile of fur and teeth and a few bones."

Jack interrupted, "How many rooms did you get?"

Andre said, "Oh yeah, that would be the Super 8. I got you a connecting room. Now, that Yeti moved that great big boulder? It took days to winch that thing in place!"

Elizabeth smiled and said, "Jack lifted it and flew it into place. He even had to turn it to match up with the hole."

Andre pulled over and said in amazement, "You've got to be kidding me! You lifted the boulder that was in front of the council headquarters?"

Jack said, "I'll tell you all about it when we get to the hotel. I need a shower, a meal and some sleep."

Andre said, "A haircut and a shave wouldn't hurt either." He fired up the Caddy. Soon they were at the hotel; he said, "Your bag is already in your room." He held his jacket open and the two fairies flew in. Then he opened the door.

Jack was standing next to the hotel, waiting. Andre said, "Key," then reached in his suit and took out a plastic card and said, "This is a hotel key." He swiped it though the slot and the light turned green.

Jack pulled the door open and asked, "Which way?"

Andre walked past and to the lift. He stepped in and said, "The penthouse," as he pushed three.

Jack asked, "Is there room service?"

Andre asked, "Don't you live here?"

Jack replied, "Did you pick up something to eat?"

Andre said with a smile, "There's a foot-long sub in the refrigerator, crisps and a biscuit on the table."

Jack rubbed Andre's shoulder, "Thanks, man."

As soon as Andre opened the room door, Jack was inside and to his room. A couple of minutes later, he came out with the sub in his hand. Andre was questioning the fairies about what had happened. Jack put his free hand on Andre's shoulder. When he looked up, Jack's eyes locked with his. They sat, looking into each other's eyes for a good three minutes. Then Jack said, "That's what happened."

Andre said, "Now that's cool! I know some of those council members."

Jack shrugged, "Hey, I have to get ready for bed. Wake me in the morning. I'll take you out for breakfast."

Andre said, "I think you should keep a low profile for a bit."

Jack stroked his beard, then said, "You're probably right."

Andre asked, "What time would you like me to wake you?"

Jack said with a mouthful of sub, "Early", then walked back into his room.

Nora followed. She landed on his shoulder. "First you drink a couple of glasses of water, then shower."

Jack said, "I'm tired. I just want to go to bed."

Nora crossed her arms and hovered right in front of his face. "You have to take a shower! Look at you your hair, your moustache! You're growing younger by the minute."

Jack huffed out a "Fine". He walked into the bathroom and looked into the mirror. He could see two inches of brown goo at the roots of his hair. He ran his finger across his cheek, leaving a streak. He just rolled his eyes and turned on the shower. When he was done, his toothbrush was sitting on the sink with an empty glass next to it and the bottoms of his pyjamas were lying on the toilet. Jack stepped from the shower. He finished wiping off, then stretched and said, "Boy, I feel great!"

Nora flew up and said, "Put your sleep wear on, brush your teeth and drink at least one glass of water."

Jack looked at her and asked, "Who died and put you in charge?"

Nora was quite pissed now. "Ivan put me in charge and you know it."

Jack smiled and said, "You're right, I'll do what you ask." He stepped into his pyjama bottoms and slammed a glass of water, then brushed his teeth, then filled his glass again and went out into the room. He opened the bag of crisps and finished eating the sub.

He said, "That's it! I'm hitting the hay."

He looked around and found Nora fast asleep on top of the napkins. He smiled and said, "Yeah, it's been a long day."

Jack crawled into bed. He lay there, sifting through all the stuff he had running around in his head. He was doing what Ivan had told him to do. Memories were just electrical, stored in his brain. He was going through everything he learned from the All-Knowing Jonathan—most of that he scrapped. John's childhood—he just kept what he needed and now he felt he was stronger still. The next thing he knew, Andre was at the door. Jack looked up. Andre said, "It's six o'clock, you wanted to be woken early."

Jack rubbed his eyes. "OK then." He quickly dressed and asked, "Do we get a continental breakfast?"

Andre looked at him. Jack said, "What? I might live here, but I never stayed here. Hell, you registered!"

Andre said, "Yes, they have coffee and doughnuts. We have to get back."

Jack asked, "Can we stop and see how Sara is doing?"

Andre said, "Why do you think we have to leave so early? That's three hours out of our way. We stay there for an hour, no more."

Jack walked back into the room. His bag was on the bed, zipped and ready to go. Jack took a walk-through and looked under the bed, in the fridge, in the bathroom. Nora said, "I got everything, let's go."

Elizabeth and Nora rode in Andre's pocket because he wore a suit jacket with the nice inner pocket.

Jack said, "First stop, coffee."

Andre said, "Take it to go."

Jack walked to the breakfast bar. There were some fruit and vegetables and a plate of doughnuts, apple turnovers, and so on. Jack filled a plastic plate and his coffee and went off to the truck. Andre had dropped the key off first and met Jack in the Escalade. Jack bit into the apple turnover and the flaky crust fell on the seat.

Andre said, "You can eat in the rentals, but not in my cars."

Jack looked at him and said, "Fine, let's go."

Soon, they were on a highway heading west. Jack asked, "Why are you going this way?" Andre pointed to the GPS. Jack said, "Take the next exit south. We can cut at least a half hour off."

Andre took the exit and the route changed. Nora flew up and stared at the screen. Then she asked, "How does it know where we are?"

Andre pointed to a series of bars and said, "Do you see the green bars right there? That shows how many satellites we have."

Nora asked, "What's a satellites?"

Andre pondered for a minute, "It's a machine that is shot into space with a rocket and it orbits the earth, collecting data and sending it back to earth. We've been through this before. That's why Jack shouldn't be flying around, blowing tops of trees off."

Elizabeth said, "So that's what those things are," she pointed to an observatory.

Andre told her, "No, those are telescopes monitoring space. We're worried about the ones looking *down* at us. Those satellites are whizzing around at thousands of miles an hour. They can see you." Jack just closed his eyes and put his head back.

Andre reached over and gave Jack a shake. Jack eyes snapped open. He gasped, "What?"

The GPS said, "Eight hundred yards, turn right and you will be at your destination."

Jack stretched and asked, "I thought you hated a woman telling you where to go."

Andre said, "The fairies think it's neat. Well, we are here. Remember. One hour."

Jack looked at his watch, "OK, one hour."

Andre slowed the Caddy to a crawl and rolled into the driveway. Jack got out. Andre stepped out and grabbed his jacket. He slid it on, leaned back and held it open for Nora and Elizabeth to scoot in. Jack was standing on the porch, ringing the bell. There was no answer. Jack said, "Damn! I wonder where she is." He said, "Nora, do you feel any of the red fairies?"

She crawled up to Andre's neck and told him, "Up in that big pine. It feels like there are a few."

Jack floated off the ground and peered into the tree. He said, "I want to talk with one of you and you don't want me to pull you out of the tree."

A red fairy flew from the tree. Jack held out his hand palm up. The fairy landed on it and Jack slowly sank to the ground. He asked, "Can you tell me where Sara is?"

The fairy said, "Thank you so very much! You have saved my life and the lives of my people."

Jack said, "Can you or can't you tell me where Sara is?"

The fairy said, "She is at the big house on the hill."

Jack rolled his eyes, "Ah yes, the big house. You can come along and tell us what has been happening around here." Jack motioned to the truck. He said, "Remember that mansion we drove by the other day? The one with the long drive and the gate? That's where we want to go."

Jack got in the truck and started to question the red fairy. "Is Sara going through regeneration? How is she? What did she think of the fight?"

The red fairy couldn't answer most of the questions; he just said, "She is working at getting us fairies used to *not* being slaves and living in cages. She wants us to move back into the big house; she says it's safe."

Andre pulled up to the gate. Jack said, "I've got this." He closed his eyes and lifted his hand. The gate swung open.

Andre asked, "How did you do that?"

Jack said "I understand electricity. This isn't a computer-operated gate. Let's just pop in and see what she is what she is up to."

Andre pulled up in front. He opened his jacket and all three fairies flew in. Jack got out, walked up to the front door and rang the bell. A couple of minutes later, Sara answered it. When she opened the door, she saw Jack, wrapped her arms around him and gave him a kiss on the lips, saying, "Thank you so very much! I have never been so happy."

Jack pried her off him, asking, "Is there anything we can do for you? We wanted to make sure you were all right."

Sara wiped the tears that started to stream down her cheeks. She sobbed, "Everything is great. I'm going to move back into my house after all these years. I get to move back in, oh, thank you, Jack!"

Nora flew out of Andre's pocket, followed by the other two fairies. She flew to Jack's shoulder and said, "We have to get inside."

Jack asked, "Do you mind?" He stepped into the place, then he whistled, "This is pretty nice. Three stories!"

Sara said, "Four. And four stories underground. Come in, I need a break. There's coffee on in the kitchen, I'll get it."

Jack asked, "Do you mind if we have it in the kitchen?"

Sara said, "Follow me." She quickly walked down the hall to another hall through a dining room and into the kitchen. Andre pulled out a chair for Sara. She sat, then he pulled one out for Jack. Jack pulled out his own and sat.

Andre served the coffee. Jack said, "I don't have much time here." He looked at his watch. "Less than half an hour."

Elizabeth flew to the table and asked, "How are the fairies? Are they making an army?"

Jack cocked his head and said, "What? This is the first I've heard of this!"

Sara said, "Yes, I have picked a general to lead, the same one you had and I am going to teach them about all the great battles."

Jack said, "An army, what for?

Elizabeth said, "Didn't you see how they handled the blues? All they need is weapons and training. They can defend themselves."

Nora flew down between Jack and Elizabeth. She asked, "How is Sara?"

Jack said, "Oh yes, that is why we are here. Sara, do you have someone capable of doing your regeneration? And can you get all the paper work for your next life?"

Sara said, "I have a couple of older fairies that can do the regeneration and I was going to go to Russia to get my paperwork."

Andre said, "This is a new world. It will take you at least ten years to get a green card to get in this country legally; there is so much red tape."

Jack wrote down the address to the Magic Castle on a piece of paper and said, "Pay attention. On the front, how old you are going to be, what your name is, who your folks are, and how you're going to inherit your fortune."

Sara was taking notes. She said, "This is going to be tricky. It never was this complicated."

Andre smiled and said, "Welcome to the 21st century, where you can't trust anyone. And you have a long e-trail.

Jack said, "I have someone that can fudge your tax records."

Andre asked, "Now really, how is it going?"

Sara said, "It is going well; I am feeling better than I have in years. I can see that I have a future."

Jack asked, "Aren't you sick and throwing up? Unable to stand? God, that first day, I felt like hell, thought I was going to die."

Sara said "This isn't my first regeneration. You have to take it slow. It will take a month."

Jack said, "We have to go. Invite me to the funeral."

A blank look came over Sara's face. "I forgot! I have to stage my death, organise my funeral and redo my will."

Jack smiled, "That will keep you busy. Just get me the information, I'll handle the birth certificate."

Sara said, "I'll see you out. Maybe next time I'll have the place clean enough to give you a tour."

Nora flew up to her and said, "We'll be back soon, Jack has to take care of his house up north."

Sara said, "Oh, you have to leave it in your inheritance."

Jack said, "That's not it. The damn blue fairies burnt it to the ground. I lost everything."

Sara put her arms around him and gave him a hug. "I'm so sorry."

Jack said, "It was just a house, but I lost everything that reminded me of Emma—my wife."

Sara asked, "How long ago did she die?"

Jack said, "She didn't die, she was killed by the blues. One night she went out to catch some blue lighting bugs; she was stone cold when I found her." He wiped a tear from her face. "She was a good woman; the blues killed her."

Sara held him tighter as she whispered in his ear, "I am so sorry."

Jack gently pushed her away and asked, "Were you married?"

Sara said, "For 133 years. He was killed in a fight with a blue guardian. If I knew how to block an attack, I could have saved him. I was just lucky I got out with my life. That's when I moved out here."

Jack asked, "How long ago was that."

Sara said, "Thirty years ago. My last husband died trying to save me from three blue guardians. That time they let me go."

Jack said, "I will send you a prepaid mobile phone so you can call me. Marvin is a little paranoid, he thinks the blues are monitoring the phone lines."

Sara said, "Stay, have some more coffee."

Andre said, "I'm sorry, we are on a timetable; we have a plane to catch."

Jack said, "A private jet and he's the pilot, but we have to go. I have more crap going on, more than I know what to do with."

Sara showed them the door. Jack said, "Go and fill out what you want on your birth certificate. I need that right away. Like put it in the mail tomorrow and put Marvin, the Remington on it. Nobody knows I am there."

They all got into the Escalade. Jack rolled down the window and waved. Andre said, "I think she's going to be a looker when she's regenerated."

Nora flew up and handed Jack a bottle of water. She said, "You're not going to match your driving licence pretty soon."

Andre said, "You know she is right you are going to have to stop using your powers and playing with fairy dust."

Jack looked at him and said, "It's not like I'm looking for a reason. I had to use it. And I wasn't going to walk miles to the fairy council."

Andre reached over and flipped down the visor. "Look."

Jack opened the mirror. The light shined on his face and he sat and stared, then said, "Shit, we have to stop at a pharmacy and get some hair dye." He ran his hand over his face.

Nora fluttered to the dash. "Jack, you are doing just fine. I have seen regeneration just like this one, nice and slow."

Jack said, "Slow? Pretty soon, my kids won't even recognise me. It's supposed to take a month or two! It has only been a week."

Jack reached up, closed the mirror and said, "That reminds me, once I'm on the plane, I have to call my boy and chew him out again for not telling me my house burnt down." He unbuckled and squirmed around, getting his phone out of his pocket. He flipped it open.

Andre said, "Why don't you wait till you calm down a bit, and you already did that?"

Jack shot a look at him, put the phone to his ear and spoke loudly into it, "Johnny, my boy, is there a reason you didn't tell me the house burnt to the ground?" There was a pause, then Jack yelled into the phone, "I don't care, I lost everything! You even had my town car scrapped! What the hell kind of a son are you?"

Jack took the phone from his ear and pushed cancel. Nora stared at Jack, then said, "Come on Jack, really, was that necessary? You yelled at him yesterday for the same thing. And Sara told you she was married before."

Jack smiled, then chuckled, "It was not necessary, but fun. He should have told me as soon as it happened."

Elizabeth flew to the dash and told Jack, "You know, I think I'm starting to like you."

Jack yelled, "Starbucks!" and pointed.

Andre said, "OK, but this is the last stop. Marvin is probably pacing the floor, wondering what is going on."

Jack flipped open his phone again, played with it and then put it to his ear. He said, "How's Boris?" Then he said, "Oh, Elizabeth did an excellent job. And there was a fire at my house while I was gone, total loss." Jack looked over to Andre and said, "A triple shot, mocha. And how long before we grace his door?"

Andre said, "Five hours, give or take." He ordered the coffee.

Jack said, "Yeah, Marv, we'll be there in about five hours, give or take. You want us to pick anything up? OK, then."

They drove for another half an hour and they were at the airport. Andre said, "Screw it, we will pay the penalty for not filling the tank. And they can pick it up at the hangar." Andre leaned over and took a small pack from the glove compartment.

Jack took it from him and told him, "Drive. I will call the rental service." The next thing he knew, they were in the plane. Jack asked, "Don't we have to fuel up?"

Andre said, "Everything is taken care of, don't worry. You're paying for it." He started the checklist before the flight. Nora sat on his shoulder as he explained what he was doing and what the gauges did.

Jack said, "Wake me when we get there."

Andre called the tower, confirmed the flight plan and they taxied down the runway. As soon as Andre gave it some gas, Jack's eyes popped open. They ran down the runway and gently took off. Andre said, "See how nice it is, having a runway that is long enough?"

Jack just closed his eyes as they climbed to cruising height. Andre put it on auto-pilot. Soon, everyone was asleep, then an alarm went off. Andre lifted his arm and shut off the alarm on his watch. He said, "OK, boys and girls! A half hour and then we will be home."

Then he pushed some buttons and talked to the tower. They gave him a heading. He punched in some numbers and the plane started to bank and descend. When Andre started to make his approach, Jack opened his eyes and asked, "Are we there yet?"

Andre told him, "We will be touching ground in about seven minutes, please check your seatbelts. And make sure your luggage is secure."

Jack checked his seat belt and asked Nora to check his bag. Elizabeth flew to his shoulder. "Everything is good." Then she asked, "What was with all the mumbling in your sleep? Did you have a bad dream?"

Jack snapped back, "Sleep? I wasn't sleeping! I was going over all the crap I got from Margaret. And let me tell you, I think I underestimated her. She is one sick bitch."

Elizabeth fluttered in front of Jack. He said, "Sit down, we are going to land."

Andre slowly set the jet onto the runway; he slowed it to a taxi and talked on the headset as he drove it to his hangar.

Jack asked, "Where is Pickupski?"

Andre cocked his head, "I think he has a flight to New York, he'll be there for a couple of days."

Jack asked, "Are you guys that busy?"

Andre said, "Marvin owns the planes; we were booked out three months ahead." He pushed a button and the hangar opened; there was a jet sitting in the corner already.

Jack asked, "How many jets does Marvin own?"

Andre smiled, "I don't know, but we have three. Two 8-seaters and a 12. The larger one needs a co-pilot." Andre pulled the jet into the hangar and parked it right in the middle. He said to himself, "Close enough." The floor was polished to a shine, everything looked to be in its place.

Jack said, "This is nice."

Andre smiled and said, "Pickupski likes a clean shop. Says it's good for business, so pick up after yourself."

Jack said, "I will grab the tugger and push you into your parking spot."

Jack pulled out his mobile phone and turned it on. Andre said, "Well, as soon as I fill out this crap, we'll be on our way." He sat with a clipboard on his lap.

Jack put his phone to his ear and said, "Marvin, whatever you do, don't leave Margaret in the house. She is evil, you don't understand—"

Jack turned to Andre. "The son-of-bitch hung up on me!"

Andre said as he took out his phone, "Marvin is paranoid. He thinks his phone is tapped."

Jack rolled his eyes and said to the ceiling, "Oh, man."

Andre put his phone to his ear, "Marvin, how you doing? I think Jack is getting paranoid, he is just worried that she would take over. We should grace your door in an hour. How is Boris doing?"

Andre told Jack, "Well, Juliet is doing well."

Jack asked, "Did he tell you his dead wife was doing fine? I thought he was so paranoid."

Andre looked up from his clipboard and said, "I asked him how Boris was doing and Marvin said he was doing a great job. So if he is doing well, then Juliet is doing well."

Jack said, "We need to stop somewhere to grab a bite."

Andre put the clipboard back into place. He got out of the pilot's seat and told Jack, "Get your luggage ready. I will pull the car around." With that, he popped the door, dropped the steps and was gone.

Jack got up and said to himself, "Ah hell!" as he walked to the tugger and pushed the plane next to the other one. He turned to hear Andre beeping the horn, just a little chirp to get Jack's attention. Jack grabbed his bag and said, "Well?" with his pocket held open. The two fairies flew right in.

Jack started down the steps when he felt a fairy crawl up his shirt to his ear. Nora yelled, "Your cane!"

Jack stopped and said, "Really? You want me to go back and get my cane? I don't need it." He turned around and went back into the plane, then he ran down the steps again in protest. "I don't need any stupid cane."

He walked to the town car, Andre stood at the door waiting for him. Jack said, "I'm riding shotgun, if you don't mind." He walked around the front of the car to the passenger side, leaving his bag close to the driver's door. Andre grabbed the bag, wheeled it to the back of the car and tossed it into the boot.

When he got back into the car, he asked Jack, "How are you going to plan your day?"

Jack asked, "Why do you want to know?"

Andre shook his head, then said, "So I can plan my day, sir."

Jack said, "Well, we have to go to Margaret's for a couple of hours. If everything is in place, it might take longer. I have to talk to Marvin and tell him what is going on in the forest."

Andre pulled the car out of the hangar, then got out and closed the hangar door, then walked out of the service door. When Andre got back to the car, Jack was talking to the two fairies who were sitting on the dash. Nora sat and listened to Elizabeth talk about how she thought if they made more weapons, she could make an army at the castle. Jack turned to Andre. "Lizard Breath here is going to make you a list of things to pick up. The same as at Sara's. We're going to arm the reds at the castle and she's going to train them."

Andre smiled as he asked, "So the razors worked?"

Elizabeth pulled her sword from its sheath. "I can fly straight though a cloud of them, leaving nothing but sparks."

Nora flew to Andre's shoulder and whispered in his ear, "She is vicious. She must have killed five hundred blues by herself."

Andre looked at the little green fairy, who was standing like a hula girl on the dash. He stated, "You're a warrior, then."

She stood and stared at him for a couple of seconds, then said, "Yes, I guess I am. I fight for right; that is the way Marvin says. If we have to fight, do it for the right cause. And those blue things are just vermin. They have to be wiped from the surface of this planet and I am the one to do it."

Jack told Elizabeth, "You are to do as you are told. Guardians are much stronger. I am running this show, do you understand? I watched you fight. You absorbed the blue power, it gave you more and more power." He said, "Let's get something to eat."

Andre said, "That's fine, dine-in or drive-though?"

Jack told him, "I don't care, just stop somewhere. I'm starving."

Andre said, "That's it, then. We'll dine in, we're not eating in the car."

They pulled out of the airport and got on the freeway. Andre said, "We'll stop at a Baha Fresh, two exits up."

When they pulled up in front of the restaurant, Jack asked if the fairies wanted anything. Nora said, "Coca Cola, not diet. The real thing."

Jack stepped out and grabbed onto the car for support, "I'm a bit dizzy."

Andre popped his head back in the car and asked, "Is he going to be OK?"

Nora shouted, "He needs food every few hours."

Andre said, "Thanks for telling me now." He shut the door and quickly stepped to Jack's side. "Hey, you should keep a Snicker bar handy. That's what I do when I'm flying. That will hold you over."

Jack walked slowly to be careful not to fall. He looked up at Andre and said, "I need a Coke and something with beans in it."

Andre walked up to the counter, put in their order and ran the Coke to Jack, who was sitting, staring at the table. Andre slid the Coke in front of him. Jack looked up and said, "I think I have make a grave mistake." He took a long pull of the straw, sucking about a quarter of the cup.

Andre sat across from him with the food; he told Jack that he looked better. Jack smiled and said, "Sugar. I needed some sugar. I think I'm becoming diabetic in my old age."

Andre stared at him for a second, then said, "You need to regenerate, your bones will be stronger. You're just making it harder on yourself."

Jack looked up with a mouthful. He said, "All in good time."

Andre asked, "What mistake do you think you made?"

Jack stirred around the beans on his plate. "Margaret. I think she is too powerful for the hypnotism to hold her. There's a good chance she will kill me or have me killed. She is evil." He scraped the plate clean. He got up, filled his soda and said, "To the castle then."

They walked out of the restaurant to the car. Jack pulled out his phone from his pockets, called Margaret and chatted with her for a minute, then turned to Andre, "Drop me off at Margaret's." Jack sat with his head in his hands in deep thought, then said again, "Yeah, you can you drop me at Margaret's."

Andre asked, "Do you think that's a good idea? Since you think she might kill you?"

Jack looked at his feet, shook his head and stared at the dash. "I have to do something. The sooner, the better."

The ride to Brentwood seemed like it took forever. Jack just sat there with his eyes closed. Andre told Jack, "We are ten minutes out." Jack just sat there. Andre stepped hard on the brakes, throwing Jack into his seat belt.

Jack opened his eyes, turned and shot a look at Andre. Andre smiled, "We are ten minutes from Margaret's place. I thought you were sleeping."

Jack said, "I heard you the first time. I was going over the stuff I downloaded from Margaret. She is one sick puppy. She has killed at least five red guardians. The only reason Marvin is still alive is that she needs a breeding programme for the reds. They don't breed in captivity."

Andre shook his head, then asked, "Didn't she know if they're not fed well, they won't have kids? The only one who stayed at the castle is Rupert. We were afraid she was going to attack and take all the fairies. The blues took them one by one, so Marvin sent them away."

Andre pulled into the driveway and up to the gate. He rolled down his window and spoke to a box. "Hello, Mr Jack Robinson is here to see Miss Margaret."

A woman's voice answered, "You can park right in front." Andre pulled the big Lincoln through the gates down a long drive to the mansion. He pulled up next to the marble lions.

Jack said, "Nora and Elizabeth, stay with Andre. I will call you when I need you to pick me up."

Andre said, "My job is to wait for you, take your time. I'll be here."

Jack said, "Well, suit yourself. This could take an hour or so."

Jack got out of the car. He walked to the front door, where Linda was standing, waiting for him. She reached out her hand and said, "Jack. We thought you were going to be here yesterday."

Jack shook her hand lightly and said, "Linda, you're as beautiful as ever. I ran into some trouble up north. Downsizing the red guardians is not an easy job."

Linda said, "Margaret is waiting in the green room. Please follow me."

Jack started to follow Linda as she walked down the hall with high heels on. She walked really fast, down the hall, then took a left and down another hallway. This one had a red marble floor shined so you could see a reflection in it. The old man kept right on her heels.

Linda stopped at an open doorway. She looked at Jack; she was breathing hard. Jack calmly asked, "This is the green room."

Linda said, between breaths, "Yes, she is waiting for you."

Jack asked, "Are you coming in? This has to do with you also."

Linda said, "I am right behind you."

Jack walked into the room. To his surprise, it was a large room with vaulted ceilings and sunroof. There were trees and hundreds of flowers. Jack walked up to see Margaret sitting behind a desk. It looked out place in the lush, forested room. She saw Jack and rose from her chair, motioning him over.

Jack walked up to the desk and held out his hand as he said, "I'm sorry I am late. Things got complicated. I actually had to kill a Yeti—Big Foot, whatever." Jack grunted, clicked and smacked his lips.

Margaret smiled, "I haven't heard someone speak Yeti in a hundred years or so."

Jack asked, "Do you have everything in order?"

Margaret said softy, "Yes, everything is in order. Linda knows what to do. The only thing is the police and coroner."

Jack smiled, "That my specialty. When the time comes, I will handle that." Jack looked over to Linda and asked, "Are you going to handle all the details?"

Linda stood and smiled. Margaret spoke for her, "She'll be fine. This isn't the first regeneration she has seen me through."

She then paused and blurted sharply, "Why am I telling? You know everything I have done, don't you, Jack? You looked right into my soul."

Jack said, "That would be rude. I have a job to do. I think you would be a powerhouse in the new order."

Margaret asked, "When?"

Jack said, "The sooner, the better. I have had my ass chewed more than once over this."

Margaret stood, walked around the desk and asked, "Would you like to watch?"

Jack asked, "How are you going to do it?"

Margaret smiled and started for the door. She stopped and turned, then asked, "Oh Linda, aren't you going to watch your boss kill herself?"

Linda said, "No, I just don't think I could."

Margaret turned, then started down the hall. She said, "Linda is a great girl, but never had the guts for this. Hell, she won't even go to a bullfight!" Margaret stepped into a beautiful bedroom which must have been a thousand square feet. She walked over to her desk in the corner and took an envelope out of a drawer.

She walked to the circular staircase and put the envelope on a small table. Then she walked over to the bed and pulled out a rope from under it. She walked back to the staircase and asked Jack, "Do you think a six foot drop would be OK?"

Jack said, "If you step off a chair, you won't break your neck. That would make your regeneration go so much faster."

Maggie smiled and said slyly, "I was just checking." She walked up the stairs and tied the rope to the bannister. Then she walked down and slid over a chair, stepped onto it and measured the rope. It hung down around her chest.

She then stepped down off the chair and said, "A foot too low." She ran up the steps and retied the rope. This time, she tied it with an extra knot. She got back on the chair. This time, she pulled on the rope.

She looked at Jack and asked, "This is going to work, isn't it?"

Jack said, "It has to, doesn't it?"

Margaret stood on her tiptoes and slid the noose over her head. She said to Jack, "I have hung a few people in my life, but never myself." She did a little jump and with one foot, she kicked the chair. She came down with the rope tightening around her throat. She looked wild-eyed. She reached up, pulling herself up the rope and croaked, "I've changed my mind, help me, please!"

Jack stood there, tears streaming down his face. He sobbed, "I can't. You must die. I am so sorry."

Margaret's hands were starting to bleed. She couldn't hold the rope any longer, it was soaked with blood. She just hung there, her mouth would open but nothing would come out. She kept blinking. Jack put his hand on her arm and pulled all the energy from her. She was cold to the touch in five minutes.

He pulled his phone from his pocket and called 911. He sobbed into the phone, "My God, she's dead! She is cold to the touch. Oh my God, she is just hanging there!"

Then he gave them the address and told them he would meet them at the door. He walked back to the study where Linda was pruning the plants. Jack said, "She did it. She hung herself. You were right, you didn't need to see that."

Linda asked, "Should I call the police?"

He shook his head. "I did that already. They're on the way. I told them they didn't have to hurry, she was already cold." He said, "You're going to have to open the gate and show me to the front door."

Linda's face was streaming with tears. She took Jack by the arm and asked, "How was it? Did she go quick?"

Jack lied and said, "Very quick and painless. You don't need to see her this way."

Linda stopped at a panel on the wall and pushed a button to open the gate and have it stay open. As they approached the door, they could hear sirens. Jack said, "For Christ's sake, I told them she was dead already."

The ambulance pulled up too; Andre was in the limo. They jumped out, ran to the back and took out a gurney. Jack took out his phone and called Andre. He said into the phone, "The stupid bitch took her life. She hung herself. Yeah, this could take a while."

An unmarked cop car pulled up. Jack held the door for the EMTs. He said to the two, "Hold up, boys. Let the cops catch up. I said on the phone, she's stone cold."

The two stopped just inside the door. They asked Linda, "So miss, where is the body?"

Jack raised his fist and shook it at them. He growled, "I told you to wait!"

He then opened the door for the two plainclothes cops who just held out their badges. Jack turned and started to walk down the hall. He took his time and walked like an old man hunched over. He caught up to the EMTs. "OK now, let's all go together."

He stopped and pointed a finger at Linda. "You don't need to see this. Why don't you whip up some refreshments?"

Jack then said, "Come on boys, down this hall, I think. This fricking place is huge." He slowly led them down the hall to Margaret's room where he opened the door. There she was—hung lifelessly. She was grey. The EMTs rushed to her side. Jack was right behind them. One quickly put on his stethoscope and listened for a heartbeat. Jack put his hand on her arm and pulled whatever energy that was building inside her. He said, "She's dead, right? When I found her, she was cold and turning blue. Now she's downright room temperature."

One EMT looked at the other and said, "The old guy is right, she is dead."

Jack said, "No shit, Sherlock." He turned to the cops, "I didn't touch anything."

The older cop picked up the suicide note. He held it up and showed the other cop. It had suicide note printed on the envelope in gold lettering. The younger cop said, "Hey, that's fancy!"

The cop then broke the wax seal on the back and took out the letter. Jack stepped over to the cop and said, "Read it out loud, please."

The cop said, "OK, here it goes: Being of sound mind and will, I, Margaret, take my life. I can't live with the guilt that I sold my only child. Jack, would you ever forgive me? My will is updated. Linda, please follow it to the letter and please go out and enjoy life. My funeral is written out in the will. You will take my body straight to the funeral home and have it cremated. You may show the urn at the funeral. That has also been picked out. Signed, Margaret."

An EMT said, "Can we cut her down yet??"

The older cop handed the suicide note to the younger, then said, "I'll take some pictures and notes. Then you can have her." He took a Nikon out of his bag and shot Margaret from all four sides, then a couple of close ones of scratches that were on her neck and the blood that was on the rope. He reached down and took her hand, turning it palm up and snapped a picture of her raw hand that had dried blood on. He then measured the distance the chair was from the body and the height of the blood on the rope. He turned to the other cop and said, "Write this: chair four feet from body, claw marks on neck where she must have tried to pull out of the noose, rope burns on palm of hands where she must have tried to lift herself. My conclusion is suicide."

The EMT asked, "Then we can take her down?"

He said, "Yeah." Then he pointed to Jack. "You, the will is on the desk. See what funeral home she wants and have them pick her up. It's pretty cut and dry. Then I need to talk to you and her lady."

One of the EMTs lifted Margaret as the other stood on the chair and cut the rope. They carefully laid her down on the floor. The older cop said to the younger one, "OK. Get that gal in here and we can get this wrapped up."

Jack was at the desk on the phone with the will in front of him. He was wiping a tear from his face as he spoke. The younger cop was listening to his conversation as he pretended to look though papers on the desk. Jack laid it on pretty thick, "It's terrible. She must have planned this all along—redoing her will, planning her funeral. Everything is here, step-by-step instructions for what to do."

Jack looked up. An elderly man, about sixty, held out his hand. "I'm the city coroner. The EMTs were right, she's dead. I hear the funeral home was contacted. I can fill out a death certificate."

One of the EMTs was doing paperwork on his iPad. "Give me his email address and I will shoot him one."

Jack said, "You have to be kidding me."

The coroner took the phone, asked for the email address, then punched it in and hit send. "OK. Everything is legal, they'll be here in ten minutes."

Jack said in amazement, "You have got to be shitting me. That easy? I was a sheriff for six years. We had a pile of paperwork." Jack was fumbling with the will. It was just instructions about how she wanted Jack to handle this part.

The EMT guy said, "As long as the cops rule her a suicide, it pretty much ends there. And let me tell you, this sure looks like an open-and-shut case."

Jack walked up to the older cop and looked him in the eye, "You are one hundred percent sure this was a suicide."

The cop said, "I am one hundred percent sure this is a suicide." Jack walked over to the younger cop and touched his hand. The cop looked at him. Jack said, "You are one hundred percent sure this is a suicide."

The cop answered with a blank face, "I am one hundred percent sure this is a suicide."

The doorbell rang and Jack sent Linda to the door. In a few minutes, she was back with two men dressed in black suits and a gurney. Jack walked to them one asked, "Which one of you guys did I talk to?"

One man stepped forward and held out his hand, "That would be me. Would you like a card?"

The undertaker's assistant reached into his breast pocket and produced a business card. "Now, I would like a proper death certificate as soon as possible."

He then held out his hand to shake it again. This time, he tipped his hand, showing a hundred dollar bill. The coroner shook and said, "Yes, sir, I will fax you a copy today." He didn't know it was already sent.

The two assistants brought over the cart, dropped it almost to the floor and slipped Margaret on it. Jack stepped in their way out the door. "Wait one second! Don't you want to know how the family wants this handled?"

One of the gentlemen said, "This is our job. We're here to pick up a stiff, make sure the right paperwork is here and get her back to the shop."

Jack said, "Well, I'm coming along to make sure you know what Margaret wanted."

Jack turned to the cops. "I filled out a statement. It's on the desk. I'm going with the undertakers."

The younger cop asked, "Do you have a mobile phone? If so, we need your number."

Jack looked at him and asked, "Do I look like a guy who would have a mobile phone? If you need me, I will be at the funeral home. And Linda, read the will, make a copy. You have a lot to do. Margaret has everything on a time schedule and I want to grant her wishes."

The older cop said, "I think I should read it quick. Nobody goes anywhere till I do."

Jack held up his hand and the undertakers assistants stopped. Jack said loudly, "Five minutes." He slowly walked back to the desk and asked, "What the hell is this about?"

The cop raised one finger, then asked, "Who is this Jack she is leaving everything to?"

Jack said, "That would be a son she had forty years ago, in a nunnery on the coast. She didn't want the child at that time so she sold it to a couple from the circus."

The old guy took off his hat and set it on the desk, scratched his head, then said, "OK, I see how Linda fits in, she's getting a pretty penny. But where do you fit in?"

Jack said, "Really, you don't see the connection? I am the father to the boy she sold. I wanted to make things right and leave him everything in my will. My kids are well off and they don't need my money. I just wanted to set things right."

The cop said, "Right, you're the father. Not likely."

Jack said, "When I was 55, I went to Las Vegas for a convention, got drunk and went on a gambling binge. I was drinking heavily and I met a girl. She got pregnant. I paid for it and it was kept secret till now."

The cop asked, "You were married, how did you keep it a secret?"

Jack smiled, "I have friends. I sold a boat for ten grand more than it was worth and sent her the cash. It took me forever to find her. I was amazed to see she was so successful. Too damn bad! She felt bad about what she did."

The cop said, "Something doesn't add up."

Jack put his hand on the desk. The cop looked up and Jack said, "You will not question this. It is a clear suicide. You will push it through."

Jack looked away from him and the cop put his hat back on and said, "OK, you can go now. I'll fill out the paperwork."

He then turned to the coroner and asked, "Are you satisfied?"

The coroner said, "There is no doubt in my mind. This was a suicide and not a good one. I've seen many just like this, but she looked like she struggled."

The undertaker's assistants asked, "Can we go now?"

The cop said, "This is done. I know there is a lot to do yet. I am truly sorry for your loss."

The younger cop asked, "So let me get this straight. The two of you were in the study. She left for a half hour. Then you found her hanging, with the note." He held up a sealed bag with the envelope.

The old cop butted in, "It's a clear suicide; we will do everything that is needed on our part."

The cops walked out the room and down the hall, followed by the two in black, Jack, the coroner and then Linda. Linda quickly caught up to Jack and put her arms around him, sobbing. Jack said, "I am so sorry this happened. Now, read the will and follow her instructions.

"I will do my part." Linda sobbed, "I can't believe this is happening."

Jack held her tight and said, "You just take it easy. I'll stop in tomorrow and we can make out a plan." He patted her back and said softly, "Everything is going to be all right?"

Jack looked up to see the younger cop, standing within earshot, taking in the conversation.

Jack pushed Linda away and said, "Stay strong," then he started to hobble down the hall.

The young cop waited for him and said, "I am truly sorry for your loss."

Jack said, half under his breath, "Would you just shut up? If I hadn't come here, she would still be alive. This is my fault; I ripped open an old wound she couldn't live with."

They reached the door, Jack stepped out and raised his hand and Andre got out of the car and stood at the passenger side. Jack walked over to it. Andre opened the door and asked quietly, "Did they buy it?"

Jack said loudly, "Follow that hearse." He got in, waited for Andre, then said, "Hook, line and sinker. They ruled it a suicide and ended the investigation."

The two watched the two men in black suits pop the gurney up and slide it onto the steel drawer that stuck out of the hearse. Then one pushed a remote that pulled in Margaret. They shut the door. Three cars sat there, watching. The coroner was the first to leave, then the cops. Andre said, "We know where were we are going. Do you want to follow them?"

Jack said, "Damn straight, we follow them. She should be powering up by the time we get there."

Andre said, "She's that strong?"

Jack said, "I pulled juice out of her twice in there."

Andre said, "I hate following a hearse. It gives me the creeps."

Jack said, "One day, we all will ride in one."

Andre smiled, "He's cutting through town. Smart boy!"

Nora and Elizabeth crawled out and flew to Jack's lap. Nora asked, "Are you OK?"

Jack said, "Yes, it was rough. For a while, they all believed she killed herself. She wrote a beautiful suicide note."

Elizabeth asked, "How did she die?"

Jack said softy, "She hung herself. She stepped off a chair and slowly choked herself. Let me tell you, it wasn't a pretty sight."

Elizabeth asked, "You said she was powering up hanging there. That's strange. She shouldn't be that strong."

Nora asked, "Why did she step off a chair? She could have stepped off something higher and broken her neck."

Jack smiled as he said, "That was my doing; I told her if she broke her neck, it would be harder to regenerate, so she bought it. I let her see how I faked Juliet's death."

The hearse pulled into the funeral parlour and around to the back door. Andre parked in the car park. He quickly got out, stepped around to Jack's side and opened his door. When Jack got out, Andre asked, "Do you want me to come in with you?"

Jack said, "You just stay here. This shouldn't take that long."

An older man answered the back door. Jack knew him, he was the funeral director. Jack quickly walked across the room to the three men. He acted like he was out of breath. He put one hand on Margaret's leg and pulled more energy from her lifeless body.

He held out his hand to the funeral director, looked him in the eye and said, "You will obey."

The funeral director said, "Yes, whatever you say."

Jack said to the two, "Your guys will take her to the holding area and you will prep her for a green cremation."

The funeral director asked Jack if he would follow. Jack walked into his office and laid down the directions Margaret had written. He then told the director to get all the paperwork done and that he would be back to sign it. Jack turned and walked back to Margaret. Everything in the room was stainless steel. The director stepped on a pedal and brought the table up to the gurney's height. The man said, "Please just slide her on here. All her jewellery is in this bag."

His assistants had her undressed and slid her onto the table. Jack said, "She doesn't want to have a showing, so no embalming. Just stick her into the crematorium."

The funeral director asked, "Are you the next of kin? Do you have the power to make this decision?"

Jack said, "You are going to cremate her now. A young lady will accompany me here to open the crematorium and pick out the urn. Now, I want to watch you put her in the crematorium."

The director walked over, pushed the intercom and called his assistants. Jack said, "Tell them to check his email."

He did that and a voice said, "There is an email from the coroner, with attached death certificate. And one saying in Margaret's will, she wants to be cremated green, no embalming. Just slide her into the oven and have the funeral without a showing."

The funeral assistant said, "OK, let's do this then. Get down here and we will follow her wishes."

Jack asked, "How long will it take to cremate her?"

The director said, "According to her body size—six to eight hours."

The two assistants walked in, one handed the director the document and the other pulled out a gurney and pushed it up to the table. He turned to Jack and said, "We are sorry for your loss."

The two men asked Jack to leave the room for a couple of minutes, so they could get Margaret ready. Jack grabbed one of the two and spun him around, telling him through clenched teeth, "You will do your job! And quickly!"

The man said, "Yes, sir." He started to tell the other guy what to do. They covered her with a clean sheet, then started to wheel her out of the prep room into a room with the oven doors built into the wall. One of the assistants stepped to the door, pushed a few buttons and opened the door. A stainless table slid out from inside the crematorium. They wheeled Margaret alongside it and slid her onto the table with the sheet still covering her.

Jack stepped up and asked if he could say a few words. He reached in and took her by the hand, pulling any energy from her and said, "Margaret, I haven't known you for very long, but I'm sorry you had to go through this."

Jack stepped away from the table and the two guys loaded her into the furnace, lifting the sheet as she was pulled in. As soon as she was in, one closed the door and flipped a switch. The digital thermometer on the wall started to fly. In a few seconds, it was up to six hundred degrees and climbing.

Jack asked, "How hot does it get?"

One of the assistants said, "1400–1800 degrees. This one goes up to 2000—that cuts the burn time down to two hours."

Jack then asked, "Why do you want me back in six to eight hours then?"

The assistant said, "There is a cool down to let everything settle."

Jack met the funeral director on the way out. He said, "I will be back to open the crematorium. Bill Margaret's estate."

The director protested as Jack brushed by him. "Wait! We have paperwork to fill out!"

Jack said over his shoulder, "Get everything ready to sign, I will be back in five hours."

Jack stepped out the back door, to his waiting limo. He opened the passenger side door and got in. He turned to Andre, "To the castle, but first let's stop and grab a bite."

Andre said, "OK, let's go to a drive-through, just this once."

Andre whipped the limo into a Micky D's. Jack said, "I'll have two quarter-pounders with cheese, large fries, a shake, apple pie and a couple of chicken sandwiches."

Andre pulled up to the sign and ordered, adding a chocolate shake to the order. Soon they were back on the 405, heading for Marvin's to get him up to speed of things. Jack wolfed down his hamburgers. He told Andre that they had to be back in five hours to get Margaret's ashes. Andre said, "You know, they will do that for you. All we should have to do is pick up the urn."

Jack held up a finger as he swallowed a handful of chips, then washed it down with a long swig of shake. He said, "I have to be there when it opens, to make sure the unicorn blood burnt. If not, that will throw a red flag."

Andre said, "Well, I guess we'll be back in five hours. You are the boss."

Jack said, "Oh no, you don't! We're in this together."

Andre smiled and said, "But we aren't alone. As soon as Marvin is regenerated, he'll take charge. He runs a tight ship."

Jack finished his chicken sandwiches and said, "We'll see about that. My job is to set things back in order." Jack noticed a large gathering on the pavement as they drove down Hollywood Boulevard. He asked, "So what is going on there?" There were TV trucks, a couple of limos and hundreds of people.

Andre said, "Aw, it's just someone receiving a star on the Walk of Fame."

Jack stared, trying to see who it was. He asked, "I wonder who it was?"

Andre said, "Ask me later. I'll ask Google, it knows everything."

Nora hopped onto his lap. She said, "Don't forget to call your kids. You hung up on them the last time. They are probably worried sick."

Jack said, "Remind me when we are at Marvin's. I have to call Linda and Dave from up north. Those loose ends have to be taken care of. Oh yes, and I have to find the number of the insurance company. That's why I hung up on him. You'd think your son would tell you that your house burnt down!"

Andre said, "You know, if you kept your phone on, or at least checked your messages, you might have known about it."

Jack said, "I only use my phone when I want to call someone."

Andre pulled into the Magic Castle and around to the back. Jack said, "We should go downstairs and eat a steak, their food is excellent."

Andre said, "You just ate four burgers, a large fry and a shake! And you're thinking of food!"

Andre got out and said, "To hell with it. I'll leave it parked right here."

Jack followed Andre into the back door. He asked, "Why aren't we using the secret lift?"

Andre said, "Because it's a secret, and we want to keep it that way."

He walked to a lift door and pushed Marvin's floor. A speaker asked, "Who is it?"

Andre said, "It's Jack and me."

Then a green light flashed and the lift started to move. Andre asked, "So what's that insurance company's name?"

Jack said, "It's Pikes Peak Insurance. My agent is Nancy Smith."

Andre tapped his phone and said, "Get a pen and paper, I got the number for you."

Jack handed Andre his phone. "Here. Could you put it in my contacts?"

Andre took the phone, turned it on and it chimed. Jack said, "Don't worry about that, it's just a message."

Andre said, "No, it's 23 messages."

The lift door opened and Jack stepped out to be greeted by Boris. He hovered with his arms crossed and snapped, "Where the hell were you guys?"

Jack looked up at him and said, "It takes a while to kill someone."

He asked, "What the hell does that mean?"

Jack smiled and told him, "You can wait for my report to Marvin." He walked passed him and went to the refrigerator, took out an apple and bit into it.

Andre asked, "Are you always hungry?"

Jack said, "Now that you mention it, yes. I think I could eat every couple of hours."

Marvin stepped into the room and said, "If you had been listening, Boris told you to feed Jack every couple of hours." He then asked, "So how did everything go?"

Jack asked, "Mind if I made some coffee?"

Marvin said, "Dropoff, run downstairs and grab a pot."

Andre said, "Don't start the debriefing before I get back." He quickly walked through the flat and poof! He stepped into a wall and was gone. In two minutes, he was back again, holding an insulated carafe.

Jack was staring into the fridge. He looked up and said, "Boy that was fast! Pour me a cup and we can get started."

Andre poured the coffee. There was a little movement on top of the fridge. Elizabeth, Rupert and Boris appeared to listen in. Jack asked, "So how is Juliet?"

Marvin smiled, "She is still in a coma. We are putting the fluids inside her and we put the feeding tube back in. Her colour is coming back. Her heart is beating stronger. A couple more days, then they're going to awaken her."

Jack asked, "Should I talk with her later?"

Marvin said, "Please do."

Jack took a long sip of coffee and said, "Andre, next time you take me with you to get coffee. This stuff is good. Do you put it on Marvin's tab?"

Andre said, "Just go down there and say it's for Marvin the Magnificent and they will get it for you."

Jack said, "OK, this is what happened. We went to Margaret's place. She was ready to fake her death. We worked out some details. Then she hung herself. The cops were there, the coroner. Right now she is being cremated. We have to be back in three hours to sweep her out."

Marvin said, "Boy, I wish I had been there to see that!"

Jack said, "Trust me, you wouldn't want to see it. She stepped off a chair and choked herself to death. I pulled all her power out of her body and she just kept powering back up. That is why I have to be there to take her out of the crematorium. That unicorn blood might not burn."

Marvin looked up to the fridge. Rupert flew down to him and said, "I have no idea if unicorn blood will burn. It is powerful stuff; it is what has kept Juliet alive for all these years."

Jack got up and got himself another cup of coffee. He stopped and looked at Elizabeth and asked, "Are you staying out of trouble?"

She told him, "All the fairies are making a good home upstairs and I am learning a lot from them, Andre brought some razors and nails to make swords, this army will be better then the one up north"

Jack said, "Please be patient, I will help you find your cousin as soon as we are done here."

Elizabeth said, "Take your time. It's safe now. I have been enjoying myself. My green friend and I have been exploring, she is in search of some key. There are small pockets of red fairies but they are well hidden, still afraid of being enslaved."

Marvin asked, "What happened up north?"

Jack said, "OK. I will give you the short story. We rescued a red guardian named Sara. Killed a few thousand blues, battled three blue guardians. Killed a Yeti—Bigfoot, whatever. Went in front of the fairy council. Everything went well. Oh yeah, and we are going to arm the fairies you have here and make an army."

Jack finished his coffee and said, "I'm going to talk to Juliet, then take a nap." He stood and so did Marvin and Andre. Jack led the way down the hall to Juliet's room. He looked back to see the fairies were also in tow. When he stepped into the room, he waited for the rest of the crew.

Jack then said, "Andre, her colour is coming back! Her hair has three inches of root colour but she is still skin and bone."

Boris flew up. "She needs to build muscle. And she will, as soon as she awakens. Her heart is stronger now."

Jack laid his hand on Juliet's forehead, closed his eyes and hummed. Marvin told him, "Ask her if she needs anything."

Jack opened his eyes and told him, "She is ready, wake her from her sleep."

He looked at Boris, "This is not a request, it is an order."

Rupert flew to Jack's shoulder and told him, "We are in need of some herbs and a fungi with a blue stem that grows in tropical climates."

Jack said, "Whatever you need, Andre will get you. And Andre, use Elizabeth if you need to. She is a very powerful tool."

Jack turned and said, "Time for me to take that nap."

Marvin asked, "Aren't you forgetting something? Like what she said?"

Jack turned and pointed a finger, his hand had fingernails that were half an inch long. "She said she is sick of lying in bed. She has been in this bed ever since Margaret attacked her. She wants out."

Tears streamed down Marvin's face. He went to her and raised her bed so she was sitting up. He took her face in his hands and said, "Honey, my love. Jack is right, we need to wake you, but it must be slowly, carefully. We need some drugs. I love you so much, I can't bear to think that I could lose you."

The room was deathly silent. Marvin turned to look at Boris and Rupert and asked in a stern voice, "What are you waiting for? Whatever you need, just get me a list. And you had better not screw this up!"

The two flew out of the room on a mission. Jack said, "Nora, you follow them. Give me a report after my nap. And you, Lizard Breath, do what you can, please."

With that, Jack walked out of the room down the hall. Andre yelled, "You have an hour and a half, then we must get back to the funeral parlour."

Andre said, "I'm going downstairs for a drink. You want anything?"

Marvin said, "Yeah, a Manhattan whiskey. Have them add a half a shot of cherry juice."

Andre said, "I haven't seen you drink a Manhattan in twenty years."

Marvin snapped at him, "Get used to it." He stormed out the door, mumbling, "Where the hell did those two go?"

Andre stepped close to Juliet. He said quietly, "You're going to be all right. Rupert is just playing it safe. And it looks like the old Marvin is on his way back."

Marvin walked into the room, opened the wardrobe and took out the big flesh-covered book and headed to the kitchen. He asked on his way out the door, "Where's that drink?"

Andre said, "My lady, the game is afoot." He pulled out his phone from his pocket, ordered two drinks and said he would be down to get them in three minutes. He walked down the hallway and disappeared, then he popped out the lift, holding a martini and a Manhattan. He stepped over to the table where Marvin was sitting, studying the book of spells and sat the drink down.

Marvin looked up at him, picked up his drink and raised his glass; Andre lowered his and clinked his with Marvin's. They both took a drink in silence, then Andre asked, "So?"

Marvin started lifting a note pad, "Rupert has been giving Juliet a mixture of cobra venom and Dragon Breath which are the main ingredients in their potion. Now we need to get the bacteria out of her system."

Andre asked, "What do you think she needs?"

Marvin took another drink, "There is a plant that grows on the banks of the Amazon. We need to boil it down for three days, concentrating the juice. That would bring her heart rate up. And with the dust from the unicorn horn, that should do it."

Andre asked Elizabeth, "Would you please go and get Boris and Rupert?"

Elizabeth flew off through the knot hole in the kitchen wall. Andre sat and asked, "Do we have that much time to run to South America?"

Boris and Rupert came flying in. Boris landed on the table, walked right up to Marvin and said, "This had better be good. We were busy."

Marvin asked, "What have you come up with to bring her out of her coma?"

Rupert walked up. "We need that mushroom and pollen from a mountain lily, slime from a dart frog and a potion from a plant grown on the banks of the Amazon."

Marvin swirled the ice in his drink, took a swig and then said, "Try this: the potion of the plant and unicorn horn dust—that should do it."

Jack came out of his room, walked up to the refrigerator, stuck his head in and pulled out a package of strawberries. He walked up behind Marvin, looking over his shoulder. Boris said, "Yes, I think that will work. The unicorn dust should knock out the bacteria and clean up whatever the bacteria didn't build on. Yes I think that will work."

Jack asked, "So why do you have cocaine in your book?"

Marvin asked, "What cocaine?"

Andre said, "That's it! I thought I knew what that plant was!"

Marvin pointed to the picture: "This is cocaine?"

Jack said, "That's what I have been taught. I have never seen it in person."

Andre said, "After Jack takes his shower, we will go and look for some."

Jack said, "Shower? I don't need a shower! I took one like six hours ago!"

Andre said, "Trust me, you need a shower."

Jack finished the last strawberry and handed the container to Andre. He turned and grumbled on his way to the bathroom. Andre asked, "How much coke do you need?"

Marvin said, "Just a small amount should do it. The book asks for three large leaves. How much coke do you get from three leaves?"

Andre pulled out his phone. In a couple of seconds, he said into it, "Pickupski, where the hell are you? Three days in Maui? That's rough. Hey, how much coke can you make out of three leaves? An eighth of a teaspoon? Are you sure? OK, don't work too hard."

He then asked Marvin, "Did you get that? An eighth of a teaspoon, but that would be straight coke, not cut with anything."

Marvin asked, "How would Pickupski know?"

Andre smiled, "About 25 years ago, we ran some drugs and put a couple of mil in an offshore account—just for a rainy day fund."

Boris asked, "Is Jack OK with this?"

Marvin asked, "What does Jack have to do with this?"

Boris said, "I promised I would run everything by Jack first. If I don't get his blessing, we don't do it."

Marvin said, "This is Juliet we are talking about! My Juliet!"

Jack walked out of the bathroom wearing a towel. Marvin yelled, "Jack, get your sorry ass in here!"

Jack turned and walked into the kitchen and asked, "What's going on?"

Marvin said, "Boris said nothing will happen if you don't OK it first."

Jack said, "Yes, I am in charge of this mission and we don't need any more mistakes. I don't know what is going on here. So what have you come up with?"

Marvin said, "We are going to use that dust from Ivan's horn and a small amount of pure cocaine."

Jack asked the two fairies who stood on the table, "What do you think?"

Rupert walked over to the edge of the table. "It should work. She will awaken, then we will slowly build more muscle before she regenerates."

Andre said, "We have to leave in ten minutes"

Jack held on tight to his towel, which almost fell off, and quickly walked to his room. Three minutes later, he stepped out fully dressed. Andre said, "Let's go." He led him down the hall to the restaurant lift.

Marvin caught up to them and shouted, "Damn it Jack, tell Boris to use the potion!"

Jack stopped, cocked his head and said, "Oh that. Let's see, a mixture of coke and the dust of unicorn horn? What the hell, try it!"

Marvin asked, "Is that it? Just try it? This is my wife we are talking about!"

Jack said, "Let me search Margaret's mind. I only kept the stuff I thought would be useful and deleted the rest." Then Jack asked, "Why are we going downstairs?"

Andre said, "I ordered you a sandwich to eat in the car. That way we don't have to stop."

Jack said as he stepped into the lift, "Good thinking, I'm starved."

When they got out of the lift, Andre took him straight to the kitchen, grabbed his take-out, walked right though the kitchen and out the back door to where the Lincoln was parked. Jack got into the passenger's side and asked, "Where are we going to find pure coke in this place?"

Andre smiled, "This is Hollywood—not a problem. Now the slime of a dart frog, I have no idea."

Jack asked, "I thought we weren't using that. Whatever. Didn't that guy with the cobra have frogs?"

Andre pulled out on the road and said, "I think you're right. Black ones with orange spots."

Jack dug into his sandwich. Andre said, "You be careful to not get crumbs in the car." Jack gave a quick nod.

They pulled into the funeral home's car park. Jack got dropped off at the back door and he rang the buzzer. One of the assistants opened the door and Jack stepped in. He asked, "Is she done?"

The assistant answered, "Yes, she has completed her journey. The crematorium is on the cool-down. It should be just a few minutes."

Jack said, "I have paperwork to fill out."

The assistant said, "This way please. There is a young lady here. She said she was the next of kin."

Jack stepped into the office to find Linda sitting the next to the desk. The funeral director stood and motioned to Jack. Jack stepped close to Linda and said, "I am so sorry for your loss—your friend—your boss! I didn't think you would be up to this."

She looked up at Jack with tear-streaked cheeks. "I had to. I am the executor, I have to sign this stuff."

Jack sat in a chair next to hers and asked, "OK, where are we?"

Linda said, "We have it done. All I have to do is write a check."

Jack looked up at the funeral director and asked, "This is done, right? Did you overcharge her?"

The director said, "Yes, this is done. Everything is in order. And yes, I overcharged her ten grand."

Jack said, "OK, you won't remember telling me you overcharged."

Linda looked at Jack, then asked, "Should I pay him the full amount?"

Jack said, "Yes, of course." She took out her check book and started to write the check.

Jack said, "I'm going back to put her ashes in the urn. Stay here, I will be right back." The old man turned and went out the door. One of the assistants was polishing a casket. Jack shouted to him, "Young man, I need the urn for Margaret Webster!" Jack hurried to the crematory; the temperature gauge said 150.

He grabbed the handle and opened the door. Sure enough, there were a dozen small balls that looked like mercury. He hit a button and the table slid out of the oven. He reached into his pocket, took out a Ziploc bag and carefully put the balls in the bag. The bag sagged from the heat; he put it in his pocket anyway. The assistant came in with an urn, whisk broom, a mallet and dust pan.

Jack turned to him, "That's pretty high-tech, hey!"

The young man said, "This is the way they want it done. I would use a shop vac myself, but I guess people don't want their loved ones stuck in vacuum filter." The assistant asked Jack, "Would you like me to help? I know I am supposed to do it, but we had one family in which everyone had to put a scoop of her ashes in the urn."

Jack took a quick scan of the room, then said, "I'll give you fifty if you do it in five minutes."

The kid smiled and scraped the ashes and bones, pulling them to the front of the table to drop into a small can. As he was doing this, he said, "This will take a minute." He took the can over to a machine, locked a top on it and put the can in like a paint shaker. He asked, "Is it OK if there are small fragments of bone?"

Jack said, "No, that's fine. We're going to bury her in it."

The kid said, "That's what I say. Who's going to dump her out and check?" He slowly dumped her into the urn.

Jack said, "That's close enough. Slap the lid on it, I have places to go."

The assistant wiped off the rim, then slowly wiped off the urn using three white linen rags. He said, "You don't want her on your suit."

Jack looked him in the eye and said, "Nothing out of the ordinary happened." He handed him a fifty dollar bill and asked, "The lid is on tight?"

The kid said, "Push down and turn. Just like your meds, it's child proof." Then he sat it into a teak box. "Thanks, old man," he said as he held up the fifty.

Jack put the box under his arm and quickly walked to the office. Linda was looking though a book. Jack asked, "Are we ready?"

Linda looked up. You could tell she had been crying. She pointed to a picture in the book and said, "This one."

Jack asked, "What are you doing?"

She said, "I am planning her funeral. I know she said to just bury her, but she's not here, so we are giving her a farewell."

Jack shook his head, "We should honour her wishes."

Linda said, "We did. She has been cremated, now let everyone say goodbye."

Jack said, "I have no problem with that. Something small."

Linda said, "I will see you at the estate."

Jack asked, "Where are you having this funeral?"

She turned and snapped, "At home."

The funeral director smiled and said, "Don't worry, she's going to pull some pictures, have a video playing, a couple of cases of Dom Pérignon, hors d'oeuvres—you know, something small."

Jack rolled his eyes and told him, "Do what you have to."

The funeral director said, "Dom Pérignon 2004 is around 250, and for Miss Linda, she said she has a few bottles of 1961 that runs around three to four thousand a bottle. So stick close to her."

Jack asked, "When is this going to happen?"

The funeral director said, "This Saturday."

Jack shook his head and said softly, "Women! They just can't follow directions." Jack walked out the front, trying to catch Linda. Once he did, he asked quietly, "What the hell? There was to be no funeral!"

She turned to him, her eyes filled with tears and said, "There has to be something! We have to give her old life a send-off."

Jack said, "She won't be regenerated for three weeks to a month." Jack asked, "Would you take the urn to the house? It has ashes that have been left over from other cremations." She opened her passenger door and Jack handed the box to her, she took it and buckled it in.

Jack asked quietly, "Did you put that house up for sale in the Caribbean, Margaret said to sell the house and keep the island?"

She shot him a look, "No, I haven't. I've been a bit busy."

Jack pulled out his mobile phone and called Andre. He told him to pick him up at the front door. Jack said to Linda over the roof of her little two-seater Audi R8, "Let's stay on track. We want to keep everyone alive. Maggie's down in New Orleans. You can't talk to her; she won't be at the funeral. You can tape it and show her later."

Linda said, "It would have looked out of place if we hadn't done something. Trust me, it will be over soon. I'll start selling things off and stick to the will."

Jack smiled and said, "This is taking too long. My people want to know, why."

Linda asked, "What she just did?"

Jack said, "I am on a timeline, there is so much to do."

Andre pulled up with the Lincoln. Jack started for the car. By the time he got there, Andre was standing with his door opened. Andre asked, "How was your meeting, sir?"

Jack looked up at him and snapped, "Shut the hell up!" He got into the car.

Andre jumped in and pulled out of the drive. He asked, "So what went wrong?"

Jack said, "Well, for the first thing, there is going to be a funeral. The second thing is, I think the unicorn blood melted through the Ziploc baggy I put it in." Jack reached into his pocket and to his surprise, a wrinkled bag was still holding a tablespoon of silver.

Andre asked, "How hot was that oven?"

Jack said, "They had it set 2000 degrees—that was max."

Andre whistled, "Boy, you would think that would have done it!"

Jack said, "I thought so too. But nobody saw it. That went well, but this funeral is going to slow everything down."

Jack then asked, "Could we stop and pick up a burger or something? I'm starved."

Andre said, "Why don't you call the castle and order a meal? We'll be there in half an hour or so. The traffic is light." Andre handed Jack his phone and said, "It's dialling."

Jack took it. Five minutes later, he was done with his order.

Andre asked, "What took so long?"

Jack explained the specials to him, then Andre said, "Call them back tell them to double that order." Then he said to himself more than to Jack, "I'm going to gain fifty pounds hanging out with you."

Andre flew down the 405. Jack said, "This is the lightest traffic I have seen here."

Andre said, "I have been here when there were just a handful of cars and I've been here sitting for hours in a sea of traffic." He jumped off the freeway. Soon they were back on Hollywood Boulevard.

Jack asked, "Would you like me to order you a drink?"

Andre said, "We can wait."

Jack got out of the car and entered the restaurant while Andre parked the car. Jack asked for his table and said that he had called in his order half an hour ago. The door opened and Andre was there. He said, "I just left it in the car park."

The two of them followed the gal to their table. Jack said, "That was no fun."

Andre smiled, "It's lunch hour. Not much is going on right now."

Their waiter showed up and asked for drinks. Jack said, "I'll try one of those Long Island iced teas."

The waiter confirmed with him, "Sir, that drink has five shots in it."

Jack said, "Make it top shelf, none of that cheap stuff."

The waiter then asked Andre, "And you, sir?"

He said, "A grapefruit stinger, and make it Grey Goose. By the way, we called in our order."

The waiter said, "Your blue cheese is on its way, with liver pâté."

Andre asked, "What did you order?"

Jack had a sly smile on his face. "Just wait and see."

The salad came out with a side of liver pâté, pickled herring and black olives. Jack asked, "Is there a show today?"

Andre started to say something and the waiter cut him off, "Marvin the Magnificent is doing a small act. They say he is pretty good—for his age."

Andre said with amazement, "You have to be kidding! The old man is working! I have to see this."

They finished their salad, then came a plate of shrimp scampi. When they were done with that, a twenty-ounce porterhouse came sizzling out on a plate with potatoes and gravy, carrots and mushrooms.

Andre said, "Really? There is no way I can eat this!"

Jack ordered a glass of water and dug in after five minutes. Andre got up with his plate and headed down the hall. Then poof! He was gone. Ten minutes later, Andre reappeared and walked over to the table, where Jack was just cleaning the plate. He was wiping up the juices with a roll. Andre sat and took a roll. It was still warm. He asked, "Did you just order these?"

Jack said, "Yeah, but they didn't bring enough butter." The waiter brought up the bill.

"I put it on Marvin's tab," Jack said.

Andre took it and signed. "Let's go catch the show."

The two stood, full from eating. Jack put his hand to his belly and said, "I can't believe I can eat that much."

The hostess took them to a small showroom, where Marvin was doing some old disappearing acts, making the rabbit appear—it was a stuffed toy. He did some card tricks, then at the half hour mark, he said, "Well, thank you for watching an old man doing some tricks." He pointed at Jack and Andre, "See you upstairs." In a puff of smoke, he was gone.

People three feet from the stage stood and looked around. In an instant, he was gone. Jack said, "He is good."

Andre said, "He is great, if not the greatest, but he can't be mixing magic in his show."

Jack asked "Why not?"

Andre said, "This is the 21st century; there are cameras everywhere. They can watch you frame by frame."

Jack nodded his head, then said, "My grandson showed me my house on Google Earth. Now, that's technology!"

Andre said, "You must always be on guard."

Jack said, "Twenty years ago, I was a cop."

Andre said, "That was twenty years ago. Technology has advanced so much since then!"

Jack stood and said, "I guess I should study and catch up on things."

Andre stood and put his arm on Jack's shoulder. "Come, let's see what Marvin is up to."

They walked toward the kitchen and stopped in the hall. Andre waved his hand and said, "Open sesame," and the door snapped open and he stepped inside. It snapped shut, then opened again.

Jack said, "You have to show me how to use this lift. You have a second and a half to step through the door!" Jack stepped in, Andre took his finger off the button and the door snapped shut.

Andre said, "When we get up to Marvin's place, I want to get you on the net, to a site that sells spy paraphernalia. You'll be amazed at the size of the cameras now. And that microphone Marvin gave you for your pocket has been out-dated for years."

The door opened, the two walked out into the hall and stepped into Juliet's room, where a dozen fairies sat watching Marvin sit with Juliet's hand in his. He was telling her of his show. Boris flew to Jack, landing on his shoulder, all excited. He said, "Jack, that piece of quartz you charged? Can you recharge it and put it under her bed? We are going to wake her up. She is starting to absorb the power."

Jack raised a hand and the quartz stone rose from the chest of drawers and floated to him. It hovered between his hands and a dark red light formed around it. Then the light brightened to almost a pink. The stone slowly floated to the floor and slid under the bed.

Andre stood there with his mouth open, then said, "See, that's what I'm talking about! Magic! How could you explain how you did that?"

Jack asked, "Is that enough power? I can put more in it."

Boris said, "That is just right; when it gets weak, I will ask you for more."

Nora flew up and asked Jack if he would charge one more to give to Marvin, just in case. Jack stepped up to Marvin and put his hand on his shoulder. Marvin snapped, "If you want to know how she is, just ask. Don't try it out of my head."

Jack took his hand off Marvin's shoulder and stepped in closer to Juliet. He put his hand on her forehead and closed his eyes. The room went completely silent; everyone watched and waited. A couple of minutes went by and Jack looked at Rupert, who was sitting on the bed post. He asked, "Is there anything you want Juliet to do?"

Rupert said, "Yes, take it slow, it would be best not to rush the process. Ask her if she thinks she can swallow."

Jack closed his eyes again, then said, "Yes, she thinks she can. And she will take it as slow as she can. And Marvin, she loves you with all her heart. She said she is so happy you started to perform again."

Jack motioned to Marvin to follow. He turned and Andre was right behind him. Followed by Marvin, Jack led them to the kitchen and went right to the fridge. He pulled out a bottle of water, then went to the cupboard and took a mug out. He filled it with the leftover coffee and put it in the microwave.

Marvin pulled up a chair and asked Andre, "So how did the cremation go?"

Andre shrugged his shoulders, "I sat in the car; you have to ask Jack."

Jack sat his coffee down on the table, pulled out his chair, then sat a bag down on the table. He said, "The unicorn blood didn't burn even at 2000 degrees. We have a problem. Her secretary is holding a funeral for her on Saturday. That is going to slow things down a bit."

Marvin asked, "Are you sure she is dead?"

Jack took a long swig of his water bottle, then said, "I pushed her in the oven. As soon as the oven heated to 200 degrees, the door automatically locks. One of the funeral director's assistants opened it at the start of the cool-down and crushed the big bones and skull. I opened it at 150 and picked out the unicorn blood. She's gone, no doubt."

Marvin asked, "What is the next step?"

Jack asked, "Did you get the cocaine and the slime from a dart frog?"

Andre pulled out his phone and pushed a few buttons, put it to his ear, then held up one finger. Then he said into it, "Yeah, did you find it? Sure, an 8 ball should be fine. Pure rock, never stepped on. Where? How much? I'll be there."

He looked up. "We got the coke. I meet him in a half hour."

Jack said, "Then we shall visit our neighbourhood snake charmer. How long before we leave?"

Andre said, "Ten minutes. Don't want to be late for a drug deal, you know."

Nora flew out the door and was back in about a minute, followed by Boris and Rupert. Boris flew up and landed right in front of Jack and asked, "How long before we get the ingredients for the potion?"

Jack said, "In two hours, give or take."

Boris streaked off to Juliet's room.

Jack asked, "What has got into him?"

Rupert explained how they were going to pull Juliet out of a coma, but if they got this potion, they wanted to keep her in for another three days. She would be in much better shape if they did. Jack stood and polished off his coffee. "Let's get going. The faster we get back, the faster I get my nap."

Jack stood and Nora flew right to him. "Can I come, please?"

Jack looked at Andre. He shrugged his shoulders. Jack said, "Why not?" He opened his shirt pocket and she crawled in. Soon, they were on the road. Jack explained to her, "This is an illegal drug that we are buying and if we get caught they could go to gaol." Then he explained what gaol was and how it worked with the legal system.

Andre asked, "When did you start speaking proper English? Gaol is jail on this side of the pond."

Jack said, "What? I didn't say gaol."

Andre said, "Oh yes, you did."

Andre stopped at a Starbucks and said, "I'm to meet him right here in front. So I shall be back in a moment."

Jack said, "Great, I'm going to get a venti—that would be a large coffee." Jack got out of the Lincoln with Nora in his pocket and walked to the coffee shop, followed by Andre. Jack turned and asked, "What would you like?"

Andre said, "Whatever you're having will be fine."

Jack walked into the shop and Andre stopped and chatted with a fellow chauffeur. Jack came out with two coffees; he walked up to Andre and handed him his coffee and asked, "Now what?"

Andre said, "To the snake charmer's." He opened Jack's door, then walked around, got in and said, "What kind of java is this?"

Jack smiled, "It's a five-shot mocha, with a hint of vanilla. So how did the deal go?"

Andre said, "No problem, it's supposed to be pure. It sure is expensive!"

Jack asked, "How did you know this guy?"

Andre smiled, "I know what you're thinking. I don't use the stuff. It's a waste of time and energy."

Jack asked, "Still. Did you find him in the yellow pages or what?"

Andre chuckled and took a drink of coffee, "When I was a full-time chauffeur, we offered a lot of services, got clients laid, got them into places that they weren't invited, slipped them in and out without being noticed. That could be tricky, so Marvin taught me a few tricks on that one. To get someone a little blow, that's no problem. Now to get them into some parties—tricky."

Andre said, "There's the snake guy's house!"

Jack said, "There's no parking. You can just drop me off. I will call you when I am done. I hope he is here." Andre turned on his hazard flashers and came to a stop. Jack got out and walked to the house. He rang the bell. A voice came from the intercom, asking who it was. Jack pushed a button and said, "I am here for a dart frog and will pay top dollar for one."

The door buzzed. Jack opened it and went upstairs. The guy was entranced as soon as he opened the door. Jack said, "I don't have much time, I have a car waiting for me."

The snake guy asked, "You're Jack, right? I seem to remember you, but I don't know from where."

Jack asked, "You do have a dart frog, right?"

The snake guy said, "You know these are poisonous? The slime on one could kill a human. The Indians of South America used their slime to coat their arrows, that's why they are called arrow frogs—from the Dendrobatidae family."

Jack said, "I'll take one." He pulled out a stack of cash and peeled off three hundred-dollar bills.

The dude took the money, then said, "I don't know how poisonous they are in captivity. They lose a lot of it though their diet."

Jack said, "Just give me the stupid frog."

The guy told Jack to follow; they went in the back bedroom where the King Cobra was, along with dozens of glass cases holding reptiles. The snake man showed Jack three cases with a dozen or so frogs in each. "These are the ones that are the most poisonous."

Jack looked in the cases. There were green ones, blue, strawberry and yellow. The owner said, "The golden poison arrow frog, right?"

Jack said, "No, the orange and black one."

The man opened the case and took a pair of tongs with cling film wrapped on them, reached in and took a frog and placed it in a bag. "These are from the last shipment." Then he lifted his head and asked, "You're not going to do anything stupid with him, are you?"

Jack looked into the man's eyes and said, "Once I step out of the door, you will forget that I was ever here." He turned and walked back to the car.

Andre was surprised when Jack opened the door. He said, "Wow, that was fast!"

Jack smiled and said, "Being a hypnotist cuts the small talk to a minimum. Let's go."

Andre pulled out. They were almost to the castle when Jack asked, "Can we get some baklava? You know, with walnuts and almonds?"

Andre asked, "Are you kidding? That coffee almost put me in a diabetic coma!" He swerved across three lanes and took an exit, pulling up at a storefront. It was a Greek bakery with a sign lit up in the front window: "Fresh Baklava".

Jack looked over to Andre and asked, "Would you want a piece?"

He answered, "Ah, no. But grab a piece for Marvin."

Jack was gone for no more than five minutes. He came back with a large take-out container. Andre was standing next to the door. He opened it and Jack handed him the container. Andre asked, "Is this all baklava?"

Jack nodded; Andre commented, "There must be five pounds here!"

When Andre slid behind the wheel, Jack said, "Wait until you taste it. That is the best baklava I have had in years." And then he said, "It's the only baklava I have had in a decade."

Andre asked, "Is Nora still in your pocket?"

A little red head popped up out of Jack's pocket. "Ask her how much sugar you should have."

Jack said, "Sugar? I don't think that even came up. Boris just said to feed me every two hours. He never said what."

Andre asked, "Are we going anywhere soon, or should I put the car away?"

Jack said, "I'm taking a nap for sure."

Andre asked, "How can you sleep after a five shot cup of coffee and a pound of baklava?"

Jack said, "Let's just get this stupid frog out of my pocket."

Jack got to the secret entrance in the back of the building and waited for Andre to say the magic words to open it. Andre said, "Watch!" He waved his arms back and forth, chanting.

Jack put his hand on Andre's arm and looked into his eyes. Then he said, "Step aside." He reached up and pushed a piece of stone, then pushed one that was next to the ground; the door swung open.

Andre said, "Never do that, never show how it is done. And never steal from my mind. All you have to do is ask."

Jack stepped into the lift, "It's been a long morning. Let's get this stupid frog to Boris." They stepped out of the lift to the smell of fresh coffee; Marvin was sitting waiting for them with his chair turned to the lift.

Andre stepped out first with the take-out container. Marvin said, "You got the frog?"

Andre said, "How about five pounds of baklava?" He sat the container on the table.

Marvin stepped over, lifted the lid and said, "Hmm, baklava, I haven't had this in years." He picked out a large piece and took a bite.

Andre said, "We got the coke and the frog."

Jack reached into his pocket and pulled out a Ziploc bag with an orange and black frog in it. He said, "We have to change the air in it or it will die."

Boris flew to him, hovering right in front of the bag, inspecting it. He said excitedly, "No, this is good. See all the slime in the corner of the bag? That's all we need. Quickly, bring them into Juliet's room!"

Everyone followed the fairy, who flew off down the hall. Jack walked through the door. He saw five fairies on top of the chest of drawers with jars, bottles and a large mortar and pestle. Rupert flew to Marvin and asked if he would help grind the ingredients. He asked Andre if he wouldn't mind helping the fairies out for an hour or so. Jack cleared his throat and said, "Before anyone touches this frog, they had better have gloves on. It's an arrow frog. The natives put the slime on their arrows to kill animals."

Andre smiled and said, "Jack, we called them dart frogs when I hunted with the chief in South America—I think it was Columbia."

Marvin chimed in, "That was Zabba Zabba, wasn't it? We bought five hundred acres of coffee fields."

Andre smiled and said, "You're still pretty sharp. How's that doing for you?"

Marvin asked, "Would you like to see a picture? I have a local guy managing it. Well, *I* don't. I have my CPA manage it. We pay the highest wage around. And it does well, there are two thousand acres now."

Jack put the bag with the frog in it on the chest of drawers and went to get Andre a pair of gloves while the guys chatted. Jack swiftly walked down the hall to the kitchen and went under the sink to pull out a pair of yellow gloves. He said to himself, "I hope these fit," and went back to Juliet's room. He stepped in, handed Andre the gloves and said, "When you are done with the frog, kill it and dispose of it. We don't need those things around."

Andre took the gloves and asked, "OK, who's in charge? Let's do this and get it done with."

Boris flew over from reading Marvin's large book of potions. "We have decided to use Marvin's. Margaret's is too strong. Her book uses a lot of human blood."

Marvin asked, "What? I thought that was the same book!"

Boris said, "It looks the same from the outside, but in fact, it is wrapped in human skin, not leather."

Jack said, "I flipped through it, it's just got potions and spells in it."

Boris said, "Yes, it is a potions book, not the black book of the dead. Now get out so we can work."

Marvin took Juliet's hand from the bed, bent down, kissed it and said softly, "Be strong, my love."

Jack said, "I am going to go shower and take a nap."

Marvin said, "Linda called. The funeral is in three days. She's just setting out pictures and news articles and a small tape of her. You left the phone on the table."

Jack looked to the floor and shook his head. "Isn't that just great? I never get downtime in this place!" He started down the hall.

Marvin followed, then Andre turned and Nora flew to him, landing on his shoulder. She spoke into his ear, "You have to handle the frog. And be careful."

Andre lifted the Ziploc bag with a half-dead frog in it. The slime was thick in the corner of the bag. Rupert flew down and said, "We will call you when we need you. This could take a while, getting everything just right."

Andre looked at the orange and black frog and said, "Don't be too long. I think our friend here is almost dead." He put the bag back on the dresser and headed to see what the guys were up to.

Marvin and Jack were sitting at the table, drinking coffee and finishing off the baklava. Marvin looked up and said, "We saved you a piece."

Andre poured himself a cup of coffee and sat at the table. Jack slid the take-out container towards him. Andre smiled and said, "That was five pounds of baklava! And you guys ate it in five minutes!"

Marvin said, "Try it. It's the best I've had in years."

Andre took a bite, then said, "You're right, it is good. But five pounds?"

Nora flew up and told Andre it was time. Andre protested, "I haven't even drunk my coffee!"

She walked right up to him on the table, looked up and said, "They want you now."

Jack said, "Well, that's it then. I'm going to take my shower and a nap. How about you?"

Marvin said, "I have a show at 5:00. It's nice to get up in front of an audience, even if it is just a day gig. Nice exercise, get to talk with people. Just some pull-the-rabbit-from-the hat stuff. My hands just don't work like they used to." He picked up his fork and spun it in his hands and it vanished. "I drop the damn thing three out of ten times."

They all went their separate ways, Andre to help Boris, Jack to shower and nap and Marvin to prepare for his show.

Chapter Twenty One
To the Circus Museum

Jack woke up from his nap to find Marvin in his tux (which looked way too big for him), practicing in the magic room. Jack stood in the doorway and watched as Marvin made things appear and disappear. He floated three inches off the floor, hovered to a table and took a deck of cards off from it and started to throw them across the room into a hat that lay on a chair. He noticed Jack and missed one.

Marvin said, "Jack, glad to see you're awake. You're going to have to pack, you're going to Wisconsin for a day or two."

Jack cocked his head and said, "Wisconsin? What the hell is in Wisconsin?" Marvin smiled and said, "The Circus Museum, that's what! Remember you were sold to the circus when you were a baby? And for some reason, they want you, like yesterday. I don't know what is up, but I've never seen Suckolofski so nervous."

Jack asked if Andre was still there. Marvin told him he was still working with Boris and Rupert. Jack said, "Well, I guess I had better go and find out when we are going to leave then."

Marvin said, "Right behind you. They threw me out half an hour ago."

Jack walked down the hall. There was a strange smell, like fish and burnt almonds and it just kept getting stronger. Jack said, "We have to open some of these windows! My God, you'll never get the smell out of this place!" Jack turned into Marvin's room and opened the window. Marvin went back to the magic room and opened the windows in there and was setting up a fan when Jack popped his head back in.

Marvin saw him and asked, "Should I put the fan blowing out or in?"

Jack said, "Blowing in. Let's go see what is making the smell."

Marvin sat the fan in the window, with it blowing in the fresh air. When the two got to Juliet's room, Andre was holding her half-naked body in a sitting position with her head resting on his shoulder. She had all kinds of weird drawings on her in reds and blues and yellows. She looked like some tribesman getting ready for war.

Jack held his breath and opened the window. Marvin asked, "How is she? Are you waking her up?"

Boris flew to his shoulder and said, "She will awaken in a couple of days, right now she needs to rest."

Jack interrupted, "What is that smell?"

Andre said, "When I crushed up the cocaine and added it to the potion, it made a nasty chemical reaction. We're talking smoke, lightning. I mean the shit is still glowing!"

Jack said, "So when are we going to leave?"

Andre said, "As soon as I am done here, we'll jump into the car. I already made the flight plan. Suckolofski is chomping on the bit."

Jack told him that he needed to take a shower. Marvin said, "I will take Juliet."

Andre said, "We're almost done here, you don't want to get your tux dirty."

Nora flew up with an eye-drop and squeezed it into Juliet's mouth. Boris said, "From now on, she starts to drink small quantities of water, day and night."

Jack asked, "Shall I ask her how she is feeling?" He reached out.

Rupert said, "Don't do it, Jack. We have to do what we have to do. It doesn't matter how she feels. This is the best way; we could have had her up days ago, but this is the right way."

Jack said, "OK then, I have to get out of here before I puke." He grabbed Marvin by the shoulder of his tux. He turned and stood there, looking at her with a tear running down his face.

Marvin said, "I love you, dear, but I have to go."

Jack led Marvin out of the room and into the hall. He said, "Oh my God, I don't think I have ever smelled something that bad. My nostrils are burning!"

Marvin said, "When you first got here, you smelled worse."

Jack stopped, looked at him and asked, "Really?"

Marvin said, "That is why Dropoff is here instead of Pickupski. Ivan couldn't stand the smell."

Jack asked, "How does it work with those two?"

Marvin pulled up a chair at the table and Jack poured a couple of cups of coffee. Marvin said, "Those two have been with me for—well, hundreds of years. Ivan joined me back in the horse and buggy days. Andre was with me, oh let me see, it was before the crusades, after I met Juliet. She talked me into saving his life, he was a Viking warrior. She wanted me to save him so I did and he made a pledge to serve me."

Jack took a sip of his coffee and asked, "Are you trying to tell me Andre is over three hundred years old?"

Marvin smiled, "Yeah, well over three hundred, it was before Christ I think, the years seem to run together after a while. Let me tell you, in the last fifty years, technology has made things so much nicer."

Jack said, "You know, you are right. Cars are so much nicer, everyone has air-conditioning. Hell, even making coffee is so much easier! Just throw in the coffee and some water, push a button and you got coffee."

Marvin took a long drink of coffee and stared at his cup for a couple of seconds, then said lightly, "Medical technology is the only reason Juliet is still here. A hundred years ago I would have had to destroy her." A tear slid down his face.

Jack said, "Now that will never happen. We have everything in control. I have faith in Boris, he seems to know what he is doing."

Marvin said, "Once, I was a great sorcerer, the only greater was my teacher. I was the most powerful man in the world; armies fell at my feet, Damn it, I can't do anything now, I can't even go outside in the dark, afraid of a blue guardian killing me!"

Jack smiled, "Well, we took care of that now, didn't we? Margaret is dead and soon we will have that mess cleaned up."

Andre walked into the room, poured himself a cup of coffee and said, "You know, it's nice having coffee in here now. I used to have to go to the restaurant to get a pot when I visited."

Marvin said, "Now I have a reason to be awake, don't I?"

Jack asked, "So how long do we have?"

Andre said, "Suckolofski is pitching a fit. I have never seen him so excited. You should never have gave me the phone."

Marvin smiled, "I could have given him your personal cell number."

Andre looked at Jack and said, "See, this is the way it works: we use Burner phones; the numbers are disposable. After this trip, we throw them away and start out with different numbers."

Jack said, "I'm packed and ready to go. All I have to do is take a piss."

Andre said, "I'll shower and finish getting dressed. And I'm always packed. The jet is fuelled and waiting. I say seven minutes."

Marvin shook his head. Andre added, "It's only a couple of hundred bucks. Come on, old man, spend a little. It will save a half an hour."

Jack looked into Marvin's face. Marvin said, "He could fuel his own plane." He shouted after Andre, "Dropoff, you forgot to tell me about Juliet!"

Andre stopped and turned. "Oh, you might want to ask Boris. Everything went well. We are pushing the saline solution in to her IV, trying to get her to drink. After she is up and about, we have to take out the feeding tube."

Marvin got up from the table and said, "Well, I had better see what the boys are up to."

Jack pointed to Marvin's wrist, "You might want to take a shower and a nap. They know what they're doing."

Marvin ran his finger across his arm and left a streak. He said, "First they are going to explain everything they have done, in great detail. Then I have a show to put on." He turned and was gone. Jack went and got ready for the flight to Wisconsin.

Andre walked right past him, saying, "Let's go, before rush hour!"

Jack grabbed his bag and met Andre in the lift. Andre said, "I don't know what we are walking into, but Suckolofski just called again."

When the lift opened, they stepped out to the car park. Jack asked, "I didn't think we were to use this exit in the day."

Andre said, "We should have been out of here an hour ago. Traffic is a big thing out here, I'll get the car. You stay here."

Jack followed Andre and said, "I'll come with you."

Andre scanned a card at the door of a one-stall garage and the door opened to an empty garage. He strolled to the back and said a few words, waved his hands and the back wall flipped up and the lights turned on to reveal twenty cars. The one in back was a big old Rolls Royce. Andre said, "To the Lincoln."

Jack said, "How about the Audi?"

Andre said, "Why not? The Audi it is." They both jumped into the little two-seater ragtop. Andre pulled out of the garage and took the top down. He drove a little faster and more aggressively with this car than with the town car. Jack's white hair flew in the breeze and he didn't think of anything, just enjoyed the ride. They pulled into the airport; Andre drove to the private side, went through two check points and to his hangar. He said, "Ten years ago, you could just wave to the gate master and drive in. Those ragheads slowed everything down."

Andre parked next to the hangar, pushed a button and the top went back up on the car. He turned to Jack and said, "This should be different, I haven't seen Suckolofski in thirty years. That was when I became Andre Dropoff and Ivan became Pickupski. You know, pick up and drop off—kind of catchy, don't you think? In the old days, I would never get this old—55 max, every twenty years regenerate."

They both got out of the car and walked to the plane. Andre said, "I always take a walk-around before I fly." He walked around the plane slowly, checking the tyres, running his hands along the wing. He shook the rudder, then walked over, dropped the door and waved Jack over. Jack walked up and went up the stairs and strapped his luggage in, then he sat in the co-pilot's seat. Andre slid into the pilot's seat, put the headphones on and started with the flight plan. He started a checklist, flipping switches, writing everything down, checking one thing off at a time. Soon, they were in the air.

Jack asked, "Who is this Suckolofski fellow?"

Andre smiled as he said, "He is a manager of some sorts now. He was a lion tamer when I first met him, in France, I do believe. A small gipsy circus. I think he always worked in the circus. He was a magician, ring master, CIA, FBI—I have known him for many years."

When the jet levelled off, Andre said, "Why don't you take a nap? It's going to be, like six hours before we get there."

Jack then said, out of the blue, "So you were a Viking Warrior, hey?"

Andre shook his head and said, "That Marvin! He is getting old. He would never talk about the past when he was young—unless you got him shitfaced. Yeah, I was a Viking. Not my finest hour."

Jack asked, "What was that like?"

Andre leaned back into his seat and rolled his head on the headrest, then said, "Boy, that was a long time ago! We were ruthless when we attacked a town. Everyone died or was enslaved. Rape and murder. Our ship was always on point. My mates were ruthless. When we attacked this small village on the way to a town, the villagers started to fight back. We walked right though them.

"Then a woman and a man appeared. The man was Marvin and he pulled out his sword, hacked his way through a hundred of us and was hunting us down. I saw him slice though a shield as well as the man behind it. I grabbed a girl and hid as he walked through, killing every single one of my mates. When he found me, I held the knife to the girl's throat. He stepped towards me.

"That's when Juliet rode up, she put her hand on Marvin's shoulder and said, "That's enough killing today. Can't you let him live?" That's when I dropped my knife and begged him to spare my life and pledged to serve him till I died."

Jack said, "You didn't think you would live this long, did you?"

Andre smiled and said, "We have had our differences over the years, but it comes down to my word. I pledged to never again kill without reason. It took years for me to sleep without dreams of massacres; it took years before I could make love to a woman without flashbacks. I owe my life to that man. He has always fought for the rights of the people and has killed many on the battlefield. Over the years my love for him has grown. I would give my life for him."

Jack smiled and said with confidence, "That's not going to happen. I hope this Suckolofski guy has all the paperwork straightened out. I mean he should have got my birth certificate by now."

Andre nodded his head slowly and said, "That *could* be it. But it sounded much more than that. You should try to sleep a couple of hours."

Nora flew up to Jack shoulder and said to him, "Andre is right. Your body needs sleep; you don't know what is going to happen."

Jack agreed; he closed his eyes and drifted off in a couple of minutes. Nora flew to Andre's shoulder and asked, "So what is going to happen?"

Andre said, "Well, I am going to call the car rental place and get a car ready for us. I will fill out all the paperwork on the net and then I will call Suckolofski and tell him what time we will be coming in. Then I will get in touch with a ground crew to refill the plane and give it a once-over."

Nora then asked, "Do you think Jack is in danger?"

Andre didn't answer right away. He finally said, "Yes, I think something is out of place. They want Jack there for something."

Andre reached over and gave Jack a little shake and said loudly, "Jack, we are half an hour out and have clearance to land."

Jack opened his eyes. "OK, I'm awake. Let's do this."

Andre said, "Just buckle up," and spoke to the tower. He flew right in and landed. He taxied right up to a man holding a red flashlight and wound the engine to a stop. He stepped back, dropped the stairs and yelled, "I'm Andre! Are you Mark?"

The guy waved and nodded. Andre turned and said, "OK, let's get out of here."

Jack stood, walked back to get his bag and said to his pocket, "This had better be worth the trip."

Andre went out to meet the Mark guy. Jack got to the bottom of the steps to see Mark jog off toward a hangar, Andre passed him and said, "I have to get my bag. We have a ride to the car rental."

Jack looked back at the hangar and sure enough, there was a golf cart headed their way. When Mark pulled up with the cart, Andre was standing right next to him. Andre said to Jack, "Let me do the talking and we can get through this pretty quick. If you start flapping your lips we could be here for hours."

Andre sat up front with the driver and Jack sat in the back. In a couple of minutes, they were at the door of the car rental. Jack watched the driver shake Andre's hand, then look into his palm. Andre put his arm around Jack's shoulder and said into his ear, "If you want good service, tip big."

The two of them walked into the rental place and Andre walked the guy right through the process like a pro. In three minutes, they were looking at a Ford Focus. Jack asked, "Why did you get a small car?"

Andre said, "It's just the two of us. I don't think we will be giving anybody a ride, do you? All we need is a GPS."

Andre punched in the address of the Circus Museum and they were off. He pulled out a mobile phone and called Marvin and said they had landed and would call when they found out about Jack's kid. Then he pulled another phone, called Suckolofski and told him that the GPS said they were forty minutes out. Then he put the phones away.

Jack said, "Does he still sound nervous?"

Andre smiled, "He said to come to his house."

Jack stared out the window for a second, then said, "Let's go to the museum first."

Andre said, "You're the boss." They pulled up to the museum. There was a building, then a bridge to other buildings.

Jack said, "Drop me off, then park. Give me a few minutes, then come through."

Andre said, "Take half an hour, then we have to find Suckolofski."

Jack walked in and paid the entrance fee. He walked right through the building and crossed over to the circus where the clowns were putting on a show for the tourists. He stepped in front of a clown, looked him right in the eye and asked, "Where is the fortune-teller?"

The clown pointed. "Third row, second trailer," he said, without thinking about it. Jack thanked him and started for the trailer park. A circus hand yelled at him, "Hey, old man! You can't go back there, that's for workers."

Jack turned and the man walked up to him. Jack didn't say a word, just looked him in the eye. The man stammered, "Yes, sir." Jack walked down the dirt road to the trailer.

The door opened and a man wearing a colourful turban said, "There you are! I have been waiting for you."

Jack asked, "You have?"

The man said, "Come and sit. I have seen and heard things from my crystal ball." There, in the middle of the trailer, was a stand with a ball covered with a red cloth. Jack stepped in, sat at the table and lifted the cloth, then peeked under it.

The man sat across from Jack. He looked Jack in the eyes and Jack said, "You will get me a Manhattan Whiskey, Crown Royal, with half a shot of cherry juice."

The man got up and headed for the door. Jack pulled the cloth off the ball and a huge puff of black smoke encircled Jack and the table. Jack sat back as a figure rose from the crystal ball. It spoke to him. "I am Gabriel. This was supposed to be my fight. I was in battle across the galaxy. You will go to the mountain called the Devil's Tower. You will not fail! If you do, the earth will fall."

He started to drift away. Jack said, "I have a request. I want to talk to my wife."

Gabriel said with a booming voice: "Devil's Tower," and started to fade away.

Jack said in a loud voice, "I asked you a question." He reached out and started to pull Gabriel's power.

The archangel turned and tried to pull away. The more he did, the stronger Jack's grip became. He turned from a pale white to a blinding white light. He was pulling all the power he could. The electricity lines burnt right through the panelling, popping all the breakers in the trailer. Then a transformer blew off the pylon. The whole circus stopped. The black smoke rolled around the trailer. Gabriel stopped and said, "Fine! You want to speak to your dead wife? Well, you can't! When the blue fairies consume a human's power, they also consume their soul. Your wife does not exist; her soul was destroyed. You truly were touched by the hand of God."

Then Gabriel, with a shot of power, threw Jack against the wall of the trailer and was gone. Jack got up, grabbed the crystal ball and stepped out of the trailer, which burst into flames. He walked away from the trailer and the fortune-teller caught up to him and held out his drink to him. Jack handed him his crystal ball, took the drink and put it to his lips and sucked half of it down in one swallow.

The trailer was totally engulfed; flames were pouring out the windows and starting to rise through the roof. The fortune-teller stood there with his mouth wide open in amazement. Jack said, "Sorry for your loss. Whatever the insurance doesn't pay, send me the bill. Talk to Suckolofski."

Andre put his arm around Jack's shoulder, watching circus folks run around and spray water on the trailer from afar. The fire was so hot that they couldn't get that close. Andre asked, "Are you ready to go? It would be nice if we weren't here when all the questions start."

Jack turned slowly and started to shuffle his feet toward the bridge. The sound of fire truck sirens filled the air. People came from everywhere to watch the fire. You think people would have fled, but when they reached the bridge, people were streaming onto the circus grounds. When they reached the building, Andre said, "This way. It would be quicker if we walked around." They took the pavement around the back of the building to the front. Then he sat Jack down on a bench as he went to fetch the car. Jack sat there with his head in his hands; he looked beat.

Andre pulled the car up to him and stepped out. He walked over to Jack, took him by the arm, helping him to the car. Jack didn't say a word, just looked up at him with hollow eyes. As soon as the car started to move, Jack sobbed, "She's gone, Emma is no more."

Andre said, "Ah yeah, she died like a month ago."

Jack said, "No, I mean she is gone! The fairies ate her soul! She no longer exists."

Andre nodded, then asked, "You didn't know that?" He said to his pocket, "Nora, you didn't tell him?"

She crawled out of Andre's pocket and flew to the dash. She said, "I'm sorry, Jack. I didn't want to hurt you, it was a need-to-know. And you really didn't need to know."

Andre asked, "OK, did you really need to burn that guy's trailer to the ground? I mean—that went fast! Here we go. I'm going to stop at this gas station and you can change. That shirt can go right into the garbage."

Jack reached up and pulled the shirt away from his chest. It was blackened and a bit scorched. He said with a smile on his face, "Boy, am I glad I was wearing a cotton shirt! At least it didn't melt."

Andre turned for a second and said, "You must have took on hell of a shot! Who threw it?"

Jack chuckled, "Well, I might have pissed him off. It was the Archangel Gabriel. He tried to leave and I held him there, asking him if I could talk to Emmy. He pulled so much power, he blew every breaker on the line and then the transformer on the pylon blew. There were sparks flying everywhere. Finally the asshole told me I will never see my love again, not in this life nor the next."

A tear slid down Jack's face as he stared out the windscreen. Nora stood on the dash and tried to comfort him, apologising. "I am sorry, I really didn't know for certain. It was something the elders would say and I thought it was just to put fear in us, so we wouldn't want to get caught."

Andre asked, "What did this Gabriel want? I mean he didn't get you there to fight with you."

Jack opened his eyes, wiped off another tear and choked out, "Right. He told me I have to go to Devil's Tower. Oh yeah, and I can't fail, the whole earth is in the balance. Talk about pressure!"

Andre pulled into a driveway of a nice house, an old Victorian. He said, "Well, this is it, this is Suckolofski's house. I hope he got your paperwork done."

Andre slid out of the car and to Jack's side. He opened the door and Jack got out. Andre said, "You can change inside. I will get your suitcase later."

Jack reached inside and took out his cane. He moved slower than usual. Nora peeked out of Andre's pocket, watching him. Andre led him to the railing of the steps. He climbed them and rang the door. An old man opened it. He said, "Your name is Dropoff now, right?"

Andre reached out and said with a loud voice, "Vladimir Suckolofski, I haven't seen you in ages! How have you been?"

The old man said, "Come in. Boy, it has been a long time!" The old man turned and Andre stood holding the door for Jack.

Andre put his hand on Jack's shoulder and said, "There is nothing you can do about your wife."

Suckolofski stood just inside the door; his smile slid from his face. He reached out for Jack's hand and Jack took it. Vladimir said, "You must be Jack! What happened to your wife?"

Jack gave him a quick update about the blues eating Emmy's soul, crushing his hopes and dreams of meeting her in another life. Suckolofski took them though the house to the kitchen, where the smell of coffee filled the air. Jack stepped up to Vladimir and held out his hand. The old man looked at Jack.

Jack smiled, "OK, let's try this again. Hi, I'm Jack." Vladimir looked at Andre, who nodded his head. He took Jack's hand. Jack smiled and said, "Take as much as you need." There was a warm red glow emitting from the handshake.

Vladimir said, "My God! You might be the one after all!"

Andre asked, "Where are the cups?"

Vladimir told him, let go of Jack's hand and stepped to the table. He put both hands on it and leaned. He smiled, "I'll be fine. Just give me a minute."

Jack pulled up a chair. Andre sat a cup of coffee in front of him and asked, "Well? Are you impressed? This is our bookkeeper. He has given me, oh, I think it has been 6 different names and lives."

Vladimir stretched his back. You could hear the vertebrae popping back into place. He exclaimed, "That feels good, thank you ever so much!"

Andre said, "You two, get to know each other. I'll run out to the car and get Jack a different shirt."

Vladimir said, "That must have been one hell of a fireball!"

Jack said, "Yeah, about that—I kind of burnt down a trailer. Gabriel pulled so much power that it fried the electrical system."

Vladimir said, "Oh, Gabriel the Arch angel, thee Gabriel, so that was what all the sirens were about!"

Andre walked back in with a shirt. He handed it to Jack and asked, "What did I miss?"

Jack took a good pull from his coffee cup and asked if he could get a refill. Andre stepped over to the worktop and grabbed the coffee pot. He commented as he poured the coffee, "You know, you should tip your waiter."

Vladimir said, "You didn't miss much. Jack was just telling me about burning down a trailer and meeting Gabriel. Are you sure it wasn't Michael? He is the warrior." He started to shuffle papers on the table.

Jack said, "No, it was Gabriel, and he was on the other side of the cosmos. He couldn't make it here on time, now the angel Michael has come up, the cosmos is getting so large, God must have a lot going on, you would have thought he would have fought this war."

Vladimir said, "I got your birth certificate. It looks really good. It is a copy of two, where is the other?"

Jack smiled, "It was in Margaret's safety deposit box. Talking about that how it is going—I mean, with computers nowadays—"

Vladimir said, "I work for the FBI still. They tried to get me to retire, but I have too much information that they don't want to get out. If Marvin is right and we are going to start regenerating again, I will start to groom a younger me to take the job. There has been talk of making me—well, you know if I fail my yearly mental test, I will be slid into an asylum. I will be questioned, tortured and then put to death."

Jack asked about his new life and Vladimir slid a folder to him. There were a bunch of papers and stuff in it. He said, "It isn't done yet. There is a lot to do nowadays—25 years of taxes, six different states. You have a rap sheet. Did you know that you didn't pay taxes for three years back in the day? And you're a bad driver. You were home-schooled and you have a GED."

Andre asked, "When do you want to go to the Devil's Tower?"

Jack held up his coffee cup and said, "Now, I guess. As soon as possible. What we are going to find there will be a surprise. But if I fail, it won't be good—so I have been told."

Vladimir turned and stared at Jack, then said, "You have to spend the night. There is so much I need to know."

Jack said, "That will have to wait. When an angel comes to you and tells you to do something—"

Vladimir held a finger to his lips and said in a hushed voice, "You don't know who is listening!"

Jack smiled and said with a grin, "I have Nora. If there was a blue fairy within earshot, she would know." Nora crawled out of Andre's pocket and flew down to the table, then a couple of old rusty-looking fairies came fluttering in. Jack asked, "Do you have a power stone?"

Vladimir nodded and told them to follow. They walked to a blank wall and he turned a light on. He pushed a knot in the wainscoting and the wall slid to the side. Jack said to Andre, "See? You don't need to make a production out of it!"

Andre shook his head and added, "Now where is the fun in that? Besides, now we all know how to open it."

Vladimir stepped inside. There was a small room with a village like the one Marvin had, but much smaller. The room itself was around six foot square. Vladimir reached up and took a small stone off a shelf. He rubbed some of the dust off and then handed it to Jack.

Jack smiled and rubbed the piece of quartz. It was perfectly round, about the size of a grapefruit; it started to glow. Vladimir said, almost begging, "Not too much, oh my God, not too much! We don't want the blues to know I am here!"

Jack stepped over to the shelf, placed the stone back into its holder and asked, "So how many red fairies do you have living here?"

Vladimir put his hand on Jack's shoulder and said, "In the old days, I had over a thousand. They lived in the old circus wagons, in the surrounding hills. Now, maybe a dozen or two."

Andre stepped out and Jack followed him. He went straight for the coffee pot and filled the cups that were left on the table. Jack asked, "Where is the nearest colony of blues?"

Andre added, "They can't be far; they are probably watching you. Oh no, you don't! We don't have time to go hunting."

Vladimir asked, "Can you kill them?"

Jack said, raising his cup, "It's more like pest control."

Andre pulled out his phone and started to play with it. He said, "Hey, here we are. There is an airport in Sundance. Should I rent an F150? 4-door saddle bags, that is—extra fuel tanks. OK. Now I'll book us a room at the Best Western Devil Towers inn. It's only 22.6 miles from Sundance."

Jack asked, "So how long before you get a flight plan?"

Andre smiled, "Oh, ten minutes. Depends on how busy Madison is. By the time we get to the airport, we should be good to go."

Vladimir said, "Whoa, hold on there! You haven't been here half an hour and you're going to leave?"

Jack lifted his coffee cup and Andre got up from the table. Jack said, "Yeah, I guess that would be a bit rude."

Vladimir asked, "How is Marvin? He speaks in code on the phone."

Jack said, "Marvin? Oh, he is doing better. Now Juliet, she's in bad shape. She was in a coma when I first got there and still is."

Andre filled the cups and asked if they were going to stay for another. Jack said, "Sure, why not?" Andre looked up at the ceiling, walked back to the cupboard and started looking though the cupboards for more coffee.

The two men sat and shot the shit, bringing Vladimir up-to-speed. Jack told him how he was enlisted in this fight against the blues and how he met a unicorn, the Bigfoot and the fairy council. He was very vague, not telling him too much. Jack then asked how Vladimir had got caught up in this.

He reached up and stroked his chin. "Well, I couldn't tell you exactly when. It was way before electricity. Marvin needed a new life for Juliet and himself. It was just so much easier to have it done by an official—I think Madison was president then."

He smiled, raised his cup to Andre and said, "You were the Jefferson brothers, all rich, at the time. Marvin gave me everlasting life. Well, I thought this was it this time. I have never been so old. Lost my wife eight years ago."

Finally Andre spoke up, "That was the early 1800s, right? Well, I'm going to the restroom. Then we can leave. I would like to get there before dark."

Jack asked Vladimir about his paperwork. He said, "I told you before. Just give me some more time—couple of days should do it. And I need pictures of you when you are regenerated."

Andre walked up and asked, "What about Marvin and the missus? Oh yeah, and Jack's got himself a lady friend who is going to be in need of a green card."

Jack stopped as he walked to the bathroom and turned. Andre said loudly, "Sara."

Jack said, "Oh yeah, that is on a need-to-know basis."

In five minutes they were headed out the door, shaking hands and wishing each other good luck. Jack apologised again, "I truly am sorry about burning down the trailer."

Andre opened the door for Jack and asked, "Are you ready?"

As soon as they were on the way, Andre asked, "So do you trust him? I mean, you left a lot out. You didn't mention Margaret, or where anything was."

Jack said, "That is a need-to-know. If he doesn't know it, he can't be forced to give it up. He thinks he is being watched and is a little paranoid."

Andre said, "You'll find anyone that deals with the red fairies is either paranoid or dead."

Jack said, "I got that from Nora the first time I met her. Anyone who sees a fairy could be killed—if that's not being paranoid, what is?"

Nora climbed out of Andre's pocket and flew to the dash. She said, "There is something about that guy—I just don't know! And if you had ninety percent of your race wiped out, you would be paranoid too."

Jack asked, "Do you think ninety percent of your race *was* wiped out?"

Andre said as he merged onto the highway, "Oh, I would say at least ninety. There were colonies of thousands in the old days. They were enslaved or killed. Marvin tried everything until one day, in the south of France, he partnered with three other guardians. They attacked a stronghold of blue fairies. Marvin was the only one to make out alive. That was, oh, a couple of hundred years ago. That's when we moved west to America. Let me tell you, that was hell!"

Jack asked, "So you just ran?"

Andre turned and looked Jack in the eye. "We survived. There was no fighting them, they were too strong."

Jack said, "We will see about that. I don't know what's going to happen in South Dakota, but whatever happens, happens."

The car went silent for a good five minutes, then Andre said, more to himself, "You know there *was* something. Suckolofski should have been more excited."

Jack said, "I didn't read his mind, dammit! I should have!"

Nora said, "Next time, Jack, just relax and think of what that white fairy said."

Andre said one word, "Gabriel."

Jack put his seat back. In five minutes, he was asleep. Nora took this time to talk to Andre and asked, "Do you think Jack is the one? You know, the one to fill the prophecy?"

Andre said, "You mean the one to send all the blue fairies off the earth?"

Nora flew to the steering wheel and said excitedly, "Yeah, that's the one."

Andre let out a sigh. "You do know that *angels* gathered the blues together and sent them in a blue column of light to a star? And let me tell you, Jack is no angel."

Nora asked, "What happened to the blue guardians?"

Andre smiled, "That was before the blues had guardians. They lived off meat and the power of the red fairies."

Andre spoke loudly, "Jack, ten minutes till the airport, time to wake up!"

Jack woke up with a big yawn, then said, "I think I'm in deep shit."

Andre asked, "Now why do you think that?"

Jack rubbed the sleep from his eyes and said, "I kept going over what Gabriel said. This was supposed to be his fight, but Lucifer knew he was on the other side of the cosmos. What I can't understand is, why me? I mean, there are all kinds of angels—look at Michael! He is known to have fought with the Devil and he is the greatest angel. Then you have Raphael. I'm not sure who he is, but he sure would be better-suited for this job!"

Andre said, "Don't be a doubting Thomas, God has handpicked you. I think he knows what He is doing." He chuckled, "Have faith, my brother."

Jack closed his eyes, then said, "This is going to be a shit-fest."

Nora flew up, landed on his shoulder and asked, "What's a shitfest?"

He said, "It is when everything goes to shit. It's going to smell really bad."

Andre pulled out his phone and started to dial a number that he was reading off a paper. Jack said excitedly, "What the hell are you doing? Give me that!"

He took the paper from Andre and waited for the phone. Andre handed him the phone and said, "I have done that a hundred times; I think I can read and drive."

Jack said, "Not while I'm in the car, you can't! Now what are you doing?"

Andre said, "I was calling the car rental place, telling them where I'm leaving the car. They can pick it up."

Jack said, "Wow, they will do that?"

Andre smiled, "They don't like to. And they're are going to charge, but they will do it."

Jack dialled the number and handed it to Andre. He lied and said his plane was taking off in ten minutes and he didn't have time to drop off the car. They would have to pick it up at Gate 24. A pause, then, "Yeah, yeah, just bill me."

Chapter Twenty two
Off to Devil's Tower

Andre pulled up to the gate where his jet was parked. Jack didn't say a word. He got out of the car and walked to the back. Andre popped the boot, Jack reached in and took out both suitcases before Andre got back to him.

Jack said with no emotion, "Let's do this." He stood tall and his hair flowed around his shoulders as he strolled toward the plane; Andre had to work to keep up. He stopped at the jet.

Andre opened the door, only to have it slam hard and bounce. "Dammit!" he muttered. Jack grabbed the railing and carried his suitcase aboard; Andre followed him. Jack slid his suitcase between the back seats and slid into the co-pilot's seat. Andre went and strapped his luggage to a passenger's seat, then did the same with Jack's. He went back down the steps and did his walk around the plane. Then he boarded the plane and pulled up the stairs, got into the pilot's seat and started to run though his checklist. He talked into the head gear, describing his flight plan, then started to roll out onto the tarmac.

Jack asked, "Is there a delay?"

Andre reached up and flipped a couple of switches then said, "Ah, maybe ten minutes." Then he said, "I sure hope nobody noticed you getting on the plane."

Jack asked, "Why would you say that?"

Andre asked Nora, "What's different with Jack?"

She flew from Andre's jacket to the console in front of Jack. "Hmm, let me see, he has a six inch scraggly beard, his hair is about 10–12 inches longer and he doesn't walk with a cane anymore."

Jack sat stroking his beard. He asked, "Is this always going to happen when I use the power?"

Nora flew up and said, "Marvin said as soon as you are regenerated, you will stop."

Andre asked, "How about the smell? When I regenerated, we did it nice and slow, I never smelt like that."

Nora said, "God, I hope so!"

Jack ran a finger across his arm, leaving a streak. He muttered, "Ah, man."

Nora asked, "Do we have water on board?"

Andre said, "Not until we are in the air."

He pulled the plane out on the runway and made a nice, smooth take-off, banking it toward the west and climbing to cruising altitude. "OK, you can get yourself a drink, maybe change. There should be some wipes in the overhead."

Jack got up and hunched over. He walked to the back of the plane, unbelted his suitcase and headed to the bathroom. He looked inside and said, "Hell, I'll just get dressed out here." He reached in, took the pack of wipes and ran a sheet across his arm. It came off solid brown. He pulled out another, that one came a lighter brown.

Nora flew to the cockpit and said, "Jack needs a shower."

Andre said, "You're not kidding! Boy, is he ripe!"

Nora said, "No, his skin is going to be clogged!"

Andre said, "We'll get a hotel room in Sundance."

Jack walked back to the co-pilot's seat and slid in. Andre looked at him and said, "OK, next time, look in the mirror. You have streaks on your face. We'll be landing in about 14 minutes."

Jack said with surprise, "What? We just got started!"

Andre said, "It's only a 75 minute flight. You were screwing around for half an hour!" Andre spoke into his headpiece, then started to descend. He said, "We're going straight in." He sat the jet down, nice and soft and rolled up to a small hangar. A man held out those orange sticks, guiding him in. Andre asked, "Now, who is this idiot?"

Andre stopped. The door to the jet opened; Jack got up and headed to the door. A young man popped his head into the plane and asked, "Could I get your luggage, sir?"

Jack got out of the co-pilot's seat and yelled, "Just a minute!" Jack took the seat belt off his luggage and sat it next to the door, then did the same with Andre's. The young man took both and sat them at the bottom of the stairs. Jack turned and asked Andre if he was coming.

Andre slid a notepad back into its place and said, "I have to keep my log up-to-date; Pickupski trips when things don't add up."

Jack climbed out of the plane and the young man standing at the bottom of the stairs said, "Your F-150 is parked right outside the gate. Keys are in it and so is the paperwork." His eyes snapped open and he took a step back.

Andre walked down the steps holding a bag. He walked up to the two and shook the guy's hand. He slid his hand into his back pocket, not looking at the tip that Andre had palmed him. Then Andre dropped the bag on the blacktop. "One more thing," he said. "Would you throw this out and see if you could get rid of that smell? Fuel her up. We're here for a day or two, we are working though his bucket list. Cancer—that is what you smell."

Jack asked, "It's not that bad, is it?"

Andre nodded, "Yeah, it's that bad."

Jack picked up his suitcase and said, "Your truck is over here."

Andre followed Jack, who was strolling at a pretty good pace. He lifted the suitcase and up and over the side of the truck. Andre asked, "Shouldn't you act your age?"

Jack smiled as he asked, "Why should I? Nobody knows me here. And let's face it, I don't look that old anymore."

Andre dropped the tailgate and put his bag in, then walked around and slid into the truck. Jack was already sitting on the passenger side. Andre pulled out his phone and started to type with one hand and power the windows down with the other.

Andre said, "You're right, we want to get him in a shower. Wow, is he ripe!"

Jack asked, "How did you get this truck? You didn't sign anything!"

Andre smiled, "It's just like the hotel room—I just book. All we have to do is get the key and sign out when we leave. Top floor with a balcony, two queen-sized beds." Andre looked at his phone and said, "It's that hotel, right over there." He started the truck, rolled out of the parking spot and said to himself, "I hope they don't charge to fumigate the truck."

He pulled into the hotel and said, "Now, don't come to the desk. Just take the lift up to the fourth floor. I'll meet you there." Andre went to the desk and a lady handed him two cards; Jack stood at the lift, watching him. He noticed that Andre didn't want to ride in the lift with him.

Jack got in and took it to the top floor; Andre was there in the other lift in a minute and said, "We're going to have to make a game plan."

Jack said, standing behind him, "The first thing is to shower, then I'm going to have to buy some more clothes. We don't wash anything and just keep throwing them away." Andre opened the room and walked right to the windows. Jack said, "It's not that bad." He walked into the bathroom and closed the door.

Andre said, "It's safe. Does he stink more than usual?"

Nora climbed out of Andre's pocket and fluttered to his open hand, "Yeah, it's different, more skunk-like."

Andre said, "He's right, I'm going to buy him some clothes, I'll be back in an hour."

Jack opened the door wrapped in a towel; his four-inch brown roots were gone. He had snow-white hair flowing over his shoulders and sporting a six-inch beard. He asked, "Where is Dropoff?"

Nora flew up and landed on his shoulder. "He's out, shopping for clothes for you. By the way, you look a lot better!"

Jack asked, "Do you know if there are any plastic bags to put my clothes in?" Jack walked over to his luggage and opened his suitcase. He took out a Ziploc bag with his shaver, deodorant and a comb. Then he unzipped a pocket and took out another bag, this one had a flannel in it.

Nora fluttered to an end table and asked, "What's in the bag?"

Jack grumbled, "It's a pair of scissors. Maybe this time I'll just trim the beard." He turned and went back into the bathroom. Half an hour later, Jack came out of the bathroom; he was clean-shaven and his hair was chopped off at the shoulder. He asked, "Did Andre come back with new clothes?"

Nora flew up to him and landed in his palm. "No, he hasn't. I pulled the garage bag out of the can. Is this large enough for your clothes to fit in? They still stink."

Jack walked over to the table where a small bag lay. "Oh boy, I'll try it, but it's going to be tight." He laid his hand down gently on the table and Nora stepped off. Then he grabbed the bag and headed back to the bathroom. After a little cussing, Jack came out with the bag, tearing at the seams. "To hell with it! I'm going to throw this in a dustbin outside."

Nora flew to his shoulder and yelled, "You can't! You're just in a towel! And you don't have the key."

Jack smiled, "Just wearing a towel, that doesn't bother me! Standing in the hall waiting for Dropoff—that would suck." Jack picked up the plastic card and headed out the door. He walked down the hall and met a cleaning lady, held up the bag and said, "Miss, I had an accident. I want to throw out my clothes. Where do you want them?"

She held out her hand, then got a whiff. She exclaimed, "Oh my God, just drop them in the bag!"

Jack stepped over to her trolley and dropped it in a large garbage bag that was hanging from it. He thanked her. She took a deep breath, pulled the bag off the trolley and tied it, then shot him a dirty look. As Jack was heading back to the room, he met Andre, who yelled down the hall, "Old man, where the hell are your clothes?"

Jack waved him off and started to the room. He opened the door and waited for Andre. Andre was carrying three plastic shopping bags. When he got close, Jack said, "I suppose you didn't get any underwear?"

Andre squeezed through the door and said, "You know, you could have told me what you needed before I went."

Jack in turn said, "Any halfwit would have looked in my suitcase to see what I needed."

Andre threw the bags on the bed and said, "You'll just have to go commando, unless you want to go shopping."

Jack just shrugged and went to his suitcase. He opened it on the bed and looked over to Andre. "You did look in my suitcase, just forgot the underwear!"

Andre flicked on the TV and said, "How the hell do you think I got your size? I'm not the mind reader here, you are."

Jack went into the bathroom and got dressed. When he came out, he was wearing a western shirt, blue jeans and tennis shoes. Andre was watching the news and said casually, "You're just going to throw them out anyway, so I bought whatever was on the sale rack.

Jack smiled and said, "No, no, this is good. So, what did you learn in town? We have to make a plan."

Andre said, "Now, you're not going to believe this shit! They are making a movie about bringing the Devil back to earth. There are over a hundred people—actors, set designers. I mean, they are making a sacrificial altar made out of pure quartz and a Stonehenge all on the top of Devil's Tower."

Jack started pacing, then said, "No, this isn't good! What the hell am I going to do?"

Andre said, "I was wondering the same thing. This was probably planned for years."

Jack looked at the weather report on the news and said, "Damn! A storm is going to come soon. Let's go, look at this mountain and get a feel for when this is going to happen."

Nora flew to Jack and said, "Tonight is a new moon; it will be dark."

Jack said, "Let's just get out there."

Nora flew to Andre and started to crawl into his pocket. Jack asked, "Why are you riding with him?"

Nora yelled, "You still smell!"

Andre said, "Yeah. The lift that you rode in? It still smells!"

They headed out the door and Jack asked, "Did you get you get a feel for when this is going to happen?"

They stopped right in front of the lift. Andre said, "You're the mind reader, find out."

Jack cocked his head and a smile spread across his face, "Yeah, I can do that, can't I?" The doors to the lift opened, they stepped in and Jack asked, "What is that smell?"

Andre said, "This is nothing, you should have smelled it before! This is the lift you rode up in. Wait until you smell the truck." They walked out of the hotel into the car park; the truck was there with all four windows open. Andre said, "I put one of those evergreen tree deodorisers in it. We will see if it cut the smell."

Jack stepped on the running board and reached in the window, which of course set off the alarm. He jumped off. "What the hell?" he shouted.

Andre hit the button on the key and said, "Security. You can't reach in through the window when the doors are locked."

Jack opened the door and hopped into the truck. He turned to Andre and said, "Isn't that amazing? Two weeks ago, I would have struggled to get in here—now I am feeling better than I have in forty years."

Andre turned to him and said blankly, "Just focus on the job on hand; this is going to be war."

Jack stared at Andre. He read his mind and said, "Do you really think we are all going to die?"

Andre turned the key and said quietly, "Damn it! Stop reading my mind! And yes, this could really be bad."

Jack said, "There's the tower! How far is it from here?"

Andre turned off the main highway and said, "27 miles, about half an hour or so."

Jack pointed at a gas station and said, "Could we stop there for coffee?"

Nora climbed out of Andre's pocket and said to Andre, "Jack has to eat meat. And he needs to drink more water."

Andre pulled in the restaurant. "OK, that was a good idea; I am hungry." Andre said, "You're an old man, act like it." Jack opened the truck, climbed down and slowly followed Andre, who held the door open for him.

A waitress came up, grabbed two menus and said, "Follow me." She just stood there looking at Jack, blank-faced.

Jack said, "Go," and she turned and walked to a table. They both slid into the booth and ordered coffee.

As soon as the waitress left, Andre told Jack, "You can't do that, people will notice!"

Jack said, "She's going to kiss your ass. She thinks you will give her a twenty percent tip. She has three kids, her husband is a drunk who cheats on her and treats her like shit, so she has been saving up to leave the jerk and move in with her sister in Colorado Springs."

Andre smiled, "All that in less than twenty seconds? I am impressed."

The waitress came with the coffee; she sat both cups down and filled them with a thermos, which she sat on the table. She smiled at Andre and asked, "May I take your order, sir?"

He pointed to Jack and said, "Steak and eggs. And I will have the Denver omelette."

She asked Jack, "What kind of eggs?"

Jack said, "I would like two scrambled and two over-medium hash browns. That steak? Make it a 12-ounce, wheat toast. And could I get a water for both of us?"

Andre asked, "So you *were* hungry."

Jack sipped the coffee and said, "OK, we go to the tower and case the joint." The waitress was back with the water and two other customers in tow. She sat the glasses down and sat the two in the booth next to them.

Andre motioned and said, "Miss? I would like a bagel with cream cheese."

Jack made small talk with Andre. He started to talk about the investments he had made and then the food got there. When Andre was done, he excused himself to go to the bathroom. As soon as he left, a commotion outside the gas station caught Jack's eye—two girls were being dragged out the door.

Jack walked quickly. Soon he was outside with the three. The cop was trying to get the girls in the back of his car. Jack stepped up and said with a commanding voice, "Now see here!" All three heads turned and looked at Jack, this wild old man with his hair flowing in the breeze. Everything stopped. Jack touched the cop's shoulder and said, "Freeze," then he cupped one of the girl's cheeks and muttered, "Demon, you will release her!"

He pulled a small quartz stone from his pocket and held it. He reached over to the other girl and cupped her cheek, closed his eyes and the stone lightened again. Jack then said to the cop, "We are going back inside. Settle this! The charges will be dropped. You will call the girls' parents and you will put them on a bus home."

Jack walked back into the gas station where the manager was standing with her arms crossed. She asked, "And where the hell do you think you're going?"

Jack looked her in the eye and said, "You will drop all charges on the two girls. They promise never to enter your store again."

The manager stepped outside to meet the cop and girls. She said, "Harry, just get those two the hell out of here!"

Both girls said, "We are sorry and we will never do anything like this again."

Jack came back out of the station carrying two rosaries. He handed them to the girls and said, "You will wear these till your faith is stronger." Then he pulled out his money clip and pulled three hundred-dollar bills from it. He handed it to the cop. "This should cover their bus fare. Feed them. They are hungry."

Andre walked up to him and asked, "What are you doing, Jack?"

Jack looked at him, grunted and walked right by him, back into the gas station and into the restaurant; Andre followed. Jack slid back into the booth and drank a half cup of coffee. Then he filled it with the thermos and asked Andre, "Warmer upper?"

Andre shook his head and Jack sat the jug down. The waitress came over with the bill. She asked, "How did you talk Harry into letting those poor girls go?"

Jack said, "I was a police officer for years. And I have kids of my own." There was a slight pause, then, "Ah, shit, I should call them! Anyway, they just needed some help getting home."

The waitress said, "I'll take that when you're ready."

Andre pulled out his wallet but Jack raised his hand. "I got it." He stood, reached into his front pocket and pulled out his money clip. He pulled all the cash out of it and handed it to the girl. He said quietly, "Take this, there are over two thousand dollars in it. Take the kids and go to your sister's. Have faith, my child."

She reached out and took the money; tears slid down her face. She covered her mouth and just closed her eyes.

Jack turned to Andre and said, "It's time." Andre stood and nodded to the girl, who was standing there in shock. Andre had to walk quickly to keep up with Jack. They went out the door and to the truck.

Andre unlocked the doors and slid in. He didn't say a word until the truck was moving. He blurted out, "What the hell, Jack? Do you want everyone to know you are here? And what is up with those two kids?"

Jack turned and said, "Let me study what the girls knew—it's happening tonight. They were possessed. Their demons brought them here. And the waitress—she needed the money to get out of a marriage. She was in danger and so were her kids."

Andre asked, "What did you see when you read the girls' minds?"

Jack closed his eyes and said, "They are demon priests, who are devil worshippers. They are the ones that run the show—they are most powerful. They are going to sacrifice a virgin, spill her blood on the altar and read from the book of the dead to bring the master back onto this earth."

Jack opened his eyes, lifted his head and muttered to himself, "Ah, man what have we got ourselves into!"

Andre smiled and said cheerfully, "OK, let me get this straight—there are a bunch of priests who are devil worshippers. They are going to kill some girl and bring the Devil back to earth. If you ask me, it sounds like the guys in charge are the Devil worshippers. But what are they up to?"

Jack looked at him. Then a smile slid across his face. "That's it! Gabriel said the whole earth was in the balance—this must be it!" Jack closed his eyes and said, "Just drop me off and wait at the hotel."

Nora crawled out of Andre's pocket over to Jack, and started to crawl in his. Jack's eyes popped open and he asked, "Where do you think you are going?"

Nora said sheepishly, "I am coming with you. I promised I would take care of you."

Jack closed his eyes again and said quietly, "This is going to be hell, you know? I'm not going to promise we'll get out alive."

Nora said, "I know. I have felt it as soon as we turned off the main road. And it's getting stronger."

Andre asked, "What is getting stronger?"

Nora said, "Evil."

Jack said, "It feels like a thousand Margarets."

Andre pulled up to a fork in the road in the shadow of the tower. He drove down a half mile, then pulled up to a guard station. Jack said, "This is where I go it alone." Jack stepped out of the truck, talked with the guard, then stepped back to the truck.

Andre said, "Good luck! If you need a hand or a lift, just call."

Jack said, "Get some sleep. Leave the balcony door unlocked—just in case I live though this."

A golf cart came putting up to him and the driver asked, "Are you the OSHA guy?"

Jack held up his hand, "That's me." He stepped into the cart. The driver started to question him. Jack held up one finger and the driver turned and looked at him. That's all it took. Jack said, "You will watch the road. You have seen all my papers and you know I have all the power to shut this place down. You will take me to one of the High Priests. Once you drop me off, you will not remember ever seeing me."

The driver just went down a path between trailers and pulled up to one. Jack got out and the driver started to look around like he didn't know why he was there. Jack saw a guy in heavy robes walk by; he quickly got ahead of him, then stepped in front of him. The priest pulled back his hood a bit to get a good look at Jack. That's all it took. Jack had him bring him to his trailer, where he questioned him and took his robes. Then he touched the man's forehead and seconds later, blood ran from his ears.

Nora excitedly crawled up to Jack's ear. "You killed him!" she yelled.

Jack said calmly, "Hide your power, we are in the lion's den! They will all die. Or we will." Jack stepped out of the trailer, he looked at his watch and started to move closer to the tower. He stepped to a guard who was holding an AK-47 and asked, "Is everything going to plan?"

He pulled his hood to one side to entrance him. Jack then said, "Open your mind. Your will is strong, yes, yes. Everyone must die." Then he said, "OK, up we shall go."

Jack walked to a golf cart and said, "It is time. Take me to the tower." The driver sped right to a cable lift. Jack got out and stepped in the wire cage. In about three minutes, he reached the top. He walked over to the set—you could see the storm rolling across the plains with lightning and huge thunderheads.

There was the girl—she must have been drugged or entranced. She said nothing, just walked up to the altar and stood as they picked her up and slid her on it. They tied her down to it. It looked like a large pool table with pockets on the corners—this one had ancient Sanskrit written on it. The stones around it were set up like Stonehenge in England.

Jack could feel the power. The rocks on the very top had tarps on them; he could tell that they were there to hide the power. Just in front of the altar, there was a cut piece of glass polished to a shine. It looked like a 13-sided pyramid, about six foot high. Jack closed his eyes, remembering what the guy who he killed in the trailer had had in his mind.

He started to step forward and the hooded ones turned to him. He stepped back to his spot. The storm grew closer and the cloud mass dropped to a couple of hundred feet. Lightning flashed and thunder rumbled across the plains. Nora started to crawl out of Jack's pocket. Jack said quietly, "I know. This is it! Stay in there! Whatever happens, do not come out of my pocket!"

All the hooded ones stepped forward one step at a time. They spaced themselves around the altar and started to chant. The storm got closer; the chanting got louder. There was screaming from the trailers and gun shots. Jack knew it was time—there was a mass suicide going on down below in the trailer park.

Jack closed his eyes, remembering what was in the guard's brain. All the followers in the camp were to be given a glass of wine to make a toast. The cyanide in it would kill instantly. If they wouldn't drink, the guards had orders to shoot them. The chanting got louder. The main man stepped in the circle to read from a huge and large old leather-bound book. The cover had raised figures on it. The hooded ones stepped back to the pillars and one of them stepped to the girl. Jack also stepped back to a pillar. They all chanted as the one in the middle yelled out ancient words. The storm's full fury bore down on them—lightning flashed and hit the trailer park.

Jack could feel the demon souls rising. The man with the knife slit the girl's wrists and legs and the blood ran toward the corners of the table. The hooded ones pulled the tarps off the quartz stones and their blue power glowed, lighting up the top of the mountain.

Jack reached out and shot a ball of white light, hitting the pyramid and blowing it to pieces. He threw both arms in the air, turning the stones from blue light to blinding white. He pulled their power down, hitting each one of the hooded ones and cremating them all right where they stood.

A lightning bolt shot down to the altar. Jack reached out and pulled the power, grounding it to the mountain. He was pulled off the ground right into the massive storm. He didn't stop pulling the power from the storm. He directed the lightning to the trailer of the guy he had stolen the clothes from, hitting the LP tank, blowing the front end of the trailer and leaving it burning. The wind circled him; he just hovered in the centre pulling the power and grounding it.

Hundreds of massive lightning strikes hit the ground. Trailers, rocks, dust and cars were whipping around him. Then a loud and thunderous "You will die!" came from the clouds.

Six large lightning bolts hit Jack. Jack just redirected them to the ground and yelled, "Come here!" He pulled power from all sides of the storm. Lightning shot from miles away and hit the tower. All of a sudden, the lightning shot away in all directions at once.

Jack dropped his arms and hung his head. The storm cloud he was in started to swirl, turning into one large tornado and Jack was in the eye. He could see the top of the mountain and the book stood out, sitting on a pulpit. Everything else was gone—the stones, the altar. Jack held out his hand and the book came to him. He grabbed it and slid it into his robes. As he flew away, he threw a bolt of lightning, blowing the pulpit to rubble. He flew straight up and out the eye of the huge tornado.

Nora crawled out of Jack's pocket. She climbed up to his ear and asked, "Why didn't you try to save her?"

Jack wiped a tear that was sliding down his face. "The same reason I didn't destroy all those demon souls—timing. I tried to kill the Devil and I failed."

Nora said, "Let's go to the hotel. There is nothing more you can do here."

Jack held onto the book in his robe with one hand and flew to the dark side of the hotel and then up and onto the porch of his room. Andre met him and asked excitedly, "Well? Did you do it? Did you stop the Devil?"

Jack walked in, dropped the book on the bed and said, "Yes, I stopped the Devil. But everyone died! For what? Nothing! I couldn't pull him together, I couldn't destroy him, dammit! I watch a young girl be sacrificed. For what?"

Andre stepped closer, grabbed Jack by the shoulders and looked him right in the eyes. "You did what you were supposed to do. That was one hell of a light show—the clouds were so dark I couldn't see though them. There must have been a thousand lightning strikes. And that tornado! All the sirens were going off."

All of a sudden, Andre said, "Oh my God, you need a shower, like, now!" He put his hand over his mouth and squeezed his nostrils shut.

Jack pulled down the hood, then pulled started to pull it over his head. Nora flew out, grabbed it with her feet and flew to the ceiling with it. Jack looked up and said, "In the garbage." He headed to the bathroom; his hair was dark brown and just stuck to his shirt.

Andre held out a garbage bag with one hand, then took his other hand off his nose and held it open so Nora could stick the robe in it. He had to help, even though he didn't want to. Jack closed the bathroom door. Andre opened it and sat the bag inside and said, "You too! Get in there!" Nora flew in with Jack.

Andre reached in and turned the fan on. He went to the sliding glass doors on the balcony and slid them wide open. Then he stood there, looking at the storm flash across the plains.

Jack stepped out of the bathroom wrapped in a towel. He grabbed his pyjama bottoms and stepped back into the bathroom. A couple of minutes later, he emerged holding the bag. He said, "This time, we take it with us. God, I hope nobody saw me!"

Andre shook his head and said, "I don't think so. The cloud cover dropped to the top of the tower. Did you do that?"

Jack took his suitcase and flopped it on the queen bed closest to the bathroom. "Nope, that was the Devil. Or a part of the Devil. He wanted to be discreet. I might have had something to do with the tornado, but I'm not sure."

Andre sat on the bed next to him. "Tell me about him."

Jack turned to him, holding his pyjama top. "There's not much to tell—I never saw him. It was like a power, I could feel him all around me. I reached up and pulled the power together and grounded him to the earth, but he just spread out over miles. I just couldn't pull him together."

Jack sat on the bed and put his face in his hands. Then he stopped and looked at Andre, with a tear running down his face. "Dammit, I failed! I should have destroyed him. Now he knows my power and my weaknesses. It was more like a test!"

Nora flew to his shoulder and said, "You did all you could! You stopped the Devil from taking human form and walking on this earth!"

Andre was still staring at Jack; he said, "You have won this battle! They had worked for years to set this up—all the people, the props, the red tape to film on the tower! And by the way, I put that thirty-pound book in a garbage bag. It reeked of burnt flesh."

Jack put his hand on the bed, closed his eyes and said softly, "I don't feel so well."

Elizabeth flew across the room with a bottle of water right to Jack. She said in a demanding voice, "Drink this! You are getting—how do you people say it—dehydrated. Boris said to feed him every couple of hours. My God, do I have to do everything?"

Jack took the bottle from her and unscrewed the top. Andre asked, "How long have you been here?"

She said, "Just a few minutes—long enough to hear that the Devil just tested Jack's strength." She paused, then asked, "Jack, why didn't you kill him?"

Jack finished the bottle, looked up at her and said, "I just couldn't pull him together. It was like he was the storm and his being was the power spread out for miles. At first he was right there—I could feel his presence. The words out of the book drew him close, I think. If I hadn't been there, they would have brought him back to earth."

Nora flew to Andre and asked him if he would get Jack some more water and something to eat. Jack stood and looked at the news. They were showing a film of the storm that had whipped through the Devil's Tower, asking for all emergency personnel to get to the tower. Jack said sadly, "They are all dead. Every single person—dead."

Elizabeth landed on his shoulder and said, "Jack, this is war. We have to focus on the job at hand. I have a message for you."

Jack interrupted, "Weren't you supposed to be in Hollywood?"

Elizabeth said, "I was told to get you this message."

Jack interrupted again, "How did you find us?"

This was starting to piss the green fairy off. She hovered right in front of Jack's face and started glowing a light green. She pointed her finger at him and yelled, "Now listen! The guy with the crystal ball—he said you have to get back to Wisconsin—to a place called Necedah."

Jack asked, "Who told you that?"

Elizabeth lowered her voice, squared off her shoulders and said, "That Vladimir Suckolofski guy—he told me to tell you to get your ass back there."

Jack smiled as Andre handed him another water. He said, "She's kinda cute when she gets mad."

Andre said, "Green fairies are the ones you don't screw with. I'll call Marvin and tell him we have to go back to Wisconsin for a day."

Jack asked, "Didn't you order room service? I am starved." Nora flew to Jack and asked him to look in the mirror. Jack got up and walked to the mirror to see his long white hair had two-inch roots of dark brown.

Jack muttered to himself, "Ah, crap!" He took off the pyjama top to see a brown ring around the collar. Then he put it back on and said, "Screw it! I'm going to eat first, then I will shower."

Andre stepped back in from the balcony and stood in front of the TV set watching the news. He said, "This isn't good. It's going to make the national news. Oh for Christ's sake, satellite imagery!"

Jack rolled off the bed and stood with Andre. He asked, "Do you think they will see anything?"

Andre said, "There will be people taking the pictures apart. Did you see that? There are trailers flying all over the place."

The TV said, "Back to live news helicopter footage of the tragic tornado at Devil's tower."

Andre said, "Look! Trailers up to five miles from the tower."

There was a knock at the door. Jack excitedly said, "Food!" He stepped to the door, took the tray from the young man and said, "Bill it to the room." Andre got up, tipped the guy and ordered some chicken and two Royal Crown Manhattans with a six-pack of bottled water. Jack tore into the meal—a 16-ounce T-bone with bacon, potatoes, coleslaw and baked beans.

Jack told Andre, "You should get some sleep. It is going to be a long day tomorrow."

Andre smiled and said, "As soon as my Manhattan gets here. You didn't think I ordered you two, did you?"

Jack wiped his face and smiled, "Yeah, I thought that was a bit weird, but tonight I could have drunk two."

Andre said, "Now get your ass back into the shower, you're getting a bit ripe."

Jack looked in the mirror and saw his hair now had three-inch roots. Muttering to himself, he walked back to the shower. When he got out, Andre was sitting on the balcony, watching the lights flash by the tower. There was a helicopter flying with a huge spotlight. Jack said calmly, "They're wasting their time. There are no survivors."

Andre held up his glass and asked, "Are you sure?"

Jack walked over and took his drink off the small table. "Yeah, I didn't feel anyone alive. They all toasted with wine laced with cyanide the ones who didn't drink were shot, they were releasing the demons that possessed them, that was power to Lucifer."

Andre said, "Marvin knows we are going to be a day late. He told me to tell you: 'This is not the only iron you have in the fire.'"

Jack turned and walked back into the room. He went to his suitcase and pulled out three phones. Nora flew to him and asked, "Are you going to call your kids?"

Jack looked at her and said, "Why don't you just go to sleep? You had a long day."

Nora stood there, looking up at him. He finally said, "Fine, I'll call them! By the way, where is Lizard breath?"

Nora put her hand in front of her mouth, holding back a laugh and said with a smile, "She is at the tower, doing damage control. Andre sent her."

Jack picked up a phone, flipped it open and hit dial. He said loudly, "Linda, Jack here. How are things doing on your end?" A pause, then, "Did that Dave Hanson call? When? I'll be there and we will start assembling the troops."

Jack looked up to see Andre standing in the doorway. He said, "I have to be in the Caribbean in two days. I have a date." Jack put the phone in his suitcase and pulled out another.

Andre asked, "Now who are you calling?"

Jack looked up and said, "This is Suckolofski's phone." Jack called and asked one question, "Do I *need* to be there?"

Jack closed it and looked at Andre. "I think all of this at the tower was just a test. Oh my God! If that was a test, we're in a world of hurt!"

Andre picked up the phone and ordered a vodka martini and a large order of onion rings, then looked at Jack. Jack took three steps towards him and said, "Another Manhattan, a cheeseburger and chips and something with chocolate."

Jack went back to the bed, picked another phone, opened it and dialled. This time he spoke softer, "Hi, just checking in. Tell your sister I'm doing as well as could be expected." With that, he closed the phone.

Andre asked, "Did you leave a message?"

Jack smiled, "You know, that's the way I'm going to do it from now on. It's a lot easier."

Andre said, "I'll teach you how to text message. Just send it to them and you don't have to talk."

Jack reached down, picked up his drink, held it up and said, "I'll drink to that!"

Elizabeth stood on the nightstand waiting for someone to notice she was back. Andre saw her and asked, "So how does it look?"

Jack turned, walked over to the bed and sat down to get debriefed. Elizabeth stood thinking, then said, "It is a mess over there—hundreds of people walking around. They are collecting human remains. That tornado smashed the bodies against rocks and threw them miles away. There are trucks and trailers scattered everywhere. I flew to the top of the tower, nobody has been there. It's clean—there is nothing up there, no small rocks, no bodies, nothing."

Jack asked, "How about the Stonehenge, there was a large glass pyrimad that shattered. Are they investigating, or are they just moving the bodies as they find them?"

The green fairy said, "No stones were standing, nothing out of the ordinary. They're just putting the bodies in the backs of trucks and taking them away. There are so many!"

Jack said, "Well, time will tell what happened here. Hopefully, they will never know the truth. It's getting pretty late, they will probably start again in the morning."

Andre asked, "What is going on with our food?"

With that, a knock came; Andre started for the door, Jack jumped up and followed him. Andre took the food and handed the tray to Jack. Jack looked around him to the server and said, "Look at me." The server looked at Jack and just stared. Jack then turned and walked back into the room.

Andre handed the waiter a tip and said, "Bill the room."

Andre walked up to Jack and said, "If you wanted onion rings, you should have ordered them yourself. And what the hell was that by the door?"

Jack smiled as he finished one of Andre's rings. "That was Ben, he didn't hear anything outside the door. I was just checking. He thinks the massacre was a tornado."

Andre took his onion rings and sat on a bed. He said, "Where is Nora?"

Jack was just taking a bite of his cheeseburger. He said with his mouth full, "She's sleeping; she's had a full day."

Andre got up, went to the mini-fridge and took out two bottles of water, handed one to Jack, then said, "You had better drink both of them." He then went back and got himself another. He said, "Eat, shower, then sleep. We are getting out of here as soon as possible. Oh yeah, your last pair of pyjamas—the ones you're wearing—garbage them.

Jack got up and grumbled on his way to the bathroom. He grabbed the garbage bag on the way there. Elizabeth flew to Andre and asked, "Does Jack smell different?"

Andre said, "The smell of burnt flesh is what you're smelling."

She said, "That is a very foul smell."

Andre sipped his martini and asked, "How's your stay on earth going?"

She crossed her arms, turned her head and asked, "How the hell do you think? This was supposed to be just a long flight; find Aurora and go back. I never would have expected the blues to be this strong and to have enslaved the red race."

Andre cut her off, "You didn't answer my question. Are you enjoying yourself?"

She stood there, looking up at him, then said, "I am here to find my cousin. When I do, I will return to my planet."

Andre asked again, "But are you enjoying yourself?"

Elizabeth said with a grin, "Yes, this is pretty interesting. I will teach those blue devils to enslave fairies, I will kill them all."

Andre said, "There's my girl!"

Jack came out of the bathroom with flowing white hair and a Santa's beard. He walked over to his Manhattan, put it to his lips and said, "It's been a long day." He slammed back his drink and slid into his bed.

Andre, who was already in bed, said, "It would have been nice if you turned off the lights and closed your door."

Elizabeth said, "Fine! I'll do it." She flew to the door and swung it closed, then to the switch, she fluttered right infront of it, trying to turn it off.

Andre said, "For crumb sakes, just take it and push it down, man some people's kids."

Nora flew down to Andre and said quietly, "You can't tease Elizabeth that way. She is stronger than you think."

Andre said, "What do you mean, she can't even turn off the light?"

The light went out and she fluttered above Andre and said, "That was the first time I have ever turned off a light. I am sleeping with Jack tonight, he wants a report in the morning. She flew to the door and went into Jacks room."

Jack said, "One day I will teach you simple electricity. Now get some sleep. Oh by the way, how did you find us?"

Elizabeth said, "I knew where you were going. Once I got here, I could feel the blues' power stronger then I have ever felt. Then you powered up."

Jack got up early. He stepped out on the balcony and sat and watched the sun start to creep across the plane. It illuminated the tower. He could see lights out in the distance; there were people who had worked through the night. Jack closed his eyes and went over everything that he learned from the Devil. He was trying to figure out how to defeat him and to sift through all the stuff he had taken in from the Devil worshipper.

Andre quietly stepped out and put his hand on Jack's shoulder. He said, "You couldn't have saved them."

Jack opened his eyes, looked up at Andre and said softly, "They were going to die anyway. The devil that was there was called a shedu, a storm devil. It's still the same devil. It is so large! How do you fight something that can spread out for miles?"

Andre asked, "What would you like for breakfast?"

Jack's snapped, "Coffee and whatever you're having."

Andre went back in the room, called room service and made a four-cup pot of coffee. He turned on the TV and that woke up the fairies. The breaking news was the satanic deaths at the tower, test showed cyanide poisoning and gunshot wounds, no survivors found yet." They showed live pictures of all the wreckage—trailers that were ripped apart, insulation blowing all over and a pickup with body bags. The news said they had run out of room to store the bodies and were using a grocery store cooler to stack them. These people were from all corners of the county and it was going to take a while to identify the bodies.

The F.B.I. was on the scene; the newswoman tried to interview a man in a black suit but he blew her off. The sheriff was happy to talk. He said there was a lot of paper blowing around. Every person had had a thousand page script and it was going to take some time. But this they knew for sure: some of the people were shot and others didn't have a scratch on them.

Andre said to himself, "Screw this." He walked to the balcony, holding a cup of coffee and said, "We have to go. This is going to be a lockdown. They don't know what's going on, but they do know people have been shot."

Jack looked up and asked, "Do you think they would shut down the airport?"

Andre asked, "How long before you're ready?"

Jack got up, sipped his coffee and said, "Ten minutes. Can we stop at McDonalds on the way out?"

Andre smiled and said, "Make it five. And cut that damn hair, it's past your shoulder blades! I'll run and check out."

Jack rearranged his suitcase, took out a pair of jeans, a shirt and socks. He said to himself, "What a waste, just going to throw them out."

Nora flew up to him and asked, "Why don't you throw them in one of those white machines?"

Jack said, "Time, for one thing. And they smell. It's just easier this way."

Elizabeth landed on the TV and asked, "What's going on?"

Jack ran scissors through his hair, cutting it off at shoulder length and put it in the bag with his pyjamas in. He piled everything that was going next to the door and did his last run-through, looking under the beds and in the bathroom.

Andre opened the door and asked, "Are you ready?"

Jack said, "Let's do it. The sooner we're out of here, the better." He grabbed his suitcase and threw a bag of clothes in it. The book was strapped to the suitcase.

Andre grabbed the other bag and said, "The truck is parked right outside."

Jack slowed his stride, hunched over and walked slowly behind Andre to the lift. Once they got in, Andre said, "Boy, something smells in here!" When they got out, Andre told Jack the truck was to the right. Jack said he had to return the room key. Andre said, "Keys are thrown away, they're coded for your room and cost pennies."

Jack said, "I should have left it in my room. Here, give it to the desk." Jack handed Andre the room key. Andre took it, mumbling, "This is a waste of time."

Jack pretended that he hadn't heard it and just stood there. Andre came back and asked, "Are you happy now?"

Jack smiled and said, "Let's just get going." Andre held the door open for Jack.

When they got to the truck, Andre took the bags of clothes and tossed them in the corner of the bed, then sat the suitcases on them. Once they were in the truck, Andre asked, "Do you know why we are going back to Wisconsin?"

Jack said, "Because Lizard Breath told me to."

Andre asked, "Miss Elizabeth, do you know why?"

She crawled out of Jack's pocket and hopped to the dash. "I told you before, Vladimir told me."

Andre asked, "So what's going on at the tower?"

She said, "They're starting to sort through the trailers that are still in one piece. There are a lot more people and trucks there—some look like soldiers."

Jack said, "Ah, Pete's sake! They called in the guard. Do they have a lot of yellow tape around stuff?"

Elizabeth asked, "How did you know?"

Jack said flatly, "That's the way they usually have detectives check out the scene. They tape off anything they want to investigate. Were there a lot of places taped off?"

Elizabeth cocked her head, then said, "A trailer, a big car-thing, around a pile of rocks—I don't know, maybe six."

Jack said, "That car-thing was a van that had the poison in it. I don't think there is anything to tie me to it. The only thing that worries me is the satellite photos."

Andre said, "Well, if the Feds investigate, the plane was registered at the airport, so they know we were there."

Jack pointed and asked, "Can we stop at Mickey D's?"

Andre said, "They are still serving breakfast."

Jack said, 'Order me six breakfast burritos, some juice, a half dozen hash browns, bacon and sausage."

Nora said, "Water, you need to drink more water!"

On the way to the airport, they passed a queue of army vehicles. Andre muttered to himself, "Please, don't shut down the airport!"

Jack asked, "So why don't you call?"

Andre looked over at him and said sarcastically, "Do we really want to bring attention to ourselves? You'll never match your ID. I put in our flight plan last night. We're just leaving a couple hours early."

The food came and Jack started right in. He had more than half the food down before they got to the airport, which was like, eight minutes from Mickey D's. Andre played with his phone for a minute as he was pulling into the rental place.

Jack asked, "Why don't you just leave the truck at the airport?"

Andre smiled as he said, "This is a small airport, with a free shuttle to the airport—ten minutes tops."

They pulled up to the front, where they met the shuttle. A man walked to the truck, took the luggage and placed it into the shuttle. Andre grabbed the two bags of laundry. Jack just sat there and ate. Andre popped his head in the cab and said, "We're ready, let's go."

Jack grabbed a bag, sucked down the rest of the juice and headed for the shuttle. When they got to the airport, the driver drove right up to the plane. Once they were loaded, Andre shook his hand, slipping him some cash. Jack watched from the doorway, then sat in the co-pilot's seat. Andre pulled up the stairway, locked the door into place and sat down in the pilot's seat.

Jack asked, "OK, how much did that cost?"

Andre smiled. "A hundred bucks, but it was worth it. He will fill it up and clean it out."

Chapter Twenty Three
To Necedah

Andre chatted with the tower for a minute or two and then taxied out onto the runway.

Jack asked, "Are they going to shut down the airport?"

Andre said, as he started to throttle up, "We're not in the air yet." He put the hammer down and they were up and flying. Jack was eating and the plane was banking back into the sun.

Andre pulled out his clipboard and started the pre-flight check. Jack asked, "Aren't you supposed to do that before we take off?"

Andre smiled, "You're not going to tell, are you?"

Jack asked Nora to get him a water. She flew back and got him one from the mini-fridge. He then asked Elizabeth, "So do you like flying in the jet better than outside?"

Elizabeth flew over, landed on his knee and said, "Look here, Jack! I am supposed to be looking for my cousin."

Jack cut her off. "We will do things as they happen. The more fairies we talk to, the better chances are of finding your cousin."

Andre, who had just taken his headphones off, asked, "You have been gone for a while. Isn't someone going to start looking for you?"

Elizabeth hopped to the dash and stared at Andre, then said, "Nobody is coming to my rescue, this planet is off-limits."

Andre asked, "So if it's off-limits, why are you here?"

Elizabeth's voice rose, "I told you I am here to find my cousin!"

Andre asked, "So why did *she* come here?"

Elizabeth started to glow, "I might have dared her to do it."

Jack smiled and nodded his head. "So this is all your fault! And you said nobody's coming to rescue you. Well, I did, didn't I?"

Elizabeth bowed her head and squeaked, "Yes, it's my fault."

Nora flew up with the water gripped in her feet. She hovered in front of Jack and said, "Thank you, Lord, if you hadn't shown up, nothing would have changed."

Jack took the water and said, "Yes, I must thank you also. I was just looking forward to death before. Now, I have a life—a reason for living."

Andre turned and looked at Jack. "Now let's not get teary eyed, things have been set in place by a higher power. We are but pawns. If we're going back to Wisconsin, something didn't work out right."

Jack leaned his chair back and said, "I had the element of surprise. That won't happen again. They know my strength. This is going to turn bad, I just know it."

Andre said, "Get some sleep. We will be there before you know it."

Jack took a drink of water and closed his eyes. He asked, "What could I have done? It looked like the Devil just spread out over miles."

Andre pulled out his iPhone and started to tap the screen, pulling up pages. Nora flew to his shoulder and asked, "What are you doing there?"

Andre smiled, "I just rented a car, booked a hotel and I was working on having the plane refuelled. They're charging a bit much to park the jet just for a day."

Nora asked, "You don't have to pay, when you use that thing?"

Andre chuckled, "That thing is a phone, it's just a smart phone—it does more than I know. And yes, I am paying for everything, Marvin will repay me."

Nora said, "Now, that's amazing! What was that satellite thing that Jack was so worried about?"

Andre told her: "They are satellites—machines that fly around the earth, take pictures and send signals. That is how TV works and if they had real-time satellite photos, they could look right down in your forest and see what was going on, right now."

Nora said, "There is no way a machine in space could see us!"

Andre said, "They can read a licence plate—oh, those things with the numbers on front of cars."

Nora said quietly, "Really? They can see us? But we can't see them."

Andre smiled and said, "Welcome to the 21st century. Now you take a nap, we will be there in 45 minutes."

Nora flew to Andre's shoulder, then asked quietly in his ear, "Where are we going, and why?"

Andre whispered, "To a town called Necedah. I googled it and it sounds like a nice town, small airport—I can land there. Last time we landed in Madison, that place brings back memories—went to college there once."

Nora asked again, "Why are we going there?"

Andre whispered, "Because we were told to. There is a shrine of our Mother Mary there—it has a bunch of small shrines. I think the Archangel Gabriel will tell Jack what to do."

Then Nora started to ask him about his life. Andre said, "You should get some rest. And my life is none of your business."

Elizabeth asked, "Who is this Mother Mary?"

Andre slowly shook his head. "OK, I will tell you. A long time ago, like two thousand years ago, God, our Creator, sent down his Son to live like a human. Mary was conceived from the Holy Spirit and she had the saviour Jesus Christ. And she and her husband Joseph raised him."

Elizabeth asked, "You mean a God was born a human being? And why was this Jesus sent here?"

Andre said, "I believe it was a test, to see if the human soul was worth saving. We have been taught to praise God. I believe millions of souls have made their way to heaven. I have seen ghosts that I believe are lost souls."

Elizabeth said, "Now that's all nice and dandy, but what is God getting out of it?"

Andre cocked his head in thought, then said, "You know, nothing is for nothing. We know bad souls go to hell, good souls go to heaven and some souls go to purgatory. Maybe there is power in souls and we are feeding God with our prayers and praise. I mean, just think of it—billions of souls, just from this planet! Well, millions of good souls, but there are billions of planets."

Elizabeth said into his ear, "It's all about power then?"

Andre whispered, "It's good against evil, that's the way it always has been. But now if you look at the big picture, I mean the real big picture, I think you are right. It *is* about power. God kicked Lucifer out of heaven in a power struggle and it's been going on ever since."

Andre asked, "Elizabeth, you have lived a long time, how didn't you know about God, do you have a God on your planet?"

Elizabeth said, "That I cannot say, I have taken an oath not to speak about my planet to anyone."

Nora smiled, "I have gone to many churches. I just wanted to hear your take on the subject."

Elizabeth said, "This is why we can't go to some of the planets! There are off-limit places like the earth and some are just banned. We can visit most of the planets that are in your so-called Goldilocks zone."

Andre asked, "Have you visited many planets?"

Elizabeth said, "Oh yes, many planets, but we can't talk about them. This one is very nice but violent. The blues were supposed to have been sent to an uninhabited planet, but some must have stayed."

Andre then asked, "Are there people like us on other planets?"

Nora who was listening, flew to Elizabeth's side. Elizabeth said, shaking her head, "I can't tell you."

Nora asked, "Why can't you tell us?"

Elizabeth said, "We, the green fairies, take an oath, don't you guys listen, before we fly from our planet: never bring anything back, and never tell one planet about the other."

Andre asked, "Do you have God on your own planet?"

She said, "And never tell anyone about our own planet."

Andre said, "I had to try." He reached over, picked up his headphones and said, "It's back-to-work time." He slid them onto his head and pulled down the microphone. The two fairies hopped to the dash, looking out the window,

Nora said to Elizabeth, "This is so exciting!"

Andre started talking to the tower. Jack stopped snoring. He sat his seat back up, then asked, "How long?"

Andre said, "We should be touching down in about 37 minutes."

Jack unbuckled his seat and announced, "Well, I have to piss." With that, he was up and headed for the bathroom.

Andre took off the auto-pilot and talked into the headpiece. Jack came back holding a water and a donut. Andre asked, "Where the hell did you get the donut from?"

Jack said, "Last one—I had it in my carry-on. So what's up, captain?"

Andre smiled. "We're going straight in. I checked with the car rental, we have a Lincoln standing by. A flight crew will fill her up this afternoon. I figure we should be in Necedah by 2:00."

Jack asked, "Can we get a hotel and freshen up first?"

Andre smiled and said with a chuckle, "Ah, I thought we would get a room after you meet whomever you're going to meet. Remember Baraboo? The fire? Next time something like that happens, call! I didn't know where the hell you went."

Jack started to lose his colour and then said, "I don't know what is going to happen or where we have to go!"

Andre said, "First, we are going to go to a shrine of the Mother Mary. There are a bunch of other shrines there too. I think that is where you will find Gabriel."

Jack said more to himself than to anyone else, "Yeah, and that went well! We didn't leave as friends, did we?"

Andre set the flaps and started to drop toward the airstrip. He said, "Necedah has an airport. At least this one didn't lie about how long the strip was."

Andre sat the jet down on the strip, nice and gentle and slowed, talking into the headset. He turned off the main runway towards a black town car. Jack said, "Nice car."

Andre said with a smile, "Nothing but the best when it's not your money!"

A man stepped out with two orange sticks, guiding them into a parking spot right next to the Lincoln. Andre said, "So far, we have had good service."

Jack asked, "OK girls, who do you want to ride with?" Both of the fairies flew to Andre. Jack said, "Yeah, I know I need a shower, this is getting old. I could shower three times a day!"

Andre said, "You're looking younger all the time, you'll never match your driving licence."

Jack looked down at his hands and wiggled his fingers. Andre stopped the plane and started the shutdown. Jack got up and said, "Meet you outside." With that, he got up and unbuckled his suitcase and Andre's. He dropped the steps and climbed out with the suitcases. The man had chucked the wheels.

Jack sat the suitcase down on the blacktop and got the rest of the luggage. When Andre came out of the plane, he stepped over to the man and shook his hand. Jack had everything in the boot and was waiting by the car. Andre said, "Well, it's off for an adventure."

Jack said, "Just get in the car."

Andre slid into the driver's seat. He pulled out his phone and sat for a second, then turned on the car and programmed the GPS. Jack said, "Give me your phone." Andre shrugged and handed Jack his phone. Jack took it, studied it and turned it sideways. "This is amazingly thin, this is one of those 4G things."

Andre held out his hand and Jack placed it back into it. Andre said, "It's a 6G and it is fast. If Marvin had an iPhone, you could FaceTime with him. What kind of phone do your kids have?"

Jack said, "Ah, nuts! The kids! No, I don't want the kids to know what I look like! Hell, I am supposed to be dying!"

Nora hopped to one of Jack's legs and yelled up to him, "You have to call them! And Marvin!"

Jack took out his phone, opened it and said, "When I get on the road, I will call."

Andre looked at his phone and said, "An hour, hour and a half—we'll take I-90 to I-94 and stop at Baraboo and see Suckolofski. We're driving right by, it would be rude not to stop."

Jack asked, "Why did you check your phone when you had already programmed the GPS thing?"

Andre reached up and tapped the GPS, turning the sound up. A man came on, telling him to turn right. Andre said, "Now watch. He will take us the shortest way, not the fastest or easiest." Andre tapped the GPS and it showed the route, through side streets to the highway.

Jack asked, "Have you noticed there is something strange about Vladimir?"

Andre smiled. "Oh yes, Vladimir—Marvin has regenerated him a few times. He has worked in the government secret services for a long time. He trusts no one. He has giving me a new life many times before. The last time, we went to Russia. It's getting tricky nowadays." Jack reached into his breast pocket, pulled out a Snickers bar and started to unwrap it.

Nora climbed out of Andre's jacket and hopped to the dash. She stared out the window for a second, then walked over to the passenger side. She stopped and watched Jack eat his candy bar. When he was done, he asked, "OK, what do you want?"

Nora asked, "Did you call your kids? And you should call Vladimir."

Jack looked over to Andre, then rolled his eyes. He sighed, "Fine, I'll call. But it's going to be the same stuff—how are you, where are you, what the hell do you think you're doing? And then I cheated on their mother and had a child!"

Jack flipped the phone open. Andre said, "Just remember, you only call your kids on that phone!"

Jack answered back with a "Yes, sir." He pushed his contacts and to his son's number, then you could hear him say, "I'm fine, none of your business. I don't give a flying leap what she thinks. Hey, it was a mistake! And I am going to find him. Well, I checked in! You be good." He pushed the off button, looked up at Nora and said, "See? I told you, same thing! I can't call Vladimir until I get to my suitcase."

Andre said flatly, "You know you can never see your kids again? You look damn near twenty years younger."

Jack smiled. "And I feel twenty years younger. And it will so much easier on them this way, no funeral or service—they'll just get a box of ashes in the mail."

Andre said, "Ten minutes."

They pulled into Vladimir's driveway and Jack said, "This is just going to be a quick visit, right?"

Andre said, "We will make it fast. He knew we were going to the Devil's Tower. The whole world knows about the storm."

Jack said, "Oh man, that's right!"

Vladimir answered the door and said, "Andre, what the hell are you doing back here?"

Andre said, "This might sound corny, but we were in the neighbourhood and thought it would be rude not to stop by."

Vladimir was excited to see them. Jack said as he passed him at the door, "We will fill you in once inside."

Vladimir said, "Yeah—that must have been one hell of a trip!"

Andre said, "Really, we are just travelling through on the way to Necedah."

Vladimir said, "The Queen of the Holy Rosary? Why are you going there?"

Jack said, "You told us, so that is what we are doing."

Andre said, "I don't think he is going to trash the place. By the way, how is that burnt trailer doing?"

Vladimir said, "Insurance is going to pay for most of it, he lost everything."

Jack asked, "So you saw the news footage? What do you think happened at the tower?"

Vladimir said, "It looked like a massive storm, but the news tried to put the spin on 'The Devil did it', with that movie getting filmed there. What the hell *did* happen?"

Jack said, "The news was right. A bunch of devil worshippers tried to bring the Devil back to earth and blue guardians tried out their Stonehenge. That actually could have worked, the key was glass though. It was six feet high, I think they took the measurements off the real one. Stonehenge—it wasn't to scale, but nobody lived to tell."

Andre said, "Well, we brought you up to speed on what happened over there. We want to get to the shrine. By the way you *did* tell us to go to the shrine, isn't that right Elizabeth?"

Vladimir said, "I did not!"

Elizabeth said, "Yes, you did. You sat right there in that chair and said, 'Jack has to go to Necedah, go get Jack.'"

Andre asked, "Was he talking in his sleep?"

Elizabeth asked, "Do people do that?"

Vladimir said "I don't and have never done it, I would lose my security clearance!"

Jack smiled and asked, "How do you know? You are asleep."

Andre said, "Someone was talking through him, I have seen it done before, Voodoo magic."

Vladimir asked, "Did you pay for the hotel with a credit card? What else could tie you to the tower?"

Andre said, "Forget it. We have flight plans, bought fuel, rented a truck—we left a lot of tracks."

Jack mumbled to himself, "Ah, whatever happens, happens."

Andre smiled and said, "Well, you are probably going to get your ass chewed for letting Lucifer go. The Devil is still out there."

Jack shot him a look. "Don't you think I'll get an 'Atta boy, good job you stopped the Devil from walking on this earth!'?"

Andre chuckled. "See, if that happens, it would be great! But if he shoots you down, you're ready for it. Sorry for leaving so soon, but the game is afoot."

Jack said, "People really don't say that anymore. Well Vadimar, I hope to get my paper work soon, so I can start my new life."

Andre said, "The bus is leaving, we will be in touch." They hopped into the car a started for the shrine.

There was a hoarding and an arrow pointing to the shrine. Andre pulled into the car park; there were a few other cars there. Jack said, "Nora, you stay with Andre. And Andre, stay in the gift shop for now."

The two walked to the gift shop and talked to the elderly lady behind the counter. Jack asked about the shrine and how many people there were today. The lady told them it was a self-guide tour and to just go out the side door to enter. Jack walked toward the door; Andre stood talking with the lady. He asked if the Mother Mary had appeared lately.

The old lady smiled and said, "Well, young fellow, I have been working here on and off for thirty years and have never have seen her. But that doesn't mean she hasn't visited. You can feel her presence."

Then she looked up and said, "She's here, don't you feel her?"

Andre said in a nervous tone, "Oh boy!"

Meanwhile, Jack walked through the shrine, stopping and looking at all the saints. He stopped and brought his hands together, saying a little prayer looking at the Archangel Gabriel. He stood there waiting and his phone went off. Jack took out his phone and answered it. Andre said quietly, "You do have your phone on! It's Mary, Mother Mary. Oh my God, she's here I think!"

Jack said, "OK thanks, I'll turn my phone off."

He walked right over to a large statue of Mary. He looked into the eyes of the statue and said, "I can feel your presence. What do you want from me?"

Jack heard in his head, "Walk with me."

They walked into a side door of the church. As they walked, Mary talked to him, just chitchat. They stepped through a doorway and the door closed. Jack turned after hearing the door shut. There was a young woman standing there with a white glow to her.

Jack dropped to one knee. Mary said, "Get up, we don't have much time."

Jack raised his head to look at her. She stood there with her arm extended and motioning upwards. Jack got to his feet and asked, "Are you Mother Mary?"

Mary said, "Yes, Jack, I am the mother of Jesus. I have been watching this planet for over two thousand years now. We are at war with the blues and Lucifer. At the Devil's Tower—that was the closest he has come to walk the earth."

Jack asked, "Was that it? Was that the purpose for which God has granted me this power?"

Mary put her hand on Jack's shoulder and said quietly, "I am afraid not. That was part of it. You have to defeat the blues; you will have to destroy them. I am here to help you, but I can just give you advice, you are strong enough. Please find Baba Yaga, she will help you."

Jack asked, "How is it you can walk the earth and the other angels can't?"

Mary smiled. "I'm special. I see over the earth till the day my God comes back in the end, I do come and go as I like. But that is in the future, and it could change. Lucifer isn't happy. There are so many good people! The end isn't coming soon enough for him."

Jack asked, "Why me?"

Mary smiled. "Well, Gabriel was halfway around the cosmos. This was his fight, but he couldn't make it on time. God had to make a move and you were it. I myself think you are a good choice. Just remember: you have to crack a few eggs to make an omelette. And never show your power."

Jack asked, "Why don't you show yourself? Everyone's faith would be so much stronger!"

Mary put her hand on Jack's shoulder again and looked him straight in the eye. "You have a lot to learn. Faith is about believing. With all the cameras and satellites, all your technologies—one picture and it would be sent around the world. You would think there wouldn't be war or starving people? Can't you people just get along?"

Jack asked, "What do I have to do?"

Mary said, "You have to do what you think is right. And you must win for the earth's sake."

Jack asked, "What is heaven like?"

Mary said, "It's time. Follow your heart but listen to your brain. You must win this." She turned toward the door and disappeared as the door opened.

Jack walked out, shaking his head and talking to himself, "Yes, it's a beautiful day. What do you think about global warming? Yeah, Dropoff, I'll tell him. Marvin, OK. Yes, love is strong. What about Buddhism, Hindus? How about the Jews? Oh, I know! What about those Muslims?"

Andre stepped up to him and asked, "Who are you talking to?"

Jack smiled. "Mother Mary, and she likes you. You have a pure heart. And she wants me to tell you: everyone has to die, so let it go."

Andre asked, "Are we done here?"

Jack smiled as he said, "Yes, I think we are."

Andre asked, "Did she say why she wanted to appear here?"

Jack shrugged his shoulders. "She has appeared here before. So maybe she has to appear in the same places. There are a few shrines around, maybe this one is quiet."

Jack walked up to the counter and said, "You are going to meet Mary tonight as you sleep. She will come and get you herself, so prepare."

As they walked to the door Andre said, "That was cold."

Jack asked, "Did you see that smile?"

Jack said, "I have to take a leak." He walked to a men's room and Andre followed.

Right before Andre entered the door, he looked to his right. A young woman said, "Andre, you take good care of Jack. Do what he says and tell Merlin I said hi."

With that, she vanished. Andre walked into the bathroom and stood next to Jack. He cleared his throat and said quietly, "I saw her, she told me to watch over you."

Jack shot him a look, then said in a pissed-off tone, "Hurry up, tell me where was she standing!"

Andre asked, "What's the big deal?"

Jack said, "Just show me."

Andre walked out first, pointed to a rack of clothes and said, "Right there. She stood about four feet in."

Jack said, "She can't be photographed. We leave no trail, no hard proof that she was here." He walked up to the counter and asked, "Where are the cameras?"

The old lady said there were a few mostly in the shrine and church. Jack asked, "Near the men's room?"

She smiled. "No, there are only these three." She pointed out one watching the cash register and one in a corner, and another in an opposite corner.

Jack grabbed Andre by the shoulder and spun him around. "I still have to take a piss." They went back to the men's room and did their business.

Then Andre said, "Jack, let's get out of here."

They walked out to the car. Jack sat and went over what Mother Mary had said—this took a few miles. Then he said, "OK. I have been touched by the hand of God and given special powers. I have to free the red fairies. I pissed off Lucifer himself, so I have to watch my back. We don't know who is in league with the blue guardians. Oh yeah, and they want to bring the blues back from that planet the angels sent them to. We knew that."

Andre said, "Yes, but you stopped the Devil from taking over the world. You have the book and were not seen. You have Marvin in your corner and now you have Mother Mary too."

Jack said, "Ah, but she is just an advisor. She told me to find Baba Yaga. But there is something weird about that—she said please, like I really don't have to, but it would be a favour to her."

Andre asked, "Really? She said Baba Yaga? She has been dead for thousands of years. She was Merlin's teacher, Marvin was called Albrich back then."

Jack said, "I thought the mission was done. But that was just a test."

Andre said, "We will be at the hotel in ten minutes. You can take a shower, then have a good meal. My God, I thought this was the end! You fought Lucifer himself!"

Jack said, "We stopped the Devil from taking over the earth, but that is just part of our journey."

CPSIA information can be obtained
at www.ICGtesting.com
Printed in the USA
LVHW080953010219
606069LV00008B/82/P